# THE
# BRADBURY
# REPORT

A NOVEL

STEVEN POLANSKY

WEINSTEIN BOOKS

ISBN: 978-1-60286-122-0

First Edition
10  9  8  7  6  5  4  3  2  1

*For Julie and Sylvia*
*For Benjamin and Michael, again.*

A Report on the Government
Practice of Human Cloning
in the United States of America
in the year 2071 a.d.,
authored by "Raymond Bradbury"

# One

I am a man who doesn't matter. The same could be said of most men. In what follows, I will make no special claim for myself, save one, for which I can take no credit. This report will not, finally, be about me. I speak carefully here, and with regret, though not, such is my understanding of the world and its disenchanting ways, with incapacitating regret.

I was born without particular advantage. I was neither rich nor gifted nor congenitally happy nor especially pleasing to look at. Neither was I born poor or disabled or deformed or given to chronic sadness. I had, at birth, generally what I needed. I was uterine, though not—I am sixty-six years old—engineered. My parents cared for me.

Had I been luckier—had I, Anna might say, been sufficiently open to the operations of luck—providentially favored, my life might have been different. I might have accomplished something that served to define me, to set me apart from the mass of men of my sort. I might have discovered some leading, sustaining, purpose. I might have been happy in the way some men seem to be. I missed my chances. Or they were denied me. I am not a bad man. I have not been altogether thoughtless. I have tried to live reasonably, to avoid injuring others, whenever I have understood injury might be done. Through no egregious faults of my own, I have not mattered, do not matter, even to myself.

I am an old man. In November—should I live to see it, which is not likely—I will be sixty-seven. This is not old, is the obvious objection. In our day, in our age, with our means, this is hardly old. But I have not aged well. I have not worked at staying young. I did not take regular exercise. I was not studious about my diet. I could not seem to get enough sleep. Or I got too much. I did not rejuvenate my teeth or hair or skin, took no treatments for adipose reduction, received no cell therapies. This was not so much lack of vanity as it was absence of enthusiasm. Like many men my age, of my means, when it became available, I did sign on for CNR replication, though I took this step without much forethought or interest. I have no progeny—that is, no sons or daughters. No one to correct or encourage me. My wife, to whom I was married only seven years in what seems a lifetime ago, died, senselessly, atavistically, I thought, in childbirth. We had chosen a boy, brown hair, green eyes—we limited our choices to these—but had not named him. I grieved. I could think of no reason to marry again. I am tired out. Seen on the streets of Lebanon, passing along, ponderously, I was taken for a man much older than I am. I have been sick. I have been, am now, and not ungratefully, near death.

I have never had a sense of humor. I have not found funny that which, for as long as I can remember, others have laughed at. I have no skill in irony, and often mistake it for something else. Typically, I mean what I say. Against the long odds I face with language, I will try to be clear and precise.

I am just old enough to remember the spate of books written in the first decades of this century about what used to be called "cloning." There were scientific texts and the attendant popularizations. At least for the brief space before all discussion was curtailed, there were books that considered the ethical, legal, and regulatory issues. None of which I read. I am here thinking of the novels and stories, the fictive, speculative works of science fiction and fantasy. I am old enough to remember a number of these. I was aware of their being read; I remember hearing them spoken about. Michael Benaaron's *To Thine Own Self* was, I recall, much celebrated. So, too, Richard Powers's *Twig*. Evan Spire's endless series of horror stories, clones themselves. Edward Manigault's *Sheep*. A gruesome book called *Zygote*, and one called *Alter Eden*: I can't remember who wrote them. There were also, so it seemed at the time, hundreds of movies, one hard upon the next, some taken from books, nearly all of them vulgar and silly, a few of which I must have seen in the effort to be sociable.

*This* book, if one can call it that, is not science fiction, or fantasy. It is, at its heart, the account, manifestly true, of a young man, and of his courage and generosity. His preternatural humanity. At this valedictory point in my life, I was not looking for a project, or time to occupy. I want neither fame nor financial gain, could have no use for either. As a result of this report, I expect nothing will change. Should I live to finish it, it will be published only abroad, where, however widely and sympathetically it is read, it will be as so much preaching to the choir. In my own country, America, it is likely it will not be read, and, if read, not believed, and certain that a strenuous attempt will be made to discredit me, and that I will be punished if I am found. The most extraordinary measures have been taken to prevent a man like me from knowing what I know. Tyranny of the right, the left, it is all the same. It is because I survive, because I am the only one (of two) able to do it, that I write this. I am not a hero, and I am not afraid.

I am—I can think nothing else—the only living creature, the only human in the world's history, to have experienced time travel. (There is one other. I do not contradict myself. For Anna, the experience was markedly different, was, I'll presume to say, less profound.) If there have been others, we do not, would not, know of them. The possibility of time travel—this hackneyed rubric will have to do for now—in the only way it will ever be possible, is, as might be predicted, an unlooked-for result, a by-product—world-reconfiguring, dangerous, sad—of Science's insuppressible chase.

Just over a year ago, in July, on the first inhabitable day following a prolonged nationwide inversion, I got a call, without video, from a woman I had known when I was in my early twenties. By coincidence, her call came on Louise Brown Day. It has been demonstrated mathematically that ours is a world in which coincidence is the rule, and this is, by some margin, not the least probable thing I will tell you. When I knew her, her name was Anna Weeks. Her name, now, was Anna Pearson. She'd been married, she told me, nearly forty years, to a wonderful, loving man (her words) somewhat older than she. He'd died, preventably, in the past year. She was still in mourning. They'd had three children, all of them now grown. She still lived in Iowa. She was retired from teaching. Disqualified for payout from her husband's life insurance, she subsisted on her pension. I learned this last fact later.

We'd been graduate students together at Iowa State, in Ames. She was a native of Iowa. She had come to the university as an undergraduate and stayed on. I was born and raised in New Hampshire, but had come to Iowa by way of William and Mary, in Virginia. We were both seeking federal licensure as high school teachers, she in history, I in math. She was a year ahead of me. For reasons I have always wanted to think had nothing to do with me, she didn't finish her degree, leaving the university, and Ames, in the middle of the second, and final, year of the program. Even without a master's, she was able to secure a teaching job in the small town where she had grown up, in the high school she'd attended. We'd corresponded for a few months after she left the university. When she called, I had not seen her in over forty years.

This is a sad story. One in which I do not acquit myself with much sensitivity or nobility. I was twenty-two, but that is no excuse. I tell it because it bears on the rest.

In late August, forty-five years ago, two weeks before classes were to start, I drove to Iowa from New Hampshire in an ancient Volvo hybrid I'd nursed through college. In the trunk were six or seven cases of canned tuna fish, which my mother, who died shortly thereafter from ovarian cancer, had purchased and stowed there for me. This was when safe tuna was available and affordable. I'd declined to live in subsidized campus housing and had taken a furnished apartment in town, above a Hmong gift shop.

I had never been to Iowa before and arrived knowing no one. My first night in town, I took a walk around the campus to acquaint myself with it. It was a Sunday evening, still light, summer break, and the campus was quiet. I thought the place architecturally undistinguished but not uninviting. I understand improvements in the physical plant have been made; I have not been back since I finished my degree. At some point in my walk I encountered Anna Weeks, now Anna Pearson. Perhaps she was sitting on a bench, reading, beneath one of the campus's signature miracle elms. Or she was sitting cross-legged on a blanket in some grassy spot. These are scenes at once recognizable from romantic simulations. I don't remember where she was, or how, exactly, we began a conversation. I do remember she joined me on my walk. She felt great affection for the place, had been there five years—four as an undergraduate—and was eager to serve as guide. We walked most of the campus that evening. I was tired from my drive, and not an energetic companion. At my best, I would not have been sparkling. But I enjoyed her company. She was intelligent, and articulate, and lively. We wound up in town, near my apartment, at a twenty-four-hour patisserie. We sat and talked for several more hours, until I was nearly stuporous. We agreed to meet the following day.

Anna was lonely. This would have been unmistakable to most people. I didn't see it. She was a large woman, a bit ungainly, though not unattractive. As an undergraduate in Ames, she had picked up the nickname "Twink," which she carried with dignity and humor. She urged me to use this sobriquet, which, I see now, I should have done but then refused to do, telling her, stupidly, it made me sad. When I heard other people call her Twink, I felt angry—at them, at her.

For the two weeks prior to the start of classes, we spent at least some part of every day together. Anna was a great help to me. She advised me on classes and professors to take and avoid, led me through the baroque registration protocols, showed me where to buy texts and supplies. She and I had become friends. We ate together at least one meal a day. We went to movies. Of her choosing. I accompanied her, pretending to an opinion while she shopped for her fall clothes. One afternoon, in my old Volvo, we drove out of Ames, making a circuit of nearly two hundred and fifty miles in the Iowa countryside—this was well before the Clearances, before the havoc-playing influx of originals from the Dakotas—stopping for beefsteaks and sweet potato fries at a vestigial roadhouse in a town called Le Mars, not far from Anna's home. I remember being unimpressed by the landscape or, better said, impressed by its uniformity. It is a wonder I was willing to undertake this trip. I found Anna affable and easy to talk to. Doubtless I was circumspect. I am more than slow to reveal myself; I almost never do it. It is not fear that constrains me, or modesty, or decorousness, but lack of interest. Even with my wife, whom I loved, I was decidedly less than intimate.

Anna talked avidly, in large swaths, without inhibition. I don't remember what she talked about. I believe much of the time I was attentive; I carried with me through the after-years a fairly elaborated sense of her. I knew she was keen on literature and film. I knew she was an only child, that her parents divorced when she was very young, that her mother had raised her in straitened circumstances, that in high school she'd had no boyfriends, in college one terrible, sociopathic suitor, that her father was absent and unkind. She was full of self-deprecating humor, full of political fervor (she belonged to several anti-government action groups), which, in her case, was authentic and not a means to sexual encounter. She was a good storyteller, and, as much as I enjoyed anyone's company at that place, in those days, I enjoyed hers.

With the beginning of term, I saw Anna less often. Because she was a year ahead of me, we had no classes in common. I did not yet have other friends, as she did, competing for my time. We met several times a week for lunch or dinner. On these occasions, we were alone. She saw to this, fending off her friends, sparing me, I assumed, their society. In all this time, which amounted to most of the first term, I did not touch her. We did not kiss or hold hands. She did not come up to my apartment. I did not see her room in the graduate residence. Whatever those observing us may have thought, between ourselves we did not characterize or speak of our affections. We were chummy. We were not romantic. I didn't think much about our friendship, apart from being thankful I had someone to talk to from time to time. I had no idea what she was thinking.

I did not tell Anna about the girl, still at William and Mary, who thought she and I were to be married soon after her graduation in the spring. We'd made no formal plan, but that was the understanding. We'd grown up together in New Hampshire. I'd known her since grade school. She'd been my only girlfriend in high school, and, after a year apart, she followed me to Williamsburg. Our families were close. We shared a history, seamless and literally lifelong. We were tied in all manner of ways. She'd had other, more advantageous options, but chose William and Mary to be with me. In her sophomore year there, with what was unconscionable slovenliness, I got her pregnant. I arranged and paid for the abortion. For much of high school, and through several years of college, I imagined I loved this girl, in the inchoate, mindless way I imagined love. I did not mention her to Anna. This was, in part, because I saw no reason to; in part, because I felt diminished by my attachment—it had, by that time, begun to feel slavish and unimaginative—to the girl in Virginia, whose name will here be Ann. That this omission was calculated and self-serving needs no remarking. But I think it is true that, had I thought it was in any way caddish of me not to tell Anna about Ann, I would have told her. That there was a girl in Virginia, to whom I was preemptively attached, to whom I bore some overriding responsibility, had nothing to do with the nature and degree of my feelings for Anna, which would have been what they were, girl or no girl. I liked Anna. I felt some unwarranted pity for her, which, I fear, might have given me a puerile pleasure I was not, at the time, above. I did not love Anna, felt toward her no physical attraction, and did not want her for anything other than friendship.

In early November, I met, purely by chance, one of Anna's three roommates, an undergraduate, who for three years had been Anna's closest friend at the university. Before she married me, her name was Sara Bird. I was on campus, in the automat, eating lunch. Anna and her roommate were already there, though the place was crowded and I didn't see them until I was nearly finished. They came over to my table. Anna introduced her.

Sara Bird. Twenty-one years old. From Indianola, outside Des

Moines. Her father, briefly my father-in-law, was a minister in the moribund Episcopal Church. In the public gaze, he was an exemplary man—learned, wise, well-spoken, elegant in bearing, reverent, refined. In private, to his wife and three children, he was despotic. I was given a glimpse of the domestic version. It was enough to eradicate in me whatever remnants of Christian faith there might have been; merely being in his presence, I was determined, as was then the expression, to throw the baby out with the bathwater. There is no question he was the principal cause of most, if not all, of Sara's emotional debilities. Her mother, an aristocratic Norwegian, born into the Lutheran Church, who, after nearly thirty years in America, spoke only a rudimentary English, was of no use in preventing or even tempering her husband's attacks, which found, as their favorite target, the eldest child, the beautiful, languid, exceedingly vulnerable Sara. For seven years I hated him. I watched him closely whenever he was around her. I was poised to intervene, eager to expose him for what he was. (I was delusional. I was in my twenties. I would have been no match for the man.) When Sara died I stopped just short of blaming him expressly. I did prevent him from presiding at the funeral. Afterwards, I had nothing more to do with him.

Sara became my wife. I lived with her seven years. I knew her better than I had known anyone before, or since. I loved her as I have loved no one else. She was the most beautiful woman I'd ever seen. From the first, I was aware how idiosyncratic this judgment was. She was thin and pale. In repose, her face was sad. There was a darkness about her. Her eyes were sunken and shadowed. She was quiet, formal, flinchy, because she was delicate, easily hurt. I talk about her this way to Anna—who is, she says now, beyond being hurt by it—and she remarks I might be describing some vaporous nineteenth-century heroine. For me, all these melancholy accoutrements constituted her beauty, which was ethereal, asexual, for all her sadnesses, serene. She was irresistible.

At that first meeting, other than to say hello, she did not speak. She was glad to let Anna do the talking. Once I knew who she was, as is the way, I began to see her frequently on campus. She was not easy to talk to, or to get at. If she was not with Anna, which made awkward any overture, she was almost always in the midst of a herd of students, her fellow undergraduates, male and female, as unlike her as they could be: noisy, raw, lighthearted savages, careering about as if they believed they would never die. She told me, later, she despised them. But among them, she said, in the thick of their rout, their collective spasm, she felt anesthetized, blanketed, needing never to speak or think.

When I went back to New Hampshire for Thanksgiving, I still had not had the chance to speak with Sara alone. The Monday before Thanksgiving, my mother died. She'd been sick a long time. A common case of extended morbidity. The end, however, was precipitous. I was her only child, very nearly her only kin, and it properly fell to me to make the arrangements for her funeral. Though we had not been as close as she'd wanted, I'd loved my mother. I did not get the chance to see her before she died. I was now alone—my father was long dead—without family. Ann had come up from Virginia for the holiday. She was a support to me at the funeral, and I was grateful for her presence there. It was the last time I would see her. Ann, Anna, Sara. Three women. A mysterious conflation: the only three women in my life, all at once. By the time I got back to Ames, obeying an animal instinct to avoid any additional pain, I had, if not forgotten Sara Bird, pretty much scrapped whatever designs I'd had.

If my work at the university had been interesting, or challenging, I might have thrown myself into it. Now I was back, the friendship with Anna, who offered me only an appropriate and genuine sympathy, began to cloy. She seemed—nothing in her behavior had changed—oppressively needful and clinging. I avoided her, fabricating lame, perfectly transparent excuses. After two or three of these, Anna felt the insult and stayed away. At the same time, without providing an explanation, I broke off communication with Ann. I wanted, I told myself, nothing to do with anyone.

In the bleak midwinter—I believe there is an old song that begins thus—walking back to my apartment late after a profitless night at the library, I stopped at the New Times Café, on the near edge of town, to get out of the cold and the snow. It was not a café, but a bar, little more than a cement bunker, with a grill, and a pool hall in the rear. It was a shithole—grim, roughneck, inhospitable. It was the first time I'd been in the place. That night, Sara was already there. She was sitting in the darkest corner of the lightless room, at a high-top table for two, with Anna.

I stood inside the doorway, brushed the snow off my coat, stamped my boots. They were talking. I could have gone back out before they saw me. By any measure of sensitivity, I should have left. Instead, without consciously deciding to do so, I walked across the room to their table. So far as I knew myself, I was no longer interested in Sara Bird. I had, certainly, no wish to cause Anna any further unease. Yet over I went, as if I was precisely the person they were both hoping, on that arctic night, to see. It was to be, in all our lives, a pivotal moment. I cannot regret it.

The place was crowded, raucous, in direct relation, it must have been, to the severity of the weather. Anna saw me approaching. She stood up. In my hearing, she said to Sara, "I'm going to the bathroom."

I smiled at them both. Before Anna had a chance to flee, I said, "Hello."

Sara looked at me reproachfully. Anna had confided in her. She put her hand on Anna's wrist. (My wife had the most lovely hands. I miss them still.) "Stay," she said. Then, to me: "What are you doing?"

Anna stood there, embarrassed and bewildered. I saw no anger in her.

I should have stopped talking, turned around, walked away.

"I'm not doing anything," I said, gracelessly. "I was going home. I was cold. I came in. I saw you both. I said hello."

"I'm leaving now," Anna said. She took her hand away from Sara's.

"No, don't," Sara said.

"It's you he wants to see, Pie." Anna's pet name for Sara. I never learned its provenance.

"I don't want to see him," Sara said.

"I'm sorry," I said. It was not clear to whom I said this.

Sara stood up. I watched, dumbly, as they gathered their things, put on their coats and hats, and stalked off.

I took a breath. I had no idea what I was doing. I looked around the place. It was not friendly. In a wash of cheap remorse, I considered staying there and getting drunk (I was then, I am now, in practice abstemious). I considered losing whatever money I had with me to the pool sharks, should there be any, in the back room. I considered dropping out of school and going home to New Hampshire to await, in self-imposed quarantine, Ann's graduation from William and Mary and, following ineluctably, a colorless marriage. I did none of these things.

By the time I caught up to the girls, who were walking uphill back to campus, I was near frenzy. When they heard me slogging after them, my boots sloshy in the snow, they turned to wait. This was a gesture of real kindness. It was still snowing hard. And though the wind had slaked somewhat, it was brutishly cold. Anna stood just behind and to the side of Sara. I stood before them. For whatever reason—guilt, cut-rate sentimentality, the cold—my eyes were full of tears.

"Forgive me," I said. "I mean neither of you harm. I like you both. It's been a bad time. My mother's death. Other things. I am not myself." I shook my head, wanting to withdraw what I'd just said. "This is no excuse. I'm sorry. There is no excuse. Forgive me. I won't bother you again."

They did not speak.

"That's all I want to say." I started down the hill. As I did, I slipped in the snow and landed, with a great pathetic whump, flat on my ass. Had I planned it, it could not have been more effective. I heard Sara laugh. It was a musical laugh, a trill really, sweet and full of mercy. It was that laugh, and her hand on Anna's wrist, that determined me. Then Anna called out: "Are you all right? Are you hurt?"

By the end of January, Sara had moved out of the graduate residence—where, owing to a dispensation procured by Anna, she'd been allowed as an undergraduate to live—and into my apartment above the Hmong gift shop. We'd been dating, if that term is apposite for our furtive meetings, only a month and a half when she decided to take this step. I loved Sara. I wanted, always, to be with her. Somehow we'd kept our assignations hidden from Anna, who had, or claims she had, no inkling about what was happening. All the sneaking around was infantile and vulgar and demeaning to us all, but I was besotted and wholly irresponsible. When, preparatory to vacating the room they shared, Sara finally revealed to Anna what had been going on, Anna was stunned, mortified. Not by what we'd done so much as how we'd done it. And she was deeply saddened. Far more by the loss of Sara than of me. But she was sad about me, too. She had, as she has said, some hopes.

Sara didn't see much of Anna after that. For what remained of their friendship, they established workable but uneasy terms. I didn't see Anna at all. Except once. Sometime in March, a matter of days before Anna left the university, after Sara and I had been living together nearly two months, I felt it was past time to resolve the situation with Ann. It was, of course, more than past time; it was inexcusably late. I should have gone to Virginia to tell her face-to-face about Sara. Instead, I phoned her. Ann was wounded, rageful. She refused to accept my explanation, my apology, whatever mongrel, disreputable thing I was tendering. She berated me, cursed me. Our conversation—I said very little; beyond the mere, for her appalling, facts, I had little to say—lasted more than two hours. By the end of it, I could barely stand or breathe. I felt as if I'd been eviscerated. I also felt—this was scandalous—sorry for myself.

I went looking for solace, for Sara. I had not wanted her to be in the apartment when I called Ann. It was Saturday night, ten o'clock. Spring was near. The streets in town were full of life. When I got to the campus, desperate to find Sara, the students were in the throes of a spontaneous, drunken, somewhat premature, end-of-winter celebration. It seemed everyone was bent on going wild. I could not find Sara. I became more and more distraught. I went to the graduate dorm, to the room she'd shared with Anna, thinking—I was hardly thinking—I might find Sara there. I had not gone to that room before.

Anna was alone, reading. There were stacks of books and papers on the floor and furniture. From Sara I knew that Anna was hard at work on her master's thesis (she would not stay to finish it) about the Second Korean War. She was in flannel robe, pajamas, and furry slippers. Her hair was gathered in back with a rubber band. She was wearing reading glasses and had on no makeup. It may have been, simply, my blinding need, but I thought she looked better than ever. I was happy to see her. I discovered I had missed her. She was startled and, as you'd expect, not pleased to see me, though she was kind. She invited me in, cleared a space for me on the daybed. Without preamble, without a trace of tact, I asked her if she knew where Sara was. She didn't. She hadn't seen Sara in days. Did she have any idea where I might find her? (It turned out Sara had met up with her old gang, and they'd gone, blithely, to a truck stop by the interstate.) She had no idea where Sara was. I spent most of that night with Anna—I left her room just before dawn—and she displayed no vindictiveness. About her own feelings she was reticent. But she did not once stoop to recrimination. Was there something wrong? Was Sara all right? Her concern was authentic. I said so far as I knew Sara was fine. Then, relieved, giddy to have someone to talk to, someone to listen to me, to comfort me, I fell apart. I began to weep convulsively. Anna sat down beside me on the daybed. She took my hand, and I collapsed into her arms, my head on her breast.

I told Anna about Ann—it was the first she'd heard of her—and our conversation. I kept nothing back. I told her things about Ann and me, things about myself, I would not tell Sara. I confessed to her my fears, rehearsed my failings and frailties, delineated, in fastidious detail, my self-loathing. I was relentless, grotesquely self-absorbed. Anna listened to all of it, the whole woeful inventory. She cosseted me. She tried to be reassuring. I was not so bad as I claimed. I was not evil, just flawed, broken. As she was. As was everyone. (These were the days before Direct Germline Intervention.) Somehow, she was neither patronizing nor disdainful. She was able, even, to evince some joy in the idea that Sara and I were together. When it was over, when I was completely purged and spent, when I had squeezed myself dry and taken everything I could take from her, Anna helped me to the door and sent me back to Sara, who was, by then, sleeping cozily in our apartment.

Within the week, Anna had left the university. I did not see or speak to her for forty-five years.

I am not a religious man. Few people are, these days, religious. I was an infant, too young to remember the tyrannous, hateful, pseudo-Christian mania that took hold of the country in the reign of George Bush ("the Pretender," now, to distinguish him from his less malignant father). I was too young to remember the violent and mass recoil that accompanied his downfall, away from a zealously theocratic state, in which regressive stupidity was institutionalized, to an equally zealous secular one, in which science was allowed to proceed unchecked. Ours was a tepidly Presbyterian house. My parents were not at all serious about matters of faith, and we barely registered these radical shifts in policy and mood.

This past year, led by the events I tell of here, I have begun reading through the Bible, in a methodical but unscholarly way, Old Testament to New, without a clear understanding of why I am doing it. I have the Authorized Version, the King James. It was not easy to obtain a copy. I bought it when we first got to Montreal, in a second-hand bookstore on the Rue de la Montagne. I have taken it with me through every move. It is with me now. It is a beautiful book, in fairly good condition. Oversized and heavy. I am a slow reader. I am finding some of it familiar, some of it utterly strange, some of it dull and useless, some of it beautiful and moving. I have not, as yet, turned to God. It is the story one comes to first, the story of Adam and Eve, which for me has been most provocative. Eve was made from Adam's rib. It follows: Adam, the first man, was also the first original. Because she was made from him, Adam would have felt a special warmth for this last, derivative animal. Through this asexual mode of reproduction—unprecedented and, until recently, unrepeated—God, as I read the story, opened up a gap in the otherwise sturdy, previously impeccable rib cage. That is, He made in Adam a highway to his, Adam's, heart. Forgive the bumptious metaphor, but I have been opened up just so. I have been re-made. I had forgotten who I once was, who I once might have become. I have been made to remember. (Eve was born knowing deep down the way to Adam's heart, and, fatefully, with the means to turn his heart from God.) In our systematically de-scriptured world, the copy is made from the genetic material of the original. The original thus serves as a new Adam, a peculiarly modern Adam, a voluntary Adam, an Adam with an enlightened self-interest, an Adam who is asked to risk not very much (a blood cell or two) in this peculiarly modern version of the biblical investment—for health rather than love, human or divine. The copy is made to serve the original, as—here it gets turned around—Adam served Eve. If it should ever be required.

Before Anna contacted me and initiated this series of events, in the twenty-one years since it had been made not only legal, and socially and ethically legitimate, but also routine—it is the exceptional case that an original does not have his umbilical cord blood collected and banked—I had not given much thought to the matter of clones and cloning. I'd given no thought at all to my clone, wherever he was. (I knew where he was, if I'd permitted myself to think about it.) In this way I was like the rest of the American populace. After a year of conversation with Anna—she did most of the talking and provided all of the knowledge—I am convinced that the government has done everything in its power to keep us from thinking about the subject. The very terms we use—"original," "copy"—were designed to be flattering to the former, dismissive to the latter, to be less scientific, less clinical, more palatable, ultimately blinding. When it is considered at all by the American public, cloning is taken, gratefully, for the centerpiece of a federal health care system. This fiction persuades and placates us (and, not incidentally, allows the government to do little else for us in the way of health care). I use Anna's language of protest. It does not come naturally to me. My involvement in this is personal, not political, but you must see, as I now do, that we are all complicit. We are guilty, individually and collectively, of a staggering narcissism. From the inception of this inhuman practice, which diminishes and defines us—we are consummate sheep; the only real public debate was about whether or not to privatize the business of cloning—there have been pockets of resistance. These groups are tolerated, co-opted, impotent. (Anna and her husband were active in the opposition. Both refused to participate in the replication program. This refusal was to cost Anna's husband perhaps twenty or thirty years of life.) There is a terrible symmetry to be noted. The United States is the only country in the civilized world where cloning is legal and state-sponsored. It is everywhere else outlawed. We are again the rogue among enlightened nations, as, for so long, we were in our refusal to abjure capital punishment. Having finally abolished that barbarous usage, the United States now reserves its sanctioned executions—few know about this; no one talks about it—only for superfluous or, in the rarest of cases, wayward clones. And their abettors.

Anna's call came a year ago last July, ominously, as I've said, on the 25th. That spring I'd taught my final semester at the high school in Lebanon. I'd been more than ready to quit, but I had not yet found the rhythm for retirement. At a low level, I was restless, bored, disoriented, but willing to loaf and idle. Without knowing it, I had begun to feel the debilitating effects of a diseased heart. I had vague plans to travel. I wanted to go back to Scotland, to the Trossachs, Loch Voil, where Sara and I had been on our honeymoon. I wanted to live for a while, maybe two or three months, in Italy, in Umbria, in, say, Spoleto, which I knew little about, except that the very expensive olive oil Sara used in cooking was made there. I'd always imagined a leisurely, picturesque drive across the northern part of the country, from New Hampshire to Washington State, taking the Minnesota By-Pass up through Canada. I thought about riding out a New England winter or two in Hawaii, or Arizona, or American Samoa. I had read too few of the major works of English literature, and I told myself this would be my chance to do that, knowing, though I actually bought a one-volume complete Shakespeare, I never would. I had people I could meet for the occasional lunch or coffee, but I had no real friends. After all my widower years of eating in restaurants, I thought about learning to cook for myself. I do not fish. I have no hobbies. Had Anna not called, I might well have simply come to a gradual stop.

It was a Saturday, 11 o'clock in the morning, 10 o'clock her time. I was still in my pajamas. The day was cool, the air finally clean, and I had the windows open. I had not slept well. I was finding it harder to get, and to stay, asleep. For no reason I could think of, my right shoulder ached. It was tender to the touch. I was sitting at the kitchen table, eating dry cereal and working the crossword puzzle in the local paper. Outside the kitchen window, two red squirrels gibbered at one another, while Sophie and Marie, the twins from next door, drew chalk figures on their driveway. The Internet chimed, an uncommon occurrence in my house.

"Is this Ray Bradbury?" the female caller asked.

To protect Anna, and myself, and anyone else to whom contact with us might lead, I have changed the names of persons and places whenever it seemed advisable. Anna's maiden name was not Weeks, nor was her married name Pearson. My name is not Ray Bradbury. When I began to write this report, Anna suggested I take this name. She is a great reader and tells me Ray Bradbury was a writer well known in the latter half of the last century. I live in New Hampshire, but not in Lebanon. Sara Bird was not Sara *Bird*. She did not come from Indianola, but someplace like it. Even Le Mars, in northwest Iowa, where I said Anna and I stopped on our outing for beefsteaks and sweet potato fries, was not Le Mars.

"It is," I said.

"This is Anna Pearson. You may not remember me."

I thought for a moment. I couldn't place the name. This happened to me quite often. "I don't."

"No," she said. "When you knew me I was Anna Weeks."

"Anna?"

"Yes."

"I remember. Of course I remember. Is it you?"

"Yes."

"How are you? Where are you?

"I'm in Iowa. I never left. I'm all right. What about you?"

"I'm okay," I said. "I'm older than I was. Old. You wouldn't know me."

"We are both old. I would know you."

"Not likely," I said. "This is a sweet surprise. Are you still speaking to me?"

"I am. Obviously." She laughed. "I was angry with you. For a long time. You hurt me, you know."

"I do know," I said. "I was a lout."

"Yes. You were."

"I don't like to think about it."

"Do you think about it?"

"Probably I don't," I said. "Probably not."

"Just as well," she said.

"It's not."

"You were in love. You were a boy."

"I was."

"And Sara? How is *she?* Are you two still together?"

"Sara died."

"Oh, no," she said.

"It was a long time ago. Thirty-five years."

"What? What happened?"

"She died in childbirth."

"And the baby?"

"He died, too."

"Oh, no," she said. "I'm so sorry. How terrible."

"Thank you. It *was* terrible."

"I don't know what to say. I've thought about Sara often."

"I have, too," I said. "Are you married?"

"I was. My husband died this past year."

"*I'm* sorry." I said. "There is no escape."

"From?"

"Sadness. Pain. It heaps up."

"No," she said. "I *am* sad. I do miss him. I miss him every minute. But we had a good, long life. We had children together. I am grateful for it. Absolutely. Glad." She was quiet. Then: "That was thoughtless. Forgive me. I don't mean to be cruel. This must be hard for you to hear."

"Not at all," I said.

At my request, she spoke briefly about her husband, who'd been a nurseryman, and about her children. There were three of them, two boys and a girl: the oldest a professor of history; the middle child, the girl, a labor and delivery nurse; the youngest, a graduate student in philosophy. One of her sons lived in the Pacific Northwest, the other abroad. Her daughter was close by. There were, so far, two grandchildren.

"You did well," I said.

"I've been very lucky. Lately I've wished the boys were nearer to home."

"They'll come back," I said, not quite knowing what I meant.

"Oh, they do. They're good boys."

"Are you still teaching?"

"I retired last year," she said.

"I just retired," I said. "This spring."

"What will you do?"

This question, it turns out, was somewhat disingenuous.

"I have no idea," I said. "What do you do?"

"I keep busy."

Then she said my name. Not Ray, of course, but my actual Christian name. She spoke it in a way—knowing, affectionate, beseeching—I'd not heard since Sara died. It startled me to hear my name said this way again.

"What?" I said.

"There is something I want to talk to you about."

"What is it?"

"I want to come see you."

"What is this about?"

"I won't tell you now. We'll talk when I arrive."

"This sounds serious, grave."

"It is," she said. "Both. It is important we talk."

"All right," I said. "When do you want to come?"

"Soon. If it's convenient for you, I'd like to come the first week in August."

"That's next week."

"Will that work for you?"

"Come anytime. I couldn't be more free."

"If it's possible, I'd like to stay with you."

"Yes. Good. I've got too much room. Tell me when you're getting in, I'll pick you up."

"I'll be driving," she said.

"From Iowa?"

"Yes. Listen. Ray." There was nothing calculated about the way she spoke my name, but the effect was uncanny. "Don't tell anyone I'm coming."

"I have no one to tell," I said.

# Two

I see how one generates suspense. I am not a novelist. I am not interested in the tricks of that trade. One of my teachers at the university remarked that my prose read like a poor translation from the Czech. More than one person has suggested to me the similarities between written language—it was usually poetry they were thinking of—and the language of mathematics. I was a high school math teacher, not a mathematician, but I think this is wrong, wishful thinking on both sides. The ends—expression on the one hand, theoretic manipulation on the other—are radically different, not comparable. I have found I am deaf, and blind, to nuance. I have been told this more than once. It is an incapacity that has made my life bearable

The six days between Anna's call and her arrival in New Hampshire, I was in suspense. I didn't like it. I found it an unpleasant, frustrating state. Why had she called me, just then, after all those years of silence? What did she want to talk to me about? What did she want of me? What would happen next? Had I had anything else to do, after I'd readied the house—I had not had a houseguest in decades—I might have been able, intermittently, to put her visit from my mind. As it was, I spent most of my waking hours those six days speculating, brooding. I let my mind run, unfettered by logic or probability. I wondered if she had waited a respectable time after her husband's death, then called to see if we might, in our later years, try again. What if she were still angry, still feeling the injury I'd done her, and was on her way, now that she had nothing to lose—in this laughable line of conjecture, I omitted thinking about her children and grandchildren, about the value of her life to her beyond her marriage—to have, at long last, her say, to take some long-meditated form of revenge? Was she coming to ask for money? Reparations? Was she dying—this notion, I admit, came as a relief—making the rounds, saying good-bye in person to all those who'd played a part in her life?

I put fresh linens on the guest room bed. I emptied several drawers in the chiffonier and cleared my winter coats, hats, and scarves out of the guest room closet, leaving a dozen empty hangers for Anna's use. Without her deftness, without taking her delight—I took no delight—I did roughly what I remembered seeing Sara do in preparation for visits from her family. (Sara's father, who would not forgive her for marrying me, was never a visitor. This was all right with me, and Sara.) I bought some cut flowers, lilies, irises, alstroemeria, arranged them clumsily in a ceramic vase, and placed them on the night table, along with a fresh box of facial tissue. I sanitized the guest bathroom, stocking it with newly laundered towels—bath sheets, hand towels, and facecloths—an unused bar of soap, and an unopened bottle of shampoo. I disposed of the few incidental and inedible items in the refrigerator and wiped down the shelves. I went to the grocery store and laid in some staples—orange juice, milk, cheese, English muffins, eggs, beer, crackers, bread. I had plenty of coffee on hand. I bought two bottles of wine, one red, one white, and a corkscrew. I mopped the kitchen floor with a lemon-scented detergent I found under the sink, and cleaned the counters with bleach. I went around the house putting away extraneous things, though, on my own, I'd acquired very little. I put off to the last the vacuuming and dusting. The lawn did not need mowing. We'd had almost no rain that summer and were under the most stringent rules for rationing water. I was not a gardener. There were no flowers to tend. Nothing remained of the elaborate perennial beds Sara had designed and planted when we moved here some forty years ago. Over the years I'd lost a number of trees—two birches, a chestnut, a red maple, and an ancient shade oak in the front yard—to weather and insects and disease. One unlikely bit of Sara's brief tenure survived: an ornamental white-star magnolia she planted just outside the kitchen window. Suddenly, each spring—I never notice the buds—for a day or two only, until a rain or stiff breeze despoils it, this tree, or bush—I don't know which it is—is incandescent, profuse in delicate white blossoms.

I found all the effort a nuisance. I was not looking forward to Anna's visit. I was lonely, unrelievedly lonely, and I had been for thirty-five years, but I did not long for company. I never sought it. Not even in a pet. Anna had given me no sense of how long she planned to stay. I had no idea what we might have to say to one another once the main subject, whatever it was, had been discussed. The prospect of living in the same house with another person, for however short a time, was to me repellant. As was the thought of a protracted bout of reminiscing, of trolling a past—my memory of Sara would, I believed, under any pressure remain inviolate—in which I would figure as more or less a villain. I was closed to all but the narrowest range of feeling and experience, and I had not the slightest wish to open up.

At noon the next Saturday, almost exactly one week to the hour of her initial call, Anna called me from a rest stop on the New York Thruway, west of Syracuse. She had been driving all night. She would nap in her truck, she said, for an hour, then come on. When did I think she'd get there? I guessed she was five or six hours away. She would see me, then, around seven. I told her whenever she arrived, I'd be happy to see her. At three that afternoon—Anna would have been in Albany or western Massachusetts—I had my first heart attack.

I was vacuuming the study. "Study" is grandiose. The room, which is towards the rear of the house and looks out, past my nondescript yard, on the back side of a teetering, aboriginal barn owned by a neighbor to whom I've never spoken, is without decoration. It is a room we meant to get to, Sara and I, but didn't. That I've left it as it was is due neither to reverence nor fetish. There is a small kneehole desk, a wooden ladderback chair, a desk lamp, a computer, and a freestanding bookcase, with room in it, still, for books. (When Sara died, I got rid of all my books and, for the most part, stopped reading.) On the floor is an oval hooked rug. There are two windows with pull-down shades. Except for a calendar, which I update each year, the walls are bare. No studying, no real work of any sort has ever been done there. When I had exams or problem sets to grade, classes to prepare—over time, there was less and less need for preparation—I set up at the kitchen table. Except to use the computer, I avoid going in.

I bent over to pull the vacuum plug out of the wall socket, and I felt light-headed. This often happened to me when I bent over or stood up too quickly. This time, the dizziness persisted. I sat down in the desk chair. I spread my left hand flat against the desk. I felt a pull, a tightening in my chest. I rested my elbows on my knees, let my head droop. I spent several minutes looking at the floor. There was no pain. The dizziness did not subside, and my chest felt heavy. It did not, then, strike me I might be seriously ill. I began to feel nauseous. Then a numbness in the two outside fingers of my left hand. My chest felt heavier. The numbness spread to the rest of my hand and up my arm. My breathing became constricted. These were common, textbook signs I failed to interpret. I stood up. I thought I'd go to the kitchen for a glass of water, that I would feel better if I could drink some water. I sagged to the floor. During none of this was I afraid. I began to wonder, in a detached way, if I might be dying. It seemed I was not afraid to die. From my knees, I reached up to the computer and struck the shortcut for emergency services. Within seconds I heard the voice of the dispatcher.

"How can I help?" the voice said. "Are you in trouble?"

Although it felt as if it were coming from a long way off, in space and time, it was a human voice, kind, dispassionate, of indeterminable gender.

"Yes," I said. "I think I am."

"What is the trouble?"

"I don't know," I said. "I think I may be dying."

"Are you in pain?"

I did not find this question bothersome. I found it interesting.
"No."

"Are you bleeding?"

"No." Then, with a clarity and concision that struck me even then
as odd, I enumerated my symptoms. "I'm dizzy. My chest is heavy. I'm
nauseous. I can't feel my arm. I'm having trouble breathing. I can't
stand up."

"You're having a heart attack," the voice said without hesitation.
"I am?"

"Yes. Where are you?"

"In the study. I'm on the floor."

"Stay there," the voice said. "Help is on the way."

What a wonderful phrase, I thought. What a wonderful system.
If I'd died then, thinking this, I would have died happy.

I lay on the floor. I was calm. I began to feel as if I—I mean, precisely, *not* the room or any part of the world outside myself—were getting smaller. As if I were pulling in, compacting. There was no element
of siege in this. It was a peaceful, pleasing diminishment. Such that I
felt some irritation when the EMTs arrived and set to work on me. I
can't tell you how long it took them to get there. It might have been
minutes, or hours. I flickered in and out of consciousness. No pain.
No fear, nor, more surprisingly, regret. An agreeable, seductive state.
I suspect they came quickly. They'd have had no trouble getting in the
house; the front door is unlocked when I am home. I have a frag-
mented sense of what happened next. There were two of them,
young men, in uniform. Competent, efficient, reasonably gentle. One
of them smelled of beets. I know they hooked me up, there in the
study, to what would have been a diagnostic machine. There was a
small mechanical noise. I heard one of the men say, "This guy's in arrest." Then I was in an ambulance, attached to an IV drip. At one
point I must have looked up. "You're having a heart attack," one of

the young men said. I was lifted out of the ambulance and wheeled into the hospital—Dartmouth-Hitchcock—to the Imaging Center, where I lay on a table for what I know was a long time. (Despite the aliases I am careful to give all persons and places, including the hospital to which I was taken, I assume it will be possible for anyone who wants to, to track me down. And I assume they will. But I would not endanger the woman I am calling Anna.) I learned later they were hoping the attack would back off, waiting to see if it would. When it didn't, they performed an old-fashioned angioplasty. I don't remember this, of course. They found that two of my arteries were dangerously occluded, one of them one hundred percent blocked, the other eighty percent. They inserted two stents. All of this standard procedure and routine, though, as they told me, the attack was massive, and I might easily have died. I was in the hospital three nights, after which I was able to walk about on my own and they discharged me. There was no way yet to know the severity of the damage to my heart. We'd have to wait six or seven weeks—"let the dust settle," was how the cardiologist phrased it—then assess my condition and, the implication was, my chances going forward.

The hospital stay was unobjectionable. The census was low, and I was given a private room at no extra charge. I slept. I ate a little. I read the newspaper. There seemed no way to turn off the television. I'd experienced no threshold revelation, had had no clarifying visions, no epochal shift in perspective. I was transformed only insofar as I was weaker, more fragile, wearier. I felt as if a tree had fallen on my chest. I knew no more about life or death than I had before I went down. Apart from the doctors and nurses and sundry hospital staff, I had no visitors, no calls. Once the sedatives and painkillers wore off and I regained my wits, I remembered Anna.

I called her cell phone, which she'd instructed me not to do. This was early Monday evening.

She was in my house. "It was wide open," she said. "I came in, and I waited for you. You didn't come. I stayed."

I explained what had happened.

"Dear God. How do you feel?"

"I feel tired. A little bit dazed. A lot dazed. Ginger."

"I would say so," she said.

"Have you been comfortable?"

"I have," she said. "Very. Thank you. I made myself at home. I'm eating all your food. I wasn't sure where you wanted me to sleep. I took the bed in what looked like the guest room. The flowers are a lovely touch."

"Good," I said.

"I've been rude," she said, "squatting like this. I couldn't go to a motel."

"No. I was prepared for you to stay. I'm glad you did."

"The house is nice. It's very clean."

"I tried," I said. "I didn't get to finish."

"You nearly killed yourself doing it."

"I don't think that was it."

"There can't be any record of my visit," she said. "We must not be connected."

"I don't understand. As you know."

"When are they letting you out?"

"Sometime tomorrow," I said. "I don't know what time. You'll stay."

"I will. I came a long way. Is there anything you'll need I can get in the meantime? You'll have to tell me where to get it."

"I can't think of anything," I said. "A new heart. Is there enough to eat?"

"There's enough. How will you get home? I'd offer to come get you, but I don't think that's a good idea."

"My plan is to take a taxi."

"Then I'll see you tomorrow," she said. "No need to call me again."

I had begun to find Anna's secrecy annoying. While I was having a heart attack, advancing on death, albeit unconsciously, this tangential old woman (she was one year older than I) had installed

herself in my house, showily withholding any explanation. I was in
the frame of mind to think she too much enjoyed being mysterious
and impenetrable and in control. If I'd had the strength, I would have
been angry. But I was, at last justifiably, preoccupied with myself, and
my affliction. I was becoming an almost perfect solipsist, intently
watching every pulse on the beeping monitor beside the bed, moni-
toring, myself, each barely perceptible, probably imaginary, tweak
and twinge.

At lunchtime, just prior to my discharge, I had a visit from the
cardiologist. He wanted to know how I was feeling.

"Mortal," I said. "Battered. Like so much meat."

"That's to be expected. You should also expect some postopera-
tive depression. I can give you a prescription for something to miti-
gate that."

"I won't need it."

"I'll write it anyway," he said. "If you do need it, you'll have it."

"Thanks."

"I want to talk with you about what comes next. Are you up to
that?"

"I'm not sure I want to know."

He understood this as a joke. I was not joking.

"First, I'd like to see you again in seven weeks. I'll have one of
my nurses call you to schedule an appointment. Of course, if anything
occurs in the meantime, if you have any concerns—you'll doubtless
have some—if you feel any discomfort, experience any pain, I want
you not to hesitate to call my office. But, in general, I think you're
good to go. At least for the time being."

"And then?"

"Well," he said, "then we have to see. We'll take a look at your
heart, run some tests, assess the damage, and make a decision about
what course we take."

"What are the options?"

"There are basically three," he said. "If the damage your heart
has sustained is minimal to, say, moderate, we might want to see if

changes in diet and exercise and, for want of a better term, lifestyle, in combination with medication, might be sufficient to keep you and your heart in reasonably good health."

"I don't exercise," I said. "I eat most every meal out."

He smiled. "You'll want to change that. In any case."

"Sounds awful."

"Maybe so," he said. "If the damage is more significant, we'll consider the possibility of a bypass. It's a simple procedure. Effective. And the convalescence isn't bad."

"Though not something to look forward to."

"Perhaps not," he said, "but preferable to the alternative."

"Which is death?"

"Oh, no. I didn't mean that. There's no reason on earth for you to die. I meant a transplant."

"Christ."

"No, no. Listen. We do four or five a month here, and we're a small outfit. I don't do them myself. But I watch them done. It's not without risk, but, if everything's in place, it can be pretty much routine. The convalescence is long and sometimes a bit tricky, but if you need it, it's not something to be inordinately afraid of."

"I'd be damned afraid," I said. "I can tell you that."

"Yes. Of course you would. But, statistically speaking, given the proper circumstances, you'd do fine."

"I'm not sure I would," I said. "I'm not sure I'd agree to do it. What are the proper circumstances?"

He was quiet for a moment. "Here's where, given your age, I need to ask *you* a question." He stopped again. "I'll be frank with you. It's a question I find repugnant. Asking it is among the more distasteful things required of me in my job." He put a hand to his face, pushed his glasses up on his brow, pinched the bridge of his nose. A conventional gesture, but the vexation was genuine. "My views on the matter are of no consequence. You should disregard them. Do you understand me?"

"I'm not sure I do," I said. "What is the question?"

"The question is, 'Is there a copy? Do you have a copy? Did you have a copy made?'"

"I did do that," I said. "I suppose there is. I don't know for sure. I don't know anything about it, really."

"No. That's the way of it. But, you remember, at the time, participating. In the program."

"Yes."

"You are sixty-six."

"Yes."

"If he exists, and from what you say he does, your copy would be, approximately, twenty-one."

"I guess that's right."

"Well, then," he said. "Those are the proper circumstances. They couldn't, in point of fact, Mr. Bradbury, be any more proper, or propitious."

When I got home, Sophie and Marie were outside in their front yard playing with a little boy their age I hadn't seen before. It was midafternoon, and bakingly hot. The girls were dressed alike, as they were whenever I saw them. This afternoon they wore yellow shorts and white T-shirts and looked—I was glad to be home, glad to see them—like daisies. They were pretty girls. I could not tell them apart, though I hadn't ever needed to do so. In the seven or eight years they'd lived there, I'd said no more than hello to them, and they'd not said one word to me. From my perspective, they were clean, quiet, untroublesome children. I enjoyed sitting in my house, looking out the window, watching them play. (I do think it curious that anyone would choose twins, though I've read more and more couples are doing so, in spite of government dissuasions. There have even been reports of triplets. I wonder, in the case of twins, is a copy made of each, or does one copy serve both?) I was sad to think they were afraid of me, that, for them, I was the bogey next door. Or—I was less sad to think this—that they'd been directed by their parents not to speak to me, to stay away from me. Whatever they'd been doing before I got out of the taxi—one of the girls was holding a large, silver-foiled star—the three of them stopped and stood quiet and watchful as I walked to my door.

I looked terrible, I knew, ghostly, ogrish, making real their fears. I was sorry about this for the children's sake and, in advance, Anna's. I had on the clothes I'd been in when I was taken to the hospital. I was wearing the chenille slippers they gave me, and the ID bracelet, and carrying a plastic bag that contained oddments I'd collected during my stay—lotions, toothbrush and toothpaste, shampoo, patient information sheets, samples, hospital receipts, and various magazines I thought Anna might want to look at. I smelled like antibacterial cleanser. I'd not washed my hair in four days, but had remembered to comb it that morning, so I would not be too unsightly meeting Anna again. As a matter of courtesy, not vanity. I was no longer vain.

Anna's truck was not in the driveway—my car, which got little use, was around back in the garage—and I could see no trucks, no unfamiliar vehicles of any kind, parked on the street nearby. The house was quiet and still. The front-facing windows were shut, the drapes drawn. The front door was locked. I didn't have a key. There was a spare badly hidden in the garage, but I was exhausted and out of breath from my short walk, and did not have the strength to get it. There was no doorbell, just a brass knocker Sara had bought, in the shape of a watering can. I lifted the knocker and let it fall several times, my predicament observed with interest and satisfaction, and, I gave myself license to think, with some reflexive sympathy, by Sophie and Marie.

There was no noise from within the house. Not a creature was stirring. (I am susceptible, lately, near death and far from home, to washes of nostalgia.) I sat down on the front step. I smiled at the children in the adjacent yard, to signify, I suppose, that though I looked like a cadaver, I was not abject. Maybe I hoped they'd come over and chat. They turned away. The twin who was holding the star dropped it on the lawn, and, as if this were the signal to take flight, the three of them scurried around the far side of their house.

Moments after they'd gone, the drape on one of the front windows was pulled back a bit, then dropped. I was impatient to get in out of the heat, to reclaim my house. The latch shifted, then the door was opened.

I got to my feet slowly.

"Ray." Anna stood behind the door. "Come in. Come in."

"Thank you," I said.

She opened the door wide enough to let me in, then closed it behind me. We stood in the small foyer, too close, really, to regard one another.

"Hello, Ray," she said.

"Hello, Anna. It's good to see you."

"Likewise," she said. "Give me that." I handed her the plastic bag. She moved past me. "Come inside."

"All right," I said.

I followed her into the living room, which was hot and dark and stuffy. The windows were shut, and, unaccountably, she had not turned on the air-conditioning.

"Might we open the windows?" I said. "It's oppressive in here, don't you think?"

"I do," she said. "Very. You sit down." She pointed to an upholstered wing chair, which, it happened, was where I habitually sat. "Do you have visitors?"

I sat down in my chair. "Rarely," I said.

"Women?"

"Never. Why?"

"I'm reluctant to call attention to myself," she said.

"I can't imagine anyone is paying attention. Who are you talking about?"

"Your neighbors. Or those children in the yard. They would have seen the ambulance. They would have seen you taken away, would have known the house was empty."

"I don't know. Say they did?"

"Well," she said, "who am I?"

"Why would they care? This is my house. I live here. Why would anyone care?"

"I want to be unnoticed," she said, "unremarkable. Here's what you say, should anyone ask you."

"Ask me what, Anna? This is absurd."

"Listen, Ray," she said. "I'm not good at this. All right? I haven't done this before. I don't really know what I'm doing. But I feel like I need to take precautions. I know I need to take them."

"What are you talking about?"

"If anyone asks you, after I leave, who I was, you tell them I was a nurse sent by the hospital to see you through the first days of convalescence."

"No one will ask. I don't speak to anyone. No one speaks to me."

"That's unfortunate," she said.

"I don't mind."

"I do," she said. "You'll have to find a way to tell them. Shall I open the windows?"

I watched her as she went around the room, pulling open the drapes and raising the sashes. She was old, which should not have surprised me as it did, though, compared to me, she had aged gently, appealingly. She was taller than I remembered her, and thinner, her face longer, more angular, her features sharper. Her hair, which, forty-five years ago, had been dark, was now a kind of gunmetal gray, parted in the middle, curling inward just below her ears. Her eyes were bright. She did not wear glasses. She had on blue jeans, a white, short-sleeve shirt unbuttoned at the neck, and running shoes. Her arms and hands looked strong, like she was used to some sort of heavy work. If not pretty or particularly feminine—she had been neither at twenty-two— she was a more than passably handsome woman, who looked to have lost none of her energies.

"There," she said. The room was lit with the withering light of a midsummer's late afternoon. The air was heavy. There was no breeze. I was sweating. She sat down across from me, on the sofa. She sat up straight, both feet on the floor, and appraised me. "So how are you? You look like hell."

"I imagine I do. I've been through it just now."

"I know you have. Are you okay? I should have asked you first thing."

"I think so. You look good. You look good, Anna." I was feeling resentful, but I was willing to say this.

"You're surprised," she said.

"No. You look good."

"For me, you mean."

"I don't mean that," I said. "You look healthy, strong. From where I sit."

"Well then, thank you." She leaned forward, her elbows on her knees. "I'm a tough old bird." She smiled at me. "You had your chance." Then: "Are you in any pain? Is there anything I can do for you, to make you more comfortable?"

"I'm okay," I said. "I'm happy to be home."

"You'd prefer to be alone."

"I suppose I would. I wish you'd tell me what's going on. Why have you come?"

"I've come to tell you. That's why I've come. For goodness sake. This isn't a social visit. I can't be as quick as you'd like. I remember you; I don't know you. I don't know how you'll respond. I'm worried about it. I need to worry about it. I have to get a sense of things, a sense of you. And with your condition, now, everything is more complicated, more difficult."

"For me?"

"Of course, for you. And for me. And others."

"Others?"

She did not respond. I saw no way to force her to talk about what had brought her. In truth, I didn't care, so long as it was done. I would have been happier if she left without telling me. I couldn't imagine it was anything, given how I was feeling, I needed to be concerned with. I was ill, perhaps critically. I was frightened by what had happened to me. I wanted to rest, to be quiet. Just that. More than once, in the course of the following day, I was at the point of asking her to leave. (It would have done no good. There was only one thing

I might have said to cause her to go, to give up on me, and I could not have known what it was.) I believed—I was surely right—that Anna's presence, made more taxing by her unexplained, inexplicable, behavior, was dangerous to me. I said this to her. "It's not good for me. It can't be good. It's too soon for me to manage this. It feels heartless of you."

"I know it does," she said. "I am so sorry. I didn't expect to find you this way. If I had known, I would have postponed my trip."

"What about that? *Might* we do this another time? Some other way?"

"I don't think so."

We had several such fruitless and circular conversations, each one more inane than the last. Anna prepared our meals. She stayed with me one week. Every morning, she drove some distance—I now participate, wholeheartedly, in the hugger-mugger—on the interstate to the giant food nexus, buying only what we needed for that day, so she could carry the stuff to the house from her truck, which she continued to park on a residential street, several streets off. I was restricted to a bland diet. She fixed me broiled skinless chicken breasts, plain pasta, boiled potatoes, toast, clear soup, green Jell-O, hospital food, which Anna rendered—I have to say—quite palatable. I slept intermittently throughout the day, sometimes several hours at a stretch. In part, because I was often unable to stay awake, in part because it was trying to spend so much time in the house with a near stranger. Anna did laundry, did the dishes, kept the place orderly and clean, read the newspaper, watched television, read the books she'd brought with her. We spent much of my waking time apart. I closeted myself in the study, which, as I've said, was not characteristic of me. When we were together, for meals and at other times, Anna talked about her three kids, her grandchildren, and her late husband. We'd both had long careers—hers evidently more satisfying—as teachers, and, though I wasn't eager, we talked some about that. She insisted I tell her about Sara, and I did, though guardedly at first. It felt good, and right, to describe for Anna, room by room, just how different the house had looked and felt and smelled, when Sara was alive, how little in it or about it, now, was telling of her. Anna was animated when we talked about Sara, and it was obvious that she, too, had loved her. It was only this shared affection, I think—whatever the difference in degree—that kept me, finally, from abjuring all dictates of courtesy and, supposing I was able to do it, throwing her out.

# Three

Before Anna's first visit—she would be back, having assured herself I could be trusted, though she remained, with regard to my safety and my emotional and physical equilibriums (to say nothing of her own vulnerabilities), apprehensive and more than ambivalent about involving me—I knew next to nothing about the universe of cloning. Except on the one day of the American year prescribed for ritualized remembrance, for the national experience and expression of what, on the occasion of the very first Louise Brown Day, some undersecretary mawkishly called "original gratitude," I never thought about it, gratefully or otherwise—not about cloning, nor about the race of clones. ("Race" is self-evidently wrong, but I can think of no other word. Species? Subspecies? Metaspecies? Paraspecies? The practice beggars taxonomy.) Least of all—model citizen, I—did I think about *my* clone. My *copy,* as we are meant to say, and to think.

About the issue of cloning, I'd been apathetic. Even so, I'd always found the holiday—I've been around for them all—discomforting and sinister. Its very name, I now see, was, like all the authorized nomenclature, cunningly chosen to mislead and trivialize. As most of us have forgotten or never knew, Louise Joy Brown, born July 25, 1978, was the first human product of in vitro fertilization. She was not a clone. She was the sexually reproduced daughter of two parents. She lived and died a postal worker in England, where human cloning has always been outlawed. She had only obliquely, "inspirationally," to do with cloning. This may be one reason why, despite governmental dicta, the day has come more commonly to be called, especially among children, "Dolly Day." Which translation—chillingly apt—led inevitably to the surreal and grisly scene of summer streets filled at dusk with flocks of children in pink or white sheep suits, in their woolly innocence folded among debauched bands of grown men and women, conspicuously drunk, in bizarre, I'd say monstrous, sheep's-head masks. (I remember my grandfather, an inveterate Live Free or Die Yankee who fought in the shameful war in Vietnam and somehow survived it, in his dotage telling me about southern boys in his platoon who'd claimed to have had, as he slyly put it, congress with sheep.) The unseemly pack of them, children and parents, prancing and cavorting, raucously bleating deep into the night. Imagine at this the sweet twins next door. Sophie and Marie. I have seen them.

I knew nothing—and still know very little—about what goes on inside the Clearances. (This name is *not* misleading. It is meant to be forbidding.) Almost no one knows anything. Not even those who, like Anna, live in contiguous towns and villages. (You'd think it would take a concerted effort for them *not* to know, living on the border. Remember the assiduous ignorance of the citizens of Dachau, the sleepy town of that name. Anna assures me the opposite is true.) Not even the sedulous, sparse, and painfully ineffectual resistance, of which Anna is a low-level part. Many of her fellow dissenters, living purposefully as near as they can to the boundary, have devoted their lives to investigating the unholy business transacted there. So far as is known, none of them has ever gained access to the Clearances. (And lived to speak of it?) None of them had ever encountered a clone or seen one from a distance. (There are two public roads in the Clearances. They bisect the territory, north to south and west to east. I have, one time, driven the length—it was go the whole way or turn around—of the north–south route, from Valentine in Nebraska, through what once was Minot, and into Canada. By design, one can see nothing from these roads, except vast open fields and the occasional collocation of abandoned houses and commercial buildings.) Not one of them has ever met or spoken with anyone even tangentially involved with cloning. No one has. In this respect, these abolitionists, Anna's compatriots, are exactly like the rest of the population, including, it is generally believed, those in the very highest reaches of government. The best the abolitionists could do, even aided as they were by anti-cloning, anti-American thinkers from abroad, the nearest they could come to an accurate or even approximate sense of life, if the word applies, inside the Clearances, was informed speculation, basing their guesses, and the elaborated schema derived from them, on what was known about the science and technology of cloning, and, more determinatively, on fundamental and empirically verifiable assumptions about the way the government thinks and acts (that is, pragmatically, cynically, venally) and about what invariably motivates it (that is, profit).

As would be true for any American my age, I remember the riots in North and South Dakota. It was a bitter political fight (in a more passionate, less fatalistic age, there would have been civil war) between the states and the federal government, over the latter's attempt—wielding the doctrine of eminent domain, pushing it far past, despotically past, it was widely felt, its legal and already flagrantly overextended bounds—to appropriate the entirety of what were the Dakotas as an integral part of the process, the government's depopulation of those two states, in the space of four years, forcibly evicting all the "original" residents—one and a half million of them: men, women, children, and their chattel—giving these flinty heartlanders top dollar for their houses (which were summarily razed) and businesses, and adequately funding their relocation. All of this in order to repopulate the subsequently renamed territory with clones, and all the high- and low-tech ordnance of the cloning enterprise. When this happened, I was in my early forties, living alone in New Hampshire, far from the theater of conflict.

When Sara and I were on our honeymoon in Scotland, in the Trossachs, on Loch Voil, I read—by pure chance—one quiet afternoon while Sara was napping, an historical novel about the Highland

Clearances. I might have been outside; the afternoon was fine. I chose instead to remain indoors, near Sara, in our bedroom, to be near her. To watch her sleep was, still, a new and almost discomposing delight. In sleep her face was—this said without irony or self-parody—beatific. Her hands by her head on the pillow were pretty and delicate. I felt blessed by this woman, by her physical presence, her spirit, by her incomprehensible willingness to love me. (The language is religious. I was not.) I felt lucky, beyond all just expectation. This was nearly two decades before the government's decision to confiscate the land of North and South Dakota. When I still read books.

We were staying in a sixteenth-century great house, what seemed to us a small castle, made of a rose-colored stone, set back maybe a hundred yards from the shore of the loch. It was mid-September. We were married September 12. It is a day, a date, that has kept its power. The mornings there were cold and misty, the afternoons clear, the light off the loch unearthly. "Fourth dimensional," Sara said, by which she meant not Time, but the supranatural clarity of things. By nature she was reticent and self-contained—I loved this in her—and not given to such pronouncements. At breakfast, in addition to the eggs and sausage and bacon, there was fried bread that came slotted in a silver rack. We had never, either of us, seen fried bread before. There was also a kind of oatcake—very dry and stiff, barely edible—squat jars of homemade preserves, clotted cream, and a quilted tea cozy done up like a Cheshire cat. We ate everything. We were a week in the Trossachs, then another week down in Edinburgh and the Borders.

The book I read that afternoon was called *The Highland Clearances*—according to the back of the jacket, it was popular in its day. It retailed a series of events, especially brutal, and entirely unknown to me, that occurred in the north of Scotland in the late-eighteenth and early-nineteenth centuries, when, by force of arms—bayonet, truncheon, pike, fire—the English removed from their homes tens of thousands of men, women, and children, in order to make room for their, the English's, grandiose vision involving the large-scale farming of sheep. The book was written by a man named Prebble—Richard or Robert or John—sometime, I think, in the second half of the last century. I remember this name, because at the end of our honeymoon, fourteen supernal, irrecoverable days, the night before we were to fly from Glasgow back to Boston, we stayed at a bed-and-breakfast, unforgettably elegant, near the English border, in the sweetly named town of Peebles.

During the abysmal, godforsaken years when the Dakotas were evacuated (another state-engendered euphemism, as if the land, itself, was dangerous), the prior and analogous event was, so far as I recall, never invoked by either side. (Is there today anyone—excepting professional historians, diehard clansmen, and those like Anna, those, I mean, with whom she is in league, who make it their business to know such things—who knows anything about the Highland Clearances?) It must be that whichever functionary came up with the new and official name for the erstwhile Dakotas was at least somewhat familiar with the Scottish instance. Was the choice of name cynical? (Could the name, the concept it revived, have given rise to the action?) Was it sardonic? Coldly, recklessly arrogant? Psychopathic? Can a state be psychopathic? We know it can.

On Wednesday evening, as we were going to bed (I need not say: she to her bedroom, I to mine), Anna told me that, because I'd been in the hospital nearly all of the first three days she was in New Hampshire, she was extending by one day her stay with me. If I didn't object. I did object. I would have been overjoyed to hear she was cutting short her visit. But I was unwilling to say so. Her plan had been to arrive one Saturday and leave the next. Now she would stay until Sunday.

However pushy or presuming I've made her sound, Anna was not once during her stay—nor has she been since—insensitive. She was, and is, careful, painstaking about my feelings. In all other ways, too, painstaking. Until the minute she began to say what she had come to say, she was perplexed about how, or when, best to say it. Rightly, she felt she needed to spend enough time with me—was a week enough time, given, especially, how standoffish I'd been in her presence?— to be able to assess the kind of man I had become. She was unwilling to rely on impressions, less so on feelings, some forty-five years old. Having heard her out, how would I respond? What would I do? I prefer to believe—Anna assures me it is true—she was not afraid I would betray her. To pose the question starkly: was I emotionally, and now, physically up to hearing what she would say, to face what she would bring me to face, up to being and doing what she would ask? She wasn't sure, despite her unwavering certainty about the justness of her cause, despite the categorical nature of her charge (which included no trace of concern for my welfare), that she had the right to involve me, to put me, in several ways, at serious risk.

That Friday night—the second-to-last night of her time with me—Anna initiated the fateful conversation, in which, for my own peace of mind, I had willed myself to lose all interest.

We had just eaten dinner, which Anna prepared in my out-of-date, underequipped kitchen. I can't remember what we ate that night; but it would likely have been meatless (chilaquile? ratatouille? kung pao mock duck?), and it would have been good. Anna is an accomplished cook. Everything she fixed for me—that visit, and later—was good. I could not have loved Sara more than I did, but it would be fair to say that as a cook, my wife was erratic, ambitious beyond the reach of her skills, overzealous in her use of spices, indifferent to matters of presentation, and odd in her ideas about what went well with what.

We were sitting in the living room, my wife's old friend and I. I had done the dishes, which was the arrangement we'd tacitly adopted: Anna cooked the evening meal, shopped for the ingredients; I cleaned up after. Since Sara's death, lunch, when I thought to eat it, was usually catch-as-catch-can. Four times a week on average, sometime after one o'clock when the lunch rush subsides, I walked into town and got a sandwich or soup at what I'll call here, for old times' sake, the New Times Café. This didn't change with Anna's arrival. If anything, I was more eager for reasons to leave the house, and did so, not only for lunch, but whenever I could come up with a plausible—and, you have to believe, perfectly unconvincing—excuse. I assured Anna she was welcome to join me on these furloughs, which, in all instances, she declined to do. Because, of course, she, too, was uncomfortable in the awkwardnesses of our cohabitation—likely more uncomfortable than I, as she was not in her own home—and happy to see me leave.

It was 7:30. I was on the couch, a lumpy, scratchy thing (I mean the couch, though I had more than a few lumps myself), looking half-heartedly at a newsweekly Anna had picked up on one of her shopping excursions. She was sitting in a threadbare old wing chair—already a secondhand piece when Sara and I came upon it early in our marriage—which was where I customarily sat. Her feet were up, shoes off, on a needlepoint-covered footstool Sara bought to dress up the chair. We had not spoken in several minutes, not an easy interval of silence to abide. I was thinking there was just this night to get through, then one more night, then Anna would leave. Then I saw she'd put down the book she was reading—I don't remember what it was, but it was thick—and was staring at me. There was nothing combative in the way she looked at me. I would have said doleful. I sought for something harmless to say.

"When did you stop eating meat?" was what I produced. "When I knew you, you were not vegetarian."

"It's mostly red meat I won't eat," she said. "I was not a lot of things when you knew me. I was not a wife. I was not a mother. Not a teacher." She listed her vocations—they were for her clearly that—with real passion, for which I envied her. She shook her head, as if to clear it of a disconcerting scene. "I don't know what I was. When you knew me. I was hardly anything. And, anyway, why? Was the dinner bad?"

"No. No. It was delicious. You're a wonderful cook."

"I am satisfactory, just," she said. "You're easily pleased. My husband was a far better cook than I am." She spoke of her husband, whenever she did, by name, which I won't give here. "He was wonderful in the kitchen." She smiled.

"You miss him." I had become, more and more with age, master of the obvious.

She laughed at me. "I do. Of course I do."

"Of course," I said.

"Ray," she said. She was turning the conversation, taking charge. Again the way she said my name made me feel a little less absent. She took off her reading glasses, put them on the occasional table beside her, turned off the lamp. We were not quite in the dark; under circumstances less tense I might have taken the chance to doze. "Probably better," she said, "if I can't see you very well while we talk. I'm afraid I might lose my nerve."

"You're not afraid of me," I said. "Goodness."

"I'm not afraid of you. It's that, for all your pretense at rudeness, you seem such a kind old man."

"I don't know how kind I am," I said. "I'm beginning to dodder. But I don't know that I feel very kind. I wouldn't depend too much on that."

"Oh, no. I do depend on that. And it worries me."

I considered keeping silent at this point, as a means, maybe, of demonstrating how contingent my kindness could be, but more as a way of forestalling whatever it was coming at me. "Worries you because?" I said.

"Because this will be hard on you. It is hard on me. It will be harder on you. I wish that weren't the case."

"Why don't we forget it, then?"

"Tell me this," she said. "What do you know about cloning?" When I didn't answer right away, she said, "This is the best I can do. There is no graceful way to start. I'm not asking what you think, necessarily. I'm asking what you know."

"I don't know anything." Which was true. "I don't think anything." Also true.

"Not an overly impressive stance." There was affection in her voice.

"I have no stance." I felt piteously little affection for her then. "I know nothing about cloning. Should I? I guess I'm ashamed to say it, but I don't."

"Your shame—mock if you want—is not the issue."

"No mocking," I said. "What are we talking about?"

"All right," she said. "Listen to what I tell you."

"I'll listen," I said, "if you'll turn on the light. Would you mind? I can't do this in the dark. It's too theatrical. Leave your glasses off if you don't want to see me. I need to see you. If we're going to do this."

She turned the lamp back on—I'd been harsh; I could see I'd hurt her feelings—and left her glasses on the table where she'd put them.

"I don't mean to be theatrical. What I mean to do, what I've come to do, is tell you what you'll need to know."

"In order to?"

"I'll get to that," she said. "Will you let me speak?"

"Please," I said.

"I am a small part," Anna said, "of a group that opposes cloning, a group for whom cloning is a national, as well as personal, disgrace. It is morally and in every other way abhorrent. We believe cloning damns the soul of this country, if this country still has a soul, and the souls of all of us who stand by, do nothing. And we are determined to use all available means, short of armed insurrection, to put an end to this practice."

I wondered here, but didn't ask, what they planned to do about the conceivably hundreds of millions of clones already in existence. Would these creatures, I didn't know how else to think of them, have the sins of their makers visited on them?

"We are too few, too covert, to be a coherent force. So long as we are small, so long as what we say and do makes no difference, we are tolerated by the government. Perhaps, without knowing it, we are even indulged. The general population ignores us. We are only loosely conjoined, intentionally so. I don't really know any of the others. I know a scant few of them only by sight. I know no one's name."

The configuration she described—the system of isolate, atomistic, say, three-person action cells designed to prevent discovery and capture of greater numbers—was familiar to me from a film I'd seen when I was a boy. It was an old, old film, in black and white—I can't imagine where my friend got the disk—called *The Battle of Algiers*. I had not heard of it then, have not heard it referred to since. It was the first foreign film I'd seen, the first time I'd had to contend with subtitles. It moved me inordinately. As I remember, it filled me with a directionless fervor and indignation, and a completely unearned sense of my own virtue, none of which persisted much beyond the afternoon I spent watching it. Was there some secret handshake or gesture, a single mutating password, or a call-and-response sequence of trigger words, with which one member of Anna's group identified herself to another? I wanted to ask this, too.

"My husband was in the group before I was. He was in it from the first. He'd had a voice in shaping it. This was before we married, before I met him, before the state took over the dirty work and made it policy. When the replication program was instituted, he refused to participate. As I did. As you did not. This is a truth hard for me to make peace with, but he would probably be alive still if there had been a clone. I believe he was right to do what he did. I believed in him, in what he believed. I involved myself in the resistance; I stayed involved through all the frustrating and fruitless years. I'm still involved, probably, because of him."

Here she stopped. She picked up her glasses and put them on. She rose. "Give me a minute," she said. She went into the kitchen, from which she called out, "Can I get you something?"

"I'm fine," I said.

I heard the microwave kick on. She came back with a mug of tea. She sat down and left her glasses on. What she said next was different in substance and tone, more confidential. It was something, I believe, she had not expected to say.

"This is too much for me, I'm afraid. Too costly. I'm no longer up to it, if I ever was. And now, with what has happened, without him, I've been asked to go past where I should ever have been asked to go. Past, really, where I'm willing to go."

I could see she was ready to cry. I said nothing. I watched while she sought to compose herself. I tried to help her by assuming, seated on the couch, what I meant to be a sympathetic posture. We are, all things considered, a ridiculous species, not worth copying.

"I don't want to be here, Ray. I can't say for sure what my husband would have wanted me to do. I don't want to bring you into this. I am not taking revenge, if that's what you've been thinking. I'm not. I'm not vengeful, towards you or anyone. I don't have it in me. Over the years, when I thought of you at all, I thought of you kindly. I wished you well. And Sara. I don't want to be in this, myself. I want to be at home, or visiting my children. I want to be with their children. I regret every minute not in their presence, one or the other of them. I want to be at ease. You understand this. I want to be easy. I'm not sick, but I've begun to wear down. As much as I can, I want to enjoy what's left. However this goes, whatever happens, this will be the last of it for me. And it will not go well."

I am not a man who is undone by a woman crying. In the seven years we were married, I watched Sara cry many times. What you'd expect in the routine course of things. Not once, I want to believe, was it the result of intentional cruelty on my part.

"You are lucky in your children," I said.

"I'm sorry for you," she said.

"No. I mean, not just now. Not just because of what you said. I think about this all the time. I try not to, but I do. I wonder what my life might be, had my son lived."

What she did next made me uncomfortable: she came and sat beside me on the couch. I recognized it as a gesture of consolation, but it felt intrusive. She was too close. I could smell the dinner on her.

"You should refuse, Ray," she said. "You should listen to me, then you should refuse. Send me home. I'll tell them you can't be trusted. That you are too great a risk. Don't do what I ask. When I ask, refuse me."

"How could I not?" I said.

Then I asked a question I was surprised I had not asked already. "How did you find me?"

As I thought she might, she smiled. "I wish I could say, 'We have our ways,' but it was one call to the alumni relations office."

"I wouldn't have known how to find you."

"You wouldn't have wanted to," she said.

I told Anna I wonder often what my life might be like if my son had lived. This is true, and not at all a recent phenomenon. What I didn't say was this: I have not wondered, or only very rarely, what, had he lived—he would be thirty-four—my son, and *his* life, might be like.

What this says about me is not something I'm happy to acknowledge. Worse, there is a broadly correlative question I ask myself with an obsessive frequency. If, like some accursed fairy-tale father, I'd been given the choice to save one or the other of them, my young wife or my infant son, which would I have spared? The question is atrocious. So, too, that I would ask it over and over again, that I would ask it at all. My response, because I have one, because it never changes, because each time it is immediate and unflinching and unequivocal, is obscene. Given the choice to save my wife or my son, I would, now and always, save my wife, whom I loved and knew and lived with and depended on.

"In twenty-five years," she said, "we've been able to gain no first-hand knowledge of what goes on inside the Clearances. Which is remarkable, given how diligent we've been. If the government is doing what it set out to do, there will be close to two hundred and fifty million clones in there, living their lives. We can only speculate. How do they live? Day to day, hour to hour. What do they do? How are they treated? What do they eat? How do they think, and what do they think about? How are the infants produced? If they are borne, who bears them? Who delivers them? Are they suckled? How are they reared? Who rears them? Who, that is, are their parents? Are they parented? Do they get an education of any sort? Are they taught to speak? Are they permitted to speak? Have they developed a language of their own? How are they governed? Are they named? Are the males and females segregated? Do they feel desire? Do they feel love? What if these living repositories of human parts themselves require medical care? Do they know they are clones? Do they experience what we would call a sense of self, whatever we might mean by that? What happens when a clone gets old? What happens when a clone dies? Of natural causes, I mean, before he or she is harvested. What happens when they've been harvested? Suppose a hand is taken? Or a leg? Or an eye? Or a liver? Their heart. What is done with what remains? Do they protest? Can they conceive of protest? Do they rebel? Are they punished? What form does their punishment take? How are they dressed? Do they know kindness? Do they know God? If so, what

God? Are clones human beings? If they are not, in what way not? What are the differences between them and us? Where, in the business of cloning—it is a business, if the government is involved—is the profit? How is the money made?"

I don't remember all the questions Anna posed in that conversation. Nor can I be sure which of the questions I've tallied here were hers, and which are questions I've come up with, after the event. We know some of the answers now. Anna does, and her group, and I, perforce, do, too. Until we (I chafe at the pronoun) make public this information—this report is intended as the first step in a broad-based, multiform campaign of disclosure—and more so afterwards (when we are exposed and no longer of use), we are, Anna and I, in significant danger.

"So far as we know," Anna said, "no one has been inside." She was no longer beside me on the couch. As she began to unroll her sample questions, she stood up, just so she might pace slowly the width of the living room, back and forth between the wing chair and the double windows. Instinctively, I spread out, legs and arms, occupying as much of the couch as I could to discourage her sitting back down. With the enumeration of each successive question, she became more and more absorbed in her task, paid less attention to me. "And not once in twenty-five years has there been a creditable report of a clone come outside the Clearances. We have waited and watched for it. Religiously. As if we were a lunatic cult."

"And you're not," I am sorry to say I said.

Either she didn't hear this, or she ignored it. She stopped pacing. She sat down heavily in the wing chair, as though she had worn herself out.

What she said next, she said quietly, without affect. "We have a clone."

For several seconds, I said nothing, I was irrational enough to think the clone Anna said they had might be Sara's, that this would explain Anna's coming to me. I confess this possibility, however macabre it might have proved if realized (Sara would be no older than twenty-one; I would be an enfeebled old man, not just unrecognizable but unknown. I would mean nothing to her. For me, after the first delusory moments, it would be killing.), filled me with expectancy and something like physical desire. I knew it was not possible; Sara died before the replication program was initiated. "Where did you get it?" I said.

"Him," Anna said. "I'm not sure. He came to us. Wandered off. Was misplaced. Found. I don't really know."

"Escaped."

"No. We don't think that's what happened. The concept of escape would have no meaning for a clone. We don't believe they'd have any reason to think there was anywhere to escape to, that there existed anything other than what they already knew. No idea of inside and outside. Escape, as an intentional act, would be inconceivable. It would be in the best interests of the government, and their enterprise, if this were so, and we believe it is so. I'm sorry. Did that sound prepared?"

"Yes."

"Does it make sense?" she said.

"If you mean, 'Can I follow the logic?' I can. But no. None of this makes sense. You came to spend a week with me because you found a clone."

"I didn't find him. I don't know who did."

"But you have him?"

"He was brought to me. He stayed with me six days. I don't have him now."

"Who's got him?"

"He's somewhere safe."

"Oh, good," I said. "I'm relieved." After forty-five years, through not a single effort of my own, I'd been given the chance to make some amends to Anna. Once again I was boorish. To this day, I have no idea why. Anna allows it might be something about her that irks me, but I will not let her take the blame.

"Listen, Ray. The entire system depends on one basic principle: originals must never meet, must never see, a clone. If such an encounter should take place, if one of us should run into one of them, the effect would be to transform what is a conscionable, even, for some of us, a reassuring abstraction, into a thing literal and real. The consequences would be disastrous."

"We believe this," I said.

"We do," she said. "We can believe nothing else. Look, you unpleasant, sullen old man. Just shut up. You will not keep me from saying what I want to say by being churlish."

She left me no space to respond.

"If one clone has somehow got himself outside the Clearances, as has now happened, and there are some two hundred and fifty million clones inside the Clearances, it is a statistical certainty that, in twenty-five years, other clones have also got themselves out."—I am mathematician enough to have known that Anna's assertion, though it might well be true, was a case not susceptible of statistical analysis, and that the very notion of 'statistical certainty' is oxymoron. "If this *has* happened, and it has, it is not public knowledge. We don't know about it. And we would. So we've concluded that the system of tracking down and capturing any such wayward clones must be swift and sure, pitiless, unerring. We also believe that when a clone is captured, he is killed. No clone who has been outside the Clearances, who has experienced, no matter how briefly, what is outside, who knows that there is an outside, can be allowed to bring that knowledge back in."

"They are killed?"

"Executed. Yes. They must be," she said. "All useful parts would be harvested and banked."

"After they are dead, presumably. You don't mean first."

"We don't know. We do know nothing would be wasted."

"You are sure about this?"

"We are as sure as we can be," she said. "We are sure. I tell you this, because I want you to appreciate the danger we're in. The danger you're in."

"Oh, for the love of Mike," I said. "I am not in danger. I am not a damned clone." Sadly, that is verbatim.

"Whenever a clone is captured, whoever is found to have helped or harbored him, whoever has recognized him for a clone, must also be taken. We don't know what happens to *these* people. Maybe they are cut up for parts, then disposed of. The government would not balk at this. It would be a penalty to their taste, ruthless and condign: originals, for their crime against the state, made copies. In any case, you are most certainly in danger. And it is my fault."

"Because of what you've told me."

"Yes. And because of what I've come to ask you to do."

"So what is it?"

"To start, we want you to meet with this clone."

"*You* don't."

"No," she said. "I don't."

"Why me?"

You will be wondering, here, how it was possible, at this late moment in the conversation, for me not to know what her answer would be. I will say only that I didn't know.

"The clone is yours," Anna said.

# Four

This is how it turns out, with me all but confined to a bed in Calgary. Writing this report.

I am in Canada, having effectively traversed—a kind of forced march—that benevolent and enlightened country. Do I miss America? I do, yes. It is my home. Though I know very little of it, it is all I know. There are parts of northern New Hampshire and the Northeast Kingdom that for me are sacred places. I continue to make this claim to myself, though I am not sure it is true. Mount Cardigan, Mount Assurance, Mascoma Lake, Squam Lake, Zealand Hut at Zealand Falls at the base of Zealand Peak, Lake Willoughby. Even Weirs Beach on Winnipesaukee. I went to such places more than once with my father when I was a boy. My mother was never along. More than all else I remember the smell of conifers, the light at dawn and the mist in the morning thick on the lakes, the lakes like pearl in the moonlight, the snapping clearness of the night sky. Conventional stuff, I suppose. I'm afraid I remember these things better than I do my father, who has been dead a long time. When we first came back to New Hampshire to live, I took Sara to the White Mountains. She had lived most of her life in Indianola; she was appreciative. (When she'd lived several years in New England and had some basis for the comparison, she admitted she preferred the less exacting Greens, and Vermont in general—

"It just seems better groomed," she said, as unemphatically as she could.) But in the forty-odd years intervening, I have not gone again to any of those spots. Maybe because they *are* sacred to me. After Sara died, and the baby, my infant son (thank God we had not named him), I pretty much stayed put. America is not easy to miss.

Too late, but I'd have liked, I think, to have lived, or died, by the sea.

*By the sea, by the sea, by the beautiful sea.*
*You and I, you and I, oh how happy we'll be.*
*I long to be beside your side, beside the sea,*
*Beside the seaside, by the beautiful sea.*

These are the only words I remember from a song my mother sang to me. As her mother had sung it to her. When my mother sang it, and I was no longer an infant, I cringed at the grammatical rectitude of "You and I, you and I," thinking she must have got it wrong, that, for every musical reason, it ought to go: "You and me, you and me, oh how happy we'll be." She was right. The mistake was not hers. After her death, in a spurt of piety and the first flush of orphanhood—November 2027, I was in my early twenties—I looked it up. The song was more than one hundred years old, written in 1914 by Harold Atteridge (words) and Harry Carroll (music). Reading what I've written here, I see I have substituted, as I do always when I think of this song, when I sing these lines to myself, the word "long" in the third sentence for the "love" of the original. I prefer my version.

I was born and raised and, after college and graduate school, spent all my adult life in western New Hampshire, as far, in that state, from the Atlantic littoral as one could be. My mother and father and I would once or twice a summer make the drive to the shore, to Hampton Beach, where, even then, the water was full of sewage and runoff, industrial and medical waste, all sorts of marine garbage, and a tarry sludge that stuck to the bottom of your feet. You would get sick swimming in that water, though hordes of very wealthy people swam there. I wasn't much of a swimmer. I didn't at all like being in the ocean. I didn't like not knowing what I might be stepping on, what might be scuttling around my feet. My mother was an enthusiast and a strong swimmer. If you wanted to swim in clean, non-toxic water, you had to drive up the coast into Maine, to be safe, as far north as, say, Boothbay, and then the water would be too cold until late in the summer. In college, I was not too far from the Chesapeake Bay, and, in the spring of my freshman year, I went several times to Virginia Beach with two boozy, showy boys from Nashville. In my sophomore year, I went with Ann—in our final, apocalyptic phone call, she used the word "discarded" to describe what I had done to her—to a place on the Eastern Shore called Chance. Iowa is landlocked, of course, and the two years I spent there in graduate school—the first of which as an engine of dismay for Anna—I didn't see the sea.

I have just ended a year on the run, living in close quarters—for me a year of unprecedented intimacy—with Anna and, in one person, a genetic facsimile of myself and a recognizable version of myself as a twenty-one-year-old. I have claimed, in the spurt of self-abasement with which I began, that this report will not be about me; but it is no accident, no surprise that, from time to time, my past will seem to intrude upon the narrative, will want to infiltrate, to subvert the express and more than sufficient purpose of this report. It appears I will not keep it out, that I will welcome it, solicit it. When your parents are gone, when your wife is gone, when you have no children who survive, no family at all, no friends, when there is no one who shares your past, no one who remembers it, then, for all you can prove, or even determine, your past might as well never have been. It might never have been. This report, whoever's idea it was I write it, whatever use others will make of it, however reluctant I was at the start, is my report now.

When Anna told me, "The clone is yours"—a crystalline, phase-shifting point beyond which nothing would for either of us ever be the same—I did not respond as you'd expect. I did not say, as might some half-cooked, pasteboard character in a novel, anything remotely like, "Mine? The clone is mine? What do you mean?" In the instant she said, "The clone is yours," I moved past any confusion, past any doubt about the veracity of her statement. "You've seen him?" I said.

"I have."

"He looks like me?" An unscientific question, more than a trace narcissistic, but I was steady. I could have had no real idea what I was facing.

"He looks just like you." She smiled. "Like you used to look. A bit bigger."

"Taller?"

"Taller. Broader."

"He's twenty-one," I said.

"That's right," she said. "You're a whiz."

"I'm not. The doctor asked me about it. About him. What is his name?"

"I don't know. We don't think he has a name," she said. "It's a terrible thing. I don't know what to call him."

"But he's all right?"

I don't think I yet felt for the clone any kind of proprietary concern, which, directed towards the clone, would also constitute a new and misbegotten opening for the propagation and expression of self-love. In the swamplands of self-love, it happens, I am a pioneer.

"He's all right," she said. "He's bewildered. Scared. He was completely narcotized when he was found. Full of drugs. That's been hard. He's just now coming off them. Just now coming clear."

"What kind of drugs?"

"All kinds," she said.

"They *found* him?"

"Yes."

"Who did? You?"

"No," she said. "I didn't find him."

"Who did then?"

"I can't tell you," she said.

"But you know?"

"No. I don't know."

"Where was he found?" I said. "What was he doing?"

"I don't know that either. I assume it was somewhere just outside the Clearances. He couldn't have gone far the shape he was in. It's a wonder he could stand. The poor boy. I don't know what he was doing."

"What do you know?"

"Enough," she said.

"You've been with him? You've been in his presence?"

"Yes," she said. "I spent six days with him."

"Where? What were the circumstances?"

"In _____." Here she named the town in Iowa. "In my house. He lived with me."

"He lived with you? "

"I took care of him. He was in awfully rough shape. It was not my decision."

"Your group." I was already sick of them.

"They brought him to me," she said. "Yes."

"Is he still there? In your house?"

"No."

"Where is he?"

"I can't tell you," she said.

"Because you don't know."

"No," she said. "But I can't tell you. Not yet."

"When can you tell me?"

"If you agree to do what they ask," she said, "I'll take you to him."

It was here, or hereabouts, our conversation stopped for the evening. I was exhausted and surly. The floor had fallen away, but I refused to drop.

We went to sleep on terms awkward and unresolved. The next morning I lay in bed ungraciously late, in a flagrant attempt—Anna would not have missed it—to foreshorten the last day of her stay. If I could have avoided her altogether, I think I would have. I came out into the living room in my pajamas and a robe. I was wobbly. It was nearly eleven. The drapes were drawn back, all the windows open. The morning was already hot. We would need the air-conditioning. I would have to go from room to room, lowering the storms and sashes, which, in my state, would entail exertion and, I let myself think, risk. Anna was not in the house. I could be dead before she returned. There was some evidence in the kitchen she'd made herself breakfast. There was no note. I sat at the kitchen table with a cup of tea and noticed that even on this sweltering morning my toes were cold and had a bluish tinge. My fingers, too, were cold, the palms, the heels of my hands, blue as well. I was not getting enough blood to my extremities. I felt the tip of my nose. I was reminded again of my own frailty. When the time came, I would not be loath to admit it: Anna, and what she'd brought with her, were too much for me. I would be unembarrassed; I would be content to plead infirmity, incapacity, to whatever she proposed, which, if she was to be believed, would please her. The kitchen smelled of toast and syrup. Through the open window I could hear one of the twins next door, Sophie or Marie, crying. Whichever one it was, she was spitting mad, pitching a whale of a fit. I hated to think of that sweet face contorted in anger.

When I was a boy, the three of us, my father, mother, and I, went to church on Sunday morning. We went twice a month, every other Sunday, to the Presbyterian church. It was a nineteenth-century brick building, an upstart church in the colonial town, set a humbling three blocks off the green, close enough to our house so we could walk to it. Over the years, the church had been subjected to a continuous and capricious architecture, as if successive building committees had played a sort of inter-generational dominos. The randomness in the style of the additions—wings perpendicular and oblique, glazed breezeways, ornamental cloisters—and in their points of attachment to the original structure was jarring. By the time we joined it, the church as a physical entity had ceased to make sense. There was a foolishness in the way it was laid out that I loved. I wandered the halls, eluding my parents, finding myself lost within its illogical precincts. I was christened there. The pastor was a giant. He was six-foot-eleven, and even as a boy—we stopped attending church when my father died—I could tell he was a fine preacher. I can't remember any music, though there must have been an organ or a piano and hymns. For the offering my father took a folded check from the inside pocket of his suit coat and put it on the collection plate. He avoided looking at anyone when he did this. After the service, there were often doughnuts, homemade baked goods, in the narthex. There was a church camp in summer I didn't go to, and every once in a while, all the kids in the congregation were invited to come and sit on the floor in front of the altar to listen to a children's sermon. I was too shy to go forward, and watched from a pew with my parents. I remember there were hand puppets once, barnyard animals—a donkey, a cow, a rooster, a lamb, maybe a dog. The pastor played the banjo. A woman who worked at the post office sang on occasion. So there was music. Of the three of us, only my father took communion.

I didn't know where Anna was, and I had not given any thought to her attitude towards God, but I couldn't imagine she had gone to church. Virtually no one in Lebanon now goes to church. On Sunday, the church bells don't ring. The carillon on the Catholic church is at all times quiet, the rectories and parish houses have been sold, the ministers are itinerant, and the churches themselves are used primarily for weddings, funerals, and various civic functions.

At one o'clock, when Anna came back, I was still in my robe and pajamas. I was sitting, still, at the kitchen table, a mug of cold milky tea in front of me. I might have fallen asleep. I had not washed. I had not gotten to the air-conditioning or the windows, and the house was stifling. Anna came in through the side door, which opened into a small mudroom/pantry directly off the kitchen.

"Sleeping Beauty," she said.

She was wearing khaki shorts, running shoes, a white T-shirt with little flowers embroidered on the neck, and a yellow visor. In each hand she had a shopping bag loaded with groceries. Her forearms and calves were sinewy and mottled with freckles. She was spry. She hoisted each bag onto the counter. She had gotten stronger, livelier with age. I was a slug, a sorely diminished thing. Watching her move about my kitchen, sorting through her purchases, putting them away in my cabinets, I wanted only to go back to bed.

"What have you got there?" I said.

"I had to lay in supplies for the trip home."

"That's right," I said. "When are you leaving?"

She smiled at me. "You know exactly when I'm leaving. You jerk. You've been counting the minutes."

"Tomorrow," I said.

"First thing. But you're not off the hook yet."

"I had that sense," I said. "How did you sleep?"

"Okay," she said. "You were snoring."

"You could hear me?"

"I could hear you. You were snoring away. Then you'd make this horrific gasping sound, and you'd stop. As if you'd stopped breathing. I was worried."

"Sorry," I said. "I didn't know I snored."

"My husband was a great snorer," she said. "The same thing. Suddenly he'd gasp and stop breathing. He went to a sleep clinic. They gave him a machine to use at night. A mask to wear over his nose. It helped him sleep. Helped me, too. If there's time, you should look into it."

"If there's time?"

"Well," she said. "Let's wait. Have you had lunch? You haven't, clearly. I'll fix us some lunch. We'll eat, you'll put on some clothes, and then we'll talk. We'll finish it up, see where we are."

"I had the thought," I said, "that maybe you'd gone to church."

"No," she said. "Not today."

Anna made a delicious chicken salad with apples and celery and walnuts and grapes. It was perhaps the most comprehensive dish prepared in that kitchen in the last forty-five years, and it took her just over fifteen minutes (when had she cooked the chicken?) to put it together. We ate without conversation at the kitchen table. The house heated up. After lunch, as she'd stipulated, I showered and dressed. She washed the dishes and, sparing me, closed the windows. I switched on the air-conditioning. It was past two in the afternoon when we reconvened. She was waiting in the living room, sitting on the edge of the couch, inclined forward, her forearms on her knees. I sat down in the wing chair opposite. We had taken our positions, but before she could start, I asked a question I'd been thinking about since the night before.

"You spoke to him?"

"Yes, " she said. "As much as I could. Whenever he was conscious and reasonably comfortable. I talked myself silly."

She smiled.

"What?"

"I even sang to him," she said. "And I don't sing."

"What did he say?" I said. "What did he tell you?"

"He didn't speak."

"At all?"

"No."

"Why not?"

"It's not clear," she said, "that he *can* speak."

"Why not?" We had just begun, and already I was the querulous child.

"I don't know. It may be that, physically, he can't speak. Or that he doesn't have language. We'll have to see."

"When?"

She looked at me, as if to say, "If you must ask questions, ask the right ones."

"What is it you want from me?" I said.

"I don't want anything from you. If it were up to me, I wouldn't be here, you wouldn't be involved."

"Yes. Yes. You've said this."

"It's important you know it. It's important I say it. It's what I mean."

"But you're here," I said. "We're talking. You've taken great pains, gone to great lengths."

"You can't imagine," she said.

"All right. So?"

"So no more questions. Here's what they," before I could interrupt, "here's what my group wants you to do. They want you to meet your clone. Face to face. They want you to spend time with him. Then they want you to write about how that feels, to write about what that means. To you. To meet your clone."

"Why? Because they think what? It will be devastating?"

"That's what they think. Obviously, there's no one who could know how it will feel. I can tell you it will not be easy, or pleasant."

"Why would they want me to write about this?"

"Come on, Ray. They believe—I have to admit I believe it, too— that when it is published, your account will be of tremendous importance to their cause." She hesitated. "It's just as much my cause. And it's worthy. Whatever else about the group may be corrupt, the cause is worthy." She came back to me. "Listen. Can you possibly think that of all the clones in the Clearances—all two hundred fifty million, or however many there are—not one of them ever dies—by accident, from illness, from natural causes—before he or she is used?"

"I haven't thought about it. As you know."

"Think about it now. Of course they die. They must die all the time. As we do. Thousands and thousands a day. More. I don't know how many. No one is ever contacted. No one ever hears his clone has died. Why do you think that is? What do you think happens?"

"I don't know, Anna. Clearly, I don't know."

"You're not meant to. But if the system is to continue, it must be that when an original needs a part after his clone is dead, he is given a compatible part from some constantly replenished store of spares and left to believe the part comes from his clone. I told you it is the key to survival for the whole business, that an original never meet his copy. Do you remember?"

"For Pete's sake."

"Okay," she said. "Well, it is only slightly less important that an original never have cause to think about his clone. At least until the clone is required. And then you don't question it; you're simply glad he's there for the taking."

"And my account, as you're calling it, will do what? Make us think about our clones? Is that it?"

"That's the operative idea," she said.

I laughed. I had not laughed, not really laughed, wholeheartedly, in decades. The idea of my writing an account, an account of anything, struck me as very funny and, not incidentally, unimaginable. But it was more than that. The larger situation, and my part in it, seemed, just then, preposterous. I laughed so strenuously I thought I would injure myself. I could not catch a breath. The word "operative." "That's the operative idea," she'd said. I found this surpassingly funny. My stomach went into spasm, my ribs hurt. I begged Anna to help me. "Help me," I said. It was all I could say. I thought my heart would stop. I thought I might die laughing this way. Right, I thought, to die, now, as I was, laughing. I had overstayed. My life was ludicrous.

"Why are you laughing?" Anna said.

I thought she could not have said anything funnier. Despite what I've just written—all hindsight—it is unlikely I had any idea why I was laughing.

"Tell me," she said. "I'd like to laugh."

I couldn't speak.

"Then stop," she said. "Please. No more."

I stopped.

"That was shabby," she said. "You make me sad, Ray. Again."

"I'm sorry," I said. "Again."

"Can you collect yourself?"

"I'm fine," I said. "I don't know why I did that."

"I need you to be sensible," she said.

"I will be. Give me a second."

"All right," she said.

"I can't write anything," I said. In part, at least, to show her I had kept track.

"You can," she said. "If you decide to."

"I can't. And why would I decide to?"

"That's not something I can tell you."

"You want me to decline," I said.

"I do," she said. "You know, this is not easy for me. More than anything I want what your account would help bring about. I despise the practice of cloning. I want it to end. I want not one other clone to be made. But I have no right to ask this of you. The risks are enormous."

"Have you asked?"

"No," she said. "I have not. I have told you what they want you to do."

"They know you're here?"

"They sent me."

"So I'm already involved."

"Yes."

"Can I decline? Can I choose not to do what they ask?"

"I'm not sure, Ray. I don't know what the consequences will be if you refuse. I don't know what they'll do. I've lost my sense of them. I no longer trust them. I can tell you they won't consult me."

"I won't be coerced," I said.

"That's admirable," she said.

"I'm not unwilling to die," I said.

"I'm sorry to hear that," she said. "You should want to live."

"Why?"

"I can't tell you that either," she said.

"If I do what they ask, if I write the account, it will be published."

"Yes. They'll see to that."

"Where? Here? In the U.S.?"

"I'm not sure. Maybe. Attempts will be made to keep it from appearing. Everywhere else."

"Who will read it?"

"Everyone," she said. "At least that's the hope."

"I can't write," I said.

"I assure you, Ray, the quality of the prose will not be an issue. What you need to think about is what will happen to you once the account appears."

At this point, I felt little fear. The dangers were wholly theoretical. They bore little connection to the real experience of, say, physical pain or extinction, if one does, in fact, experience extinction. Now, as I write this, the situation is decreasingly theoretical, and, though I've felt no pain as yet, nothing out of the ordinary, the real stuff is close. Still, I am not afraid. This is not a function of courage. I've discovered, too late for it to be of any use to me, that I am not without courage, but I believe my present lack of fear, a species of detachment, has more to do with the sadness and fatigue that fill me. There is little room in me for fear.

"What will happen?"

"They will kill you," she said. "They will find you, wherever you go, and they will kill you."

"We're not talking about your group now."

"No," she said. "Though once *they* have your account, I expect there's nothing they'll like better than your death. It would be a great boon for them. Maybe more powerful than the report itself. As a martyr you'd be very useful. You'd be eloquent."

"If you've thought of that, won't they?"

"The government, you mean?"

"Yes."

"Yes," she said, "they'll think of it. Of course."

"But it won't stop them."

"No. They won't let you live. They can't. You will know, you will have seen, too much."

"So either way," I said.

"Oh," she said, "I don't know. You could refuse and take your chances. I can't say for sure what my group will do. The other way, you'd have no chance. It's not a happy choice."

"Then your coming here . . . ?"

"Yes," she said.

"Thanks."

"I'm sorry," she said. "Whatever happens to you will happen to me. That's a small consolation, I know."

"It's no consolation." I said. "It is all the more reason to refuse. Why on earth would I do this? I won't do this. Go home. Tell them that I won't do it."

"Listen, Ray," she said. "Put aside any concern you have for me. I knew what I was doing when I came here. I've already made my decision. If it were my clone, if it were my report to write, I would. I wish it were my clone. I wish it were. That would be easier. It wouldn't be easy, but it would be easier. I would be frightened. I would be sad. I am frightened, and sad. But I would do it."

"You would do it," I said.

"Ray. I'm saying what I would do. I'm not saying what I think you should do."

"I know," I said. "You would do it?"

"Yes."

"What about your children?"

"They have nothing to do with your decision," she said. "I won't talk about them now."

If I could have managed it, I would be buried beside Sara, and we'd both be buried in New Hampshire. On a hill in the country just out-side the town where she and I lived is a small cemetery that would have been cozy. My parents are buried in a churchyard just fifteen miles to the south. Sara is buried in Indianola. Her father insisted Sara's body be brought back to Iowa. She is buried there, with her par-ents, in the Bird family plot. I have not been to her grave since the funeral. We had lived together so short a time, I was persuaded they had more right to her than I did. I was easily persuaded, because I was, really, indifferent about where she was buried. Her father could do her no more harm, and I would not see her again.

I was with her in the hospital when she died. I sat by her bed, held her hand. I told her I loved her. I had lost a son I never got to see. There could be little doubt I would soon lose my wife. I was blasted, separated from myself, yanked out of my mind, unable to think or feel. Sara was not conscious of me, for which I am grateful. I don't remember much about the time I spent with her in that hos-pital room. I don't remember the moment she died. I don't remem-ber what the doctor said, or how he said it, or what I did after that. I ought to remember it all, but I have only one discrete memory from those cavernous hours.

Her parents had flown in for the birth of our son. The baby was already dead by the time they arrived. They were in the waiting room.

They were distraught. I was sorry they were there. Her father was loathsome. Her mother was inoffensive; she had done nothing to earn my enmity. For her sake, I tried to keep them informed. I came out at regular intervals to bring them word. There was never anything to say. Sara's condition continued to worsen, and then she died. At some point, after six or seven hours of this deathwatch, I left the room with the vague intention of getting a candy bar and a drink from some vending machines I thought I'd seen on the way in. I didn't know what I was doing, or where I was going. I wandered off. When I got back to the room, having to be led there by a hospital volunteer, having forgotten why I'd left, Sara's father, the Reverend Bird, was standing over her. The room was dark; he had turned off the lights. He had some kind of prayer book in his hand, and he was reading from it aloud. I don't know what he was intoning, though I've told myself, subsequently, he was performing the last rites. I knew that if she were awake, if she could hear him, see him standing there in the dark, Sara would be terrified. She would not want him there, doing that. I was furious. I told him to get out. He could see how angry I was and, wisely, did not resist.

# Five

The heart is a vulgar thing. For all its symbolic currency—it is the only organ that so resonates (imagine a comparable poetic fuss made over the liver or lungs)—it is ignoble. A deep red mass of muscle tissue—quadripartite, not heart-shaped—with pipes and valves. On the streets of Calgary, *my* heart, already damaged, already rickety and winded, for the second time in a year threatened to shut down altogether. The cardiologist who saw me there, meaning, I think, to ease me of blame, said, "It may simply be your heart was programmed to last you until now, and not much longer."

I might have taken a new heart. It need not have come from *my* clone. Had I asked for one, it would have been taken from some superfluous clone. The heart perfectly homologous—the government has no cause to be sloppy; its supply of hearts is inexhaustible—but still a stranger, a disrupter of whatever sense of intimacy I might have had with my own body. (In the days before cloning, there was inculcated between donor and recipient—with the aim, largely, of promoting organ donation—the notion of solidarity. In the current mode of exchange, where the "donation" is in no respect volitional, no permission sought, among other things we have lost, we have lost that.)

In what way, for whom, is my extended survival necessary? Or good? What is my presence here, that my absence would be significant?

And these questions are beside the point. Even if my life were worth prolonging, I could not have taken a heart from my clone. Or from any other.

I am writing this report. There may be value in that.

In this one respect, at least, it seems I cling to life: I am aware of my heart, alert to it, as never before. I attend to its systoles and diastoles, its firings and misses, as if I were leaning in to catch the last whispers of someone I loved. I have earned the metaphor. This one, too: What would my life with Sara have been like, her life with me, if I had had a different heart?

The texture of our brief life together—I mean the whole, not just the surface texture—was, until the very last, peaceful and easy. We were congenial. We did not fight, or rarely. There was never any anger sustained between us. We worked well and productively together. We kept a clean and orderly house, and took comfort in our thrift. We traveled when we could. We enjoyed each other's company. I was faithful. By rule and nature, but also because I could not believe my luck. She was a fine and beautiful woman, and, to risk belaboring the point, I was, in all ways, ordinary and undistinguished. I believe she was faithful to me. (I mean in saying this to cast no doubt.) I know—I always knew—I was less than what she needed me to be. That as her husband, principally in the quality of my love, day by day I failed her. I believe she loved me, and that her capacity to give and receive love was far greater than my own. I see now I didn't do enough to help her realize that capacity, come full into her endowment. To love me in the way I asked to be loved, in the way, perhaps, I permitted her to love me, she didn't need to love enough, at a pitch sufficiently high or a level sufficiently deep, to love the way she could. The waste of it is what, after all the years, I can't stop feeling. I taste it still on my tongue. It is what I see, too often, when I close my eyes. Our life together so short. My obtuseness. My reserve. Unforgivable.

Though I didn't see this at the start, she came to me sad and broken. Beyond what I could imagine, watching her with her father, I don't know much about her childhood in Indianola. For good reason, she was not eager to talk about it. The truth is, I'm not sure I cared to know more than I did. She was the eldest of three children and the primary, I'd say obsessive, focus of her father's attentions. She had a brother and a sister. Her father left the two of them all but exclusively to the care of their mother, who, in return for this sop, seemed willing to surrender all parental rights and influence with respect to Sara. When he knew she would be beautiful—I've seen the pictures: Sara *en pointe* in *Sleeping Beauty*; Sara with her violin; Sara sitting on her Connemara pony; Sara in her cotillion gown—her father, the Reverend Bird, a desperate Anglophile, had a vision for Sara. In imagining her become what he wanted her to become, in fashioning her for his own delight, I believe he conflated two types, neither of which he'd ever bumped up against in the flesh: the nineteenth-century squire's daughter and the southern belle (the second, of which there was a surfeit at William and Mary when I was there, is, I'm guessing, just a poor copy of the first). He enrolled her at St. Agatha's, a K–12 Episcopal school for girls. He insisted she take lessons on the piano and violin. He had her study dance with a teacher in Des Moines, and, by the time she was fourteen, Sara was lead dancer in that city's youth ballet company. He bought her the pony, Finn (alas, even the pony gets an alias), which he boarded on a farm west of Indianola, and paid a matronly Devonshire woman, married to a fellow priest in the bishopric, to instruct her in equitation and dressage. He took an avid, unnatural interest in her clothes and hair and makeup and jewelry. It was he who decided her ears should be pierced. He insisted she get biweekly manicures. Even after we were married, he persisted in appraising her appearance, and continued to send her expensive jewelry and clothes, which, by then—this made me very glad—she would not wear.

I met him for the first time at Easter, 2027. It had been only since late January that Sara had been living with me in my apartment above the Hmong gift shop in downtown Ames. She had not told her parents about our arrangement. She was expected home for the holiday. She asked me to drive her to Indianola and stay the weekend. She wanted her family to meet me. We would be married the following September, on the 12th, but, at that point, Easter, neither of us had yet mentioned the prospect of marriage, and I, at least, hadn't given it a thought. I don't know what she was thinking. She neglected to brief me about her father. I knew only that he was an Episcopal priest. If I expected anything—I don't know that I bothered to form expectations—I expected to find the family not especially well off, living humbly and simply, in the proximity of the church, in a house provided for them by the parish. Sara never spoke about money and didn't seem to have much of it.

They were wealthy. Growing up in New Hampshire I knew no one so manifestly affluent. The house was in a new and demoralizingly sterile subdemesne called Thrushcroft, and nowhere near the church. Palais Bird, as I liked to think of it. It was an architectural monstrosity. At base a sort of ersatz and hypertrophied English Tudor, with a roof meant to look, very broadly, like thatch, perversely combined with, among other anomalies, a quasi-Corinthian colonnade on either side of the front door, ultramodern casement windows in the façade, and a Victorian cupola center top. Inside, it was opulent—crystal chandeliers, marble floors, hand-knotted oriental rugs, gold-plated fixtures. In one of the formal reception rooms there was an ornate, working harpsichord—I heard Sara play it—from, I think, the sixteenth century. In another, even larger room, which opened out on a brick-and-stone terrace overlooking the formal garden at the back of the house—it was still too early in the Iowa spring for much of anything to be in bloom—was a Steinway grand her father made sure to mention had been played during an American tour by Rachmaninoff. Coming through the front door and standing face to face with a staircase that might have been lifted from a Venetian palazzo (I have not been to Venice, and know nothing, firsthand, about the palazzi there, or their staircases. I take it they are sweeping and grand.), I was bedazzled. Sara's mother was waiting for us in the entryway, which, I discovered, looking up into a glazed and gilded dome, was an atrium three stories high. Where did the money come from for this garish and profligate display? It as sure as hell did *not* come from the salary paid her father by the church. Though it made her family situation even more repugnant, I took great satisfaction in learning from Sara that her father contributed almost nothing to the pot. He absolved himself of any real financial responsibility on the grounds that he was a man of God, at the same time he spent wantonly the money that came, almost without limit, from his wife's family, who had, for several generations, owned a shipping line back in Norway.

We arrived late afternoon on Maundy Thursday. Sara's mother met us wearing a black velvet dress with a single strand of pearls. Her hair was pulled back severely and tied off with a black velvet ribbon. She was small and plain. She was in her mid-fifties, but looked much older. The skin on her face and hands was dry and papery, her knuckles prominent, her fingernails, beneath the polish, ridged and bitten. Her hair, which had been blonde—Sara had a picture of her mother as a young girl in Bergen; she had been pretty—was now pure white. She was thin, even gaunt, and curved inward. She was skittish. She didn't say much; after twenty-five years in America she was still not comfortable with the spoken language, especially not before strangers. When she saw Sara, she began to cry. After a suitable delay, Sara's brother and sister drifted into the entryway. They were both still in high school and living at home. They were unambiguously glad to see Sara and, though not overtly impolite, paid me little attention. They were good-looking, relaxed, confident kids. They are both still alive and have, I believe, fared reasonably well. Except for the dutiful Christmas card from the brother's wife, to which I don't respond, I have had no contact with either of her siblings since Sara died. Sara's brother is an electrical engineer. He lives in San Diego and has a daughter. Her sister is married, in Minneapolis, to a Somali with whom she's had five children. Though we are not related by blood, these children are my nephews and nieces, whom I will never know. The last I heard, Sara's sister had converted to Islam, which I was happy to hear, imagining her father's reaction. Sara's father and mother are long dead.

What explains Sara? How could she have come—so fine and sensitive and graceful—from the commingling of two such parents, one of them positively malefic? So our genes are *not* our fate? Persuade my clone of that. I didn't meet her father—the house was big enough that I didn't run into him—until Saturday afternoon. The reason for his absence, given me by Sara's mother—she was anxious to soften any possible offense I might take—having to do with the various offices and functions attendant on Holy Week that required his presence and ministration, seemed plausible enough. We'd been assigned separate bedrooms: Sara her old room on the second floor, and me one of the several guest rooms on the floor above. He had come to Sara's room, in the evening, after I had gone to sleep, and again in the morning, before I'd emerged for breakfast.

We all went to a Good Friday service at the church, where I saw Sara's father for the first time, and heard him deliver to the assembled and somber few a brief meditation on the meaning of the Passion. I was predisposed to admire it, but I found his meditation platitudinous and bland—on the Passion!—found *him* affected and smug.

After lunch on Saturday afternoon, Sara told me her father wanted to see me in the library. I would be in his house four days—he was there, too, off and on—and this was to be our only meeting. Sara led me—silently, guiltily, I thought, very much as if she were leading me to a special doom in which she was complicit—to a part of the house I'd not yet been in. It was, as they'd all been instructed to call it, their father's wing, and contained, in addition to the library: his bedroom—her mother had her bedroom in another part of the house; his bathroom—he liked to take long baths and often did not complete his morning toilet until early afternoon; his sitting room, which I could see as I passed it, was spacious; and an indoor stationary lap pool, for his use only.

He was waiting for me in the library. The room was a hexagon, which is an odd and disorienting shape for a room. Except for the door through which Sara and I entered, and the large sash window in one of the western walls—the drapes on this window were tied back, and the afternoon sun streamed through it—the rest of the wall space was taken, floor to ceiling, by bookshelves. These shelves were made from a kind of pickled pine. They were simple and elegant. Whatever the merits of the individual books it contained—for anything I knew, he'd bought them by the yard—the collection was extensive. I'd estimate there were two to three thousand volumes, maybe more than that, some of them leather-bound sets, almost all the rest clothbound. Here

and there, space on the shelves was made for small, effeminate porce-
lain figurines—florid little shepherds and shepherdesses—and also for
various diplomas and awards Sara's father had earned, and photographs of him with assorted luminaries from the larger ecclesiastical
world and the local political scene. The floor was made of wide un-
varnished pine planks. Much of the floor was covered with an oriental rug, clearly old, its colors muted and quite beautiful. Near the
center of the room, not quite facing the door, was a large, dark oak
double desk with a deep-red leather inset top. One could sit on either
side of the desk, or, as originally intended, share it. From the late Ja-
cobean period ("Sheffield, circa 1625," he said to me, when we were
alone), the legs and edges of the desk, elaborately carved and detailed,
looked almost medieval. The desk chair was straight- and high-
backed, of the same dark oak. There was a green-glass reading lamp
on the desk, an old-fashioned and ornamental inkstand, a framed pho-
tographic portrait of him standing behind his wife and children, and
a silver tray with a crystal pitcher, several tumblers, and a silver bowl
for ice. In one of the room's six equal angles stood a large antique
globe, in another a simple Shaker-style reader's stand (when I was a
young boy I drove with my parents into Maine, to Sabbathday Lake,
to hear the very last of the vestigial Shakers sing their hymns) with,
open upon it, an oversized and illuminated bible. Beside the window
was a scuffed brown leather wing chair with matching footstool, and
a tall brass standing lamp. It was the kind of room in which one might
expect to encounter, if not Erasmus or Galileo or one of the lesser
Medicis, at least a man with some education, a modicum of discern-
ment, and unconstrained access to cash, who had an overweening interest in appearing connoisseurish (how to explain those figurines?),
old-moneyed, and learned.

Sara's father, the Reverend Bird, stood beside the wing chair. He
was holding a book, as if he'd been reading and had just risen to
stretch his legs. His back was to the door, and he was looking out the
window. For our benefit, I thought, he'd struck a prayerful, medita-
tive pose. Though he could not have helped but hear us open the door,
he did not turn towards us, until Sara said, "Daddy."

Then in his mid-fifties, Sara's father was handsome, tall and slim and graceful, his posture faultless, his complexion fair and smooth. His hair was silvery and fine. He seemed to me to be more conscientiously groomed than any man I'd ever seen. He was wearing a suit, dark gray with a pale chalk stripe, and a black clerical shirt with the priestly notch of white in the collar. His shoes had been brought, by someone, to a high black shine. I could see, when he turned to face us, that the book he was holding—he kept his place in it with his index finger, to suggest he intended, shortly, to continue reading it—was Pascal's *Pensées*.

"Darling," he said to Sara. Without moving in our direction, he lifted his empty hand and held it out to her, his palm up, his fingers extended, a flourish, as if he were asking her to dance. Or, as I think of it now, as if they had already been dancing and were in the middle of some tricky break step that had taken them, briefly, apart. Sara went to him, took his hand, leaned in, raised up on her toes, and kissed him chastely on the cheek. Still holding his hand, she looked back at me—I had remained standing just inside the door—and said, sunnily, without guile, "Daddy, this is my friend. Ray Bradbury."

"Ray," he said.

"Mr. Bird," I said. I intended no slight, though on the drive back, Sara told me he'd been displeased by the lack of form in my address, had taken it as a sign of disrespect. He expected me, she said, to call him "Reverend Bird." When I knew what it was he wanted from me, the precise code of deference required, I could not, thereafter—not once in all the time I knew him, no matter that it might have made things easier for Sara—bring myself to do it. I am embarrassed now to confess I was, for seven years, to take heart in this paltry line of resistance. "It's nice to meet you," I said. Then: "This is a beautiful room. All these books. Amazing." This was fawning of the worst sort, nearly pure obsequiousness.

"Thank you, Ray," he said. "That's kind of you to say. Though perhaps more modest, more ascetic than we might have come to had my wife been given her head—you have seen the rest of the house—it is for me a beautiful room." It was not easy to think of it as modest. "A place of quiet and retreat," he said. "Of study and prayer. Of sanctuary. Which I find I more and more need. I'm at peace here, among my books. As I'm sure you will understand. I hope you've been comfortable so far in your stay with us."

"I've been very comfortable," I said. "Thank you. And extremely well fed. I'm glad to get to see where Sara grew up. It helps me imagine her as a little girl. I'm also happy to be away from school. If you could see the way I live, you'd know I'm not used to," indicating the room, "this level of," I would attempt an ingratiating joke, "modesty."

Given my usual reticence, this was a veritable aria. I saw Sara stiffen as I finished, without, at the time, understanding why. He would soon hear from Sara herself—I didn't know she'd come home to tell him this—that she and I were living together. When she told him—I was not present, and probably should have been—he was furious with her. On moral, and other, less admirable grounds. There was no reason for him to hear preemptively from me—the agent of his heartbreak, the unworthy, uncouth, godless graduate student who would separate him from the girl of his dreams—even an intimation of the truth: that we lived, his daughter and I, like squatters in a rat-trap apartment above a Hmong gift shop on the shabbiest street in downtown Ames.

"I trust, then," he said, "you will do your best to make yourself at home."

"I will," I said, without any idea what we were really talking about, though I felt again, for the first time since my mother's death, the pang of orphanhood. As a graduate student, my present state was impecunious, but I was not starving or freezing or without shelter. Going forward, there was for me some likelihood of gainful, if not bountiful employment. But I had no one at my back. In the face of small favors, I would be grateful and dimwitted, slow to take umbrage. Too slow at times. Too grateful. A shriveled nut of civility.

I can't remember what Sara said, how she managed her exit, but it was graceful. She was standing beside her father, then she was beside me, the back of her hand brushing the back of my hand, then she was gone, the clean smell of her still in the air, promising, I think, to be right back, after she did what she was pretending she needed to do. I was the perfect stooge—mildly suspicious I was being set up, too good a guest, too fatted a goose, too stupid with love, to protest. The subsequent and very unpleasant conversation between Sara's father and me lasted no more than fifteen minutes. At which point, as if she'd been watching the clock—we were done talking, and I felt pretty much dispatched—Sara, who made enough noise coming down the hall to alert us to her approach, gaily blew into the room, expecting, I suppose, to find us joined in an embrace of mutual and manly affection. She was so fine, so ungodly innocent, to see her all at once like that was a detonation in the heart, a clearing shot to the brain.

"Hello, you two," she said, before she could take an accurate reading of the scene. "Miss me?"

Below, I provide an arrantly stark reconstruction of my conversation with Sara's father. I dispense with all interpolated notation of gesture and action, and I do this more for the sake of accuracy than of ease. During our conversation there *was* no action or gesture. At his bidding, so we would not have to call from across the room, I came closer. Hard as this is to credit, we stood, like duelists, facing one another at an uncordial distance of five or six feet, and talked back and forth.

> HIM: So. I'm glad to have this chance to speak with you. Without Sara present.
>
> ME: All right.
>
> HIM: Would you prefer to be sitting?
>
> ME: No. I'm fine where I am. Thank you.
>
> HIM: It is my practice in situations like this one to speak candidly.
>
> ME: Please do.
>
> HIM: You are a graduate student at the university. Am I right?

*ME:*  In my first year. That's right.

*HIM:*  In math.

*ME:*  Yes.

*HIM:*  At present you are not a candidate for the Ph.D.

*ME:*  No. I'm not interested in a doctorate. I don't like math enough, to tell you the truth.

*HIM:*  Which is to say you are pursuing a Masters' degree.

*ME:*  That's my plan. Yes.

*HIM:*  Your plan is to teach.

*ME:*  Yes.

*HIM:*  To teach at what level?

*ME:*  High school. At least, that's my thought at the moment.

*HIM:*  Well. If teaching is worth doing, then it's worth doing at any level.

*ME:*  I suppose that's right. I hadn't thought of it quite that way.

*HIM:*  Sara tells me you are from New Hampshire.

*ME:*  Yes.

*HIM:*  You were born there?

*ME:*  And bred.

*HIM:*  What part of New Hampshire?

*ME:*  The western part. Not too far from Vermont. It's a small state. Have you been to New Hampshire?

*HIM:*  I have not.

*ME:*  It's a nice place.

*HIM:*  I'm sure it is. And it is true that neither of your parents is alive?

*ME:*  Sadly. My father died when I was young. My mother died this past Thanksgiving.

*HIM:*  I'm sorry for your loss.

*ME:*  Thank you.

*HIM:*  Have you any brothers or sisters?

*ME:*  No.

*HIM:*  You are alone.

*ME:*  More or less. Yes.

*HIM:* Who were your parents?

*ME:* Who were they?

*HIM:* What did they do?

*ME:* For a living, you mean?

*HIM:* Well, yes.

*ME:* My father was an accountant. He worked as an auditor. My mother, when she worked, worked at the high school, in the attendance office.

*HIM:* I'm interested: What was your parents' faith?

*ME:* I'm not sure what you mean.

*HIM:* I mean, son, in what form, if any, did their faith, if any, express itself? I mean, *did* your parents worship? *How* did they worship? *Where* did they worship? Which God did they pray to?

*ME:* Let's see. They were Presbyterian. My mother was a Methodist, but she switched when she married my father. I assume they prayed to the same God you pray to. They were good people. They had a good marriage. We were a happy family.

*HIM:* And you? What is your faith?

*ME:* I can't answer that question.

*HIM:* Because?

*ME:* Because I don't know what my faith is.

*HIM:* You don't know.

*ME:* I don't. I don't think about it. Maybe I should.

*HIM:* And what do you think of Sara?

*ME:* I think she's remarkable.

*HIM:* And it is not her money you are interested in?

*ME:* Of course not.

*HIM:* She stands to inherit a great deal of money. Do you pretend that you are unaware of this?

*ME:* I don't pretend anything, Mr. Bird. I *was* unaware of it, until just now. And I'm sorry, but I don't give one hoot.

*HIM:* What is the nature of your relationship with my daughter?

*ME:* I'm not sure it's my place to say. What has Sara told you?

*HIM:* She has told me very little. I'm hoping *you* will tell me. That you will be man enough to tell me.

*ME:* I will speak only for myself. I like your daughter very much.

*HIM:* You like her.

*ME:* Yes, I do. Though I wonder why she'd bother with me.

*HIM:* Yes. Well. I have to say I wonder the same. I mean, to speak frankly, on what basis do you permit yourself to think you are worthy of her?

*ME:* I don't think I'm worthy of her.

*HIM:* Yet you pursue her. You allow her to involve herself with you to the extent that she is no longer likely to explore other options.

*ME:* I wouldn't say it's a matter of my *allowing* Sara to do anything. She does as she pleases. I don't know that I have much, or any, say in what she does.

*HIM:* I assure you, you do.

*ME:* I don't know how you could know that.

*HIM:* Please. Don't underestimate me. I also know, for instance, that Sara no longer lives in the dorm. That she now lives with you.

*ME:* She has told you that?

*HIM:* *She* has not. I'll say this simply. I want you to discourage her. Sara's judgment may be faulty, but she is not a fool. She has seen something to value in you, and I will believe it is there. On the face of things, you seem reasonably intelligent, and not unkind. You might be pleasant to sit next to on a plane. But you are not the man for Sara. Not by a long shot. I won't let you let her so radically undervalue herself. I won't sit passively by as she makes such an egregious mistake. I want you, on your return to Ames, as soon as it is possible, to bring to an end your relationship with her. I want her to return to the dorm. I want you to leave her alone. I wish you well in your studies. Chances are you will make a fine high school teacher. But you have no earthly business with my daughter. You can't possibly imagine that you do. I don't want to hear about you again.

ME: Should this not be Sara's decision?

HIM: Absolutely not. My plan for Sara is that she go to Paris in the fall to study at the Sorbonne. I expect you to do nothing to interfere with that plan.

ME: Have you talked about this with Sara?

HIM: About Paris?

ME: Yes.

HIM: That is not your concern. I will assume that we have come to an understanding, Ray, you and I. And I will ask that you keep what was here said between us in confidence. There is nothing to be gained from including Sara in this conversation.

ME: I don't agree, Mr. Bird.

HIM: Whether you agree or not is of no consequence. I expect you to do as I say.

ME: That's ridiculous.

HIM: And if I find that you have betrayed this confidence, I will take the steps necessary to have you dismissed from the university.

ME: You think you can do that? You can't do that.

HIM: I can. And, be clear, I will.

He didn't take the steps necessary to have me dismissed—whatever those steps might have been, and assuming he could have done so—because, when it became clear, as it soon did, that Sara had thrown her lot in with me, to injure me would have been also to injure her. In the car on the way back to Ames, before we were even out of Indianola, I told Sara exactly what her father had said to me.

She was appalled. "How could he have said such things to you?" she said. "How dare he do that? And, think, I brought you to him. I am so sorry. My poor boy."

"I have to admit," I said, "I was a bit overmatched."

She smiled at me, leaned across the front seat, and kissed me on the ear. "Of course you were. Will you forgive me? He said he wanted to meet you. He said he just wanted time to talk with you alone, to get to know you. And then he told me how much he liked you.".

"I don't think he liked me," I said, with some glee.

In *their* final conversation, which had occurred in the library on the morning of our departure, her father said he'd "very much enjoyed" our talk. Sara took that moment to tell him she had moved in with me.

"He flipped into a rage," she said

I wondered, not aloud, how much of it was feigned. "He already knew," I said.

"What?"

"He already knew you were living with me."

"You told him?"

"He told me."

"How did he know?" she said.

"I have no idea."

He told her how disappointed in her he was. That he could not condone her behavior. That her behavior was scandalous. That he was embarrassed for her, embarrassed *by* her. Had she forgotten who she was? Then, as if to punish her, he told her she would be going to Paris in the fall. She said she wouldn't go. She would go, he said, because he had decided she would go. No, she absolutely would not go. Would she defy him? he asked. If she had to, she said. He wanted to know, was it because of me? That was part of it, she told him. She was determined, then, to stay with me? She said she thought she was. He said that if she defied him, he would have no recourse but to disown her. "Go ahead," she said.

I loved her for that. By that time, I needed no more reason to love her.

It was the evening of the last day of Anna's visit. She would leave for Iowa first thing the next morning. It was after we'd eaten a cold supper at the kitchen table, after I'd done the dishes, before we said good night. We hadn't talked much since the afternoon. No mention of my clone, or her group, or anything else of any seriousness. Not since the conversation in which she told me what they wanted me to do, and how dangerous it would be for me to do it. She'd left the house for several hours. I don't know what she did while she was out. The day was very hot. I was feeling a bit shaky and oddly chilled, and stayed inside. I watched out the window for the twins, Sophie and Marie, but they didn't appear. When Anna returned, she went straight into the guest room to begin packing her things. It was obvious she meant to leave me to myself. I tried to take the time she gave me to think about what she'd proposed. I was dutiful, but more than usually diffuse. When there was nothing left to do with the day but call an end to it— it was what my mother, for reasons unexplained, called the violet hour—we wound up sitting quietly together in the living room. Anna was finishing a cup of tea. I was idle. It was as if *we'd* been married for forty years. It was then—the question came to me only after I'd stopped thinking—I asked her: Wasn't I the very first person the government would look to when they discovered my clone was missing? Wasn't I, therefore, the very last person her group ought to want anywhere near their clone, now they finally had one?

What I asked was something she and the others had thought long about. Her response was seamless and more thorough than seemed necessary—she told me more than, at the time, I wanted to know—as if, as part of her charge, she was bent to the service of logical completeness.

Figure the odds, she said. The likelihood of a clone escaping from the Clearances was negligible. In any case, she said, it would not be an "escape." The clone would have no concept of escape, no way of planning or imagining his survival outside the Clearances, no idea there existed anything outside the Clearances he might escape to. The clone would have no idea about the possibility of sanctuary, in Canada or any other place. Because, of course, the clone would have no idea about political boundaries or nation states. Should a clone find himself somehow outside the Clearances, she said, he would be absolutely unable to deal with the world. The clone, I must remem-

ber, would not know he was a clone, would not understand the concept of clone, would not know there were originals and copies of originals. The clone would likely not have sufficient language to tell
anyone he might encounter who, or what, he was, or where he was
from. The clone would likely not understand roads, or cars, or shops,
or money. More to the point, the clone—this they knew, empirically,
was true—would be medicated to the edge of catatonia. He would
very possibly be hit by a car or truck on any road he was unlucky
enough to wander on to. Should he survive, he would most likely be
reported to the local police as a vagrant, or a drunk, or a lunatic. In
which case, he would be picked up and taken into custody. If he then
happened to be seen by someone who, observing the barcode on the
inside of his left forearm, could deduce its meaning, the clone might
be handed over to an official connected with the Clearances, where,
because the clone had seen, however dimly, the world outside, he
would immediately be executed. If, as was more likely, the clone was
not recognized as a clone, and if he did not find some way to kill himself first, he would, sooner rather than later, end up in an institution
for the insane.

The chances of any of this happening, she said, were infinitesi-
mal. Even so, there was far less chance that the clone would, before
anything else happened to him, come into contact with one of the
smattering of resisters—however vigilant they were—who lived on the
margins of the Clearances. Far less likely still was the possibility that
one of the resisters who recovered the clone would recognize in him
his original. The government would have figured that the odds against
a wayward clone being found by, or given to, a member of the resistance who just happened to know the clone's original, and who could
recognize that original in the clone, were staggering, way too small to
be given any consideration at all. Factor in their general operating
principle—that an original must never think about his copy, is never
contacted, not even when his copy dies—and it is certain that the
clone's original would be the very *last* person the government would
suspect, or communicate with, when that clone went missing. It was,

thus, precisely me, Anna said, the Dolly Squad (should such an entity actually exist) would come for last.

"But, eventually, they will come," I said.

"They will come," she said.

The next morning, early, we were in the kitchen. I'd watched dully, while Anna ate a quick breakfast. Now she was ready to go. I'd done nothing to help her get ready. She had beside her on the kitchen floor a suitcase, a shopping bag filled with food and drink for the trip, and a small black satchel I'd not seen before. "I'll call you in three days, when I get back to Iowa," she said. "You can tell me then what you've decided."

"What if I need more time?" The question was false. I had, I believe, already made my decision.

"We don't have more time," she said. "If you decide to do what they've asked, I'll be back to get you exactly ten days from now. You'll have to be ready to go with me."

"Go where?"

"Canada."

"Where in Canada?" I said.

"I can't tell you that until you've made your decision."

"I have an appointment with the doctor," I said. "In six weeks. He needs to see the damage to my heart. To see how bad it is."

"There are doctors in Canada," she said.

"Would I bring along my medical records?" I was nothing other than a feeble old man, standing in the kitchen in his bathrobe and bare bony feet, with his hammertoes and poor circulation, whining about his feeble heart.

"No," she said. "Listen, Ray. You'll have to leave everything behind. You won't have time to sell your house. Or your car. Or in any other way settle your affairs. You must do nothing of the sort. For as long as possible it must look as if you have not actually left, that you are still living here. If someone notices you are gone, it must seem you will be back shortly."

"I won't be back."

"No," she said. "I have something for you." She reached into the satchel and pulled out a sheaf of printed pages held together in a green plastic binder. It looked like the kind of packet I might have given to a class. She put it on the kitchen table.

"What is it?"

"I don't know what to call it exactly," she said. "A notebook."

"Yours?"

"For you," she said. "If you want to, read it."

# Six

*Ray.*

*If you are reading this, then I have been to see you, we have talked, and you are at least considering what they have asked you to do. I had hoped you'd reject their request out of hand. I'd thought there'd be no question you would, once you understood, and I'd go home, face my own music, and that would be that. But if you're reading this.*

*I trust it was good to see you. I imagine it will be. You were very kind on the phone, very gracious. You will be not so gracious or happy to see me when you find out why I have come.*

*I am sorry I will not see Sara. I am so sorry about Sara and the baby. What sadness that must have been. My husband died in the spring, as I told you. It is not the same thing, I know.*

*Can it be forty-five years since I've seen you? Well, I will see you soon. I am nervous about it. I have gotten old. I am gray and gristly. I hope you will not be too alarmed. It is the first time in forty years I have traveled anywhere without my husband. I am leery, but I will get there. I have maps, and I have my husband's truck. It's almost new, a big, hulking thing. He bought it for the nursery just before he died. As I've planned the trip, I will be three days on the road. I admit there have been times, especially this past week preparing to come to you, when it has all begun* to feel like madness. Like a dream I might have had when I was still young. I will get there.

As I write this, I don't yet know anything about you, besides what little you told me told me on the phone, and besides what I remember from the year we spent in Iowa. It wasn't even a year, and most of the time you were preoccupied courting Sara. I sit here with no sense of who you have become, how you think, or what you know about things in general. More to the point, I don't have any idea what you think or know about cloning, or about your politics, or about your basic sympathies. In the brief and faraway time I knew you in graduate school, setting aside the crummy way you treated me, you seemed to me a decent guy, though, I have to say, somewhat self-absorbed and confused.

It is one a.m. and I can't sleep. I am jeeped up. I miss my husband tonight, as I do most nights. This afternoon it rained hard. Now the air is cool, fresh, sweet-smelling. It is a beautiful night here. The street outside my window is bright under the moon. My windows are open. The night is calm, despite the party going on half a dozen houses down. High school kids on summer vacation, living it up. Would I want to be their age again? That blithe? (Just young again. I was too ungainly and clomping ever to have been blithe.) I think I would. So long as what was to come was my life with my husband. The same life. There would even, briefly, disappointingly, be you. I'd take it all. I'd want nothing to change. The music is loud but inoffensive, maybe because I can't make out the words, and there are the sounds of revelry only partly drunken. On this night I am grateful for the noise, glad for their company. Later this morning, sometime after breakfast, I leave for New Hampshire. I am packed and ready. I should sleep. I'll keep at this a while longer, then go back to bed.

I did not write these journal entries for you, or for anyone else. Before they delivered the clone, I was warned there must be no record, no evidence at all of the clone having been in my house. Which makes the entries a kind of contraband.

The clone was taken from me a week ago. They took him just after he'd suffered through the torments of withdrawal and had started to become aware of me and his surroundings. What must he have thought? I can't say I miss him exactly. With or without you, I will see him again.

I don't know where, or how, or by whom the clone was found. I don't know where he was, who had him, what was done for him, before he was brought to me. I do know he hadn't been out long. Not more than two days, if that.

It was late in the evening when I was called, given the word that a clone had been found, and that before the next day was over the clone would be in my care. I had been out to a movie, which is something I rarely do now I'm alone. My daughter had just seen this movie, a clever farce about two men, one sloppy, one neat, trying to live peaceably together, and she'd called that afternoon to recommend it. It was her little girl's third birthday. That was the main reason for my daughter's call, so Grandma could wish a happy birthday to her little pudding pie. My daughter and her family live two hundred miles away. I had thought to drive down to be with my grand-daughter on this day, but, at the last minute, didn't feel up to the trip. There are days when my body reminds me how old and finicky it is. And think, when this night is over, I will set off on a three-day drive to New Hampshire.

(My heart sags as I write this. There is no way to protect them. They will be easy to find.)

No. This must be in the report. Whatever else there is, Ray, this must be in it. Boldface. **My children, my grandchildren, know nothing about any of this. They know nothing of my activities. They are not involved. They have no part in it. I have told them nothing. None of my children, or my grandchildren, knows anything. After I disappear, I will not communicate with them. When you come for me, they will not know where I have gone.**

The man who called that evening was one of the group. I did not recognize his voice, and, the way things are structured, I'm sure I would not know him if we passed each other on the street. He said, "Hello, Anna. This is Jimmy Valentine." I knew exactly what that meant. A clone had been found. However minuscule the chances of this ever happening, an elaborate code and set of procedures was in place, and I was well versed in *them. I said back, "Hello, you, mister," which was the pre-scripted prompt, meant to let him know I was in the game and had my wits about me. Then he said, "What are we having for dinner?" Which meant they would, contingent on my next response, be bringing the clone to me sometime soon. "Your favorite," I said. "Grilled pork chops," which told him I understood the question ("glazed," if I hadn't), "with applesauce," which signified I was willing and prepared to receive the clone ("with horseradish," if I wasn't). "Yum," he said. "I'll be there in four shakes," meaning the clone would be delivered the following day at eight p.m. "I'll keep it warm for you," I said, which requires no gloss. He said, "That's my girl," which confirmed the transaction and ended the conversation.*

*The local texture of our work against cloning might be foolish and overwrought, but the work is noble and necessary. I believe it is God's work, and I am not a "true believer," not in God, or even in the work. You must understand, Ray, the danger of the most minor indiscretion or nonchalance, to us as individuals and as a group, is real and potentially ruinous.*

*It is interesting. You expect never, never expect, to get the call. No matter how earnestly you prepare for it, you know the chances of the call ever coming, to you or anyone else, are virtually none. Then it comes. You answer it, and it is "Jimmy Valentine." The instant you say, "Hello, you, mister," consenting to your part in the action, the political, subversive, revolutionary action, you step extravagantly out of the only world you have known till then. You get the call, and a hatch in the floor opens like a gallows trap. You fall through, and your life is utterly changed. I heard the unknown voice on the other end say, "Jimmy Valentine," and I gave all the right responses. When the call was done I felt calm and outside myself. This is what is happening to me, I thought. This is who I am now, and what I do. Something like that. I had much farther to fall.*

*I have to believe there were other people in the group living near enough to where the clone was found who might have been called on to receive the clone, provide him with food and shelter, and for a week or so (it turned out to be six days) attend to his immediate physical and emotional needs. We are widely dispersed along the perimeter of the Clearances, among villages and towns in Iowa and Nebraska and Wyoming and Montana and*

*Minnesota. There aren't very many of us all told, three thousand tops, and sparse few in any one area. We don't know one another, or only one or two others. This is a function both of geographical circumstance, and design. We don't do much, besides watch and wait and, in a studiously uncoordinated way, badger our congressmen. An anonymous anti-cloning newsletter, called* Original Sin, *is published monthly on the Web, but I'd bet we are the only ones who read it. Even I don't read it very often. It doesn't much change, one issue to the next.*

*I suspect they wanted a woman for the job. Someone in my group would have been aware my husband had recently died, and that I was living alone, inconspicuously. The local operatives (I don't know what else to call them; we don't know what to call ourselves) knew, too, I'd raised three children, and probably felt I could be counted on to nurse the clone through the rigors of withdrawal. I was a longtime member of the group. My husband was instrumental at its beginning. Maybe they thought, by calling me, to honor him.*

*As I mean to do.*

*I spent the next day laying in provisions I thought I might need taking care of the clone. I had no idea what kind of shape he'd be in, what I'd wind up doing for him. I hadn't yet been told how old he was or how long I'd have him. I bought basic stuff, staples: meat, vegetables, fruit, cheese, bread, eggs, juice, cereal, rice. I bought two pints of chocolate chocolate-chip ice cream, and some real maple syrup, in case I made him pancakes. I picked up some first-aid supplies: rubbing alcohol, cotton pads, bandages, adhesive tape, anti-inflammatory tablets, hydrocortisone and antibiotic creams, antacid tablets, a bottle of milk of magnesia, an emetic, laxatives, over-the-counter sedatives and painkillers. I already had a fair sampling of this stuff on hand, but figured I might need more. I bought a toothbrush and toothpaste for him, shampoo, deodorant, body wash, a comb and a brush (and a bowl full of mush), a razor and shaving gel and aftershave, trying to replicate the toiletries my husband used.*

*I enjoyed shopping for the clone. I wanted him to have new, fresh things. Except for visits from my children, who were tender and solicitous, and my grandchildren, who were tonic, I'd not had a guest in the house since my husband died.*

My husband's clothes were all clean, hung neatly in his closet, or folded and put away in his dresser drawers. I'd seen to that soon after his death. My husband was such a big man. I couldn't imagine the clone would be able to wear much of his stuff, but I got out a robe and some underwear and socks and pajamas. I tried my best to anticipate the clone's needs. As it happened, very little I did to prepare for his stay with me was of any real use. Pretty much all I'd need would be diapers and wipes, and those I didn't think to get.

The next evening at seven I backed my husband's truck out of the garage, drove it around town for a few minutes, then parked it on the street in front of the house. I left the garage door open, the garage light off, these machinations all pre-arranged. Outside it would be light, still, for an hour or more, but I closed the drapes all through the house. Then I sat down in the living room with a raspberry tart and a cup of tea and waited. I thought about my husband. I think about him as I write this. What would he say about what I'm about to do? What would he advise?

His kidneys had failed. We could not pay for dialysis. Our decision, more than twenty years ago, not to have ourselves cloned, meant that we were able to get only minimal insurance, and that my husband was not eligible for a transplant, unless he could, on his own, find a compatible kidney. He'd made his peace with this; I had not. I begged the doctor to take a kidney from me, but in this way only were my husband and I incompatible. He insisted we not tell the kids he was dying until it was too late for them to be of use as donors. (Am I willing, ready, to die for this cause? As he did? It seems I am.)

Just before eight o'clock, I stood at the kitchen window, looking out over the front yard through a split in the curtains. I'd left the kitchen dark so I could see without my being seen. A car stopped in the street directly opposite the house, idled a moment, then came slowly up the driveway. It was an ordinary car, small, Chinese. It was light enough out that I could see there were three men in the car, the driver and two men in the backseat. The car pulled into the garage. I heard the garage door shut. I turned on the kitchen light. I opened the kitchen door, which communicated with the garage down a small set of stairs. From inside the kitchen I turned on the overhead light in the garage. I remained in the kitchen and looked down into the garage. The garage light seemed unusually harsh. The driver got of the car and came around it to the passenger side, the side nearest me. I didn't know him, as I knew I would not. He was short and bearded, younger than I, in his early forties, I supposed. He looked up at me. He did not smile. A huge, leathery moth was flapping around the garage light. The driver asked me to turn off the light, which I did. Those were the last words he would say. He opened the rear door of the car on the passenger side. The car's interior light went on, but faintly. The man inside the car closest to the passenger side door, I now could see, was the clone. He looked to be asleep, or dead. He was motionless, his arms limp at his side, his head thrown back, his neck stretched tight, his mouth open. I could not see his face. The man in the car sitting beside the clone worked with the driver as he, the driver, took hold of the clone by both ankles and began to slide the clone, feet first, out of the car. The clone appeared to be inert. It was clear he would not be able to move or stand under his own power. He was unconscious and did not visibly react to anything done to him. The man inside the car positioned himself so that the clone's head rested on his lap. Then the clone was out of the car, the driver holding him by the ankles, the other man holding him underneath the arms. As if he were a strip of sod. They stood him up. They were neither rough nor gentle with the clone, merely expeditious. The clone's head sagged, and all I could see was the top of his head. When he had got the clone's feet set flat on the ground, the driver, the smaller of the two men, let go of the clone's ankles. He put his shoulder to the clone's midsection and lifted the clone, draping him over his shoulder. Carrying him like that, the clone's head hanging upside down behind him, he brought the clone up into the kitchen. The other man followed, shutting the door as he came through. He was older than his comrade (my comrade, too), my age perhaps, tall and thin and nearly bald. I noticed his hands, which were scarily large and long-fingered, as if he were acromegalic. His head, too, was disproportionately large and bony.

We did not speak. It was as if we'd been told to keep silent, or beforehand had agreed not to talk, neither of which was the case. I led them out of the kitchen and up the stairs to the guest room, which I had prepared for the clone's arrival. I'd made up the bed with clean sheets and pillow slips, emptied the drawers in the painted dresser, even put a vase of cut flowers on *the night table. (What did I imagine I was doing?) The shades were drawn, and the room was unlit, except for a nightlight in the shape of an angel I'd plugged into the wall beside the dresser. The nightlight had been my daughter's. The room had been her room. The driver, still carrying the clone, stooped and, with the help of the taller man, let the clone fall onto the bed, laying him face up on top of the bedclothes before I had a chance to pull them back.*

*It was my first opportunity really to look at the clone. Our recent thinking was that a clone's daily uniform would be designed to coincide with the current mode of everyday dress in the towns and villages bordering the Clearances, modified when necessary to keep pace with trends in local fashion. (In Iowa, fashionwise, we are ten years behind the coasts.) So that should the impossible occur and the clone find himself, or be found, outside the Clearances, there would be nothing visual to distinguish him as a clone. I don't know what he was wearing when they found him. By the time he was brought to my house, our clone, your clone, did look like most any young man in his early twenties in rural Iowa in the middle of summer. He had on a pair of blue jeans, white socks, and white running shoes, which were brand-new. Someone had put him in a white cotton T-shirt, which—the only anomaly—had long sleeves, in order, I assume, to cover the code on the inside of his left forearm. They had cleaned him up, and maybe even given him a haircut. His hair was short. He was clean-shaven. His fingernails were clean and trimmed. When you looked at him, there was nothing to cause you to suspect you might be looking at a clone.*

*I knew, at once, it was you. Your clone. The moment I saw him on my daughter's bed, I did not make the distinction. I was looking at you. It was you, Ray, a bit bigger than I remembered you, broader in the chest, a touch leaner in the face, but there was no doubt it was you. I had gotten old, along with everyone else, and you had remained exactly as you were when I knew you forty-five years ago. It was the only way I'd ever known you. I had not seen you age. So there was no chance I might have misremembered you. It was you. It was disorienting, shocking. Terrifying. At the moment of recognition, I was, all at once, overcome with grief—for everything, in that instant, I felt I'd lost seeing you still young. Time collapsed. It was as if, suddenly, see-*

*ing you, I'd lost my husband again. As if I'd had no husband, no children. I was, at once, embarrassed by how old I was, by how old I looked, by how old I would look, now, to you. I was, at once, furious about how young you looked. I was envious. I was not, then, angry you had a clone. I am now. Disappointed. Not surprised. At that moment, looking down at you, I missed you terribly. I felt guilty, treacherous, missing you. It's been two weeks, and I am still in shock.*

    *I must have blanched, or gasped. The tall man looked at me. "What is it?" he said. He said this in a kindly way.*

    *"I know him," I said.*

    *"You know him?" he said.*

    *"I know who this is."*

    *"This is a clone," he said.*

    *"Yes."*

    *"Do you mean you know the original?"*

    *"Yes," I said. "I mean that."*

    *The driver looked at me but didn't speak. The tall man shook his head. "Christ," he said. "How is that possible?"*

    *"I don't know," I said.*

    *"It's not possible," he said.*

    *"I'm sorry," I said. "I'm so sorry."*

    *"No," he said. "Of course not. Are you sure?"*

    *"Yes."*

    *"What's his name?" he said, and I knew he was the one in charge.*

    *"His name is Ray Bradbury. We were in graduate school together."*

    *"Maybe you're mistaken," he said. "We can check this. We can find out."*

    *"I'm not mistaken," I said. "I know him." I had a brief snip of clarity. "I knew him."*

    *"Is he dead, then?"*

    *"I don't know," I said.*

    *He put his hand on my arm. My arm was bare, and his fingers were elongated and knuckly, vegetative. I tried not to recoil. His touch was gentle. "Ray Bradbury, you said?"*

    *"Yes."*

*"Okay. Good. We can check this. Will you be all right?"*

*"I hope so," I said. "Yes."*

*I hadn't signed on for this.*

*What follows, Ray, are the notes I made during the time your clone was with me. I put them down in an attempt to keep my thinking straight, borderline functional and sane. I had no one to talk to. It is an account of my time with your clone. It is dismal stuff.*

*Tomorrow I leave for New Hampshire. Who knows how this will go? Good luck to us both, Ray. Good luck to us both.*

### Thursday. July 16. 9 p.m.

*Jesus God, how am I to do this? For seven days. It makes me too sad, makes me tired at the thought. I feel old. Today all day I was thinking about quitting. One night, one day, and already I want to quit. I do. I want to give him back. Let someone else take him. I'm not the right one. Not for him. It's not human to ask me. I almost put out the rake. I saw him at eight this morning drive by in the Chinese car and I was ready to get the rake and put it out. An hour ago he drove by again. Right on time. I should have been outside, waiting for him to drive by. I should have put out the rake. I was too ashamed. Tomorrow, first thing, I will do it. How can they ask me to do this? For goodness sake. There is no choice. Calm down.*

*It's hot in here. He was drenched in sweat, poor thing. If I opened the windows maybe we'd get a breeze, but he'll start up again and the neighbors will think I'm killing him. Who will they think he is? They are your friends. Some of them you've known all your life. Do not think ill of them. What a racket. The poor boy. I've never heard such noise. Like some wild creature, something dying in the woods. I know nothing about things dying in the woods. What about all my howling? I may howl again. You'd think I was killing him. Trembling. Twitching. His arms and legs jerking around. I couldn't keep a blanket on him. It was piteous, his hands flying all over the place. He nearly got me. Coming off the sedatives they gave him for transport. I don't think he ever woke up. On top of all the other stuff he'd been on, you'd think they'd have shown some mercy. The poor boy. Clone.*

*What is he? What am I to call him? How am I to think of him? You are confused, you stupid old woman, because he is not who you think he is. He is someone else. You don't know him. If I opened the windows, we could get a breeze, if there is one.*

*I'm thinking of the first night with _____, the night we brought him home from the hospital. We had no idea what to do. We had the equipment, the supplies, all the baby stuff, and no idea how to use it. We were terrified. He slept through, lucky for us. Sweet little thing. His head like a pumpkin. He didn't cry. I checked on him every five minutes to make sure he was breathing. Thank God my mother was nearby. Little pumpkin head. He's turned out okay. He's turned out better than okay. Lucky in my children. A mother is only as happy as her saddest child. I've got used to being alone. The house feels alien tonight, dangerous. I'm afraid to leave the kitchen. I'm afraid to get out of this chair. What if he gets out of bed?*

*I went shopping today, early, before eight. He was resting quietly. I dashed out and back. I grabbed some disposable underwear, a 24-pack of adult diapers, diaper-rash cream. I was embarrassed to be in the incontinence aisle. My friend wears them. She's my age. Not me, not yet. Just keep my uterus where it belongs. I was surprised to see they work like the baby ones. I had nothing to use to change him. Some stuff my daughter left when she was here last, baby diapers, a packet of wipes that had dried out. So far he has had nothing to eat. I was able to give him a little water from a sippy-cup. He hardly woke. I looked in on him in the middle of the night, before three sometime. Even from outside the room I could smell it. A terrible smell. Much worse than kids' poop. My kids' urine was like water, odorless and clear. He was asleep on his back, his arms at his side. The blanket was on the floor. He was breathing, moaning with each breath. Shuddering. I undid his belt, unzipped his pants, got them down around his ankles. The smell nearly knocked me over. He was already in a diaper. They'd brought him in a diaper. Why didn't they tell me? They told me nothing. What will he be like when he wakes up? How will I restrain him if I need to? The inside of his pants was covered with poop, the seat, the legs. He must have had more than one bowel movement in there. Explosive. His stool was loose and watery, greenish gray, smeared all over his legs and his stomach. It was on his socks. I tried not to breathe. It was terrible. I got a pile of hand towels and wet washcloths. His poop was on the bed. It was on my arms and hands, on my shirt. This is an awful job if it is not someone you love. I cleaned him up. In the middle of his belly, where it belonged, he had an ordinary navel I'm not sure why I was surprised to see. I will ask about this. I looked at his thing. Poop? Thing? What is wrong with me? He was uncircumcised, which made it much harder to clean. I had never seen one uncircumcised before up close. I didn't like the look of it. I cleaned it with a washcloth. He became erect in my hand. I felt guilty. He was asleep, poor thing. I put a beach towel over him, then the blanket from the floor. That dog we had from the pound, always humping your leg. Leo was the name it came with. I didn't like him. We didn't have him long. When the dog got worked up, my husband called it the red rocket. The sight of it coming out, twanging there, red and nasty. Appalling. Too much for me. I'll put the rake out tomorrow morning.*

*Throw the washcloths and towels away. Don't try to launder them, for God's sake.*

### Friday. July 17. 10:15 p.m.

*Another day. It looks like I'll keep him the week. I didn't watch for the car today, either time. The rake is still in the garage. I feel like a new mother all over again with a colicky baby. _____ cried nonstop the first three months. We had to hold her, rock her, walk her up and down the room. Nothing else soothed her. I can't remember how I got through it, though on either side the boys were relatively easy. Now she's got children of her own. Sweet, placid girls, thank God, because her husband is no help to her. I am not a fan of my children's spouses. Is any mother really?*

*This is worse than colic. I must have emptied the pail ten times. There was nothing left in him to bring up and he kept retching. After each spell he fell back asleep. We've got a thunderstorm. It rained off and on all day. Now it's really coming down. I pray we don't lose power. I couldn't open the windows even if he'd stay quiet. You'd think he'd be exhausted from all that throwing up. I held the pail for him, kept him from falling off the bed. I dabbed his forehead with a damp washcloth. I offered him ginger ale and ice in a sippy-cup, which I couldn't get him to take. It seemed to make him an-*

gry. This afternoon for an hour he didn't stop sneezing. I didn't know what
to do for him. I'm torn. That boy up there, that man, is the product of a
system I detest. I hate that there are any clones at all. And this one. Of all
of them, this one. You must tell yourself he is not Ray.

He is not Ray. He is a human being and you have agreed to care for
him. You can stick it out one week. You can stick anything out one week. Forget your politics. Do the human thing. As if I had a choice. Shit, he's yowl-
ing again.

It's midnight. I might never get to sleep. He threw up all over the floor,
before I could get up there, then again into the pail. He hasn't eaten a thing.
How does he have anything left? I changed him. He doesn't like having me
change him. He doesn't like being in diapers, that's clear. I don't blame him.
He swims in my husband's pajama bottoms, but they're easy off, easy on.
What am I to call him? I need to stop thinking of him as Ray. I'm reluctant
to give him a name. He's not a stray cat I've taken in. Maybe he has a
name and will tell me what it is when he speaks to me. When he is able to
speak. When he is ready. If he even can speak. If he can speak, what
language will it be? What might we call him? What would you call him,
if he were yours? What would I call him? Sonny? I wanted to call our
daughter Sonny, but my husband wouldn't go along with it. Something biblical? What about Jacob, who pretended to be his twin? Something sadder.
Job or Jonah or Jeremiah. All the J names. I've got to think of something to
call him. Temporarily. I don't want to think of him as Ray. You could call
him Puke.

Maybe Sonny. We'll see. I have no idea what drugs, how many, he
was on before they found him, what drugs he's coming off of. Or how long it
will take. Apart from the sedatives we gave him, and I don't know what
those were, or how much he got. We assume the male clones are drugged, but
we don't know. I'm sure they drew some blood from him. I never used drugs,
never knew anybody, not really, who did. I never saw anyone go through
withdrawal, except in movies. Maybe they're new drugs, experimental, not
available to us, drugs we've never heard of. Designed specifically for clones.
Just so I don't do him any harm. My back hurts. I spent most of the day sitting in a chair beside the bed. I watched him while he slept. Looked at his

*face. Watched him quiver and quake, as if he were electrified. I held his hand as long as he would let me. I talked to him when he was quiet. When he wasn't throwing up or sneezing. When he wasn't making those animal noises. I wanted to keep him company, let him know he wasn't alone, that I meant to help him. I told him who I was. Where he was. I talked to him about my children and grandchildren. I told him about the town. About Ray, what I could remember. Of course I didn't tell him what he was. Is it possible he knows what he is? Was any of it calming, reassuring? Maybe it was. I couldn't tell how much of it he heard or understood. I remembered sitting beside Ray one night, all night, holding him while he wept about some girl in Virginia he'd broken up with. We'd never heard of her, Sara and I. Surprise. I hadn't seen him for months. He couldn't find Sara, and he showed up at my room looking for comfort. Nervy. I comforted him. He was pathetic, how could I not? I told the clone the story. I talked about my husband. I recited a poem my mother read to me and I read to my kids. A long poem. James James Morrison Morrison. I was happy to see I still remembered it all. At some point in the late afternoon he opened his eyes and looked at me. It was the first time since I've had him I felt he really saw me. I believe he was curious. Maybe he was alarmed. I don't know what he felt. He seemed most interested when I held up a framed photograph that was on the night table of my three children in their bathing suits up at Spirit Lake, so that for a moment I thought he might reach out to take it from my hand. Had he ever seen a woman before? We think probably he hadn't, but what do we know? You're the first woman he sees? Poor guy. Don't despair, Sonny. There's better to come.*

### Saturday. July 18. 7:30 p.m.

*While I can still see straight.*

*He had a seizure. This morning just before dawn. I happened to be in the room. I had just changed him. I sat in the chair beside the bed and waited to be sure he had gone back to sleep. He'd had a peaceful night, waking only twice. His bowel movements are coming less frequently. His stool is getting firmer, less soupy. I take this as a hopeful sign. I know more about his stool than I'd care to. The smell is not quite so noxious as it was, which is a mercy to me. I tried to be as quiet as I could going out. I made it to the door, and then blam. His arms shot up. Like he was reaching for the ceiling, his arms stiff, locked at the elbows, his fingers fluttering. His head flopped to one side. His legs went completely rigid. His back arched off the bed. His whole body was in spasm. It looked as if it were trying to levitate. He didn't make a sound. The only sound was the creaking of the bedstead. I went to him. His eyes were open enough that I could see they were rolling. There was a honeycomb of spit foaming out the corner of his mouth. I knew what was happening. I had seen this before. _____ had several seizures when he was three, three and a half. After the first he was diagnosed with BCE, which they said he'd outgrow. He did. He had only three seizures we knew about. Three that same year, then none after. I knew basically what to do. Really, what not to do. I didn't try to wedge his mouth open, or stick anything between his teeth. I wasn't overly worried about him biting his tongue. I didn't try to restrain his movements. I thought about getting him off the bed and onto the floor, but scrapped that idea. I moved everything out of his reach and watched that he did not hurt himself. I would say the fit lasted fifteen seconds. When it was over, he was exhausted and limp. I rolled him onto his side, which is what they tell you to do. For the next four hours he hardly moved. When he woke up, sometime in the late morning, I could see he was in considerable pain. Most likely, among other things I couldn't begin to guess at, a whopping headache. I tried to give him some aspirin but couldn't get him to take it. By that time he must have been coming off the sedatives they gave him. Maybe that in combination with withdrawing from God knows how many drugs he was on caused the seizure. I don't know. I pray it will be the only one.*

*Saturday night. I should get out, but how can I? It would be nice to laugh once in a while. Your husband dies and you become scary to your friends. They shy away. I need to run to the store for some disinfectant at least. Not tonight. I'm too tired. It's quiet outside. The calm after. We suffered some damage here, in town. Tree limbs down, patio furniture blown around. There'll be some cleanup. I didn't get the chance to check on my garden. One week to Dolly Day. Jesus. What an embarrassment. Let us all make total fools of ourselves, why don't we? I'll be in. I have to figure out something he'll eat or he'll starve to death. He drank some grape juice for me today. I'm forcing fluids. With all the sweating and shitting he's doing, he must be dehydrated.*

*They just called. A man. I didn't recognize his voice. He wanted to confirm that they'd be picking up the clone Wednesday night at eight. They have verified the identity of the original. From the tattoo. You were right, he said. He is your Ray Bradbury. Not my Ray Bradbury, I told him. He told me how to read the code. The number on the clone's arm, which I didn't really see until this morning, is 1123043468. The first six numbers give you the birth date of the clone's original, in this case November 23, 2004. The last four numbers, 3468, are the last four numbers of the original's social security number. Easy when you know the key. They are sure Ray is still alive, which I'm happy to hear, though they haven't located him yet. I wonder if he and Sara still live in New Hampshire. I didn't mention that. I'm not sure why, but I didn't want to give that information, to be of that kind of help. I wonder how many children they have, what their life has been like. Then he said that because I knew the original, they'd been considering a new course of action, one that would further involve me, which they'll tell me about Wednesday when they come to get the clone. I said I didn't think I wanted to be further involved. That may be, he said. Condescending jerk. We'll talk about it Wednesday, he said. There'll be nothing to talk about, I told him. I was angry. I still am. The fact that I know the original is the very reason I ought not to be further involved. I should have said that. We'll see, he said. Then he hung up. He didn't even ask me how things were going.*

*I went up to check on him sometime midmorning. He was asleep. I'd left him on his side, but he'd rolled onto his back. He was breathing through his mouth, making little snoring noises. He was still wearing the shirt they'd brought him in, and it was filthy. I managed to get it off him without waking him up. It was soaked with his sweat and spattered with his vomit. I put it straight into the garbage. I need to brush his teeth. I could not have waked him if I'd tried, but it is not easy to get someone's shirt off when he can't cooperate. It is like making a bed with the person in it, which I learned to do when my husband was near the end. I saw the tattoo. We'd thought the clones must bear some mark of identification, but I was still a little shocked, really, to see it. The numbers were bigger and darker than you'd expect.*

*They'd clearly been tattooed. They looked aggressive and mean. I sat down in the chair by the bed and watched him lying asleep on his back with his shirt off. I let him air out. I've seen the clone, now, all over, top and bottom, back and front. I've touched him in the most private places. We'd believed the cloning process might result in some physical deformities, that the clones might be clubfooted or harelipped. Maybe worse than that. Not this clone, anyway. His body is beautiful. It is flawless. Everything is where, and as, it should be. He is more beautiful than I remember Ray being, though I never got to see Ray with his clothes off. Am I seeing him now? As he was then? Was he this beautiful? I was thinking about how he'd got an erection when I was cleaning him, about how I'd held it in my hand. I felt a long, deep tug down there. I touched myself. I hadn't thought to do that in a long time. Not since my husband died. Not when we were together.*

### Sunday. July 19. 9:15 p.m.

*An odd day. They've all been odd, these days with the clone. I've given up on calling him Sonny. It doesn't suit him. He's too grave and sad. Uriah. Maybe it's Sunday. Sunday has always been unsettling for me, from the time I was little. I'm off kilter on Sunday. Even with my husband I felt aimless and empty. A free-floating anxiety, a niggling sense of some menace gathering, of something impending. Maybe Sunday is like this for everyone. I don't think it is. I didn't go to church today. It's worse when I skip church. Maybe it's dread, left over from childhood, about the start of the next week of school. But I loved school. Maybe something bad happened to me on Sunday once, and I've forgotten or repressed it. Maybe I will die on a Sunday. Sunday nights are especially hard. All the nights are hard now, clone or no. Even so, there is something different about Sunday night. I'm mournful, wary. I miss my children. I wish the clone would talk. Tonight I would like the company.*

*The vomiting has stopped. His bowel movements appear normal. Two times today, both times his stool was solid. I checked it for blood or worms. Why did I check? I'm a scatologist, a coprophile. I can't tell anything about his urine. And I am constipated, which I almost never am. Whatever the opposite is of sympathetic reaction. I'm eating dried prunes. I offered him some, and he ate them. The poor thing was starving. He gobbled them up. I sautéed a chicken breast for his lunch. As if he'd been taking regular meals. It was noontime, anyway, and I took it up to him. He made a terrible face. It was a visceral response. The sight and smell of it disgusted him. I had two jars of baby food in the cupboard left from when _____ was here in June with the kids. Vegetable beef, peas with rice. I tried feeding him with a spoon. He wouldn't open his mouth. I microwaved a pizza, cut it up in bite-sized squares. No go. Then he saw the prunes and ate them. I brought him a banana. I peeled it for him and broke off a small piece. He ate it and the rest of the banana without hesitating. He ate a floret of uncooked broccoli that had started to brown. He ate a whole carrot, which I held for him between bites, and a wedge of pear. I wondered where he got his protein. At dinnertime, as an experiment, I cooked some lentils with celery and carrots and ginger. He liked that and was willing to take it from a spoon. He ate some brown rice, also from a spoon. I gave him a slice of bread and butter. He drank some more juice from a sippy-cup; I am down to fruit punch, then water through a straw. I will try milk tomorrow. I have to get to the store. I looked at his teeth. They seem perfect. Straight and white. No sign of any dental work.*

*We are through with diapers. Hooray for that. The clone, it seems, is fastidious, left to his own devices. Or it's his dignity at issue. I wouldn't wonder. In the early evening, after dinner, I went up to check his diaper. I looked in. He was asleep. I leaned over the bed and began to pull down his pajama bottoms. He opened his eyes. When he saw me, saw what I was intending to do, he pushed my hand away. He tore off the diaper, which happened to be clean and dry, and threw it to the floor. He was angry. Offended, I now believe. I feared he would become violent. I am physically no match. Except that he is feeble. He pulled up his pajamas, covered himself, then sat up in bed. He would not look at me. He slowly rearranged himself on the bed so that he was sitting on the edge of it, his feet on the floor. He held his head in his hands. He stayed that way for what seemed a long time. I thought he might be crying, but he didn't make a sound. Then he stood up. It was the first time he'd been out of bed. He was shaky on his feet. I was afraid his legs would not support him. I went to him and took his arm. I spoke to him as reassuringly as I could. I said, It's all right. You're all right. You'll be all right. He began to walk towards the door. He moved very slowly. I kept my hand on his arm to steady him. Would you like to use the bathroom? I said. I was guessing. Maybe he just wanted to get away. I couldn't tell if he understood. He did not look at me when I spoke to him. Let me show you where it is, I said. We walked together down the hall. He could barely shuffle. He was very weak, obviously disoriented and dazed. I went with him into the bathroom. I raised the lid on the toilet, lifted the seat, then flushed it once to show him how it worked. He looked at me. His face was full of sadness. It broke my heart to see his face. Ray's face. He stood in front of the toilet. His knees were trembling. He was like an old man, hunched over. He just stood there. I was thinking it might be he had never peed in a toilet before, that male clones urinated in those long metal troughs they have at ballparks, that they used toilets only to defecate, or maybe they sat down to pee. It might be he'd never used a toilet. I had no idea how to show him what to do. It did finally occur to me he might be waiting for me to leave him alone, that he might want me to give him some privacy. I went out into the hall. I left the door open and stood where he could not see me. After a few moments he closed the door. I was afraid he'd fall and smash his head against the sink or the tub, but I stayed outside. I heard the toilet flush. I heard the water running in the sink. When he opened the door, I took his arm. He wouldn't look at me. We made our way down the hall and into the bedroom. I helped him onto the bed. That's better, I said. He lay back down, turned his face to the wall.*

*The oddest thing. I was sitting with him while he lay in bed. Sometime after two, midafternoon. It was hot. He was in my husband's blue shorty pajamas, lying on top of the spread, somewhere between sleep and waking, I'd been singing to him for half an hour, trying to soothe him, show him kindness. Human kindness I almost wrote. Three Little Fishies in that silly voice. Never Never Land. Show Me the Way to Go Home, both versions. Songs my mother sang to me, her mother to her. I tried to think of lullabies, but couldn't. Good thing I didn't think of Rockabye Baby, because I would have sung it. I sang Norwegian Wood, an old Beatles song my mother loved. I wondered if anyone had ever sung to him, if he'd even ever heard singing. Out of nowhere he began to shriek. Like a cat in a fight. I stopped singing. He sat up. He looked at the backs of his hands, then he rubbed them furiously against his legs. In an instant he was frantic. He began to claw at the skin on his arms. Then the same on his shins and ankles, in a frenzy back and forth between his legs and arms, flaying himself. I could see he thought there was something alive and moving on his skin. I didn't know if he was asleep and dreaming, or awake and hallucinating. I put my hands on his shoulders and pushed him gently back against the bed. There's nothing there, I said. Go back to sleep. There's nothing there. As soon as I took my hands away, he was back up and scrubbing at himself. He did this for about five minutes, shrieking all the while. Then he stopped. He lay back and fell right asleep. Maybe he was asleep the whole time. I don't know.*

*We are in for it now. I was sitting at the computer in the kitchen half an hour ago, writing these notes. I looked up and he was standing just inside the door from the dining room. He was watching me. I hadn't heard him come down. He hadn't made a sound. He didn't seem at all threatening, just interested in what I was doing. It was unnerving to see him standing there in my husband's pajamas looking exactly like Ray. Father, Son, and Holy Ghost. I poured him a cup of fruit punch. It was all I had. He drank it where he stood, right from the cup, no straw, no sippy-top. He opened the refrigerator, as he'd just seen me do. He poked around inside. When he touched something, I named it, bread, cheese, butter, eggs, as if I were teaching him the language. Who knows what he knows? He opened the cupboards, and I named the things he touched. He was very careful not to disturb or break anything. He turned the water on in the sink, then turned it off. He looked at my computer on the table, but didn't touch it. He seemed most interested in the framed photographs hanging on the wall by the cookbooks, and in the ceramic cookie jar on the counter in the shape of a bear. When it seemed he had seen and heard enough, we walked back upstairs. Climbing the stairs was hard for him. I led him back to bed, and sat with him until he was asleep. All of it very peaceful and sociable, as if we were old folks at home. One of us mute. He is up and about, on the loose. What do I do now?*

### Monday. July 20. 10:30 p.m.

*No hallucinations today. None I witnessed, anyway. I believe we are over the worst. He was awake for longer stretches at a time. We have dispensed* with diapers. When he needs to urinate or defecate he uses the bathroom. He seems to know what to do, seems grateful to be allowed to do it. No more howling. He is with me now in the kitchen, sitting beside me as I write this. He is watching me write without much interest, sipping hot tea from a mug. Still not talking. What if he can read? _____ didn't talk until he was three. The other two talked early. Our pediatrician said he'd talk when he was ready, and he did, and then we couldn't shut him up, and now he's a philosopher. Maybe the clone isn't ready. For goodness sake, he's not a toddler. I can tell he is, by nature, gentle and calm, particularly so now he is off the drugs. He is stronger today, but still weak. It is late. He should sleep. I should walk him up to bed, but I like having him near me.

They called this morning. Exactly at eight. The clone was still asleep. I was just back from a quick trip to the store. I was afraid to leave him alone. I loaded up on produce and juice, and bought a cheapo intercom so I could hear him downstairs when he was in bed. There has been a change of plans. They are coming to get him a day early. Tomorrow night at eight. I am to have him ready to go, though they failed to tell me what that means. I will make sure he has clean clothes to wear. I'll pack a bag with some things for him to take with him. I think I may be sorry to see him go. I think I may want the extra day with him. Oh, well. Lose one Ray, you lose them all. I don't feel quite so glib.

He slept through the night. He needed the sleep. Do clones dream? is a question we've asked. They do, of course. I have seen him dreaming. It is, when you think about it, a foolish question. It would be comforting if we could believe they didn't dream. I can't know anything about the nature of his dreams. I can say that last night he seemed clearly to be dreaming, and, given the noises he was making in his sleep, the dream I watched him have was not a happy one. Since he has been with me, my dreams have not been happy either.

I spent much of the day with him, walking around the house, showing him things, naming them. Whenever he's awake now he wants to be on his feet. There is no way to keep him in bed. I sympathize. He's been in bed too much. No way to keep him from getting up and wandering around the house and quite possibly hurting himself. Either inadvertently or intentionally, though he's given me no reason to fear that. I can't lock him in the room.

*The door locks from the inside. Even if there were a way to do it, he's not a prisoner here. The only answer is not to let him out of my sight, as if he were a toddler, except when he is asleep, and then I have the intercom. So far he's shown no desire to leave the house. I am thankful for this. He listens when I tell him what things are, but he does not repeat what I say. It is eerie being with someone who doesn't talk, but not altogether unappealing. He seems content to be silent, and probably wishes I'd say less. It's hard to tell what he's seen before, what he's familiar with. We watched a little television together at noon, a cooking show, while we had our lunch. I couldn't tell if he'd watched television before. He seemed only mildly interested in it. I sliced an apple for him, which he ate. I stir-fried some green beans and onions and celery and carrots, but he wouldn't eat the vegetables cooked. I gave him a whole peach and some raw beans and a peeled carrot and several celery stalks, and he ate these. He had several slices of bread and butter and drank a full mug of milk. For dessert I gave him a small bowl of chocolate chocolate-chip ice cream. He liked it, he really liked it, and I gave him a second helping. I had some myself. He was perfectly comfortable using a spoon. I am reluctant, still, to give him a fork or knife.*

*We've had some awkward moments. This morning, after I'd been to the store, after they'd called about the change of plans, I thought I'd grab a shower while he was still asleep. I left the bathroom door open so I could hear him if he cried out. I was out of the tub and had just had time to wrap my hair in a towel when he wandered in. I was naked. He wasn't at all embarrassed. He stood fast and looked at me. I could tell he was especially interested in my breasts, which, at their best, were never very pretty, and are now, you'd have to say, unsightly. He also seemed taken aback by my genitals. I wonder if he'd been struck by my lack of a penis. He is of the first generation of clones, who we believe are not of women born or bred, so that he may well never have had contact with a woman before, or even seen one. Strangely, I wasn't embarrassed to have him look at me, and I made no immediate move to cover myself. I've always been modest, to a fault. My body has always been big and clumsy. Even with my husband, with whom I was otherwise uninhibited, I was shy about letting him look at me. I pray it is not that I was free with the clone because, however unconsciously, I was able to think of him as something less than human.*

*When he woke up from his afternoon nap, he was soaked in sweat. He is still not through withdrawing. He agreed to let me give him a sponge bath. He submitted to it really, all the negotiation done without him saying a word or giving any sure indication he understood what I was talking about. It would have been easier for him to shower, but I couldn't let him go in there alone, and I wasn't going to go in with him. Even though he'd already seen all of me that he could see. I took off his pajama top, left the bottoms on. I spread a beach towel out on the bed and got him to lie down. I filled a mixing bowl with hot soapy water. I didn't have a suitable sponge, so I used a washcloth. I washed his neck and arms and shoulders and chest and stomach. Then I washed his legs from the knees down. I washed his feet. Very biblical. I wanted him to flip over so I could do his back, but he wouldn't. I sang to him while I washed him. I felt like something between a nurse and a geisha. I bent over him, dabbed his forehead with the cloth. He reached up and touched my breast. He put his whole hand over my breast. I was wearing a crew-neck pullover. I wasn't showing any cleavage. That's a laugh. I'd been careful not to rub against him. He'd already got a good long look at my breasts, and I suspect he wanted to see how they felt. There was nothing aggressive or overtly sexual in the way he touched me. He was tentative and gentle. I took it as a purely exploratory, investigative move. He was curious. It was sweet. I named it. I was wearing a bra. I let him keep his hand there a while.*

### Tuesday. July 21. 11:30 a.m.

*I did something this morning I wish I hadn't done. I'm fairly confident I meant well, but I feel creepy now. It is not something I will do again.*

### 8:45 p.m.

*The clone is gone. The same two men came and took him away. If they do not change the plans, I will see him again. I will not count on it. For all their preoccupation with system and protocol, they are capricious. I am furious with them. It was a terrible scene. They came at eight. The clone and I were in the kitchen waiting. I'd explained to him what was about to happen.*

*He listened, but I don't believe he understood. Before they arrived, he was calm, which seems to be his natural, unmedicated state. I'd packed him an assortment of toilet articles from the supply I'd laid in before he arrived, in an old leather dop kit of my husband's. I put this in a nylon duffle bag, along with some of my husband's warm-weather clothes—T-shirts, sport shirts, khakis, cotton socks. The shirts are short sleeve. I worry they will not let him wear them. All of it will be too big. I packed some food for him to take along in a brown paper shopping bag. Fruits and vegetables, as many as I could fit, and some oatmeal raisin cookies I'd baked for him that morning, which he seemed to like. They let him take the clothes. They would not let him take the food, not even the cookies. They wouldn't say why. I had him ready to go by 7:30. He was cooperative with me, tranquil. I wanted to spend some unpressured time with him before they arrived. I'd like to think he was in pretty good shape. I felt I'd done well by him. He was certainly better off than when they'd brought him to me. He was clean and rested and reasonably at peace. The last couple of days he'd eaten well. If you factored in all he'd been through, and how bewildered he must still be, how frightened, wherever they've taken him, you'd have to say he was, at least towards the end of his stay with me, surprisingly happy. I don't know if what I'm calling happiness had anything to do with his relief at being outside the Clearances. Maybe he was happy inside there, too. Maybe he didn't want to be out. Maybe what I'm calling happiness was really a sort of shock-induced semi-stupor. He didn't say a word. How can I be sure? I'd dressed him up a bit for his trip, gray seersucker slacks and a white knit polo shirt. I made sure his face and hands and fingernails were clean, and I combed his hair for him. He looked like a golfer. What was this impulse? Was I trying to impress these men with the quality of my care? When he saw the two of them come in, he became agitated. He was unconscious when they'd brought him; it's not likely he recognized them. They were brusque, unfriendly. Gratuitously so, I thought, and I told them that. They did not bother to disagree.*

*The clone seemed unwilling to leave me. Maybe this is just what I want to believe. They were in a hurry to take him. I asked them to slow down, to go easy. I wanted time to tell them about how he was doing, about what he liked to eat. I wanted to tell them he knew how to use the toilet, that he was in dire need of a shower and some new clothes, that the clothes I'd packed didn't fit him, that most of all he needed some underwear. They wouldn't listen. I watched the clone getting more and more upset. I told them I was willing to keep him a little longer. I asked them, please, to give me one more day. They refused. I asked them to let me take him out to the car. They refused that, too. I was afraid he would not let himself be taken. I put myself between the men and the clone. The shorter, bearded one pushed by me. I said, Stop. Please stop. I pleaded with the other man, who seemed less of a brute. Please tell him to stop. He wouldn't. The bearded man took the clone by the arm. Don't you hurt him, I said. I could see the clone was frightened. I didn't know what he might do. He did nothing. He did not resist. As they led him out, the clone did not look at me or make a single sound.*

*After they'd got him in the car, the older man, the tall one with the scary hands, came back into the kitchen to tell me about the new plan. He said he could give me only the basics, that I'd be given more detail in the coming days. They want me to contact Ray. They want me to go see him. They want Ray to meet his clone, face to face. They want Ray to spend time with his clone, then write about how it feels, what it means. They don't even know Ray. Neither do I, really. They want me to persuade him to do this. When it is published, he said, Ray's account will be of tremendous importance. I am to act as liaison, as chaperone, as nurse. I am to see to the clone's needs. I am to teach him survival skills, teach him about the world, about who and what he is. I am to make him presentable. They want me to teach him to speak, if he can't already, well enough that one day he might speak all over the world about the evils of cloning. Until he is ready for that, the tall man said, and until Ray's account is written, I am, no matter what the cost, to keep the clone alive and safe. I won't do it, I told him. You will, he said. We need you to. I won't, I said. And please leave my house.*

*He did leave then. On the kitchen table I saw the photograph I'd intended to give the clone to take with him. It was a picture of my daughter's children, a fairly recent one. He'd seen it on the dresser in my bedroom when we were walking around the house looking at things, naming them. Of all that he saw, he seemed to like this picture. It's a nice picture. The kids are cute. They are wonderful kids. I don't know why he took such a shine to it. I took it out of the frame and put it on the table in the kitchen so I'd be sure not to forget to give it to him. When I saw it on the table, I wept. I was pretty much undone. I heard the garage door open. The car started up. I knew I would do what they'd asked.*

# Seven

Yesterday was September 12. I spent the day as I have spent every day the last month, in the apartment, in bed, writing my report. My report. Makes me sound like a clerk, a scrivener, a petty bureaucrat. What do I *think* I am?

September 12 is a hard day for me. In New Hampshire it was almost invariably hot, and weeks before the leaves turned color. School had started, and most years I spent much of the day in the sweaty, smelly classroom, negotiating the rules of engagement with my students, the majority of whom were sweaty and smelly and also mulish. Each year I looked for small ways to distinguish the day. I never found a way—something explicit I might do, some ceremonial or commemorative gesture—that felt sufficiently dignified (with regard to Sara's dignity, not mine), that didn't feel contrived or false. Anyway, the day would distinguish itself. For the part of the day I was awake, especially when the 12th fell on the weekend and I could find no distraction in work, I was plainly sad, mournful. Without needing a conscious effort to do this, I held Sara in my mind. At school or out, I kept her face before me, and it filled me with regret. Conversely, no matter how I tried, I could no longer hear her voice, or feel the skin of her hands, the shape of her fingers and nails, and this, too, pained me. Her face by its presence, her voice, her hands, by their absence, I was boxed in by longing and sorrow. Was this not true for other days? All other days? It was easier this year, for whatever reason. It would have been our forty-third anniversary. Perhaps it was not being in the house in New Hampshire. I lived in that house forty-two years. Sara was there with me seven years only, but the house was hers. From the start. She chose the house. It was her money that permitted us to buy it. She made of it a home, and it remained hers all the years I lived there, a guest, a pensioner, without her.

I didn't read Anna's journal right away. I could not bring myself to pick it up. I was annoyed she'd left it for me, annoyed she'd written it. When, finally, I submitted—the thing occupied the kitchen table, Anna-like, demanding to be read—I found it moving and very disturbing. I felt sorry for the clone, sorry for Anna. I felt intimidated, scared, about the prospect of meeting and spending time with my clone. I also felt curious—curiosity more than a little prurient—to know what Anna had done that she wished she hadn't. But these were largely superficial feelings. (There is no way I could have known, or even have begun to imagine, what it would be like to encounter, in the mind-bending, time-trumping flesh, my own clone.) On what I'd like to believe was a somewhat deeper level, I felt ashamed of my essentially mindless, but now quite momentous decision to participate in the government's CNR program—to have, that is, in plain English, myself cloned.

I read the first section, the preamble, straight through. Then, after a break for soup and a sandwich downtown, I read the journal entries. As, to a much greater extent, is manifestly true, too, of me, Anna is unable to forego references to her personal life. I was happy to read these passages. On the drive to Montreal, and afterwards during our brief stay in that lovely city, though I'm sure we spoke of other things, it seemed all Anna wanted to talk about was her husband. Her love for him was impressive, admirable. For me it was also chastening. Then how is it that, just three months after his death, she seemed already—in these pages, on the road, in Montreal—to be easy talking about him, already to have made her peace with his loss? Perhaps she made this peace, and kept it, precisely by talking about him as freely as she did. Hers is a mature response. It has been more than thirty-five years, and I am still not easy talking about Sara. Nor have I been able to find anything like a similar peace. Maybe because, compared to Anna and her husband, Sara and I were together so short a time. Maybe the way she died—tragic, anachronistic, like some pioneer wife—explains it, and how young. Maybe I am simply pathetic and weak. More to the point, solipsistic. There is no grief loftier, more important than my own.

(My son died, too. I never saw him. Anna spoke about cloning the dead. Imagine. I might have raised my wife and my son, a little girl and little boy, together.)

I find not much honor or consolation in this enterprise, but I will honor, if I can, my agreement with Anna's group and try to finish this account, as expeditiously as I can.

Anna called me, as she said she would, three days from the time she left New Hampshire. It was Thursday, August 13. She was back in Iowa. The conversation was short.

"How was your trip?" I said.

"Long. Tedious. Flat. I'm glad to be home. How are you feeling?"

"The same as when you left. I feel decrepit. I feel fragile. Moderately bewildered. I was waiting for your call."

"Here it is," she said. "I didn't want to call you."

"But you did."

"I told you I would," she said. "I'm sorry."

"I read your journal. What did you call it, your notebook."

When she didn't respond, I said, "It was hard to read."

"Sorry to put you through it." That had some edge. Then she softened. "It was hard to write."

"I'm sure it was," I said. "No. It was good."

"Good?"

"I mean remarkable. Sad. I've tried to think what to say to you. It was very moving. It was helpful. Incriminating. It made me feel trifling. Worse. I've been cavalier, oblivious. I've been inexcusably ignorant. There's a human being here."

"There are three human beings here," she said.

"Yes. Of course. Anyway. It was really something to read."

"Good," she said. "Then good. Then it's good you read it."

"It *is* good."

"Now be smart," she said.

"Listen. Anna." I said. "I'm not all that steady. If you try to dissuade me, you might succeed. Why don't you just ask me if I'll do it, and let me answer?"

"Have you given this enough thought?"

"Definitely not," I said. "You called to ask me."

"Wait," she said. "I have to say this. If I'd had the presence of mind, when I first saw the clone, to keep quiet, they'd never have known about you. You wouldn't be involved."

"Probably true," I said. "But irrelevant. I don't blame you, Anna. As far as I can tell, I'm not sorry. Maybe I will be."

"You will," she said.

"Maybe I will."

"Meaning you want to do this?"

"Do I *want* to? I think I do. I'm willing to do it," I said. "If you ask me to. And provided you and your group accept my conditions."

"I'll have nothing to do with it," she said. "For goodness sake, it will not be up to me. You must believe that."

"I do believe it," I said. "Then provided *they* accept my conditions."

"What are they? Your conditions."

"I want no direct contact, at any time, with anyone in your group. Excepting you. I am not one of them. If I do this, I do it because I've chosen to, for reasons of my own. Which are none of their business. They need to agree they will try to exert no influence over what I write. Will they agree to that? Whoever they are?"

"I don't know," she said. "I don't know what they'll do."

"Will you tell them what I said?"

"I am sorry to hear this, Ray," she said. "I am very sorry."

"But you'll tell them," I said.

"I don't know that I will."

"Well, that's *your* decision," I said.

In truth, I had given *my* decision very little thought, considering the nature and putative risk of what was asked of me. I made the decision so quickly and casually—I believe I knew what I would do before Anna left New Hampshire—I wonder now at my nonchalance. It was, I have to say, less a decision, really, then a relinquishment, a relaxation. I relaxed into the idea that I would do this. I mean, almost involuntarily, I let fall away all resistance to the idea. Was it because I felt, not altogether wrongly, that I had nothing now to lose, and the very same to live for? (Are these two calculations always equal?) To state the obvious in the obvious way, I was living on borrowed time. If I allowed it to, my heart attack (the first one) might mark the beginning of a new epoch for me. The final epoch—brief, intense, possibly even meaningful. Might I, who had never given off a single spark, go out in a blaze? Was it that, finally, I didn't believe the danger—about which, from the start, Anna had been so insistent—was real? How much had my decision to do with my taking the opportunity to make some amends to Anna for the way I had treated her so long ago? Even I could see how much she was putting at risk. As it was *my* clone who had been found outside the Clearances, perhaps I felt, however ill-definedly, I ought to do something. Or did I, in some bizarre, unprecedented way—had anyone, before me, been in this position?—feel as if I owed it to my self?

No need for this plurality of explanations. The truth here is most likely simple. I had nothing better, nothing else, to do. And I wanted to see my clone. To see myself, again, as I was at twenty-one.

I had exactly a week to settle my affairs before Anna came back to get me. (She asked me to do it. I said I would.) I continued to believe I would eventually return to New Hampshire, notwithstanding Anna told me I was to take nothing with me but the clothes and personal articles I might need. Anna was all benevolence, but you'd have to say, given the apocalyptic contexts in which they'd been issued before, the sadists and more ordinary run of killers who had issued them, those instructions had a dread resonance. At the very least, they suggested that what we were about to do would not end happily.

A word about money, a subject I haven't before now had reason to talk about, and to which I have rarely given any thought. It is not that I consider the subject of money vulgar and dull. I am not above the subject, just outside it. I don't think about money, because I have a lot of it, and because very little of what I have comes from any effort of mine. I am the beneficiary, ongoing, of Sara's familial wealth, relative to which my salary as a high school mathematics teacher was pin money. Had I not been so freed from pecuniary concerns, I would, I'm pretty sure, have been as grubbing and as boorish as the next. I can too easily imagine being the kind of man who thought about, and strived for, not much else.

Anna told me we could not use personal checks or traveler's checks or credit cards or cash machines during our time in Canada, as any of those would leave a trail easily followed. How would we live? How would we eat? I felt entitled to ask. When we got to Montreal, she said, a sufficient sum would be waiting for us. Who from? Her group? Yes, she said. She explained they assumed the government would make sure I did not live long enough after the publication of my report to enjoy any of the profits that might accrue. These profits, per an agreement she would bring with her for me to sign, would revert to the group and, they were confident, would more than defray their investment in us. How sufficient? I asked. Enough for us to live on, she said.

I was not reassured. One of the first things I did in the time I had before Anna came back was to go to the bank and withdraw from my account sixty thousand dollars. Such a sum would, I knew—when, ultimately, the government's attention turned towards me—be suspicious, even damning. I did not tell Anna I'd done this until after we got to Canada. She was angry and alarmed, as you'd have expected her to be, though it was too late for her to do anything about it. When I came to pack my bag, I put the sixty thousand—I'd asked for it in hundred-dollar bills—in three old L. L. Bean boot socks I had in my drawer, twenty thousand stuffed in each sock.

I was to leave my house as if I'd gone on vacation and intended to return. I was not to sell my car, or anything else I might think of selling. (Besides the house, I owned not a thing anyone would want.) When I quit New Hampshire I would leave behind, presumably for good, my adult past, the signal period of which—the only period I cared about—was my time with Sara. Most of *that* time, we were in the Lebanon house.

Before we moved to New Hampshire, we were in Iowa together at the university just shy of two years. We were married in September, on the 12th, at the start of my second academic year there. Sara had graduated the previous June. (By then, Anna had left the university.) For Sara's sake, so she need not fret, and so her father could cut a stylish and sacerdotal figure without having to contend with me, I stayed clear of Commencement. Afterwards, Sara assured me she was willing to hang on in Ames another year, while I finished my degree. I knew—how could I not know?—she was desperate to get out of Iowa and away from her family. Had it not been for me, she would have been on her way to the Sorbonne. Yet I was happy to keep her there.

Contact with her father had become unbearable, an already strained and ambiguous relationship then made much worse by the fact of our marriage. Which fact her father found, in every way, appalling. I had not before in my life been by anyone brought so close to hatred, for all that Sara was his daughter, of his blood. He went mad. He flew into a frenzy, a rage, which, it was plain to see, was chiefly jealousy. He would not talk to Sara about our marriage, in the lead-up to it, except to say that in marrying me she was not just stooping, but slumming, trawling along the bottom. He characterized Sara's choice of me as, his exact words, nothing more than a postpubescent gesture of rebellion. (Which, at least in part, it *was,* however full of heart and nerve.) If she married me, he said without a touch of humility or charity, she'd be condemning herself to a life without refinement, without grace (he meant this not in the theological sense), without meaning or value, to a life spiritually, and in all other ways, impoverished. He refused to give her his blessing.

We'd decided on a civil ceremony, in Ames. He was convinced her decision to be married outside the church, outside *his* church—he communicated this to Sara through her mother—was intended as an insult to him. He didn't come to the wedding. After we were married, he would not talk to Sara at all. (It was only six years later, when Sara told her mother she was pregnant, that he spoke to her again.) He attempted to prevent Sara's mother and siblings from going to the wedding, insisting that their presence would constitute a flagrant betrayal of him. For what might have been the first time in their conjugal life, Sara's mother opposed him. She came to the ceremony in Ames, and brought with her Sara's brother and sister. It was not an easy or joyous occasion for her or for Sara's siblings, but they were there with us. I was grateful to her then, and I would have further reason for gratitude. When Sara and I moved to New Hampshire, her mother gave us, as a housewarming present, the down payment, and considerably more than that, for the house in Lebanon. This, as we were to understand, without her husband's approval or knowledge. Similarly, all the money Sara came into upon reaching the age of twenty-one—more money than we could conceivably spend—derived from a long-standing, generation-skipping trust established by her mother's side of the family. This was money over which her father had no say, and it was this aspect of Sara's inheritance, about which money I felt some misguided and prideful ambivalence, that allowed me to reconcile myself to what a chimp could have seen was my great good fortune. Sara's father disowned her. We received gratuitously formal notice from his attorney.

While she waited for me to finish my degree, and though we didn't need the money, Sara worked the day shift as a waitress at the faculty club. Later, in New Hampshire, she would work at a local stable, mucking stalls, grooming and exercising the horses, giving an occasional lesson, and at a wholesale greenhouse, tending to the plants. She said she enjoyed earning a wage, enjoyed this kind of work.

For the seven years we were married, she persisted in loving me as if I was worthy of her love. From the start, I suspected she was determined to prove to her father . . . what, exactly? That she had picked the right man? That she could love someone of whom he didn't approve, someone he didn't like? That, given her choice, she would choose a man radically unlike him? That, unlike him, her capacity for love was such that she would love as fully and as generously as she could—I can tell you it was glorious to be loved by her—whomever she chose? That *her* love was not contingent? (This, I think, is reductive, making her feelings for me all about her father, and does her a disservice.) I think it is truer to say she could love no other way. My luck.

For her sake only, I bemoan each uninspiring, ungracious, ordinary minute she spent with me.

The last time I'd done a thorough job of it, my heart stopped, so I resisted the impulse to clean the house. I didn't know how long it would be once Anna arrived before we'd be setting off for Montreal, but, as she was the last one to sleep in them, I didn't change the sheets on the guest room bed. I wiped off the toilet and the tub, put out some fresh towels, sprayed some scent.

I had a vague idea I might take something of Sara's with me. I walked around the house, making ready, room by room, to leave it. The truth was, I needed no memento, no tangible thing, to help me remember her. I thought about saying good-bye to the twins next door, Sophie and Marie. Those pale, enigmatic daisies. If they were enigmatic, it was only because I knew nothing about little girls. By the time they reached my classroom, they were young women. As I faced the imminent prospect of leaving the house once and for all, I was surprised to find how much the twins meant to me, how much I'd miss them. I'd watched them play outside my window, watched them sprout, from the time they were infants, though I wasn't sure how old they were now and could never tell them apart.

I'd lived in that house, in that town, more than forty years, and

I had to acknowledge there was no one for me to say good-bye to, no one whom I would tell (if I could) where I was going, or even that I was going.

"I remember that day we spent driving around Iowa in your old Volvo," Anna said. We were in her truck, on Interstate 89 in Vermont just the other side of White River Junction. It was ten in the morning. We'd just gotten started. We'd been on the road half an hour. Anna was driving. She was eager to talk, nearly irrepressible. Mostly, she wanted to talk about her husband. I would have preferred to sit quietly, and if we were going to talk, to talk about the clone. I had any number of questions.

"I took you to _____," here she named her town, "showed you around. We went for steaks and sweet potato fries at the roadhouse in Le Mars. You paid. You were very gentlemanly."

"I remember," I said. "That was a good day. I enjoyed myself."

She'd arrived in New Hampshire the day before, Thursday, August 20, late in the evening. She was exhausted. That day she'd driven five hundred miles—it had taken her twelve hours—all the way from Dunkirk, on Lake Erie, in far-western New York, most of the way in a pelting rain.

"That place is still in business," she said. "If you can believe it."

"I can't," I said.

We had a good day for the trip to Montreal. The rain had quit, the sun was out, it wasn't too hot, and the traffic was light.

"It is," she said. "My husband and I went there often. On Tuesday nights they had a salsa band. We'd go with friends and we'd dance. Did you and Sara dance?"

"We didn't," I said. "Sara was serious about her dancing. She'd done ballet." I'd never been to a ballet; I'd seen only snippets on television and in movies. About salsa dancing, I had only cartoonish notions.

"Did you ever see her dance?"

"She wouldn't dance with me." I said. "She hated to be clumsy."

"I mean ballet."

"No," I said. "I never saw her dance. Did you?"

"Once. She was beautiful."

Anna reached across my lap and opened the glove compartment. She took out a pair of sunglasses and put them on, then looked at herself in the rearview mirror.

"How do you look?" I said.

"I'd say, pretty darn good."

"I'd say so, too."

"That's a lie," she said. "We all took some lessons, so we didn't make complete fools of ourselves. I wasn't very good. Though I wasn't the worst of us by a far cry. My husband could dance. Big as he was, he could dance." She turned to look at me. I couldn't see her eyes behind the dark glasses. "I know how and when and where you met Sara. You know nothing about my courtship." She smiled. "Does anyone still use that word?"

"I would use it," I said, "if I needed to."

"You would," she said. "We were in high school together. He was three years ahead of me. I didn't really know him. I knew *of* him, everyone did, because he was the star of the various teams. He was recruited in two sports, football and baseball. He went to the University of South Dakota for one year. He didn't like school. He didn't like being so far from home. His father had died in the Second Korean War, and his mother was failing. He came home, took a job in town, helped out coaching at the high school. He and his mother took care of one another until she died. He inherited the house, and that's where we lived after we were married. It's where I live still. I remember your mother died at Thanksgiving the year I knew you."

"She did."

"And you lost your father when you were young. Like my husband."

"Yes," I said. "Not to the war."

"I was lucky in this way," she said. "My parents were divorced. I didn't see much of my father, but I had my mother close by until I was into my fifties. She was there when my kids were born, and she got to see them grow up. My father never saw them. He had died by then."

"That's too bad," I said.

"You think so?" she said. "I'm not sure."

There was nothing I could say to that. Anna took a breath, then continued.

"My girlfriends and I had crushes on the older boys, but my husband wasn't one of the ones we dreamed about. He was too big, and intimidating. He had a man's face, a man's body. He was old-fashioned. He dressed like a man. Anyway, he paid no attention to us. We were too young, too silly. I was always a big girl, as you know, what we called in Iowa a rawboned girl. I didn't do well, romantically I mean, with boys my age, though I had some friends who were boys. I was clumsy, ungainly. You know?"

"No," I said. "I don't know."

"You're being kind."

"I'm not."

"Well," she said. "I was bigger than most of the boys and was shy around them. It wasn't until my second year in college that I had my first boyfriend, my first sexual experience. A really bad guy. I probably told you about him. He was confused and angry and very cruel. I stayed with him more than a year, thinking he was the best I could do. I was frightened the whole time. I did things with him I can't believe now I did. Do you mind me telling you this? Do you want to hear this?"

"I don't know," I said.

"Since I've already started," she said. "It was he who decided to call it off. I begged him not to leave me."

She was quiet for a few moments. I closed my eyes, hoping the silence might take. Then she said: "You understand, Ray, that when you came along, and we seemed to hit it off, and you appeared to be kind and sensitive and appreciative of me, how I might have got my hopes up."

"I wasn't kind or sensitive," I said. "But I was appreciative of you."

"*Maybe* you were," she said.

I couldn't resist. She had brought the subject up, if obliquely. I took my chance.

"Anna. Will you tell me what you did with the clone?"

"What do you mean?"

"In your journal," I said. "What you did that made you feel creepy."

"Oh," she said. "That's what you want to know."

"Not just that," I said. "But I do want to know that."

"Why?"

"Because I'm neither kind nor sensitive," I said. "Because I'm curious."

"I won't tell you," she said. "Not now." She thought a moment. "It was no big deal."

"All right," I said. "Forget I asked."

At eleven o'clock, Anna declared she was hungry. I was hungry, too. Neither of us had eaten anything that morning; Anna had been anxious to get out and going. We stopped for breakfast at a small café in Montpelier. The café was cool and bright with big windows that looked out on the State House. There were, maybe, a dozen tables, only two of them taken when we got there. At one there was a middle-aged couple. Younger than we were. Obviously married. They were in a booth, sitting side by side, studying a road map spread out before them. They were both wearing khaki shorts and walking shoes. They seemed happy. Wouldn't they, I thought, looking at Anna and me, think the same—that we were married, happy? There were four teenage boys sitting at a square table in the middle of the room. They were eating eggs and pancakes and dressed in uniform—red baseball hats, gray baseball pants, red stirrup socks, red T-shirts with a number on the back and the name of a local sponsor across the chest. They had not worn their cleats into the café, but their mitts were on the floor beside their chairs. One of the boys had lampblack under his eyes. You could tell they hadn't played yet that day, because their uniforms were clean.

We took a table by the window. We could see the granite State House, its gold dome with the sun on it. When we sat down, Anna indicated the statue that appeared to guard the front doors of the capitol. "Who's that?" she said.

"This is Vermont," I said. "It's probably Ethan Allen."

It was Anna's first time in Vermont.

"It's beautiful here," she said.

"It is."

Over the years, on trips with my parents, and later with Sara, I'd passed the exit for Montpelier—usually we were on the way to or from Burlington—but I had never been in the town. For all but six years of my life, New Hampshire had been my home. I felt sad to leave it. I have to say, at the same time, I felt capable and free. I wasn't giddy or optimistic, but inside I was light, or lighter. I couldn't have articulated it then, sitting in the café in Montpelier, where these thoughts had just started to gather, but I think I thought that what had just begun was a kind of coda, or encore, to what had been a mostly dull and plodding performance.

And I was glad to be with Anna. We were companionable. This was a great surprise. On her first visit to New Hampshire, it was like being with a stranger. Though she was, at all times, a considerate guest, I'd found her presence in my house oppressive. When she showed up for a second time, after a ten-day break, it was different. I can't explain the change. When she came back, it was as an old friend. Someone I'd known and very much liked a long time ago. Someone I was happy to see again.

I didn't know what to think or feel about the clone. About meeting him. No categories of thought or feeling seemed to apply.

Anna was just finishing her coffee. I was drinking tea, which I preferred to coffee, on doctor's orders decaffeinated.

"I'll tell you now," she said. "But I don't want to talk about it."

"Tell me what?" This was pure coyness. I didn't need to ask.

"I serviced him," she said.

"The clone."

"Yes."

"What does that mean?"

"Don't be dense," she said. "I serviced him. With my hand."

I was neither surprised nor shocked. It was roughly what I expected to hear. Clumsily, stupidly, I looked at her left hand, palm down, on the table. Her fingers were long, a bit thick, the knuckles pronounced. Her fingernails were clean, cut short so that the tips of her fingers showed above them. The back of her hand was spotted, the skin waxy and thinning, the veins prominent. I couldn't help myself. I imagined being touched by her hand, as the clone had been touched. I remembered noticing her hands when I first met her in graduate school, and not liking them. I was more sympathetic now. Her hands were old. They were, one could say, full of character. No doubt they'd been tender, solicitous, astute. No doubt they'd done good and loving work. She saw me looking at her hand, but she did not take it away.

At one o'clock we were north of Burlington, not more than five miles east of Lake Champlain, the Green Mountains farther to our east. Though it was Friday, and you would have expected weekenders to be out in force, the traffic was negligible. That far north the day was still cool and the air perfectly clear.

"The air is wonderful here," she said.

"I'm used to it," I said.

"And the light. Clean and sharp. Fourth dimensional."

"Sara said that to me once," I said. "'Fourth dimensional.' We were in Scotland, on our honeymoon."

"We used to say that about days like this."

"You and Sara?"

"No," she said. "My mother and I. I may have said it to Sara."

When we'd set out that morning, back in Lebanon, I'd expressed a hope that we might drive north through New Hampshire, in order to pass by, or near at least, the places I'd gone as a boy with my father. Failing that, I suggested we take the less-traveled route, Interstate 91 north through Vermont, and cross into Canada at Derby Line, where the business of customs would be quick and easy. Anna was determined we take the most direct route, I-89, and that we make the border crossing at Highgate Springs, a busier station. *Because* it was busier.

"Did you notice the couple in the café?" she said.

"The map readers."

"Yes," she said. "They were sitting side by side. They looked happy."

"I thought the same thing."

"I like doing that," she said.

"Sitting side by side?"

"Plotting a course. I'm good at it. Whenever we took trips in the car, I was navigator. My husband did pretty much all of the driving, no matter how far we were going. I had to wrestle the wheel from him. He didn't like being a passenger."

Before we left Montpelier, I'd offered to drive, but Anna had refused. Now I said, "Will I have to wrestle you?"

"I'd win," she said. "Are you flirting with me?"

"No."

"Don't," she said. "Because I'm oblivious to your charms."

She reached over and touched my wrist, to let me know she was joking. Which I already knew.

"When we were first married and without children," she said, "we spent a lot of time in North Dakota. Whenever we could get up there. With the kids it was a bit far to drive, and after they came along we stayed closer to home. We took them to South Dakota, and did all the touristy things: Mount Rushmore, Crazy Horse, Deadwood, the Black Hills. Were you ever there?"

"No," I said.

"The government claims it maintains the important sites, but there's no knowing what they do. In Las Vegas . . . Have you been?"

"I've not been anywhere," I said.

"On the strip," she said, "outside one of the hotels. They've built a gigantic mock-up of Mount Rushmore."

"I heard about that," I said.

"Which," she said, "I plan to die before I see."

We were approaching Highgate Springs and the Canadian border, when Anna said, matter-of-factly, "I think someone is following us."

"You're joking," I said.

"I'm not."

I turned around in my seat to look out the rear window of the truck. There were several cars within striking distance. "Are you sure?"

"I'm sure," she said. "It's the green car. In the left lane. Two cars back."

I looked again. I could see a green car. "How long have they been there?" I don't know why I said "they." The car was far enough back that I couldn't see how many people were in it.

"Half an hour," she said. "Maybe a little longer."

"Do you know who they are?"

"I can guess," she said.

"Is it the government?"

"It's far too soon for them."

"Have we got a gun?"

She laughed. "Don't be ridiculous."

"The whole situation is ridiculous," I said. "For all I know, we *do* have a gun and now's the time for me to start shooting."

"I'm quite sure it's my group," she said.

"Do you know them?"

"I'm sure I don't."

"Seriously now," I said. "Are we in any danger?"

"I can't imagine we are."

"What are they doing?" I said. "What do they want?"

"I trust we'll find out."

"You're a cool customer," I said.

"I expected this," she said. "We're just at the start."

There were four cars in line ahead of us when we got to the inspection booth. The green car was two cars behind us. We were stopped, and Anna could look at me when she spoke. She'd taken off her sunglasses.

"I want to tell you something, Ray," she said,

"I have to say, Anna, knowing that car is there makes it hard for me to pay attention to much else."

"We'll be fine," she said. "Think of it as an escort. There will be plenty of time, and reason, to worry."

"You'll tell me when."

"I will," she said. "Listen. I haven't said this to anyone else. I'm not sure what to make of it. I'll tell you only because it seems to have some at least tangential bearing on what we're up to." She hesitated, then shook her head. "That's not true. I don't know why I want to tell you this. I just do."

"I'm flattered," I said.

"As you should be," she said. "My husband died in late March. He's been gone only four months, and I'm okay. If I'm not back to my old self, then I'm on to a new one. Is this heartless, faithless of me? Is it indecorous, do you think?"

"I don't think anything," I said. "I'm sure it's not."

"I don't think it is," she said. "I think my ability to cope with his loss, to incorporate it into a workable, purposeful life, does him honor."

"Probably so," I said.

"I mean, I was inconsolable at first. I was crippled with grief. People say this, but in my case it was true." She smiled. "I know people say that, too. The day after he died, when I came out of shock, I stood in the middle of my kitchen, threw my head back, and I wailed. A noise came out of my throat I had never heard before and wouldn't have believed I was capable of making. It felt exactly like my body was trying to turn itself inside out. We had been together nearly forty years. I could see no way of going on without him. I believed I would not go on. Do you know this feeling?"

"Something like it," I said.

"It so damaged my voice I could barely speak, but it seemed to bring me relief, to make such an ungodly racket. By the third day, I'd got myself under control and reasonably composed. My kids were a comfort. I was embarrassed by my behavior. And it's true, you have no real choice but to go on."

"I've heard that," I said.

"At least when you've lived such a sweet and privileged life as I have. I told myself there were still things to do. Though I have to say I had no idea what would soon be asked of me.

"Up until the time he died," she said, "my husband was the manager of the town's baseball team. He'd been gearing up for spring practice. All his present players and many of his former players were at the memorial service, with their families. He had coached the fathers and their sons. I can think of no one who didn't like him. He had a few good friends, men he had known since grade school. But there were many more, most of whom I knew, who had relied on him. I was moved by their affection for him."

"He sounds like a wonderful man," I said.

"He died of complications resulting from near-total renal failure. I haven't told you this. He was somewhere between six-foot-three and six-foot-four, and, when he was not careful, he could weigh upwards of three hundred and fifty pounds. I tried to help him eat smartly, but I wasn't forceful or fastidious enough. His weight had always been a problem. All the men on his father's side were big. By the time he was fifty, he was Type 2 diabetic. It didn't slow him down one whit. He was tireless. We monitored his blood sugar, and he took his medicine most of the time, when he remembered to. Then his kidneys failed. There are strict limits to how long they'll let you stay on dialysis. Do you know this?"

"No," I said.

"Three or four days, at most. Just enough time to harvest and transport the replacement kidneys. But we would not have been able to afford the treatment, even for so short a time. We'd both refused to participate in the government's replication program, and the medical insurance we were able to get covered only the most minimal and routine of services. When he was taken to the hospital, the first question the doctor asked him was if he'd had a copy made. Because there was no copy, he was simply not eligible for a transplant, no matter how many serviceable kidneys might have been obtainable."

"That's hard to believe," I said.

"It's absolutely true," she said. "Insult to injury, he had a life insurance policy for one million dollars, which the insurance company refused to pay out. They claimed his death was preventable, that by choosing not to be cloned, he had voluntarily chosen not to avail himself of the appropriate and necessary treatment. We'd begun to make plans to go to Canada, to Winnipeg, where, if they could find a suitable kidney, they would do the procedure. He was dead before we'd completed the arrangements. He died quickly, which was a mercy.

"He was very brave," she said. "I'd say he was heroic. He wanted it clear he would rather die than in any way benefit from a practice he found so abhorrent."

We were the next car to be inspected.

"Have we got anything to worry about here?" I said.

"Through customs?"

"Yes."

"Like what?" she said.

"I have no idea, " I said. "Are we illegal?"

"Not yet," she said.

I did not mention the sixty thousand dollars I had stuffed in boot socks in my bag. There was nothing criminal about this, but had the customs officials discovered that much cash, stashed like that, it would certainly have necessitated an explanation. In the event, we were not asked to open our bags.

"Here's what I want to tell you," she said.

"Be quick," I said. "We're next."

Anna would not be rushed. "My husband had been dead no more than two weeks when I began to think in surprising and troubling ways. I began to wonder about the choice we'd made. I knew there was no question he would still be alive and with me, with his children, with his friends, looking forward to grandchildren and a longer life, if there'd been a clone. Even at my weakest, my most uncertain, I had no real doubt we'd made the ethical choice. But I questioned the depth of my own conviction. I wondered if I would, or could, make the same choice again, now, facing the rest of my life without him."

It began to sound like something she had planned to say.

"I had thoughts stranger and more disturbing than this," she said. "At the very point when the government stepped in and preemptively took control of cloning, outlawing it in the private sector, the biotech companies were ready to make available to individuals a whole array of cloning possibilities. These included the cloning of the dead. If the cloning industry had been allowed to proceed as it had planned, it would then have been relatively easy, though expensive, to purchase a copy of a deceased parent, or child, or spouse, or friend. For that matter, if the cellular material, and the rights to it, were available, you could buy a copy of anyone you could think of, dead or alive. After my husband died, I wondered what would it be like if it were now legal to clone the dead? Would I want to see my husband alive again, as an infant? Would I want to raise him as my son? When he was thirteen, I would be eighty. What would it be like to be so old myself and see him so young? I know enough to know his clone would not *be* my husband. And it would certainly not be my son. But I wasn't sure how I would answer these questions if they were more than hypothetical."

An official waved us forward. We did not move. The car behind us sounded its horn.

"Of this I *am* sure," she said. "I am grateful this grotesque, incestuous version of resurrection is no longer a possibility."

Anna put the truck in gear and pulled forward. She'd told me what she wanted to tell me. Then she said, in an offhanded way, meaning to change the subject, "You'd figure there must be a black market somewhere for this sort of ghoulishness, but I'm not aware of it."

# Eight

More and more, I have begun to feel I am running out of time. There is, for one, my heart. Should there be another incident, of any moment, I will assuredly die before help reaches me. For another, there is the government, what Anna calls, without a hint of levity, the Dolly Squad. It has been more than a year since Anna and I crossed into Canada and received the clone. If her group can be believed, the Dolly Squad was after Anna even before we got to Winnipeg. And there is no question that, by now, the government will have had to investigate the possibility that I was involved in the disappearance of the clone. Finding me not at home, my absence inexplicable, my whereabouts unknown, they will have begun—long since, perhaps—to track *me* as well. It is who I am, what I know, what I have seen, what I might say. If the government knew about my report, it would be simply another reason for them to want me dead.

What happens to this report if they find me, or my heart gives out, before I've finished it? I am confident my report will, in the end, be far from what Anna's group hoped it would be. I take pleasure and satisfaction in that prospect. I'm not sure I want them to have it, though, having written as much of it as I have—and not for that reason only—I would be sad to think I won't finish it or, should I finish, that it will not find a sympathetic readership.

\* \* \*

Our time in Montreal—we spent three nights and all or part of four days there, arriving Friday afternoon, leaving for Ottawa Monday noon—was a sweet, happy, easy time. Innocent. Idyllic. Even, I am in the frame of mind to say, Edenic. A time just before my hitherto nondescript life lapsed suddenly into meaning and menace.

We were both untethered and fearful. I had no idea what to expect; Anna was only slightly less unsure, though, constitutionally, much braver. In Montreal, we shared one hotel room—we registered as man and wife—and it was awkward. My health was a problem. Anna was eager to walk all over the city. I was still weak and quickly tired. Walking any distance, particularly uphill, was hard for me. I went back to the hotel room each afternoon for a nap, because I needed one, and also to give Anna the liberty to walk out at her own speed. She wanted to eat at exotic restaurants; I had to be careful what I ate. She missed her children desperately.

Still, I remember our brief stay in Montreal as one last good, uncomplicated time before we took charge of the clone, a time when, no matter how anxious I was to meet him, the clone—his life, his needs, his significance—remained almost entirely theoretical. The weather was perfect: sunny and breezy and cooler than it had been down in New Hampshire. Our time was our own, and we had lots of money to spend. In addition to the subsidy we'd be given by Anna's group, we had my stash.

On the border, on the eastern shore of Lake Champlain, the Canadian customs official who processed us was cheerful and efficient. We presented our driver's licenses. The official asked the purpose of our trip, and Anna said, "Pleasure." The day was clear and bright. The station was not busy. We were an elderly couple, on vacation. That's how he took us, whatever our last names, however far apart we lived when we were at home. He asked, somewhat perfunctorily, if we were bringing any food or plants into the country. He did not check our bags, which were in full view, or ask us to get out of the truck, which he expressly admired. He made some notes, handed back our licenses, wished us a safe trip in English and French, and sent us on our way. We were through in no more than ten minutes.

We drove north on Route 133 towards Montreal. We'd gone fewer than twenty miles, when, just before a town called Sabevois, the green car came up behind us and sounded its horn once.

"The green car," I said to Anna.

"I've been watching it," she said.

"They want us to pull over." There were two men in the car, the driver motioning us to the shoulder. "What do we do?"

"We pull over," she said.

"Are you sure?" I said.

"What do you have in mind?"

It was clear I had nothing in mind.

"I was mistaken," she said, looking in the rearview mirror. "I do recognize one of them."

"Is that good or bad?" I said. "For us."

"It doesn't matter," she said. "Stop fretting."

Anna pulled off the road. The green car stopped on the shoulder, right behind us.

"Why don't we get out?" Anna said.

We got out of the truck. On both sides of the road, where we were, there were fields. A hundred yards ahead was a white clapboard farmhouse set back from the road. Running alongside the house a windbreak, a line of tall evergreens. Otherwise, there was nothing within view. The traffic passing in either direction was light. As they came upon us, a few of the northbound cars slowed to see what might be going on.

The two men in the green car got out and walked our way. I recognized the taller of the two men from Anna's journal. (*She* should be writing this report.) The other man, a black man, had not appeared in the journal. He, too, was tall, and thin, but—there was no reason to expect otherwise—his head and hands were normal size. The four of us stood by Anna's truck, on the side away from the road. The man with the scary hands—they *were* scary—looked at me. He did not speak. What was it like for him to look at me? Except for Anna, he was the one person who had seen the clone and also, now, his original. It would have been disquieting for him to see, in such swift and stark relief, the effects of age—the abrupt passage of a man from undiminished youth (however narcotized and helpless) to the penultimate stages of disintegration—the skull just beneath the skin. All very gothic, a convention of nitwitted horror films, yet, in this case, my case, real and no doubt shocking.

He spoke first, to Anna.

"Here you are," he said.

"And you, as well," she said.

"How was your trip?"

"Not bad," she said. "Yours?"

"Trying."

"Well, it's beautiful today."

"It is," he said. "It's beautiful here. Have you been into Canada before?"

"Once," she said.

"In Quebec?" he said. *"Dans cet endroit même?"*

"No," she said.

He did not introduce the black man, who, in any case, kept his focus on the road.

I looked over at the green car. There was no one in the backseat. Did they have the clone in the trunk?

"Shall we have some more conversation?" He spoke only to Anna. "Before we get down to business?"

"Not on my account," she said.

"You don't feel friendly towards me."

"I don't," she said. "You're right."

"People generally don't," he said. He smiled. "Something to do with my appearance."

"Not at all," she said.

"No. I accept it," he said. "But there are a few things we must do. And we are on the same side."

"I'm not sure," she said. "I'm not sure I know what side I'm on."

"I knew your husband," he said. "I mean you no harm."

"What things must we do?" Anna said. "Why don't we just do them?"

"All right. Now we swap cars."

"Here?" she said.

"Yes," he said. "You'll go on to Montreal in the car. We'll drive your truck back to Iowa. We'll leave it parked in your driveway. For a while at least, it will appear you are home."

"Where is the clone?" I said.

"The paperwork for the car," he said to Anna, "title and registration and insurance, is in the glove box."

"In whose name?" she said.

"Your new one," he said.

The black man handed him a manila envelope, which he gave to Anna. "A new passport for you, and a new driver's license."

"What about him?" she said. She meant me. I have to admit, the way she said it felt, at that moment, gratuitously impersonal.

"Tomorrow morning at eleven," he said, "take him to Centaur Office Supplies on the Rue de la Montagne. Will you remember that? Or shall I write it down?"

"Remember that, will you?" Anna said to me. She was teasing now, wanting to salve my feelings, which she had, in fact, hurt.

"They're expecting you," he said. "They'll take his picture. We'll make him a new passport and driver's license. You'll have it before you leave Montreal."

"I have a driver's license," I said. "I won't give up my driver's license."

"No one's asking you to," the man said, speaking to me for the first time. "Just use the new one." To Anna, he said: "We have the money you'll need for your time in Canada." The black man handed him another, smaller, manila envelope. He gave it to Anna. "Wait until you're back on the road to count it. Please be frugal. If you need more, we'll try to provide it."

"How much is there?" I said.

Again, to Anna: "You should have enough."

"Tell them to keep their money," I said to Anna. Then, to him: "Keep your money."

"Don't be ridiculous," Anna said.

"We don't need it," I said.

"Of course we do," she said.

"In Montreal," he said, "you'll stay in the Hotel Bonsecours on the Rue St.-Paul. Pay with cash. There's a street map of Montreal in the envelope with your passport and driver's license. I've written the name of the hotel and circled its location. Park the car in their garage. We've reserved a room for you, under your new name. You'll register as man and wife."

"That's no good," Anna said.

"I agree," I said.

"It will be only a short stay. We'll send word to you there about where you go next."

"What do we do until then?" I said.

"That's up to you," he said to me. "If I were you, I'd calm down and try, while I could, to enjoy myself. You've a long way to go. It will be difficult."

"That's hardly reassuring," I said.

He laughed. He put his big hand, palm down, on top of my head. "So are you," he said. "Hardly reassuring."

We were in the green car. I was driving. Anna had opposed my taking over, but I told her I wouldn't get in the car unless she consented. We'd gone not much more than a mile when she said, with some urgency, "Slow down."

"I'm fine," I said.

"Please, Ray," she said. "You're going way too fast." She put her hand on my right knee, to let me know she was serious and, by her touch, to coax me to ease up on the pedal.

"I'm angry," I said. I slowed down.

"Thanks," she said.

"I *was* going too fast."

"You were. You're a bit of a kook. You know that?"

"I'm really not," I said. "I've never been a kook. Not at all."

"Well, take it easy," she said.

I took a breath. "I will. I'll take it easy."

"All right. Hotshot." She patted my knee, then took her hand away. "There's no rush."

I took a few moments to adjust the side mirrors and the rake of my seat. I had dropped below the speed limit. "Let me just say, I didn't like that guy."

"I could tell." She smiled at me. This was a good woman I'd been thrown in with. "He didn't like you either."

"This is a lousy car," I said.

Anna turned in her seat, away from me. She looked out her window. We were passing an industrial park that extended for what seemed like half a mile. "I miss my truck," she said.

When she said this, I tried to remember (I couldn't, still can't) the figure of speech in which a part stands in for the whole.

"What kind of car *is* this?" I said.

"I have no idea," she said.

"Korean."

"Maybe," Anna said. "I don't know about cars."

She picked up the smaller of the two manila envelopes and opened the clasp.

"How much did we get?" I said.

"Watch the road," she said. "I'll count it."

There were four stacks of bills, each stack bound with a thick rubber band. Anna counted one stack. "Looks like there's ten thousand dollars, Canadian."

"Total?" I said.

"It looks like it."

"That won't last very long."

"We'll have to see," she said. She picked up the other envelope and took out the passport and the driver's license.

"What's your name?" I said.

She looked at the license. "Jane Grey. I'm from Hastings, Nebraska."

"Have you been to Nebraska?"

"I've been to Omaha," she said. "I don't know where Hastings is."

"I've not been in Nebraska."

"I like my name," she said. "Makes me sound like the heroine of a Victorian novel." She opened the passport and looked at her picture. "Dear Lord."

"Let me see," I said.

"Not a chance," she said. "Where did they get this picture?"

"Let me see it."

"Just drive," she said.

I would get my passport and driver's license Sunday afternoon, at the hotel, the day before we left for Ottawa. My new name was Oliver Grey. Maybe because it sounded so fusty, the name pleased me. The picture was, I thought, flattering. Anna thought so, too. It was the same pose on the driver's license. This was my first alias, long before I adopted, for the purposes of my report, a pen name, long before Anna gave the name to me, before I'd ever heard of Ray Bradbury.

As we neared Montreal, the drive became exacting. I had little experience driving in a city of this size. It was Friday afternoon, three o'clock. On the outskirts of the city, traffic was already heavy, and angry, in both directions. My fellow drivers seemed maniacal. The road signs were in French. Anna navigated. She had a road map opened in her lap, but even she was tentative. At the junction of Highway 133 and Highway 10, against Anna's clear directive, I pigheadishly went east when I should have gone west. We drove almost five miles before I would admit I'd made a mistake. When we were going in the right direction, heading back towards the city, Anna, who seemed to me unflappable, asked if I'd been to Montreal before.

"I have been," I said. "One time. With my parents. Before my father died." I'd been young enough, I told her, that I had no memory of the place. I did not tell Anna—I'm not sure now why I withheld this information—that I'd been to Montreal one other time, still many years ago, with Sara.

Sara and I spent a long weekend there in early spring. We saw the sights, ate at some good restaurants (I can remember a Portuguese restaurant, near McGill, where I had sea bass for the first time), and generally enjoyed ourselves. We were celebrating the news that Sara was pregnant. In a long overdue attempt at rapprochement (this is the chapter for French), Sara's father offered to pay for our trip, but Sara turned him down.

When we were in Montreal, Sara had not yet begun to show. Nor had she experienced any morning sickness. She was in perfect health—there would be no signs of preeclampsia until a week and a half before her due date—and very happy. I was happy, too.

It was past four when we found, mostly by accident, the Rue St.-Paul and the Hotel Bonsecours, a narrow, four-story brick building, its exterior characterless, among a crowded stretch of small antiques shops and ethnic restaurants. The entrance to the Bonsecours was well-hidden: a single glass door—the hotel name stenciled in small black letters on the glass—which opened onto a steep flight of cement steps. The hotel lobby, small and purely utilitarian, was on the second floor, the guest rooms above on the top two floors. I parked the car in front of the hotel in a space reserved for unloading. I tried to help Anna with the bags. It was as much as I could do to carry one bag up the stairs, and I had to rest halfway. Anna made several trips. I left her with the bags to register at the reception desk—it was she who had the newly forged driver's license and passport—while I went down to move the car to the hotel's garage. By the time I'd rejoined Anna in the lobby, I'd had to climb three flights of stairs out of the garage, and then the daunting hotel staircase from the street. I was pretty much spent. Our room was on the fourth floor, Anna said. There was no elevator.

"You'd better give me a minute," I said.

"Are you all right?" Anna said.

"I'm okay." In a corner of the lobby there were two fake-leather chairs on either side of a low table. On the table, someone had left a magazine. "Can we sit there?" I said. "Just until I catch my breath."

"You sit," she said. "I'll take the bags to the room."

"No, no." I said. "I don't want you to do that. Stay with me. Let's sit and talk. Then I'll help."

We sat down. I tried to take some deep, long breaths.

"Pretty crummy place they send us to," she said.

"Maybe the rooms are nice," I said.

"You think so?"

"We're the Greys now," I said.

"You're Bud."

"What do you mean?"

"I had to think of a first name for you," she said. "I picked Bud. Mr. and Mrs. Bud Grey."

"Why Bud?"

"I don't know," she said.

"Where did you get that?"

"It's what came to me. Seemed to suit you."

"It won't be Bud," I said. "They won't give me Bud."

"I'm sure they won't," she said.

"I'm not a Bud," I said.

"Oh, I don't know," she said.

Our room on the fourth floor of the Bonsecours was airless and close. There was no air-conditioner, no drapes on the window, just a pull-down shade. A television, too big for the room, was bolted to a blonde-wood credenza. There was also a shabby club chair, and two beds with padded headboards separated by a nightstand. Over each bed was a reading light. The bedspreads looked old and worn. The room smelled of cigarette smoke. From the ceiling in the far corner by the window, a swag lamp hung above an empty space where a table and chair must once have been. I was relieved to see we had a bathroom en suite, with no tub, but a decent stall shower and enough clean towels.

"How much are we paying?" I said.

"Too darn much," Anna said. "It's a dump."

(Over the next year, as we moved with the clone westward in Canada—Oliver and Jane Grey, with their grown son, Alan—we would be provided with better lodging: after Montreal, compact, usually clean, minimally furnished apartments with kitchenettes, leased by the month.)

By the time we'd unpacked our bags, and settled in, it was five o'clock. It quickly became awkward, sitting together in that cramped and comfortless room with nothing left to do. We were grateful to be able, now that it was five, to talk about dinner. Anna had seen a Vietnamese restaurant almost next door to the Bonsecours. She suggested we eat there. I wasn't hungry, but I was willing, if only to get out of our room and into a larger, more public space. The restaurant was good enough. At that early hour we were the only customers. I can't remember what we ate, but Anna would have had something spicy with vegetables, and a Coke. (Everywhere we went in Canada, Anna asked for Cokes, "with lots of ice.") I would have had something unspiced with chicken, and a sparkling water. Anna was a sure hand with chopsticks; I used a knife and fork. When the waiter delivered the check, I took out my wallet.

"Don't," she said.

"No. Let me."

"I've got the money," she said.

"That's all right."

"Are you sure?"

"I'm sure," I said.

"You have cash?"

I had three hundred dollars, American, in my wallet.

"I do," I said.

We thought to take a short walk along the Rue St.-Paul. After four blocks—I was aware of Anna slowing her pace for me—I was winded and dreading the four flights of stairs. "I need to turn back," I said. "I'm sorry. If you want to walk some more, I hope you will. I don't mind going up alone."

"I'm tired, too," Anna said. "You know, why don't we just go up? We can watch TV, get into bed early." It was six-thirty.

I sat on the bed closest to the door—I chose that bed in accordance with some precept of chivalry I thought I remembered but may well have made up—and watched television while Anna took a shower. She came out of the bathroom wearing a flowered cotton robe over a nightgown. She was barefoot. It was the first time I'd seen her feet. She wore toenail polish. Plum color. Her feet were not pretty. (I was sympathetic. They were the feet of a woman in her late sixties. My feet were not pretty either—I had hammertoes—though I did not willingly expose them to view.) Her face was flushed, her hair still wet. Her hair, as I've written, was gray and cut short. When it was wet, as then, you could see her scalp. "That's a good shower," she said. "There's a fresh bar of soap in there. And shampoo."

"Yours?" I said.

"Feel free," she said. She began to dry her hair with a bath towel.

"Sit, will you?" I said. "There's something I should show you."

She pulled the window shade down and switched on the swag lamp, which gave off a jaundiced, ineffectual light. Then she sat on the other bed, the one closest to the window. As if she knew what I'd been thinking, she tucked her feet beneath her.

"What is it?" she said.

"Wait." I opened the top drawer in my half of the credenza and took out the three L. L. Bean boot socks. I removed the stack of bills from one of the socks, and tossed it on her bed.

"What is this?" she said.

"Money."

"Where did you get it?"

"I took it out of the bank," I said. "It's mine."

"Ray," she said. She didn't call me Ray, of course. Nor did she call me Oliver, or Bud. When she spoke my name, it was my real name, always. "I told you not to do this."

"I know you did," I said. "I didn't trust your group. I wanted us to be able to live up here."

"This is bad, Ray," she said. "We would have been fine."

"I didn't think so," I said. "Anyway, it's done. I can't imagine it will matter."

"It might very well matter. It won't look good."

"To whom?"

"How much is there?" she said.

"Sixty thousand."

"Truth?" she said.

"Twenty thousand in each sock."

"You're crazy."

"Again," I said, "not at all."

"You are," she said. "We have to be careful, Ray."

"So you say."

"We do," she said. She looked at the money. "Take it all out."

I emptied the other two boot socks onto her bed.

"I've never seen this much money close up," she said. She laughed, but she was not happy. "At least we're rich."

"We're hardly rich," I said.

This was to be the first of many nights in Canada—a year's worth nearly—Anna and I were, broadly speaking, to cohabitate. We were never in the same bed, but always close. After the clone joined us in Ottawa, except for a single night in a Thunder Bay motel, Anna would sleep in one room, the clone and I in another. It was awkward. For all of us, but especially, I think, for me. (I don't really know how the clone felt about it. He never said.) I was more fastidious than Anna, primmer, tighter-laced. She told me often she was grateful for how modest, how unobtrusive I was when we were cooped up together. "Let me tell you," she'd say, with what looked and sounded like glee, "my husband was not a dainty man." For Anna, the charade of our living together, pretending to be man and wife, father and mother to the clone, was a constituent part of the project to which, at great cost, she'd given herself. I suspect the arrangement was for her amusing, as well. For me, it was a travesty, an inconvenience I could barely abide. The first night I barely slept at all, I was so aware of Anna in the other bed, so alert to her. It had been a long time since I'd slept with anyone else in the room. Anna was a quiet sleeper, that night and afterwards. She didn't thrash, didn't move much, didn't snore. (I snored, "like a walrus," Anna said.) Still, her presence in the room with me made it hard to sleep. That first night in Montreal I lay in bed homesick and stiff with inhibition, afraid, should I start to drift off, I would make some unseemly noise. In the last several years my prostate gland has palpably enlarged, and I have typically to urinate two or three times in the night. I was embarrassed by this and also worried I'd disturb her sleep. I hadn't thought to bring pajamas with me; at home I slept in boxers and a T-shirt. I was embarrassed, too, by the state of my body, my general flaccidity and creakiness and pallor.

Saturday, our second day in Montreal, we were both grateful for the morning, which seemed slow to come. It was dark in the room when I got up at six-thirty, as I always do, to use the toilet. I was careful to pick up the seat and, when I was through, put it down again. I worried about whether or not to flush the toilet, then chose the lesser indelicacy and flushed. I came out thinking I'd get back into bed, but Anna was awake.

"I heard you get up," she said. "What time is it?"

"Six-thirty," I said. "Sorry."

"No. I'm glad to be awake. Open the shade a bit, will you? Let's have some light."

I raised the shade halfway. "What's it like out?" she said.

"I can't tell."

"Open it all the way," she said. "We're up."

I did as she asked. The sun was not yet fully risen. The room filled with a cool, silvery light. "Looks to be a nice day."

"It was a long night," she said.

"Did I disturb you?"

She smiled. "You snored up a storm."

"It was bad?"

"It was pretty bad," she said.

"I didn't know I snored," I said.

"I'll get used to it," she said. "Or I'll murder you. What do you say we get up and going?"

"All right," I said. "Will you want breakfast?"

"I will. I'm starving. And you're buying, Mr. Moneybags."

"Happy to," I said. "So it was really bad?"

"Your snoring?"

"Yes."

"I told you. It was bad."

"What will we do?"

"We'll figure it out," she said. "We'll be okay."

"I'm sorry."

"Stop," she said. "I get the bathroom first. You already went."

"That's fine," I said.

"Did you pick up the seat?"

"Please," I said. "Of course I did."

When Anna had finished, emerging in her robe and nightgown, I showered and shaved, confining myself to the bathroom until I had completely dressed.

Not far from the hotel, on a street off the Rue de St.-Paul, we found a café. She asked me if I remembered the name of the office supplies place, and the street it was on. I remembered Centaur, but I'd forgotten the street.

"Rue de la Montagne," Anna said.

"I didn't bother to remember," I said. "I knew you would. You're so diligent."

"Yes, I am," she said.

We took a taxi to the Rue de la Montagne, a long north–south street. We didn't have the address, and it took the driver a while to find the place. When we got out of the cab it was nine o'clock. According to the posted hours, Centaur Office Supplies opened Saturdays at ten. Our appointment was not until eleven. The day was still fresh and, though I hadn't slept much, I was feeling energetic. We decided to walk along the Rue de la Montagne, north, away from the train station, back the way we'd come in the cab. From my two prior visits—the most recent of which, more than thirty-five years ago—I suppose I'd retained some impracticable sense of Montreal's geography. But this third time the city felt to me more strange than if I'd not been there before. Because I was there with Anna.

We came to a used bookstore, some of its stock already out on the sidewalk in discount shelves. Anna wanted to go in. "We need to get some books," she said. The shop was teeming with books, so cluttered it was difficult to move through the narrow aisles—impossible if another person was already there—on both sides of which books were shelved floor to ceiling, excess volumes stacked knee-high on the floor. The air was full of dust and, from the smell of it, more than a few of the books had begun to molder. Whatever principles of organization had once been in place could no longer have any bearing. Everyone, it seemed, was speaking French. Within a minute of going in, I wanted to get out. Anna seemed energized and disappeared into the maze. Even if I'd wanted to, there was no way to go after her. I stood as close to the entrance, and the outside air, as I could, without being absolutely in the way. After ten minutes of standing there, with no sight of Anna, I got tired of being jostled and rubbed up against, and, intending to stake out my piece of ground, I picked up the book nearest me, taking it from the top of a pile precariously stacked on the floor just inside the shop.

It was a thick, heavy volume, bound in black cloth, the pages gilt-edged. On the spine, in gold letters, was "Holy Bible"; farther down the spine, "Authorized King James Version"; and, at the very bottom, "Michelangelo Edition." On the front cover, dead center, was the somewhat primitive engraving, in gold again, of a lamb in profile, looking back almost coquettishly over its shoulder, standing hoof-deep in a pool of something—water, milk, blood—holding in the upraised curve of its right foreleg a cross. I know now this edition was published over a century ago, in 1965. By the inscription on the inside of the front cover, I also know it was given by her parents, Bruce and Susan Kolberg, to Lisa Suzanne Kolberg, on the occasion of her birth, January 15, 1969, at St. Joseph's Hospital in St. Paul, Minnesota. I was not often or easily moved, but the inscription, commonplace enough, touched me. The infant, Lisa Suzanne Kolberg, would now be long dead. I hoped her life had been, on balance anyway, a good one. I had not bought a book in years. I bought the bible and took it outside. (I would carry it with me across Canada. I have it with me still.)

When I was outside, I opened the bible again. It was big enough that I had to brace it against my chest. I let it fall open in my hands somewhere near the middle of the book (Kings II, as it happened) to a glossy, full-page color plate—the edition, for which I paid eleven dollars, includes more than a hundred such plates, all of them quite beautiful—of a ceiling fresco from the Sistine Chapel, depicting the destruction of the statue of Baal. I might well have looked to passersby like one of those God-struck old cranks who stand on the sidewalk calling up the end of days.

Anna came out of the bookstore lugging a shopping bag. I closed the bible. I was happy to see her.

"What have *you* got?" I said. I held the bible up before me as if it were one of the tablets indited with the Decalogue. "Top this."

"Very impressive," she said. "What came over you?"

"I felt I had better buy something. It's a beautiful book. You should look at it."

"I will look at it," she said. "I bought books for the clone. What a great store. I could have stayed in there all morning. Let's find someplace to sit, and I'll show you what I've got."

Two doors down, we found a green metal bench, unoccupied and large enough for two, set in the boulevard beneath a thick-leaved and fragrant tree.

"It's nice here," Anna said. She put the shopping bag between us on the bench. "Smell that," she said. "This is a lovely city. If I'd lived where you live, I'd have come up here a lot."

"I should have," I said.

"Let me show you," she said, and, one by one, she produced the books she had bought, praising each. (Anna kept a scrupulous account of all purchases she made with the money her group had given her.)

What she'd got were books she intended to read to, and perhaps with, the clone, books she meant to use in her capacity as his teacher. (As she understood it, in addition to keeping the clone alive and safe, this was a critical part of her charge.) These were all old books, books she had loved as a child, books her mother had read to her, books her mother had, herself, known as a child. Over the years, Anna had read and reread these books. Then she'd read them again to *her* sons and daughter, often reading from the same copies, copies she'd lovingly conserved, that had been read to her and to her mother before her. There were *Peter Pan*, *The Water Babies*, *Oliver Twist* and *Great Expectations*, *Alice's Adventures in Wonderland*, *Wind in the Willows*, *Winnie the Pooh*, *Pinocchio*, *The Prince and the Pauper*, *Adam Bede*, *Uncle Wiggily's Story Book*, *The Mouse and His Child*, a volume of Hans Christian Andersen's fairy tales, the first two books of *The Boxcar Children* series, *The Secret Garden*, *James and the Giant Peach*, *The Adventures of Lucky Pup*. I would get used to seeing these books around in the various apartments we rented. Most of them I didn't know. Anna assured me they were all "great books." Her plan, she said, was to use them to help teach the clone to read—should he need to be taught—and to help him acquire the language, should that be necessary, as, so far, it appeared it would be. (What Anna, too cagily for my taste, didn't mention was this: her group's long-term intention for the clone; that he become a presentable spokesman for their anti-cloning agenda. She saw, as I did—as the clone would come ultimately to see—the radical cruelty in exploiting the clone this way, asking him, shaping him to speak out against his own existence.)

After she'd shown me the books she'd bought, I wondered aloud what good they would do the clone, who, after all, was not a child, even assuming he'd ever be able to understand the language in which they were written, and who, more than anything else, would need to learn about the world as it was, not as it was imagined in the out-of-date fantasies Anna had assembled. What we, and he, would need, I said, were books that graphically explained the actual world and helped him locate himself in it. For the purposes of language acquisition and reading skills, I had in mind books for beginning readers, with a limited and repetitive text, and lots of illustration. To teach him the names of all the things and creatures he might never have seen, I suggested a word book or two—by which I meant those books that have, on every page, a hundred drawings of things, with the name for each thing printed beneath it—and a paperback dictionary of the English language. I suspected we'd want simple primary school textbooks in arithmetic, and science, and social studies. A comprehensive atlas of the world would be helpful, and some text, at whatever level, full of color plates, on anatomy and physiology. I thought the clone would be better served by books of this explanatory, denominating, more explicitly didactical sort. I did not press the point—my opinions were based on almost no knowledge of the clone—but I was proved right.

When he joined us in Ottawa, the clone had only a minimal number of English words, with which he could generate a minimal number of short, simple sentences in the declarative, interrogative, and, less frequently, imperative modes: "I want to eat." "When can I eat?" "Feed me." (In truth, I can't imagine him saying that last. He was a good eater but always patient and passive about mealtimes.) We didn't know whether he'd been taught to form these sentences, inside the Clearances, or whether he'd picked them up in the short time he'd been out. In either case, it was clear the government had developed some means—perhaps by keeping them sedated half the time—of preventing or, at the very least, stunting the development of language among the clones. He could not read, and had never been read to. He had no notion of reading, or of books. In the year he was with us he would be very quick to understand language spoken to him. He was slower, but still quick to acquire a speaking vocabulary and a facility with grammar and syntax. (In writing of the clone's aptitudes, there is no way for me to avoid the appearance of self-congratulation.) Despite Anna's best efforts—she was, I saw, a skillful and dedicated teacher—he still hasn't learned to read beyond, say, fifth-grade level. He was miserable trying to learn to write (as I had been)—nothing we asked of him made him angrier—and Anna was satisfied when he could print his name.

At eleven, we went into Centaur Office Supplies. To the first employee we came upon Anna identified us as Bud and Jane Grey. He seemed to understand and, without any delay, led us to the back of the store where, in a small space behind a curtain, another man took my picture. When Anna offered to pay, they assured her, in English, they'd already been paid. By this time I had begun to flag. We took a cab back to the Bonsecours, and ate a quick, light lunch in a cafeteria across from the hotel. After lunch, I went up to the room to nap.

Anna came up with me, stayed long enough to freshen up, then went down to explore the city at her own pace.

I was still asleep when Anna came back to the room, sometime after five. I'd pulled the shade down, and the room was stuffy and dark. I was not at all ready to wake up, but Anna, making no effort to be quiet, raised the shade with a snap and opened the window, letting in the air and the noise from the street.

I was not happy to be rousted this way. "What's going on? What are you doing?"

"I've come back," she said.

"I'll say."

"Because I want to talk."

"I'm asleep."

"I need to talk, Ray, please. You're all I have."

"All right. Will you let me go to the bathroom? I'll be right back."

"Go ahead," she said. She sat down on her bed to wait.

I took my time in the bathroom. When I came out I sat down on the edge of my bed and faced her. "Some things take longer now," I said.

"I see."

"So. Talk."

"Don't be that way," she said.

"Sorry. I meant: 'Let's talk.' What is it you want to talk about?"

She stood up and walked over to the club chair, on which, before leaving for her walk, she'd deposited her shopping bag. She took out several of the books. "These are wonderful books, Ray. My mother read them to me." She named the books in her hand. "Her mother read them to her. I read them to my children."

"Yes, you told me."

"I know I did. Just listen. I don't want to read them to the clone. That's not who I want to read them to. I want to read them to my grandchildren. I've been waiting to read them to my grandchildren. I've been looking forward to that. You can't imagine how much I've looked forward to that."

"I can't," I said. "You're right."

"This is not about you, Ray. All right? Can this not be about you?"

"It can."

"I miss my kids," she said. "I miss their kids. Sweet little things. I want them. I want to read these books to them."

"I'm sure you do," I said, trying my best to be compassionate.

"Will I see them again?"

"I don't know," I said. "I mean, how would I know? I don't know anything. Except what you tell me. You tell me. Will you see them again?"

"I don't know," she said. She was silent a moment. She put the books back in the bag. "Maybe I will."

"I'm sorry," I said. I *was* sorry.

She sat down again on the bed. "What am I doing here?" she said. "What am I doing?"

"I don't know, Anna," I said. "I mean, if you don't know, I certainly don't. Shall we go home?"

I believe she gave this possibility some thought. Then: "No," she said. "No. We can't go home."

"We can't? Or we won't?"

"Both," she said. "Neither. Be easy on me, Ray. I'm sad. I'm coming apart."

"What can I do?" I said. "I don't know what to do."

"Just be quiet for a minute. Let me sit quietly."

I was glad to do that.

After a while, she said. "We can't go home."

"I believe you," I said, though I didn't quite believe her. Whatever *she* might or might not be able to do, I believed I could still go home, that if, for me, a point of no return existed, I had not yet gone past it.

That night at dinner Anna said to me, "They will be after me sooner than they will be after you. I am known to them. Known to be in opposition to their program, known to be part of a dissident group, known to live at the edge of the Clearances. They will figure out I am involved with the clone long before they even begin to consider the possibility that you might be with me. Depending on when I am found, there might still be a chance for you to escape, and continue."

"With the clone, by myself?"

"If that is how it goes," she said. "Yes."

"I don't think I could do that, Anna. I don't think I would."

"You'd have to. You'd have no choice."

"I could let him go."

"You couldn't do that, Ray."

When I said this, I had not yet met the clone.

"Listen," I said. "Here's one thing I can do. I can take you to dinner. Would that be good?"

She smiled at me. "That's sweet, Ray. Can we go someplace nice?"

With a cheap and easy gallantry, already thinking about getting back to the room after dinner and going to sleep, I said, "We can go anywhere you like. So long as I don't have to walk there."

"Can we dress up?" she said.

"I'll do what I can."

On her afternoon walk Anna had seen a restaurant in Old Montreal she thought looked good.

"We'll go there," I said.

"I looked at the menu in the window. It's awfully expensive."

"It will be fine," I said.

It was Saturday night, but we showed up early enough to get a table without a reservation. It was a spectacular place—a two-hundred-and-fifty-year-old stable that at obvious cost and attention to detail had been converted to an elegant and very expensive restaurant—dark wood, exposed beams, starched white tablecloths, fine china and silver and crystal. Candlelight. The waiters expert. The space was large, but someone had given careful thought to the disposition of the tables and to the acoustics, so that although most all the tables were full, the dining room felt intimate and hushed. Anna had put on a sleeveless linen sundress with a vertical green and white stripe that made her look even taller than she was. (The dress had a special resonance for me. I'd bought one very like it once for Sara.) She was wearing makeup, lipstick and eyeliner and the like. If she had worn it before, I hadn't noticed. I had on a short-sleeve plaid sport shirt and khakis. I have always dressed the way I remember my father dressing. I'd brought two sport coats with me to Canada, both wool, a glen plaid and a navy blazer, and I carried the blazer over my arm.

When we'd been seated, I said, "Your French is pretty good."

"I had it in high school," she said. "I'm butchering it."

"They seem to understand you."

"Yes, because they all speak English."

At dinner, Anna did most of the talking. I thought perhaps she talked as much as she did—then, and at most other times—as a way to stave off grief and despair. That night, she was more voluble even than usual.

"This place is amazing," she said. "I've never been in a restaurant this fancy. Have you?"

"Maybe once or twice."

"With Sara?"

"It would have been with Sara, yes."

"Well, it's lovely here," she said. "I feel glamorous and rich. Thank you for taking me."

She talked again about her husband, and about the trips they had taken together. Conspicuously, she did not speak about her children. I knew she was trying to avoid the pain of that. At some point in the meal, she turned serious and dark. She looked at me across the table. "In the car, yesterday," she said, "you didn't respond when I told you what I'd done for the clone."

I had not been thinking about this. "I didn't know how to respond," I said. "When I read your journal, I assumed that's what it was."

"It was wrong of me," she said. "I know that."

"You hear about nurses doing that sort of thing for their male patients, the invalids, the terminal cases. Angels of mercy."

"It's not the same. I shouldn't have done it. I'm not sure why I did. The poor boy didn't know what was happening to him."

"You gave him a little pleasure," I said. "You brought him some relief."

"I don't know that I did," she said. "I hope you won't judge me too harshly."

"I don't judge you at all."

"What does that mean?" she said.

"It means, I'm grateful for your company."

"It's my fault you're here in the first place."

"True. But, as I'm here, I'm glad you're with me."

"That makes no sense," she said.

"I know what I mean."

"Anyway," she said, smiling, obviously unburdened, "don't get any ideas."

"That's the second time you've said that to me."

"Which reminds me," she said. "I want to tell you something. When I found out that you and Sara had been married . . ."

"How did you find out?"

"Sara told me. She wrote me."

"I didn't know that," I said. "Good. It's good she did that."

"I have to say," she said, "when I found out, I was sorry. Though I liked you, Ray, you know I liked you, I felt Sara might have done better."

"She could have," I said. "There's no doubt about that. I agree with you."

"I'm not saying this to be cruel," she said. "I just wonder what it means about me, that I could have felt that way and still have wanted you for myself. In whatever way I wanted you, which I don't think I really knew. But I was happy for you guys when I heard. I was married by then. Even if I wasn't, I would have been happy for you. You should have invited me. I don't think I would have come. I don't know. Maybe I would have."

That night, though I was well-fed and bone tired and longing for sleep, with Anna in the room, in a bed so near mine, sleep, as it had the night before, eluded me. I don't believe I slept at all until after four. It was Sunday. We had a lazy morning. We slept in, which was lucky for me, ate no breakfast, and didn't really get going until just

before lunch, which we had in a tiny café called Titanic. I remember
the name because it seemed, both, so witty and so hopeless. Afterwards, Anna wanted to do some sightseeing. I agreed to see one sight
with her. On a piece of hotel stationery she'd written a list, culled from
a guidebook she'd bought in Iowa, of things she wanted to see in Montreal. She proposed the Basilique Notre Dame. I had been there with
Sara, but I remembered nothing about the church. It was, in the way
of such things, big, splendid, gaudy, cold. Sara was always anxious in
churches, no matter the size or grandness, and it's likely we hadn't
stayed long. When Anna and I arrived, sometime near one o'clock,
there were few visitors. We had to pay to get in. We made a desultory
circuit of the interior. It was hard to know what we were supposed to
look at. We'd made our way back to the narthex. I thought we were
ready to leave, but Anna said, "Give me a minute."

"What for?"

"Just give me a minute," she said, and I watched as she walked
quickly up the central aisle through the nave towards the chancel. Anna
slipped into a pew near the front. She sat for a few minutes—I could
just see the back of her head—then came back down the aisle, her head
slightly bowed, the posture and the walk unmistakable. Watching her
it came to me—news, I'm sure, only to me—that the word "prayer" can
be used to denote what is prayed and the person who prays it.

"You were praying," I said.

"Yes. Do you mind?"

"No. Did you put in a word for me?"

"I did," she said. "I always do."

When we got back to the Bonsecours it was midafternoon. A
large manila envelope had been left for Jane Grey at the reception
desk. My driver's license and passport, under the name Oliver Grey,
were inside, along with a hand-drawn street map and a note giving us
our instructions. We were to leave Montreal the next day at noon. We
were to drive west to Ottawa, making no stops, and, at precisely three
o'clock, show up at the address given. The note stipulated that Anna
was to do the driving, which stipulation, a deliberate insult, I was determined we would not heed.

\* \* \*

Sunday night, our last in Montreal, after an early dinner, during which neither of us spoke about the next day, we returned to the hotel and packed our bags. It was the right time, Anna said, for her to brief me on what it was like for a clone inside the Clearances. What it would have been like for my clone. I told her I was sleepy. She said I wasn't sleepy, that I'd slept most of the day. With that, the idyll, such as it was, ended, and class began.

"From the start of the government's program," Anna said, "as I believe I've told you, we have tried to think, as near as we could come to it, the way the government thinks. All the evidence points to thinking that is pragmatic, self-interested, and venal, but who can be sure how the government thinks? All I can tell you is what seems to us the most probable of what has been guessed, deduced, imagined. We believe we have come close to the truth."

Although I had slept most of the day, I *was* tired. My feet hurt. My scalp itched. I was worried about my heart. I wanted to be in bed, in the dark, alone in the room. I wanted to think about things—however beside the point—without Anna's voice in my head. Why did I need to know this? I would meet the clone. I would see what I would see. I would do what I could for him. I would stand beside Anna. If I still saw the reason for it, I would write the report.

"Everything within the Clearances," she told me, "the most densely populated area on earth, is designed and engineered to keep the clones physically healthy and emotionally placid, to keep them manageable and docile, without the instinct or means for procreation, or self-preservation, or aggression. Every day the clones get long bouts of regimented exercise, though there is no game-playing, no sports, no activity that might encourage a spirit of collaboration or teamwork, nothing to inspire a collective sense. They get an optimally balanced, low-calorie, inexpensively delivered diet. They eat vegetables and fruits grown on the Clearances by the clones themselves. They eat very little meat, and no red meat. The poultry and pork they eat is from pigs and fowl raised inside the Clearances. The fish, too, is farmed there. No sweets. No coffee or tea; nothing that might jazz them up. Plenty of water. Wholegrain breads. A glass of purple grape juice with supper. They eat the way we might eat if our one concern was maximum health and longevity. So that, on average, the health of the clones is far better than that of their originals. It is certain," Anna said, "that the government cares far more about the health of the clones than it does about the health of its citizens, in whom it has little investment.

"As long as they live, adult male clones are administered daily a massive and uniform course of psychotropic drugs meant to keep them subdued, oblivious of sex (homoerotic), well-rested, and not discontent. I'm sure my group will have analyzed samples of blood taken from your clone, and will know the nature and extent of this medication. In any case," Anna said, "I have witnessed the horrific emotional and physical effects of its withdrawal.

"At birth, each clone is tattooed on the inside of his left forearm, with what appears to be a scannable identification number. Though it is not, in fact, scannable, at least not with any of the equipment we tried, the number simply and unmistakably identifies the clone with its original."

One way or another I already knew this, and I told her so.

"Clones are not given names," she said, "just these ID codes. They live in enormous prefabricated hangar-like structures, barracks, each of which houses ten thousand clones."

"That number can't be anything but arbitrary," I said.

"Our best guess," she said.

"Adult male clones and adult female clones never see one another; the male and female barracks are set hundreds of miles apart. The clones are warehoused, inventoried, grouped by age, according not to *their* date of birth, which might vary some from those of their barracks-mates, but to the birth date of their original. Before he got out, however that happened, your clone lived with other male clones whose originals were all were born on November 23, 2004."

"You remember my birthday?"

"When you need a part, your clone is easy to locate."

"He's not now," I said.

"When the male clones have finished their exercise and their work, whatever that is, for the day, they are sedated. Either they are working, exercising, eating, or they are sleeping."

"What does your group think?" I said, without facetiousness. "Do clones dream?"

"I can tell you they do," Anna said. "At least when they are coming off drugs.

"That the clones do not have names, that there are so many of them in any one 'residence,' that they have no 'free' time—we don't have the language to describe this universe—would certainly discourage," she said, "if not absolutely prevent, anything that resembles social interaction.

"When they reach the age of twelve or thirteen, male clones are put to work. Some do agricultural work on farms inside the Clearances. Some work at the cleaning and upkeep of the buildings and grounds. Some do road and infrastructure repair. Some see to the maintenance of vehicles and equipment. Some prepare the food. And some are involved in the process of cloning itself, so contrived that the fewest possible originals need be connected with it.

"Female clones require very little medication to keep them pacific and are not sedated at night. They do only one sort of work: they carry and give birth to infant clones, and they nurse them and care for them through infancy and childhood. The process is designed to obliterate the dangerous mother-child bond. Each female nurses and tends to a different child each day. An infant clone might, on any given day or night, be assigned to one of ten thousand 'mothers' who reside in a particular 'rearing' complex. As the clones are not named, the transient mother would call her charge 'Boy' or 'Girl' (or some version thereof in the language given the clones to use), and the child, when he or she was old enough, would use the appellation 'Nurse.' We find some comfort," Anna said, "in the belief that, under even the most severe and harassing of circumstances, the maternal instinct will prove irrepressible, and that a certain portion of mother-love, of tenderness and kindness, could not be rigged out of the situation.

"Among the clones, children have no fathers. This will be important for you to keep in mind, Ray. The boy clones have no interaction with adult males, until they leave the world of female clones. The girl clones never in their lives see an adult male.

"Artificial means of inducing and sustaining lactation, and of delaying menopause, will have been developed. When she is no longer able to give birth, the female clone is shifted to the care of young clones, between the ages of three and thirteen. After which, clones are no longer considered children. The male clones are moved to residences for adult males and committed to adult male work. At the age of twelve or thirteen, the female clone's life is given over, for as many as forty years, exclusively to child-bearing. She becomes an incubator, a factory for producing babies. When she is not having them, she is nursing them (though never her 'own'). She is almost continuously pregnant, with a respite between pregnancies just long enough to prevent the process from becoming life-threatening."

I understood, and Anna was at some pains to make this clear, that when she spoke about what went on inside the Clearances, she was dealing almost entirely in speculation, however reasoned and astute it might have been. For instance: this conception of the life of a female clone had to be, at this point in the history of the enterprise, purely speculative, as the first generation of clones, of which my clone was a member, was just now reaching adulthood. Still, when she spoke this way, declaratively, authoritatively, using the present tense as she did, it was hard to keep from taking speculation for fact.

And I wondered if she, and her group, were afflicted by the same confusion. "If a female clone is pregnant, and her original needs a part, the extraction of which would jeopardize her life and, perhaps, that of the fetus, the original is given a compatible part from a store of spare parts frozen and warehoused for this purpose, and allowed to believe it comes from *her* clone. Except in the most extraordinary cases, the babies are delivered by clone midwives (who train by watching other clone midwives). Pain medication is liberally administered; the notion of natural childbirth is irrelevant. Caesarean sections are rare. For emergencies, and for serious illnesses, the government operates within the Clearances' two hundred and fifty hospitals—we estimate one for every million clones—staffed by doctors and nurses and support personnel taken from the U.S. military, and sworn to the strictest secrecy."

"Anna. I haven't given this any thought, and even I can see there's a hitch here."

"There are a lot of hitches," she said. "We're guessing."

"Okay, but you put enough chickens in the coop and they'll get aggressive. In addition to all those medical people, your guess would require a great many others, originals, working inside the Clearances in supervisory and security positions, folks who know what goes on there, who've seen the clones, engaged with them. How does the government make sure none of these people talks?"

"We don't know what the mechanism is," Anna said, "but given that whatever goes on in there has been going on for more than twenty years without a hint of disclosure, it must be pretty near foolproof. Besides, we assume the clones are kept tractable by other means, and also that the clones, themselves, are used as guards, as police."

"It would only take one."

"It hasn't happened yet," she said. "Sadly."

"Well, somebody screwed up."

"What do you mean?"

"The clone is out," I said.

"Yes. He's out. Will you give me a second?" Anna said. "I need a sip of water." She got up off the bed and went into the bathroom. I stood up and stretched. I went to the window and looked out. The view was dismal: on the opposite side of a dark alley a line of derelict sheds.

"I'm almost finished," she said when she came out.

I sat back down on the bed. "Take your time. I'm interested."

"They closely examined your clone," she said, "and found no tracking device. In case you were worried."

"I wasn't worried," I said. "Not about that."

"Anyway, when a clone is used, and if, after surgery, the clone remains viable, still able to provide spare parts, he is not returned to his original residence. This is true, whether or not the loss suffered by the clone is conspicuous and disfiguring, or unobtrusive, as in the removal of a kidney or a lung, where only an incision scar is visible. In all cases, the clone is taken to one of many special residences, postsurgical holding pens, set apart. For a clone who is intact to see a clone who has been harvested is to confront his own destiny. For obvious reasons," Anna said, "an unused clone must never know what he has been made for.

"When an original dies, his or her copy is summarily put to death, no matter what its age. Everything that can be used for spare parts is salvaged and banked. What happens to the body of that clone? What happens to the body of the clone who can no longer survive repeated surgical diminishment? Or to the body of the clone who dies of 'natural' causes? Is it buried? Burned? Our current thinking about this is that it is composted, fermentation in some way accelerated so as efficiently to produce methane, which, converted to methanol, the government exports beyond the Clearances and sells at enormous profit."

"Waste not," I said.

"As you may not know, Ray, those who could not afford hospital birth, or those unable to pay the steep original cloning fee, were, from the start of the program, 'permitted to opt out.' Despite the strong correlation between poverty and the need for serious health care, it was rationalized that the poor—we're talking here about a quarter of the population—would not have the means to afford a procedure that required a replacement part and, thus, could make no use of a clone.

"As human beings, the clones would have an instinct and congenital capacity for language. In any human society, the rise of language is pretty much unstoppable. In any case, the clones would require a minimal language for their work, and for simple communication having to do with exercise and eating and rest. The government's problem is that once the clones get this much language, they would inevitably develop more. Would a clone dialect evolve in spite of the government's efforts to prevent it? What if a language of feelings was to appear? A language of desires? We had thought the government might be compelled to cut out the clones' tongues. Now we have empirical evidence they do not, and we wonder why. I have not yet heard your clone speak. I heard him moan and grunt and howl.

Not quite animal sounds, but not quite human. I heard him cry. But I heard nothing from him that even approximated language. Do clones talk to one another, or is verbal communication, outside of what is needed for work, proscribed? It would be far easier to prohibit access to information and knowledge than it would be to stop the spread of language and speech. And with language, ineluctably, comes thought and, possibly, understanding.

"Right there, for the clones," Anna said, "is the hope, and the horror.

"The clones get no education. They are trained to do only the work they are assigned. Once a month, male and female, adult and child, they are given haircuts. Male clones shave once a week. Clones brush and floss their teeth twice a day, and the water they drink is heavily fluoridated. Menstruation is a significant problem for the government: of the ten thousand post-pubescent female clones in any residence, most get their periods on the same day.

"Do clones love? Do they know love? *About* love? Do they have a word for love, or any sense of the concept? We couldn't even begin to speculate about this.

"Here's the catch," she said. "The government's cloning operation is still in its infancy. What I've drawn for you is the shape we think things will take inside the Clearances if the program is allowed to continue, as all indications suggest it will be. You wouldn't need to be a mathematician to have figured out that most of this could not have happened yet. The 'mandatory' program for all new births began in 2049, the year you signed up for CNR. Your copy, Ray, will be, give or take a year, among the oldest copies in existence. Except for the relative few made prior to the government's institution of the process, no clone will be older than twenty-two. This first generation of clones will have been produced without human mothers. There will have been no female copies old enough to carry the cloned fetuses. Until there was a sufficient number of female clones of child-bearing age, another method of incubation would have been found. The generation of clones to which your clone belongs was gestated in synthetic womb environments. The more 'natural,' less expensive gestation process will have been in place, now, less than ten years. There would have been no female clones old enough to care for your clone as an infant or young child. We don't know who raised your clone, or if he was cared for at all. In every meaningful sense, he, like his coevals, was born without parents. Orphans all. Adams and Eves. It is possible that, until he came to me, your clone had never even seen a woman. If anything, your clone's life inside the Clearances, lived in the main before things had coalesced, might well have been worse than it would be were he to be born there today."

# Nine

In the more than a year, now, Anna and I have spent with him, we have not learned from the clone enough about his life inside the Clearances for me to say how close Anna's group was in its speculations to being right. By the time the clone had acquired language skills necessary for him to speak usefully about his experience, he was unwilling—maybe still unable—to do so. Who could blame him? Judging by his behavior early on, and from several things he said in less guarded moments—later in the year, when he'd grown more comfortable speaking to us, especially to Anna—I can say that on at least two counts, in their efforts to think as the government thinks, Anna's group did not go far enough to get the details—where the devil, indeed, was—quite right.

To take one instance of their coming up short: Anna's group imagined there would be special, separate, segregated residences for clones that remained viable after being harvested for parts. The group assumed that, thinking pragmatically, towards the end of keeping the clones oblivious and docile and manageable, the government would not incur the risk of inciting the clones by letting them live among their counterparts returned from surgery. From what Anna and I were able to gather, there are within the Clearances no such special residences. However mutilated, used clones are sent back to live among their unused fellows, who, seeing the disfigured, maimed, to varying degree diminished clones in their midst, could think only: "This is what happens to some of us from time to time." Having known no other order, no other world but theirs, they would have no way of knowing, of imagining why it happened to them, or what it meant, no way of conceiving the single reason for their existence. The effect of this grisly, ruthless practice, which would certainly have been calculated, would be—far from riling the clones, provoking in them protest or rebellion, or even revelation—to dispirit the clones, to bring them to a kind of apathy and despair, in which state, as the government would surely know, the clones, used and unused alike, would be all the more subjugateable.

A second instance: Anna's group believed there would be regularly administered to the clones, to the adult males at least, a course of psychotropic drugs meant to suppress their sexual—in the circumstances, specifically homoerotic—impulses. It would appear—we were to infer this from the clone's behavior as much as from anything he said—this is not the case. Whether it was that the government saw in the clone's sexual impulses and behavior no meaningful threat to its dominion, or that the government saw some practical advantage in withholding its intervention, pharmacologic and otherwise, choosing instead to let sexual activity among the male clones take its natural course, is impossible to know. But after several months of watching and listening to the clone, Anna and I were convinced that homosexuality was rampant among the male clones, and that in practice it was, normatively, brutal. We were convinced that my clone had from a young age—say thirteen—been routinely sodomized by, and made to perform fellatio on, bigger, stronger clones. And that, as he got older and stronger, he had routinely sodomized, and been fellated by, clones younger and weaker than himself.

We drove away from the Bonsecours at noon—we were embarrassingly obedient—and headed west towards Ottawa. It was Monday, August 24, the day on which I would meet my clone. Outrageous I persist in calling him that, though it at least connotes responsibility, complicity. We tried using the name the group invented for his driver's license. So far as we could determine, until he came to us he'd had no name. It was possible he knew no one who was named, knew no proper names at all, did not know what a proper name was. Like an infant, in this regard. Though he already knew the names for certain things. (Isn't this different altogether from the business of human names? The difference between "chair," even "Morris chair," and, say, "Bud." The difference—I'm no philosopher—between "What is this?" and "Who is this?") At the start, we made a concerted point of saying the name to him, Alan Grey, as much as we could, so that should he wander off, and then be found, he would give to whomever found him the right name. We did what parents do, so I assume, with their babies. We pointed to ourselves and said our names. I pointed to Anna and said, "Anna." She pointed to me and said, "Ray." I pointed to myself, etc. The clone was able quickly to learn our names. (The clone would have borne a latent genetic capacity for naming.) Not Anna and Ray, or Oliver and Jane, but our real names, the names we called each other in his presence. (Anna suggested—but only once—inasmuch as we were posing as a family, and to give the clone, as she said, "a surer sense of belonging," that we refer to ourselves also as "Mother" and "Father." I rejected this idea.) We pointed to him and said, "Alan." I'm sure he understood what we were proposing, but we could never get him to point at himself and say, "Alan." We had trouble, too, thinking of him as Alan, or Al, though we were absolutely unable to come up with a name that seemed right and natural. At one point, Anna tried to revive the name "Sonny." A few times, unpremeditatedly, I called him "Sport." Both names were eminently unsuitable—"Sport" was so wrong it was funny—and neither stuck. For occasions that involved the clone with other people (there were several of these), we continued to use the name Alan Grey.

I think he did not, or could not, think of himself as sufficiently individuated to warrant a name. He didn't object to being called Alan, or Sonny, or even Sport; he seemed not to care what, if anything, we called him. Neither did he care, when we urged him to do it, to choose a name for himself.

What was *my* problem? Wasn't it that, no matter how I might have wanted otherwise, I couldn't think about him as fully autonomous, fully human? This is deplorable, beyond a doubt, but one can almost be forgiven feeling this way at the very start of things. He had no name.

Going forward, I will call him Alan.

I was determined to drive. The day was overcast. By noon it was already hot, the air soggy. The green car—we'd gotten a bum deal in the swap—was tinny and cramped, and the air-conditioner just barely worked. I missed the stalwart comforts of Anna's truck. We'd been told to make no stops on the way, but after a monotonous hour of highway driving in the heavy air I was sleepy and needed to close my eyes. I pulled off onto the shoulder, and Anna and I switched positions. We did very little talking en route, for which silence I was grateful. We observed no one following us.

We made it to Ottawa in less than two hours. It took us a while to find Friel Street and the building in which we were to live the next three months, but we were sitting in the car outside the place at least half an hour before the stipulated time. I was for going in anyway, the time be damned, though by now both of us knew my bluff was merely that. To help me save face—something she was good at, God bless her—Anna suggested we drive around the neighborhood to get a sense of what might be available to us nearby.

We were back in Friel Street at three. On the dot. The Tall Man—we were never to know his name—was waiting for us outside on the sidewalk.

He helped get our bags out of the car. "From now on," he said to Anna—this exclusionary tactic wore thin—"whenever you can remember to, try to park the car around the corner, or down the block, will you?"

The building was one of a row of connected, three- and four-story brownstones, probably put up sometime in the twenties or thirties of the last century. It had, as did its neighbors, eight or nine cement steps leading to its front entrance. There was no elevator in the building, not even for freight. Luckily for me, our apartment was on the second floor. It was in the rear, overlooking an unexpectedly capacious courtyard, shared with the buildings adjacent, in a section of which brick-walled enclosure some of the tenants had established a kind of community garden, consisting of a dozen or so small, rectangular plots. This stretch of Friel Street was entirely residential; it was quiet and well kept, lined with mature shade trees. At first sight, I liked the place. So did Anna.

"This is good," she said.

"I didn't pick it," the Tall Man said. "You should be reasonably comfortable."

"How long will we be here?" I said.

"I can't tell you that."

"Because you can't," I said, "or because you won't?"

"Both," the Tall Man said. "Why don't we grab your bags and get in off the street."

I carried my own bag up the front steps; the Tall Man carried Anna's. When we were inside the vestibule, a small space where the tenants—there were three apartments on each of the four floors—received their mail, the Tall Man put down Anna's bag. He positioned himself, blocking the front door, with his back to the street. "Before we go up," he said to Anna. "I'm afraid you will find the clone is not who he was when he was last with you."

"In what way?" Anna said.

"Pretty much every way," the Tall Man said. "I want to tell you. He's a handful. He's a regular little shit."

"We'll be okay," Anna said.

"I'm not sure you will," he said. "Look, he's very strong. When he's angry, and that's a good share of the time, he's almost impossible to control. I don't know, even with two of you, that you'll be anywhere near strong enough. As I say, I'm concerned."

"Well find a way," Anna said. "I'm not too worried."

"You should be. He's not a child," the Tall Man said.

"I'm aware of that," Anna said.

"There's no telling," he said this now to me, "how he'll react to you. He seems not to like men."

(Anna and I would talk about this. We agreed that part of the reason for his fierce antipathy towards men—however small a part, and not

discounting what might have happened to him inside the Clearances—
was that, since they'd found him, the men of Anna's group had treated
him more harshly than was called for. It is not illogical to think that one
can hate cloning, without hating the clones. Admittedly, he was not easy
to like. I, myself, am not easy to like.)

"He doesn't like *you*?" I said.

"Not one bit," he said. "I'm not the only one he doesn't like."

"What would you have us do?" I said. "Shall we hire a bouncer?"

"Be careful. Keep him as quiet as you can. Don't let him out of
the apartment." Nodding at Anna: "Let her do most of it, would be
my advice. You keep to the background. Try to stay out of his way. For
the first while, at least."

"He's up there now?" I said. "In the apartment?"

"Yes."

"Is someone with him?"

"What do *you* think?"

"Let's go up," Anna said.

Our apartment, 2R, was up a wide set of carpeted stairs that switched-
back at a small landing midway, then to the right at the end of the hall.
The Tall Man knocked on the door. Three discrete raps with his
knuckles, several seconds apart. Within, a man's voice said, "Who's
there?"

"You'll have to teach us the code," I said.

The Tall Man said, "We're here."

The black man we'd seen on the road outside Sabevois let us in.

"We're quiet now," he said.

The apartment was in the shape of an inverted L. We entered
into a small foyer. To our right was a hallway, off which were two
long, narrow bedrooms of identical size, each with a single sash window in the far wall. At the end of the hallway was a bathroom, win-
dowless, with a tub and shower. To our left was the kitchen, a galley,
large enough for one person to work in. (Though the clone was always hungry, there were whole categories of food he would not eat.
He would eat no fish or seafood, and could not stomach the smell

of Anna cooking either. He'd eat nothing creamy, though he would drink milk. No soup or stew. He'd eat chicken, but not red meat. He would tolerate pasta served with olive oil. He liked vegetables, loved broccoli and carrots, raw or cooked. He'd eat cereal or eggs or pancakes for breakfast, but was happier with frozen waffles. For lunch he'd eat a peanut butter and jelly sandwich, or a cream cheese and jelly sandwich, with potato chips, so long as we cut the crusts off the bread. He liked French fries, though he didn't get them often, and pickles. In Winnipeg, once, we let him try beer. He liked it, which made us leery. Of all things he liked cheese best, especially Muenster. Sometime in the first two weeks, we made the mistake of ordering out for pizza. For a month afterwards, the clone would settle for almost nothing else, and preferred it come out of the microwave. In general, we ate what he ate.) In front of us, past the kitchen, parallel to the bedrooms, was the living room, also deep and narrow, with two sash windows in the far wall that overlooked the courtyard. Beneath a pass-through from the kitchen, there was a rectangular table with three chairs. Along the living room wall to our left was a tall, freestanding bookshelf, empty except for a legal-size envelope on one of its shelves, a fireplace that had been bricked up, and a television on a low table. On the opposite wall, facing the television, was a sofa and, in front of that, a glass-top coffee table. In the space between the two windows, against the far wall, was a high-backed upholstered wing chair and matching ottoman.

The clone was sitting on the sofa, Alan was sitting on the sofa, his stocking feet up on the coffee table, his hands folded in his lap. His head lay back against the top of the sofa; his eyes were closed.

The black man moved into the living room and stood beside the sofa, placing himself between us and Alan.

"Is he asleep?" I asked. We were still in the foyer with our bags.

The Tall Man answered me. "We'll be lucky, if he is. So, look. Here's what you've got. There are two beds in the far bedroom. You'll want the clone in there, with Mr. Comedy. You," he said to Anna, "take the other bedroom. Sleep light, both of you. Stay alert. We don't want the damn thing running off. Now come with me a minute." So far, Alan had not moved, or shown any indication he was aware of our presence. I was, I confess, afraid to look at him.

The Tall Man led us into the first bedroom, the one that would be Anna's. Against the wall separating the bedrooms there was a queen-size mattress and bedspring in a metal frame with no headboard. Above the bed hung a faded landscape in oil, giving a generic view of a mountain lake. There was a night table and a lamp and a chest of drawers. The floors in all the rooms, except the kitchen and bathroom, were covered in the same light-brown carpeting, which looked brand-new and smelled chemical. Anna put her bag on the bed. "The only closet," the Tall Man said, "is in the other bedroom."

"I'll make do," Anna said, though this would prove a nuisance.

"There's a linen closet in the hall," the Tall Man said, "with sheets and towels and things. In the kitchen there are plates and pots and pans. Silverware. Cups. You've got all that kind of stuff. Utensils. You'll need to lay in some food. Otherwise, you should be set for a while."

"Thanks," Anna said.

"I'll put my bag in the other bedroom," I said.

"Not yet," the Tall Man said. He took out of his pants pocket a small black thing that looked like a cell phone. "This is for you," he said to Anna. He handed it to her. "It's a reader."

"What is that?" Anna said.

"It finds the clone," he said. "In Iowa, after we took him back from you, we implanted just under the skin a tiny silicon capsule, inside of which is a microchip. If you look closely at his arm, in the front, just below his shoulder, you'll see a blue dot. It's barely visible. It won't need charging for at least a year."

"He *does* have a tracking device," I said.

"Yes," he said, "but ours. If you lose him, if he gets away, you'll know where he is. As will we."

"You have one of these?" I said.

"More than one. If he gets lost, just press this button." He showed Anna a button on the side of the reader. "You do that, and we go get the clone. You don't try to get him yourself. In case he has it in his mind not to be gotten. Do you understand?"

"Yes," she said.

"Keep this in a safe place, where the clone won't find it. Listen carefully to what I tell you next. You listen, too," he said to me. "If, at any time, you feel you are about to be taken, then you let the clone go. Don't wait. Take no chances. Set him loose. Tell him to get as far away from you as he can. Make sure he does it. Then, press the button. When you've done that, destroy the reader. Smash it with your foot. When we lose your signal, we'll assume things have gone bad. Once we've collected the clone, we'll try to help you."

"Where will you be?" Anna said.

"There will be someone nearby."

"What do you mean, *our* signal?" I said.

"There's a chip inside your reader," he said. "So we'll always know where *you* are, as well."

"That's a comfort," I said.

He stuck two fingers—his fingers were bony and skewed and as long as tongs—into the pocket of his shirt. "And this." He'd removed from his breast pocket a small envelope, which he held out for us to see in the flat of his elongated palm. "There are two pills in here. One for each of you. If you are taken. They are instant and painless. No need to suffer. Nor any virtue in it."

"No thanks," I said.

The Tall Man laughed. "Do you imagine you are being brave?"

"I know I am not," I said.

"I'll hold on to them," Anna said.

"To be kept away from the clone."

"Of course," Anna said.

"Don't leave him alone," the Tall Man said. "One of you should be with him at all times. Another thing. This shouldn't need saying, but if you take the clone out of the apartment, which I don't recommend, be sure his tattoo is covered."

I carried my bag into the other bedroom. There were two beds, separated by a nightstand. Close enough that we might have slept, Alan and I, each in his own bed, and held hands across the divide. It was clear neither bed had been slept in. Alan had not spent the night in the apartment. I put my bag on the bed nearest the door—this seemed to me strategic—claiming it as mine.

When I came back into the living room, Alan was still on the sofa, and appeared still to be asleep. The black man continued to stand watch over him.

This was the first chance I'd had to take a real look at my clone. There was nothing intimate, or epiphanic about the moment, constrained as it was—though I wouldn't have wanted Alan to myself—by the presence of two strangers, one of them, the black man, all but blocking my view. Alan's head was canted back against the top of the sofa, his neck stretched to its limit, the underside of his jaw exposed. I could not see much of his face, and the perspective I had on it was distorting. He was absolutely still, giving virtually no sign he was breathing. He was inanimate. I might have been looking at a wax figure.

Anna and the Tall Man were by the bookshelf, on the opposite side of the room. The Tall Man picked up the envelope that was on the bookshelf and took from it a driver's license. "For the clone," he said. "But you keep it for him." The name on the license was Alan Lewis Grey. His address was the same Hastings address the group had fabricated for Anna and me. His age was given as twenty-one, and his birthday—too coincidental to be credited—September 12, the day Sara and I were married.

"We'll come by at least once a month to see how you are doing, to check on the clone's progress." He looked at me. "And his."

"My progress is none of your business."

The Tall Man smiled. "Of course it is. So you get to work."

It would be a year before I started my report.

"We'll be here a month?" I said to Anna.

"You'll be here at least that long," the Tall Man said. "If all goes well."

"What if we're not home?" Anna said. "When you come."

"We won't come when you're not home," he said. "You'll find two keys to the apartment on the kitchen counter by the stove."

"Yes. I saw them," Anna said.

"Don't lose them. Keep the door locked. We have our own keys in case we need to get in." The Tall Man looked over the room. "All right then," he said. "I think that's about it. There's nothing more I need to say. Except good luck to you. Good luck to you both. To the three of you." Then, to the black man: "Let's leave them to it."

As soon as they'd gone, Alan lifted his head off the back of the sofa and opened his eyes.

It is right here, at the moment in which Alan opened his eyes and looked at me, and I looked back and saw him, really, for the first time, that I am, in this report, most at risk of serving the interests, the polemical purposes of Anna's group. What I write here, now, more than a year after the event, about my initial response to seeing my clone, Alan, to inhabiting with him the selfsame spot in space and time, will for them stand and serve as the very heart of my report, its reason for being. My reason for being, too, so far as they are concerned. It is probable I am the only human being to have been brought face to face with his clone. To say it another way: it is probable I am the only human being ever to come face to face with a significantly younger, but identical copy of himself, made by the government, with his knowledge and consent, and to have survived long enough to speak of it. To stand and look at his clone, and to be looked at by him, simultaneously to see, and be seen by, himself, as he was, forty-five years in the past.

Alan opened his eyes. He looked at me, though fleetingly and with much less interest than I brought to the exchange. To him I was just another older man, and, as such—the Tall Man was right about this—threatening and unwanted. Not just another older man. I believe he felt, at the start, a special enmity for me. He would have been able to tell right off I had a prior relationship with Anna, a prior claim. I was in the way of his desire to be alone with and close to her. It is one thing—though not an easy thing, I can tell you—to look backward and see yourself as a young man. Quite another, to look forward in time. He would have had no idea who I was. He could not, and did not, see himself in me, which was merciful. Imagine how it would feel, at twenty-one, to see standing before you the old man you would become. Your doom.

He was sitting on the couch. His hands were still folded in his lap. He looked frightened to me. Confused. Perhaps I imagined he was frightened and confused because if I'd been him, that's how I'd have felt. Perhaps he was merely bored. Or numb. Or calculating his chances of overpowering us and making his escape.

Standing there, looking at a facsimile of myself at twenty-one, I felt a sort of ecstasy, a feeling of standing outside myself. I did not speak to him. "Hello there. I'm Ray, your original. Glad to meet you. I mean you no harm." I suppose I might have said exactly that. I said nothing, nor, no surprise, did he.

Alan was wearing a dark green, long-sleeved polo shirt, unbuttoned at the neck, a pair of loose-fitting blue jeans, white socks, and white running shoes. All of it brand-new. He was wearing a baseball cap, one of those replicas, with the old Montreal Expos logo on it. I remember feeling sad, looking at that hat, to think he had never played, or even watched, baseball. Later that day, right before the clone went to bed, Anna got him to take off his cap. It was she, in fact, who, after telling him what she was about to do, took hold of the brim and very carefully lifted it off his head, as if the top of his skull was a soufflé she didn't want to disturb. He made no motion to resist. He was surprised to see the hat come away in her hands; it seemed he hadn't known he was wearing it. I noticed, then, that he parted his hair on the right. I have always parted my hair on the left. (I still have most of my hair, though it has thinned and lately gone all gray.) I wondered why Alan's hair seemed to lie, naturally, in the opposite direction. I wondered, further, if all these years I'd been parting my hair on the wrong side, combing it against the grain. There was no question it looked better the way Alan combed it, and I resolved—could I have been more fatuous?—when things settled down, to try it his way.

I'd had plenty of time to envision this meeting, and my clone. I'd read Anna's journal and listened to her talk on the subject. Though I should have known what to expect, I was surprised to discover, at this first glance, that Alan was absolutely indistinguishable from an original (I could come up with no other way to say this), that nothing about him visible to me betrayed him as a copy. He was much better looking than I was at his age. That was immediately clear. As Anna had observed, he was broader than I'd been, and certainly more muscular. His face was more angular, his features better defined, the skin on his face clear and soft. His eyes were mine, I thought, and his mouth.

Taking him in, I was struck, vertiginous—such that my knees almost gave way—and deeply saddened by how young he was. He looked new, as if he'd just been made. He was, I would have said, shiny. It turned out—sometime later, when he was less hostile towards me, Anna got us to stand back to back—he was also an inch taller.

I wanted to see him with his clothes off. My belly had never been flat. My arms and legs and shoulders were strong enough, but never muscly. I'd told myself I wasn't programmed for definition. I wanted to see his belly. I wanted to see his chest, his shoulders, his upper arms. I wanted to touch him. To feel his skin. To feel his muscle. I admit I wanted to see his penis. Anna had written he'd not been circumcised. I wanted to see how that looked on him, how big it was. I'd never had much body hair. I wondered how much hair he had on his chest, his back, his legs. I wanted to see his toes. I have especially ugly toes.

I was self-conscious in front of him in those first moments, and was to remain so. In an ongoing way he made me feel shapeless and old. He made me feel obsolete, unrealized. I imagined him thinking to himself about me, in whatever language it was he thought in, "So this is all you've made of yourself. This is what, with all your advantages, you've come to." Ridiculous, really, to feel this way, but hard not to. Less trifling, harder to dismiss, was this: in his presence I couldn't help but feel all the loss I had suffered since I'd been his age. All that had been wasted. All that I'd wasted. The attendant pain. Neither the losses nor the waste were trivial. The pain was well founded and, with Alan to remind me, often disabling. Looking at him there were times I wanted to take him in my arms and weep, and not for him.

At the same time, I knew I was never really like Alan. Not at twenty-one, or at any other time, excepting, perhaps, the moment of birth. He'd had no parents to raise him. Looking at him made me think—if not at that first instant, then later—about what I might have become, how much less I would have been, without parents, or with different parents than the ones I'd had. My father, the short time he was with me, likewise my mother for a much longer stretch, were diligent and thoughtful with me. When I looked at Alan, I was grateful for them both. In the past year I have become an old man. I am owly. I have an all but defunct heart. But I think, now that I am about to lose it, I have always been grateful, in spite of its inescapable torments, its horrors, its grotesqueries, for the world at large. A world in which Alan had never lived.

I have to say, though I would have come to the moment predisposed neither way, I instantly disliked him. It was not that he so patently disliked me. It was not that he was ignorant and ill tempered and coarse, though he was all that. Nor was it that I felt demeaned, misrepresented by his behavior, or personally responsible for it. You might think it was that I didn't like who I was, myself, at twenty-one. I don't believe that entirely explains my aversion. There may have been a kind of territorial instinct in play. Reflexively, I believe, I saw Alan as a younger, stronger, better-looking double, a creature perversely made in my image, perversely manufactured to be my rival—competitive, acquisitive, usurpatious. If he exists, I may have thought, can I also exist?

I was about his age when I met Sara. I could not imagine him with her.

In that first moment, I felt no guilt or shame. I did not then feel convicted, or even implicated, by Alan's existence. Nor did I take any pride or comfort that afternoon, or later, in having given Alan life. (What, for Christ's sake, had I done? I'd given a test tube's worth of my blood, and then, for twenty-one years, not a single thought.) Looking at him, I never once felt, not then, not ever, the sense of self-perpetuation a man might feel in gazing upon his son. Nothing in my response that first day was paternal; I felt nothing for him that I might have felt for a son. He was a clone, a fact that effaced all other facts, and rendered any knowledge or wisdom I might have acquired along the way pretty much irrelevant. From time to time, in later months—

when I had come to like Alan, to care about him—in moments when he was relaxed around me, I caught myself musing that he was what my son might have been like had he lived. (Had he lived, my son would have been much older than Alan, who had, of course, nothing of Sara in him.) Anna's maternal instinct ran strong. From the first minute she spent with Alan to the last, Anna was tender with him. She was patient and solicitous, compassionate, and as loving as any-one in her situation could have been. Watching her with Alan, watch-ing her teach and tend to him—watching her soothe him when he was wild, distraught—I wondered more than once whether she'd ever, way back when we were in Iowa together, felt maternal towards me. I asked her about this. She laughed. "Not at all," she said. "Though you could have used a little mothering. And anyway, how could you ask me this? I felt amorous, you clod. How could you not know this? I wanted to sleep with you. I wanted you to take me to bed. How could you not have figured this out?" She told me that her maternal feelings towards Alan were dampened somewhat by her sense, always with her, that she had her own children to care for, to worry about, her own grandchil-dren. "I mean, finally," she said, "what is he to me?"

"I used to feel this way sometimes," she said, "when I was teach-ing and trying to raise my kids at the same time. Though, thankfully, not all that often, I found myself resenting my students for not being my children, for taking from them my best time and energy. It is hard to have anything left for your own family, when you spend your days teaching other people's kids. Hundreds of them. You know this." (I didn't know it, but Anna meant no harm.) I take no satisfaction in the supposition that this—it was not quite resentment—this grudg-ingness, would have been mitigated, at least a little, by the fact that he was *my* clone.

"He is not a child," the Tall Man had said. He was right and, I am obliged to say, right to warn us. It was easy and convenient to let yourself think of him as a child. Much of his behavior, much of his emotional repertoire, was childlike. But he was a twenty-one-year-old man. He'd been alive and sentient for twenty-one years. He'd had twenty-one years of some sort of experience. He'd been for twenty-one years in the world of the Clearances, whatever kind of world that might be. If Anna's group was correct in its assumption, he had done some kind of work since he was thirteen.

In the early going, while we were still in Ottawa, Anna was distressed by the tension in my relationship with Alan, the open hostility. She remonstrated with me, appealing to my age and putative wisdom. "Really, he is little more than a child," she would say, impatiently. "You're old enough to be his father. His grandfather. You ought to know better. It's your responsibility to fix this."

"Yes, well, he doesn't despise you."

"You don't have to take it personally," she said.

"Is it possible he knows?"

"No. It's not possible. He doesn't know."

I looked at Alan sitting on the couch, wearing his Expos cap. He looked at me, saw nothing he liked or needed, and quickly looked away. Then he looked at Anna. He stared at her. It took him a while to figure out who she was. You could see him working for the connection. He'd been in rough shape when he'd seen her last. When he did, finally, recognize her, his response was galvanic. He sat upright and began to bounce on the sofa cushion. His eyes were wide open. His mouth moved, as if to speak. He quivered. He opened and closed his fists, as if he were flashing a signal. Then, though she was on the other side of the room, standing with me by the empty bookcase, he leaned towards her—a kind of phototropic sway—cantilevering off the edge of the couch as if he might stretch himself to the opposite wall. He made a freakish sound. It was not a gasp, though the catch in his breath was audible. It was a whimper, plaintive and piteous, from far back in his throat, high-pitched, cat-like. Once he'd seen her, he did not look at, nor could he see, anything else in the room.

We talked later that night about his response to her, and what it might portend. Anna wanted to explain his reaction as a case of "belated imprinting," a term she had to invent for the occasion. "Like those little ducklings," she said, "those hatchlings, who, the first thing they see when they break out of the egg isn't their mother, but a big orange ball. So they think this ball is their mother, and they attach themselves to it, follow it around, do everything they can to be close to it. I was the first woman he saw when he came out of the Clearances. I might have been the first woman he ever saw. He bonded with me."

She cited another experiment. Baby monkeys who were given surrogate mothers, inanimate and of varying degrees of softness.

"He got the wire cage," she said. "I was soft."

Clearly there was truth in this. He was, at first, fiercely attached to Anna and possessive. He wouldn't let me near her. But it seemed to me her explanation too conveniently passed over the erotic component in his feelings for her.

The question of Anna's physical bearing with Alan was a knotty one and a matter of concern for both of us. In Anna's mind, the process of civilizing Alan, grounding him, gentling him, necessarily involved her touching him, deliberately and with circumspection, but as much as possible.

"He needs to be touched," she said.

"He seems to *enjoy* it, in any case," I said.

"He needs it. He's desperate for it."

"Just be careful."

"No, I know. I am careful. I try to be. Cripes. I certainly don't want to give him the wrong idea. It's absurd, really," she said, "to imagine me, at my age, capable of exciting a man."

"I don't know," I said.

"Look at my hands," she said. She showed them to me. "Garden tools. Simple friction. That's all it was."

"Probably not so simple," I said. "For either of you."

"Maybe not," she said.

Anna took a few steps towards Alan. I stayed where I was and watched them. She approached him slowly, so as not to frighten him, though you could see he was not at all frightened. She slumped a little and bent at the knees to make herself smaller, less imposing. Needlessly. If he'd wanted to, he could have snapped her neck like a twig.

"Hello, you," she said to him.

Alan was rapt. The closer she came to the couch, the more frenetically he bounced, the more rapidly he opened and closed his fists. His whimper changed to a monotonal series of short, staccato peeps, hoos. Monkey song. He began to toss his head side to side. It would have been jarring, dismaying, to see any normal-looking twenty-one-year-old man behave in this way. Because he looked so much like me, as I had once looked, it was harder to watch his antics. And it wasn't a question, merely, of how he looked. Had I ever had any dignity? Any grace? Watching him, I was appalling to myself. The thought of being me was appalling. At that moment, I pretty much lost all hope. For any of us.

Anna sat next to Alan on the couch. He stopped tossing his head so he could look at her. "Shush now," she said. "Hush." He stopped hooing. "It's okay," she said. "You're okay." She laid her palm flat on his thigh. He stopped bouncing. She touched his wrist with her fingertips and his hands grew still. It was like watching an exorcism. "That's better," she said. "That's good. You're good now." She smiled at him. She gently rubbed his arm, just below his shoulder. "It's okay. You'll be fine. Everything's fine." She took his hand in hers. "It's good to see you again. I missed you." With the back of her fingers she brushed his cheek. "You've had a rough time, kiddo," she said. "You're okay now. Things will be okay."

He looked at her, wanting and waiting for more.

"You know who I am," she said. She was smiling at him all the while.

He did not answer. Or blink. If he'd been any more intent on her he might have turned inside out.

"You do. Of course you do. You know. You remember. We spent some time together, you and I. In my house. You stayed in my house. You remember. You were sick. We had a time. You stayed with me. In my house. Can you remember?"

He did not speak.

"Do you understand what I'm saying?" she said.

It was hard to say for sure, but he appeared to nod.

Anna looked at me. I had not moved. "Won't you say something to him?"

"What should I say?"

"Say, 'hello.'"

"Hello," I said. I could barely bring myself to look at him. He did not look at me.

"Speak to him," Anna said.

"I have nothing to say. He's not interested in me. He doesn't know I'm here."

"Say something. Let him know you're not a danger."

I could think of nothing to say.

"She sells sea shells by the seashore," I said.

"Pathetic," she said.

"I've heard a lot about you." I pointed to Anna. "I'm a friend of hers. We are old friends."

"It's the best I can do," I said. "Give me a chance. This is awkward for me."

"How do you think it is for him?"

"We are your friends," I said to Alan. Then, to Anna: "Should I come closer?"

"You'd better not," she said.

For Anna, it must have been confusing to see us, Alan and me, come together in space and time (the universe did not explode): a version of the young man she'd known, looking just the way she'd known him; and the young man she'd known, an old man, looking so much different. Watching her with Alan that afternoon, I must have thought seeing him would have waked in her a memory of what she felt for me back in graduate school. I do remember thinking she might prefer Alan to me. She might have permitted herself to think—she was in for more sadness, if so—that, unlike me, he would not choose another woman over her. That she need not compete for his favor or affection. That Alan was a version of me not susceptible of wooing. However unconsciously, she might have seen in him a safer, denatured, at-one-remove way to experience at least some form of the intimacy she was denied back in Iowa, forty-five years ago. Cavalier, the way I posit myself at the epicenter of her thoughts and feelings.

Anna put an index finger to her breast. "My name is Anna," she said to Alan. 'Anna. I'm sure I told you this. When you stayed with me." She pointed to herself again. "Can you say, 'Anna'?"

Anna held for his response. She waited what seemed to me a long time. Good pedagogy.

"That's okay," she said, when it became clear he would keep mum. "You don't have to speak. When you're ready." She pointed to me. "That's Ray. Ray is my friend. Your friend, too."

You'd have expected her next to point to him and say his name, his new name, but she didn't.

"When you stayed with me," she said, "you were in Iowa. That's where I live. It's far from here. In another country, called America. You've traveled a great distance." She stood up. "Here," she said, "come here with me." She took his hand and bid him stand.

This was the first time I'd seen Alan on his feet. He was bigger than I expected. His forearms were ropy with muscles and veins, his neck was thick. Standing still—this would be true of him always—he was awkward, ill at ease, as if he didn't know how to distribute his weight evenly. In motion he was easy and loose, athletic.

(I was never easy, or loose, or athletic. Except for baseball, and bowling, I was not even marginally good at sports. My father, who was almost always encouraging, told me I ran like Groucho Marx. I didn't know what that meant. Later, a gym teacher told me I ran as if I had nails in the bottom of my feet. A middle-school football coach told me I had no heart. Alan looked like he would be good at anything he tried.)

She led him to the window on the right side of the wing chair. "Look out there," she said. Alan looked out the window with her. "This is Ottawa. You're in Ottawa now. Ottawa is a city in a country called Canada. It's a good place. You'll be safe here. We'll be with you now."

It was impossible to tell how much, if anything, he understood.

Standing at the window, she said, "Down there, that's a garden.

Those two people live here. They are growing vegetables. Tomatoes. Beans. Carrots. Squash. Good things to eat."

He continued to look out the window, shifting his weight from side to side. "Did you work in a garden, I wonder?"

He didn't answer.

"You eat vegetables, I know," she said. She touched his arm. "What is *your* name?" she said. "Will you tell me *your* name?"

He didn't answer.

"Were you given a name?"

Again, he did not speak.

"What shall we call you, then?" She said this hopefully, then looked to me for help. I shrugged my shoulders. She smiled at him, gave his arm a squeeze. "Don't worry, kiddo. We'll come up with something."

She left him at the window, and moved towards me. "I can't bear the way I'm talking. I sound so condescending. No wonder he won't answer. It's beneath him."

"You think?" I said.

"Absolutely," she said.

"Well, you're doing better than I could."

"But what next? He's here. We're here. What do we do? How do we start? How do we spend the next five minutes? The next hour?"

"You got me," I said, though how to pass the time had latterly emerged as the most salient question in my life.

"Would you like to see your room?" she said to Alan. "Let's see your room." Alan stayed where he was, his back to us. "Come on, you," she said. "I'll show you where you sleep. Let's go see your bed." Still, he didn't move.

"Why don't we put your clothes away," she said. "Shall we? Do you have any clothes?" He did not budge. "Well, I'm going to see your bedroom." She crossed the living room and started down the hall.

Alan turned away from the window. He looked unhappy.

"Wait," I said to Anna. "Do you think I should be alone with him?"

"I had hoped he'd follow me," she said from the hallway.

"He hasn't," I said.

She came back into the room. "Come on." She implored him.

"Go," I said to him. "Scoot."

He paid no attention to me.

"Please," she said. "Please come with me."

I was not convinced there was any correlation between the way she asked and his compliance, but he did, then, go with her. Though I was not in his way, he managed, as he passed, to ram me with his shoulder. It was as if I'd been hit in the chest with a medicine ball. I caved in. The breath rushed out of me and I stumbled backwards. By the time I was able to say, "Hey. Watch it," he was out of the room.

I went over to the window. There were two women in the brick-walled garden below, bending together over a single plot. They looked to be about the same age, somewhere in their late sixties, early seventies, and might have been sisters. One of the women had on a broad-brimmed straw hat; the other wore a red visor. They were in shorts and T-shirts and both wore gardening gloves. I watched them while Anna and Alan were in the bedroom he and I were to share, which, at that moment, was a forbidding prospect. One among many. The two women looked happy and peaceful. I wanted to open the window and call to them. I wanted to tell them what was going on up here. I'd never liked gardening—too many bugs, too much dirt. I'd left it to Sara, who was inspired. But I wanted to be down in the garden with those two old, happy sisters, engaged in unexceptional activity, passing the time in the midafternoon sun, with the bugs and the Canadian dirt.

Anna came back into the room, with Alan right behind her. He seemed pleased. She was carrying a brown paper grocery bag, crumpled at the top. "These are all his clothes," she said. "He needs everything. He needs underwear, socks, shirts, and trousers. He's got nothing. I can't believe it. What were they thinking?"

"He can wear some of my clothes for the time being," I said.

"If they fit," she said. "It will be autumn soon. He'll need warm things."

"We'll be okay," I said.

"We'll have to take him shopping."

"Not right now," I said.

She laughed. "No. Not right now."

(We'd take him shopping a week later. Foolishly. Apart from a brief midnight walk around Friel Street to give him some air, it was the first time he'd been out of the apartment. In that week's time he demonstrated that, when he wanted to, he could speak, at least a little. He was willing to say Anna's name. He would not speak my name, nor would he speak directly to me. When he was hungry, he'd ask for food. He'd say, "I'm hungry," or "I want food," or "Give me food," or "I want to eat." He had no trouble with pronouns, never confused I and you, or me and you, the way, Anna told me, little children often do. He'd say, "I'm tired," when he was sleepy, and, to Anna, "Good night," before he went to bed. He'd say, "I have to piss," and "I have to shit." Anna begged him to substitute "pee" for "piss," and "poop" for "shit," but he wouldn't. Sometime during that first week he discovered TV, then asked for it constantly. "I want TV," he'd repeat, loudly, and we had to turn it on to shut him up. When he was sick of being in the apartment—those first few weeks, not without reason, we were reluctant to let him out, and we'd find him pacing the perimeter—he'd say, "I want to go out.")

We went on a Monday morning, choosing a day and time when we figured the stores wouldn't be busy. We drove out to a mall in a western suburb. We'd forgotten to account for the back-to-school shoppers, and the department store, a three-story megalith on one end of the mall, was crowded with mothers and their children. I watched to see how Alan would react to the mother-child relationship, which was so multifariously on display, but he seemed unstruck by it. He had no interest in the kids, but he was embarrassingly interested in the women, especially the young mothers, and spent a lot of the time gaping at them in what looked like a broad parody of amazement. Anna had to keep tugging at him to get him to close his mouth and move on. After brushing too close by a young blonde woman with large breasts—she might still have been nursing the toddler clinging to her leg—Alan leaned over and said something in Anna's ear. Whatever he said—she wouldn't repeat it—upset her, and made her angry.

After that, Anna took charge. She summarily gathered some socks and undershorts—I insisted he have boxers—and a pair of pajamas, then grabbed some shirts and slacks for him to try on. Also a woolen V-neck sweater. None of the stuff she chose, save for the sweater, was to my taste—it was all voguish and cheaply made—but he was indifferent, as, by now, was she. We located the bank of men's fitting rooms. Though we would have been happy to get him off the floor, we were afraid to send him into one of those curtained stalls by himself. That I would go in with him was not an option. That past week I'd had to sleep out on the couch, because he'd refused to let me in the bedroom. Nor would he let me see him unless he was fully dressed. He slept in his underwear—he shunned the pajamas Anna bought for him—and even after he agreed to let me sleep in the room, I had to wait until he was in his bed, and under the covers, before I could enter. Anna, who had lost heart, decided we would just pay for the clothes and take our chances. Except for the slacks, which, though wearable, were half an inch too short and snug in the crotch, the clothes fit him okay.)

"He must be hungry," she said

"Are you hungry?" she said to Alan.

This time he quite distinctly nodded his head.

"Progress," I said.

"He's hungry."

"Do we have food?"

"We don't," she said. "The refrigerator's empty. We need to get some things."

"I'll go."

"I think that probably would be best," she said.

On our time-killing drive around the neighborhood earlier that afternoon, we'd seen a small market not too far from the apartment.

"What should I get?"

"Oh, you know. The essentials. Bread and milk and eggs and butter. Olive oil. Get some fruit and vegetables. Maybe some pasta and sauce. Tea, coffee. I don't know. Some boneless chicken breasts. Get whatever you want. Whatever looks good."

"Okay," I said. "But I'm not much for shopping. I warn you."

"Get something."

"I'll take the car."

"Of course," she said. "Oh, and get some paper towels and napkins and a couple of sponges. And some toilet paper."

"Okay," I said. "I'll be back."

"Please," she said. "And maybe some cereal. Something you like. For breakfast. Some juice."

"You'll be all right?"

"We'll be fine. Don't take *too* long, though."

"I'll be quick as I can." I looked at Alan, standing behind her. He was smiling. "Anna, do you want me to stay?"

"No. Just get going. And bring me back some magazines."

"What kind?"

"I don't care. Any kind. You choose. Something to read. And something for dessert. Crackers. Cookies. Some ice cream. Chocolate chocolate-chip. We like that."

"Anything else?"

"Ha ha," she said. "Do you need a list? Or can you remember?"

"I'll be lucky to remember where we live."

The green car was still out in front of the apartment, and I was able to find the market without much trouble. I'm sure I forgot to pick up half the things Anna asked for. I do know I brought back the chocolate chocolate-chip ice cream, because that night at dinner Anna gave Alan a bowl of it for dessert, and then he expected it with every meal, even breakfast. When he didn't get it, when we were out of stock, he could be unpleasant and vulgar. As was, in those early days, his wont.

I had a dark moment in the grocery store that afternoon. It would not be the last of such moments. I was in the middle of some aisle or another, my cart full of stuff. I looked at the cart, looked at the stuff, and I couldn't remember having taken any of it off the shelves. I didn't know what it was: all the stuff in the cart was to me unrecognizable. If, in fact, there were tomatoes in there, I could not have told you what they were. My heart began to race, and I experienced shortness of breath. Or I imagined my heart was racing, my breath coming short. I was hypervigilantly aware of my body and how it was working. I heard

ringing in my ears. I thought I might be stroking—I still had all the medical lingo—but there was no pain, no real discomfort. I was overswept
by dread. I wanted to flee. The cart. The store. The city. The country.
What was I doing there? I was shopping for groceries on a Monday afternoon in Ottawa. Who could believe it? There were groceries in a cart,
and I couldn't have named them. What did I think I was doing? Who
did I think I was? These were all real questions. I wanted to get in the
green car and drive, without stopping, back to New Hampshire. I knew
where I lived. Seven hours, I'd be home. What I didn't want, more than
anything else in the world, to do, was to go back to that apartment, in
which Anna and the clone were waiting.

I didn't flee. I stood by my cart, unheroically, and waited, without knowing I was waiting, for the paroxysm to subside. Which it
did. I wheeled my cart—it was helpful to have something to hold on
to, to lean on—to the checkout lane and paid for the groceries in
cash. When I was outside, I took a few deep breaths in the late-af-
ternoon air. It was still hot and muggy. I'd finished with five bags of
groceries. I was surprised by how much I'd bought. I loaded the bags
into the trunk of the green car, then I drove back to Friel Street. I
parked the car in front of our building and made three trips up the
stairs, resting between trips, leaving the bags outside the apartment
door. When I'd got it all up, I knocked on the door. Three short
raps—I was not feeling at all ironic—as the Tall Man had done.
There was no answer, and I could hear no movement within. I
knocked again, three times, waited, then tried the knob. The door
was unlocked. I picked up two of the grocery bags and went inside.
Anna was seated at the far end of the couch, the clone sprawled its
length, his head in her lap. She was stroking his hair. She touched
her index finger to her lips, then smiled at me. The clone was asleep.
*La Pietà*, I thought, feeling suddenly aggrieved. I brought in the rest
of the bags, as quietly as I could.

Anna stayed on the couch with Alan's head in her lap. I put the
groceries away. We didn't speak. Neither of us, though perhaps for different reasons, wanted him to wake up.

There was not much left of the afternoon. Alan slept, while Anna watched him. She may have dozed, too. I unpacked my clothes in the bedroom. Alan woke up. Anna made dinner. While she was in the kitchen, I gave Alan as wide a berth as the apartment permitted. I don't remember what we had for dinner. Alan's manners at table were better than I'd have thought. He was proficient with a knife and fork. He chewed with his mouth closed, sat up reasonably straight, did not make inordinate noise with his cutlery, and kept his napkin on his lap when it wasn't in use. He ate earnestly, and as much as there was to eat, including two bowls of the ice cream for dessert.

I did the dishes after dinner, and Alan spent a long time in the bathroom. He was in there long enough with the door locked that Anna got worried and knocked to see if he was all right. We watched some TV, the three of us. I sat in the wing chair, Alan and Anna sat on the couch. I don't remember what we watched—something anodyne—but, from all appearances, it was Alan's first time with television. He was very interested in whatever was on, and upset when, after a couple of hours, we turned it off.

Anna got ready for bed first. Alan stood outside the bathroom door while she was in there, and I watched from the other end of the hall to see that he didn't do anything untoward. When Anna came out of the bathroom, in her nightgown and robe, Alan went in. This ad hoc procedure—Anna first, then Alan, then me—was to become, because Alan would have it no other way, codified. Anna and I stood in the hallway.

"Long day," I said.

"Yeah."

"And weird."

"Pretty weird," she said.

"What do we do tomorrow?"

"We start."

"Start what?"

"We start working with him."

"That's what you do," I said. "What do I do?"

"You help."

"I'm not sure I'll be any use."

"Then you'll stay out of the way."

Anna enjoyed, and took very seriously, her role as Alan's teacher. But she was pulled two ways about the project. For his sake, for her sense of herself as well, she wanted him steadily to prosper under her charge. And he did. At the same time, she found her group's plans for Alan, the ways they intended to use him once he'd become articulate, literate, presentable, so odious, so cruel, that no small part of her wanted to slow his pace, impede his progress, keep him useless as long as she could. It was more knotted even than that. She believed, without doubt, that Alan could be a determinative factor in the effort to subvert the government's cloning program. She had equal faith in the ultimate importance of that effort. Teaching Alan, she thought, was a chance for her to participate in something of major, transformative significance. She had found herself—she spoke about it as a function of providence—if not at the front, then at the very heart of a revolution. She was not, herself, interested in power, not at all, but, despite what was a principled commitment to ordinariness, to life lived as plainsong, Anna was at heart a revolutionary. Long may she . . . what? Reign? No. Live. I didn't buy into the idea that Alan, or Anna, or her group would be able to effect any substantive change in government policy or practice, and I wanted no part of *this* revolution, or any other.

Alan came out of the bathroom. He was still wearing his clothes.

"Hold still," Anna said. She took the baseball cap off his head.

He went into the bedroom, our bedroom, and closed the door. Anna waited a bit, then knocked—expecting, and getting, no response—and went in. I stood outside the room. Alan was in the bed farthest from the door. He was under the covers. Anna sat down on the side of his bed. She put her hand on his chest.

"Let me say good night to you," she said. "I hope you sleep well. I want you to have sweet dreams. Things will seem better to you in the morning. Less strange. So go to sleep. And don't worry. If you need me, I'm next door." She turned off the lamp on the nightstand between the beds. "Good night now. Rest well." She came out of the room and closed the door behind her.

"You think it'll work?" I said.

"Do I think *what* will work?

"Do you think he'll sleep?"

"I hope so," she said.

"Me, too," I said. "Do you feel at all like talking?"

"I don't know. Not much. Do you?"

"I wouldn't mind."

"Okay," she said. "Let's go in the living room."

We talked for about an hour. We talked about Alan. We talked about his response to her—I expressed my concern—and about his response to me. We were both concerned about that. I didn't tell her about what had happened to me in the grocery store, but I did worry out loud about my health.

"So you know," I said. "At some point, I'm going to have to find a doctor. A cardiologist."

"Fine," she said.

"I was supposed to go back to my doctor after seven weeks. To assess the damage."

"It hasn't been seven weeks," she said. "It's barely been two."

"Is that true?" I said. "Jesus. I guess that's true. I need to do it, though. Will you help me remember?"

"You're worried."

"Yes," I said. "Wouldn't you be?"

"I would."

We talked about the Tall Man. I complained about the green car. We talked about the next day. While we were talking, so far as we knew, Alan was in bed, asleep.

"Did you notice," I said, "that his hair was parted on the right?"

"No," she said. "What about it?"

"I part mine on the left. That seems to be the way it wants to go. Do you find that odd?"

"I don't know," she said. "It hardly seems to matter."

"No, I know," I said.

We said good night, and Anna went into her bedroom. I washed up, then checked the door of the apartment to see that it was locked. I turned off the lights; I left the bathroom light on, and closed the bathroom door most of the way, so the hall was not completely dark. I opened the bedroom door. I could see Alan in bed. He appeared to be sleeping. I undressed as quietly as I could and got into bed. As soon as I'd drawn the covers around me, Alan sat up.

"What's the matter?" I said. I sat up, too.

He did not respond. He got up off his bed. I could see that he had not taken off his pants.

I got out of bed. "What's the matter?" I said. "Are you okay?"

He crossed the room to the door. He turned down the hall, away from the bathroom. I went with him. He stopped in front of Anna's door. He put his hand on the doorknob.

"Hey," I said. "Where are you going, Sport?"

He opened her door.

I took hold of his arm, just above the elbow.

This was the first time I had touched my clone. What was it like for me to touch flesh that was of my flesh? The most radical consanguinity? When we were in New Hampshire, Anna spoke to me about what it was like for her to touch her children. She said it was reassuring. She said it was like forgiveness, like coming home after being away a long time, having done your best. I felt nothing of the sort. His arm was hard and thick, and I felt only the baleful power beneath my hand.

"What are you doing?" I said.

He wheeled on me, ripping his arm from my grip. He scowled. I swear he bared his teeth. Then, clear as day, he said, "Ass fuck!"

(These were the only words he was to speak that first day. We were to discover that his stock of the language of sexual, especially homosexual, depravity was abundant.)

He raised his fist to hit me. I cowered and covered my face.

Anna opened her door.

"Stop it, you two," she said. "Just stop it. What's going on?"

He lowered his fist.

"You get back into bed," she said to Alan. "Right now. And you," she said to me, "go sleep in my room."

"Where will you sleep?" I said.

"In there."

"Absolutely not. He's wild. I won't let you do it."

Alan stood there watching us.

"Go to bed," Anna said to him.

He obeyed.

"What the hell was going on?" she said.

"He was about to hit me."

"Why? What did you do?"

"I tried to stop him going into your room."

"Why did you do that?"

"I didn't know what he was up to."

"I told him if he needed me," she said.

"I wasn't sure what he had in mind."

"What did you think would happen?"

"I had no idea," I said.

"Nothing would have happened," she said.

"You don't know that."

"I do," she said.

"Did you hear what he said?"

"Yes."

"What do you think?"

"Just words," she said.

"Oh, I don't think so."

I slept on the couch that night, and for a week to follow. Anna slept in her room. I insisted she lock her door, which she agreed to do. Once I'd vacated the room, Alan was content to sleep by himself.

Somewhere near the start of this report I remarked on an improbable moment in time—I was twenty-two, in graduate school—in which three women, Ann and Anna and Sara, were interested in me, two of them, Ann and Sara, professedly in love with me. Given my, I believe realistic, estimation of myself, and my scant experience with girls, it was a flabbergasting moment, really. I didn't know then what to make of the convergence and, after a year of looking at Alan, trying to understand his/my/the appeal, I don't know what to make of it now. Take Ann from the mix (which I did unceremoniously): we'd been friends since childhood; the love we felt for one another was as much filial as anything else and not—this must, anyway, have been true for her—contingent on physical appearance. But how to explain Anna's response, and, more unfathomable, Sara's? Neither, as I see it, had any compelling, even legitimate, reason to love me.

Anna assures me Alan is good-looking, often adding—not only in the interests of accuracy—that he is better looking than I was when she knew me when. I will agree he is not bad-looking, and that he looks better than I ever did, but when I look at him, especially with the intent to compare—I try to do this as little as possible—I see mostly the things I don't like in myself.

Like me, he has almost no body hair. (As a teenager, this was the cause of recurrent embarrassment, and, via a series of variations on the theme, earned me the nickname "Bean," which stuck.) After several months with us, Alan began to be less vigilant, and I did, a few times, see him in his boxer shorts. Like me, he has no hair on his chest or stomach, except for a thin vertical line of hair on his breast bone, which I've always thought looks like the scar from an incision, and ugly wires of hair, like hairs on a mole, springing from his nipples and unexplained navel. As is true of me, the only hair on his legs is in small ridiculous tufts above both knees. Though when I first saw him in Ottawa, he had some color on his face and arms—an indication that before he came free of the Clearances he'd spent considerable time out of doors—by the time we reached Winnipeg, and winter, his skin—everywhere but his face—was, like mine in all seasons, bleached and waxy. His fingers, like mine, are short and thick and small-nailed, his thumbs, like mine, stunted. While not grotesque like the Tall Man's,

Alan's hands and mine are less than comely. Two fingers on my right hand, my throwing hand, are crooked, as a result of baseball injuries incurred while catching; all of Alan's fingers are straight. My feet, arches fallen, soles splayed—I take this as a great indignity—are a size 12 now and bigger than his, though when I was his age I, too, wore size 10. Except for the big toe, my toes—the result of ill-fitted shoes?—curl under, my little toes barely visible, the nails like horn. Alan's toes are trim.

Our eyes are hazel, our noses long and thin. His hair is darker and fuller than mine, wavier, but I remember having hair like his. His teeth are whiter than mine, which have gone gray like the rest of me. I have a slight overbite; he does not. He looks down when he smiles—which he does grudgingly and not often—as I do. I've often wondered, about myself, why that is. A gesture of shyness? Submissiveness? Fear? It is a move, in any case, deeply ingrained and beyond my control, and watching Alan reminds me I have spent too much of my life looking down and away.

One rarely gets to hear his own voice as others hear it, but Anna confirms Alan's voice has the same timbre, I suppose you'd call it, the same—not unpleasant, I find—throaty quality. His laugh, less frequent than his smile, is short-lived and through his nose, as, equally infrequent, my laugh is. When he is perplexed, which is much of the time, he scratches the side of his head with his index finger, like a chimp imitating a human in thought. That, as Anna has noted, I do the very same thing makes me cringe. He mimics me ceaselessly, though without meaning to. It was hard, the first few months of our cohabitation, not to feel ceaselessly mocked.

In this way Alan is lucky: he does not see himself in me.

I am circumcised. Alan, as I know from reading Anna's journal, is not. I do not use my hands when I speak. I'd have thought this would be learned behavior, a matter of decorum. Maybe it is, but Alan does not use his hands when he speaks. Genetically determined or not, when I watch him, his hands still, stiff at his sides, it seems unnatural.

When he listens, when he is interested in what is being said, and especially if it is Anna saying it, he tilts his head to one side, like a puppy. I pray to God I don't do that. I have only once seen him cry. I don't cry either.

We stayed in Ottawa, in the apartment on Friel Street, three months, until the end of November. We were also to live for extended periods in Winnipeg, Regina, and Calgary. Of all these—if, I mean, I could have been there by myself—I liked Ottawa best, a stately, calm, work-able city.

We spent most of our days in Ottawa in the same way. In the morning, after breakfast—while I ran errands and did other tasks, many of them unnecessary, that took me away from the apartment— Anna would work with the clone for several hours on language skills, speaking and reading. She quickly forsook the books she'd bought in Montreal. They were beyond him. She did spend some time each night reading to him from *The Prince and the Pauper* and, when they'd finished that, from *Oliver Twist*, neither one of which he seemed to mind. (He'd pay no attention to books in which the main characters were animals or toys, nor to fairy tales or blatant fantasies.) At the first chance, we picked up a shelf's worth of easy-reading books, wordbooks with pictures, etc., which seemed to suit him. Anna saw quickly, though, that what was most productive, most educative, was for her to talk to him, systematically and at length, which she did as often as he was willing to listen. He was not desperate to learn the language.

She named the world, starting with the apartment and, with the help of a children's atlas, moving outward. When, in her judgment, Alan's behavior had become more civilized, less erratic—it took just a couple of weeks under her tuition—and when he showed himself less openly hostile towards me, allowing me, for example, to sleep in the bedroom, we were willing to take him out in public. After lunch, if the weather was good, he and Anna would walk the streets, first sticking near the apartment, then venturing farther afield. I'd go with them occasionally, though Alan was less predictable, harder to control, when I was along. He enjoyed the changing of the guards. He liked to walk along the canal, and to stand in the concourse outside the Chateau Laurier. He liked to watch people milling about. He liked to watch couples, groups of young men and women, going around together, though he would become anxious in the vicinity of a group of men, young or older. Anna talked to him about what he was seeing. We bought the closest thing we could find to a child's guide to human anatomy and physiology, and after she'd named for him her body parts and his—I was careful to absent myself for this lesson—they turned to the text. She talked to him about history, about, for instance, the Second Korean War, which had been her specialty. He liked it when she spoke about war. From time to time—this did not much please Alan—she enlisted me to talk to him about arithmetic, the idea of numbers, matters of simple addition and subtraction. Neither of us spoke to him of death.

He enjoyed it most—she enjoyed it, too—when Anna talked about herself, her life. (She tried to tell him about me, what she knew, but he was less interested in that. Though he took a meanspirited pleasure in the story, which ended with me flat on my ass, of my chasing Anna and Sara up the snowy hill in Ames.) There were stories he asked to hear again and again. He was delighted when she'd elaborate or embellish the story, but he would brook no hint of abbreviation. He particularly liked one story, which he asked for obsessively, about a crabapple tree. The story in its simplest form was this:

"When I was a little girl, six or seven years old, I was sitting in the house one morning. It was summertime. I had nothing to do. I asked my mother if I might play outside in the backyard. I had it in my mind to climb the ancient crabapple tree that was back there. This was something I was always wanting to do. My mother said I could go out, so long as I didn't try to climb the tree. 'The branches are thin,' is what she always said to me, 'they are brittle, and if you climb on them, they will break.' I assured her I would not climb the tree. I went outside. There was not much to do in my backyard if you were alone. I decided to climb the tree. I had been up in the tree before, despite my mother's prohibition, but I'd never gone very high in it.

"I climbed up to the first tier of branches and wedged myself in. The branches were thick and sturdy. I sat there for a while looking at the yard, at the house, watching the kitchen window for any sign of my mother.

"I climbed higher in the tree. I found a perch where I could sit. The branches were thinner here, but easily bore my weight.

"I climbed higher. Now I was as high up as the second floor of my house. Still the branches didn't break.

"I climbed higher. I climbed to the very top of the tree. As I got to the top, I heard the branch I was resting on crack and give way. I fell. Somehow I didn't hit any of the branches on the way down. I landed on the lawn with a splat." [This was the word in the story Alan liked best.] "I missed a brick barbecue by inches. I was not hurt at all. I stood up and brushed myself off. My mother had come to the kitchen window just as I fell and saw it happen. She was very frightened, then, when she saw I was unhurt, very angry. She scolded me, then sent me to my room for the rest of the day. I did not get any supper that night."

I'm afraid I've done the story justice. As a storyteller, Anna was no great shakes. (I am hopeless when I try to tell a story out loud, and never do it.) And unless one chose to marvel at the fact that she emerged unharmed—which, I believe, was not what interested Alan—and not, as I did, to doubt, because of that fact, its veracity, the story was, to my mind, relatively innocuous. There's no knowing why Alan prized it.

Sad to say, but, in spite of Anna's industry and skill, it was clear Alan got most of his language, most of his sense of the world, from television, which he watched as much as we'd let him, and more. Anna and I disagreed about this, Anna arguing for television—with limits—on the grounds of language acquisition, socialization, acculturation, while I argued against it, on the grounds of inanity. For Anna, the time Alan spent watching TV served another purpose. Alan hardly moved when the TV was on, and it was the only time when she felt it was safe to leave me alone with him, the only time she could take for herself.

# Ten

Alan was captivated by mirrors and pleased by his own reflection. Even assuming there are no mirrors to be found inside the Clearances—hard to think why the government would want the clones to see themselves, to whatever extent mutilated or pristine—Alan's fascination with them seemed not a function of their novelty, rather a genuine and durable delight. We would find him gazing at himself in the mirror over the sink—standing transfixed more often and for longer periods than one could imagine—in the full-length mirror on the bedroom door, in the hall mirror, in Anna's hand mirror. In all the apartments we lived in (before this one), he would, when we gave him nothing else to do, shift from one mirror to the next, savoring the severally framed and sized views of himself. He looked at himself in shop windows, in car windows, in puddles, in cutlery. We found this activity, at which he was tireless, disconcerting, and did what we could to discourage it. I asked him, once, about this preoccupation. I don't remember how I put the question—rude, no matter how I put it—and all he would say in response was, "You look at yourself." Although it is strictly true that I do look at myself—shaving, brushing my teeth, etc.—it is with almost no interest and never with satisfaction. (I shave pretty much every day now; my beard comes in gray and coarse. But like Alan, when I was his age I hardly needed to shave. Alan shaves once a week, and he is skillful at it.) However it might sound, I think in Alan's case it wasn't a function of vanity. It wasn't, I mean, that he particularly liked the way he looks, though he may have. He seemed to me mostly indifferent to his appearance and to the appurtenances of his dress. Standing before a mirror he did not fix his hair or strike experimental poses or, say, check his teeth. He seemed not to care how he might look to others. I think he simply liked to look at himself, liked to see himself, because, fundamentally, he liked himself. Not what you'd have expected. You'd assume he had not been taught or encouraged to like himself. Still, until we told him who and what he was—Anna told him, I stood by, an avatar, at once, of his innocence and the curse into which he was born—he continued to find himself lovable.

I have been thinking about this question of self-love, wondering about my responses to Alan. Could any of these responses be simply, purely, responses to Alan alone? Isn't every one of my responses bi-directional, going both outward and inward simultaneously? When I am responding to Alan, aren't I, at the same time, responding to myself?

There are two things I mean when I talk about "self-love." I mean the love of self that motivates us to act in our own interests (a form, I suppose, of selfishness). And I mean a genuine love of oneself, which motivates us to act in our own *best* interests, such that we love ourselves, such that we are loved, in the way we'd, in our right minds, most want to love and be loved. I am talking, with regard to Alan, about the second. Is this kind of self-love innate? It must be. Consider Alan. It must be. And yet, though I had loving parents, I can't remember ever having felt it. It is precisely in my lack of self-love—all the disclaimers and qualifications, all the apologies, the relentless self-depreciations—that I can be most boringly self-indulgent.

Other questions I cannot hope to answer: Does self-love equal the desire to love another? Can a person who loves nothing be loved by another person, or by himself? How might it feel to live wholeheartedly?

Nearly as much as he liked his own reflection, Alan liked also to look at photographs. "In Iowa," Anna said, "when he was with me, he was keen to look at all my pictures. All the ones in frames I had around the house. Pictures of my husband, my children, my grand-children. My mother. Family vacations. Prom. Graduation. Team pho-tos. He came back to them again and again. He looked through my wedding pictures page by page, very slowly. Albums I'd made for the kids, scrapbook kind of things. A lot of these pictures were goofy, you know, comical, but he didn't once smile. He was serious. It was weird to watch." Until Anna started to take pictures of Alan, a thing we'd been explicitly warned not to do—as evidence, if it came to that, these pictures would be damning—he had only one photograph of himself to look at it. This picture, on his driver's license—sullen and stamp-sized—did not begin to satisfy his appetite. In her wallet Anna kept some snapshots of her grandkids, and these Alan asked to see a cou-ple of times a day. In Winnipeg the three of us went to a flea market set up in the parking lot of a suburban ice arena. It was early in our time there, December, and the day was sunny and dry but painfully cold. Alan, who by that time would behave inconspicuously in pub-lic, seemed immune to the weather, to all weathers, as if for most of his life he'd been kept outside. We were able there to pick up seven or eight random old photographs, a few of them framed, most of them black and white, one sepia-toned. Of these flea market pictures Alan liked best the framed sepia print: a man in his early twenties, sitting, his legs crossed somewhat effeminately, on a sidewalk bench set in the boulevard of a city street. The trees visible around him are in thick leaf. He is in dress uniform. Army, I would have said, definitely World War II. The man is very handsome, movie-star quality, but looks sad, wistful, as if he is waiting for someone he knows won't appear. As if he is alone, on his last day of leave. Guesswork, of course, but fun to do. I don't know what Alan thought when he looked at this picture, how he interpreted it, if he interpreted it, which I suspect he didn't, but he could not get enough of it.

Anna decided we should encourage this affinity of his. In the in-terests, she said, of enlarging his powers of artistic appreciation. I didn't think Alan's avidity had much to do with art, but, at the time, couldn't marshal a competing theory of my own. (Now I'd say that Alan is en-thralled by photographs because they are faithful, if misleading, copies of reality. As he himself is.) In a bookstore in downtown Winnipeg we bought him four oversized and very expensive books of photographs by famous photographers. I'd heard of none of them, and two of them, both women, were long dead. The work of one of these women, named Diane Arbus, from the middle of the last century, was quite remarkable: there were giants and dwarves and bearded ladies and pinheads and transvestites and transsexuals. Mongoloids of indeterminate age and sex dressed in what looked like baptismal gowns. Little white angels. Her pictures were grotesque, some of them frightening; at the same time they were beautiful and moving, full of compassion. She was Alan's clear favorite. Mine, too. (There was a photograph of a maniacal little boy holding a toy grenade that scared the stuffing out of me.) The other woman, Annie Liebowitz, whose work came later in the century, did glossy, stylized portraits of celebrities, most of whom I didn't recognize. The two male photographers—both with the surname Lynch—were more contemporary. One of them seemed to specialize in grayish, monochrome photos of small, blighted Canadian towns, the other in pictures of discarded machines, scrap. After buying at Anna's insistence a number of other outrageously priced volumes, we learned that Alan was not at all interested in landscapes or townscapes. Nor was he in-terested in still lifes or pictures of animals. What he wanted to look at, all he would look at, were pictures of people, individuals and groups, the more posed and formal the better. In Regina, Anna bought a cam-era and began taking pictures of Alan, of Alan and me, recording our time together. She took pictures at a zealous clip, until she'd used up the camera's internal memory. We had no way to upload these pictures, nothing to upload them to. When there was a picture she felt she had to take—Alan and I in Regina, standing shoulder to shoulder, like friends (we *were*, by that time, friends) in Victoria Park—she'd delete one she'd taken previously.

True to his word, without advance notice, the Tall Man visited us once a month. He came back to Friel Street towards the end of September, the end of October, and the end of November. He followed this pattern the three months we were in Winnipeg and, again, the three months we were in Regina. Though we were not to see him at any other time, it was clear he was traversing Canada along with us, living in the city we were living in, always close by. Did he have a wife? A family? Were his children also misshapen? Did he have any life outside his service to the group? Did I? On some of his visits the Tall Man showed up alone; on others he brought an accomplice. We saw the taciturn black man two more times. On one visit the Tall Man was accompanied by a young woman. This was in Winnipeg, the apartment on Goulet Street. The girl was Alan's age, and very attractive. She was not his daughter, not, the Tall Man made a point of saying, in any way related to him. She was a tall, angular girl with dark hair and a seductive overbite. She had beautiful hands. Long, thin fingers, shapely nails. I noticed them right off. What on earth was he thinking, bringing a girl like that to see Alan? Was it meant to provoke, torment him? If this was the Tall Man's purpose, he achieved it. "She wanted to see the clone," was his explanation, which the girl, disappointingly, let stand without objection. Alan, who, until Calgary, would say nothing to the Tall Man on any of his visits, sat still and quiet on the couch, his hands pressed tightly between his thighs, a Winnipeg Jets cap (his team) on his head, watching the girl. She knew he was watching her and, I thought, played to him without mercy. I could see she was driving him wild, enjoying doing so, and I was relieved—I was proud of him, too, poor guy—that he did not act on his impulses, which were visible in every anguished inch of him.

On each of his visits, the Tall Man said to me, "How's the report coming?" And I responded, "It's not coming. I'm not writing it." Then we'd enact some sort of brief, pugnacious conversation.

"What are we paying you for?"

"I haven't taken a dime from you."

"That's right. The last of the heavy hitters. Mr. Moneybags."

"And who are you?" I said. "Jack the giant?" The man flustered me.

"It's Jack the giant *killer*. You want to try again?"

These exercises in provocation and intimidation were ancillary

pleasures for the Tall Man. His main business each month was to monitor Alan's progress. Anna would willingly provide for him her own assessment. She was proud of Alan, proud of her work with him. "Day
by day, he's more comfortable with the language. More proficient.
He's speaking in complex sentences. Idiomatically correct. Picking up
all sorts of colloquial expressions. What did he say the other day?
Something he saw really pleased him. 'That takes me away,' he said.
Television definitely helps in this regard, though we try not to let him
watch too much. He likes hockey. Last night he was watching a game
with Ray. I don't know anything about hockey, but I heard him say,
'He top-shelfed that one. He buried it.' He seems to know the name
for everything he sees. Understands pretty much whatever we say to
him. He thinks well, though he can't always articulate his thoughts
to his own satisfaction. He's easily frustrated when he can't think of
a word, or doesn't know it. He's quite able to conceptualize. Understands notions like love and friendship and kindness and gentleness.
Sometimes he tries too hard. He's ready to learn. Humble about what
he doesn't know. But he's quick. He's really quick. I just hope I can
keep up with him.

"He's emotionally astute. He watches me closely, gauges my feelings. 'Are you sad?' he'll ask me. Most of the time, you know, he'll
have it right. 'Are you happy now?' He's very solicitous. Not as much
with Ray, though they're coming along.

"He's reading pretty well, though he prefers being read to. We've
been onto chapter books for a while. We're reading *The Boxcar Children* now. We've got seven of them. He likes these books, though he
wouldn't admit it. I can tell he knows they're for younger kids, but
he finds them moving. The family attachments. He could almost read
them on his own, but he's still not reading silently, and he's self-conscious. So we take turns. I read a page, he reads a page.

"I've tried to introduce it, but he doesn't want to write. I don't
force him. He'll try when he's ready. And if he doesn't write, well then,
he won't. He's getting the hang of arithmetic. Ray's working with him.
He can add and subtract, multiply and divide small numbers.

"He's interested in the world. He's a sponge. He loves to be out and about with us. He's good now in public. He's sociable. Calm. But he's watchful, still wary of groups of men. We've taken him to restaurants, and he does well. He likes to eat, I'll tell you that. His table manners are good. What else can I tell you?"

"I'd like to see some of this," the Tall Man said. "Can I hear him talk? Can I see him read?"

But Alan would not speak to the Tall Man or perform in any way, and neither Anna nor I would ask him to. While the Tall Man was in the apartment, Alan sat quietly on the couch watching television or looking at a magazine. When the conversation turned to him, usually he went to his room.

"What's with you?" Anna asked me after one of the Tall Man's visits.

"He doesn't like me," I said. "I don't like him. I won't be part of your group, Anna. I will not take orders."

"Fine, Ray," she said. "But your behavior is childish. What do you think Alan thinks when you act that way?"

"I don't know what Alan thinks," I said.

"You should think about it. You should be better than that."

I did think about it. I wasn't better than that.

On his third and last visit to the Friel Street apartment, the Tall Man told us we'd be leaving Ottawa soon. (This was the end of November. I'd turned sixty-six the week before. Anna and I decided not to mark the day. We thought it better not to raise the subject of birthdays with Alan.) We were sorry to hear this. We'd gotten to know the city, and liked it. We were comfortable there, more or less.

"*Why* must we leave?" Anna said. "What's going on?" By this time I did think it the better part of something—valor, discretion— to leave all such negotiations to her.

"We think they may be getting close."

"Do you mind if I ask," she said, "what makes you think so?

The Tall Man liked Anna. He had liked her husband. He was only sorry she was saddled with me. "They've looked into your whereabouts," he said. "They've been to your house. They've talked to your neighbors. They know how long your house has been empty. We believe they've been all through the place, and your truck, poking around. They're aware of your involvement in the group. They remember your husband."

"They should," Anna said.

"They have been to see your children, your daughter in Iowa, your son in Washington State."

"Are you sure?"

"Yes."

"Are they okay? Are my kids okay?"

"They're fine. Your children don't know where you are or what you are doing, which is good, and they were eager to cooperate with the government in helping them find you. Which is also good."

"Okay, then," Anna said. "So they're okay."

"For now," the Tall Man said. "Obviously, for their protection, and yours, you must continue to have no contact of any kind with them."

"No. I won't. Are they after Ray?"

"It seems they're not. Which is what we'd expect."

"Good," she said. "That's good, at least."

"We'll do our best for you," he said. "And him," nodding at me.

"And you think they're close?"

"That's what we think."

I could keep quiet no longer. "This is the Dolly Squad?"

"Call them whatever you want," the Tall Man said. "They won't mind."

"What makes you think they're close? What makes you think they exist? Have you got tangible evidence they're closing in?" It was embarrassingly easy to collapse into the jargon.

"They're here," he said. "And if they're not here, they'll be here soon."

"Fine," I said, "but how do you *know*?"

"An epistemological question, or just another one of the pedestrian things you're prone to say?"

"Listen," Anna said to him. "This is important. You must not speak this way to Ray. Especially when Alan is around. Do you understand?"

I was grateful for her intercession.

The Tall Man smiled at her. "I do understand," he said. "You can have three days. That's all I can give you."

"The sad part is Alan likes it here," Anna said. "He's just beginning to feel at home."

"I'm sorry," the Tall Man said.

"Will we be going far?" she said.

"Depends on what you mean by far."

"Oh, for Christ's sake!" I said. "Where are we going? Just tell us and cut all the crapola." I surprised myself: this was my father speaking.

"When you need to know," he said.

Though you'd have to say our moves were scarcely unpredictable—west on to the next city of any size—we would twice more have to suffer this "for me to know" charade: at the end of three months in Winnipeg, and again, after three months in Regina.

"How's the money holding out?" he asked Anna on a later visit. "Are you doing okay?

"I could use some more," Anna said without any hesitation. "Is there more?"

The Tall Man looked at me, by his look meaning me to know that he knew I still had plenty of money. I had more than he imagined. "I think we might be able to scratch some up," he said to Anna. "You'll have it before you leave."

This was at the end of May, right before we departed Regina for Calgary, and right before my second heart attack. I remember this exchange about money, because I counted it as one of my few victories, but more so because it was that evening, just after dinner, that we decided to tell Alan about himself.

Alan watched a lot of TV. Far more than I thought good for him, but Anna's claim for its demonstrable benefit prevailed. At first he was amazed by it and would watch spellbound pretty much whatever came on, but by the time we got to Winnipeg he'd become discriminating, had mastered the remote control, and memorized the time and channel for the shows he liked. As I've said, if we'd allowed him to, he would have watched television sixteen hours a day, sitting cross-legged on the floor up as close to the set as he could get, the thing at top volume. For the sake of our sanity, we were forced to impose certain rules, which were hardly ungenerous, but by which he only grudgingly agreed to abide. He could watch one hour in the morning before breakfast, one hour in the late afternoon, after his "lessons" and whatever other activity we might have planned for him, and two more hours—if a Jets game was on, we'd let him watch it to the end—when we'd all finished dinner and he'd done his share cleaning up. There was no television during meals, no cartoons or anything else infantilizing, no horror films—this last injunction grievously belated, considering what he'd lived—nothing, if we could help it, that celebrated violence, or sanctioned it. (We made an unprincipled exception for hockey.) One of us would be in the room with him when the television was on. We did not think to prohibit pornography, which, after midnight was all too available. We were most afraid, I suppose, that before we'd raised the subject, he would see or hear something that had to do with cloning—a news report (every once in a while, you'd see in one of the Canadian papers an anti-American op ed piece that included cloning in its catalog of our evils), a feature film, a throwaway remark in one of the silly comedies he watched—but we need not have worried. Even in Canada there was little public awareness of the subject.

Alan was a great fan of the Winnipeg Jets. He was a zealot, really. He was euphoric when they won, despairing when they lost, and that season, inconveniently, they weren't very good. My father had a similar relationship to the Boston Red Sox, similar responses in both kind and occupying power. But my father had grown up playing baseball and watching the Red Sox. Before Alan watched his first game—he happened upon it flashing through the channels after dinner—he knew nothing about hockey. (I suspect, in his quick-set and utter commitment, his self-abnegating fealty to a thing that was void of any real meaning, there was some anthropological truth to be found.) To take it back a step, such concepts as sport, game, athlete, competition—

the concept of play, even—meant nothing to him. There was no doubt the fighting was an appeal. But he might have been watching a form of dance, or politics, or courtship, or war, all of which, likewise, he knew nothing about. In the town where I grew up, there was a park at the end of our street, with a rink and warping, waist-high boards that appeared overnight and a warming house, where I learned to skate pushing a kitchen chair around the ice and, though I could never skate backwards without falling and didn't take to checking, played a bit of pickup hockey. I knew the rules, but none of the subtleties. Played at the professional level the game had no appeal for me. But Alan loved it—he was a fan only, never showed any interest in skating, himself—and by the time he'd watched, say, his sixth game, knew most of the Jets players' names and numbers, and understood enough about what was going on to deliver, win or lose, an earnest, if faulty, blow-by-blow. Most of the time, in the interests of fellow-feeling, I'd watch with him.

In the middle of February, before we left Winnipeg, we took him to a Jets game. The night was clear and dry, the snow on the ground like laundry soap. It was dangerously cold, the temperature, not figuring the wind, further below zero than I'd ever experienced. Breathe in through your nose and your nostrils froze shut. Any area of exposed flesh was, in minutes, frostbitten. Anna tried to beg off. She had no interest in hockey. "It will be a good chance for you and Alan," she said, "to have an outing on your own." I insisted she come. Things, by then, were cordial between Alan and me, but I didn't think we were quite ready for that. I was worried being at the game might over-excite him and cause him to come unstrung. As it happened, Alan was in a frenzy from the dropping of the first puck to the final horn, but, despite the discouraging score, it was, if such a thing can be, a joyous frenzy. The worse things got for the Jets, the more the fans around us, drunker by the minute, screamed and moaned, the more Alan joined in with them, the more, in their collective distress, he enjoyed himself. I'm afraid it may have been the happiest three hours of his life.

We bundled up—Alan refused to wear anything on his head but his Jets cap—and took a cab to the arena. The Jets were playing the

Ottawa Senators, their archrival according to Alan, and the much su-
perior team. The game was my idea, and I paid for the tickets. Our
seats, which we'd bought at the last minute, were bad: we were in the
uppermost tier, in a section towards the back, but Alan didn't com-
plain. To his great delight, the Jets stayed close for half the first period, and even scored a goal on a power play. (It was to be their only
goal.) In the two minutes before the break, the Jets goalie, as if he'd
been bewitched or bought off, fell apart, letting in three straight goals.
"He's a sieve," Alan said to me, and with the rest of the fans raucously
demanded he be benched, and then executed. Alan had his first Coke.
In the lobby on the way in I bought him a souvenir program and a
felt pennant for the wall above his bed. After the game—despite the
dismal result, he was still elated—I bought him a jersey, lettered on
the back with the name of his favorite player, an American winger
named Finnegan, who'd spent most of the night in the box.

By the end of the second period the score was 7 to 1 in favor of
the Senators, who were, by then, skating their fourth line every other
shift, and had replaced their star goalie with his backup. In the break
before the final period more than half the fans went home, most of
them season ticket holders from the choicer seats. At the start of the
third period, I pinpointed a whole row of vacated seats in the Jets end,
where most of the action was, on the curve, up against the glass. I told
Anna where I was going, and to watch for my signal. I found the usher
at the head of the section. I pointed up to where we were sitting. I told
the usher, an old man asleep on his feet, it was my son's first hockey
game. As matter-of-factly as I could, I offered him twenty dollars. He
snatched the money. He told me if we wanted to come down, he
couldn't condone it, but he'd look away. I waited for Anna and Alan
to join me. When the usher saw Alan, he looked surprised. He may
have thought he'd been deceived, but he said nothing.

When Alan found himself so close to the ice, he was delirious. I
have to say, it was very exciting. Even Anna was thrilled. We could smell
the ice, feel the chill. We could see the players' faces, their sweat, hear
them grunt and swear. Up that close you got an accurate sense of their
speed and power. The force, the rage with which they slammed each

other against the boards, against the glass, which seemed that it would shatter, was, the first few times, quite shocking. Alan banged the flat of his palms on the glass. He shouted insults at the Senators' players, harangued the refs, but saved his loudest, most indignant catcalls for the hapless Jets.

When we were in the cab on the way home, in the backseat huddling together for warmth—Anna in the middle, Alan and I pressed against her on either side—Alan, who had not stopped chattering since the game ended, went abruptly quiet. Then he looked over at me and said, "Thank you."

He may have said that to me before—Anna insisted on politeness from him—though he would rarely talk to me, and almost never when Anna was around to talk to instead, but it was the sincerity with which he said it that floored me.

"You're welcome," I said.

"Thank you, Ray," he said—he wanted to get it just right—"for taking me to the game."

"It was my pleasure," I said.

"I had fun," he said.

"I'm glad," I said. "I'm glad you had fun." I *was* glad.

"Did *you*?" he said. Coming from him, this was more than perfunctory. "Did *you* have fun?"

"I did," I said. "I sure did. Thanks for asking."

"You're welcome," he said.

I could see Anna was gratified.

"Sorry they lost," I said.

He smiled at me. "They were bad."

"Yeah, they were."

"Weren't they bad?"

"They stunk," I said.

He laughed. "They stunk," he said. "They did." Then he conjugated the verb. "They did stink," he said. "They stink."

That was the end of our epoch-marking conversation. Alan did not say another word the rest of the way home. Back in the apartment it was business as usual, Alan focused exclusively on Anna.

It was when we were in Winnipeg, on Goulet Street, that Alan discovered pornography. By the time I caught him at it, he might already have been watching several nights, or several weeks, I can't be sure. After midnight there were three or four channels on which one could watch hard-core pornography, films and live action, continuously until just before dawn, with short respites for ads, most of them for sexual devices or online sex clubs and the like, the ads themselves unabatedly obscene. By law these channels are located only in the upper reaches of the 400s. The rationale given is this: as there are rarely active channels above 300, there is a smaller likelihood of anyone—an unsupervised child, say, up late—coming upon the stuff accidentally. These laws, no matter how they are framed, are notoriously ineffectual. The only thing they seem to prevent, so far anyway, is the showing of pornography that involves children. Alan might have been the one sentient being in Winnipeg not to know exactly where these channels were and what they offered.

I don't know how Alan happened on the channels—intuition driven by desire? a perverse providence? monkeys and typewriters?—but for however long it had been going on, he got out of bed around midnight, after I was dead asleep and snoring, and went quietly into the living room, where he watched with the sound nearly off, out of consideration for us or merely protecting his privacy. He sat on the couch, the room dark except for the tawdry light from the TV, the cinch of his pajama bottoms loosened. He was masturbating when I came in, and apparently ejaculating into paper towels, a wad of which he held in his free hand. He had the whole roll beside him on the couch.

When I saw him like that, I was embarrassed. I was also glad, for Anna's sake, I'd been the one to find him.

"Excuse me," I said. "I didn't know you were in here." What could I have said? "Cut it out?" "Carry on?" Stupidly, I stood there, as if waiting for his response. Alan was not the least bit embarrassed. He immediately stopped what he was doing and turned off the TV with the remote. In the forgiving dark he retied his pajama bottoms, gathered up the used paper towels, and left the room without speaking or looking at me. I went to the bathroom. When I got back to the bedroom, he was in bed and asleep, or pretending to be. As I'd hoped.

I didn't say anything to Anna about what I had seen. The next night, when I woke at two a.m. needing to use the bathroom—Alan didn't know what a prostate gland was and couldn't have figured mine would be enlarged and hard as a nut—he was not in his bed. Again I found him in the living room, sitting on the couch, the TV on, the paper towels, etc. I'd had a day to give some thought to what I might do, and I'd come up with the idea that I'd offer to sit and watch along with him (so long as he didn't continue to abuse himself), even talk to him about what he was seeing ("And here we have . . ." ), thinking, thereby, to strip the situation of any illicitness that might be part of its allure. But it was not its illicit nature that drew Alan. He felt neither ashamed nor accused by my intrusions. Alan simply wanted to watch people, men and women—I'm sure there was nearby a channel wholly devoted to male-male sex, but this would have put him off—young men and (O brave new world!) young *women*, engaged in sexually explicit acts, the more explicit, the more closely, clinically, microscopically exhibited, the better. For him this was educational TV, and, I now think, necessary. When he became aware of my presence, he turned off the TV, gathered his supplies, and, without a word, went straight to bed. I watched him to see if he was angry at my infringement, but he was neither angry, nor embarrassed. His attitude was one of acceptance and accommodation.

I woke the next night at one a.m. This was premeditated. I was on the case. Like some Puritan elder. I could have let him be. I was not his father; but—this is the truest way to characterize my relationship to him—I *was* his keeper. His keeper's assistant. However I might have construed my role, it surely did not include this kind of surveillance and intervention. For the third night in a row that I knew of, Alan was not in his bed. I peeked into the living room. He was there, and busy. I did nothing to make him aware of me. I went to the bathroom, then straight back to bed. After a while I heard him pottering around in the kitchen. It sounded like he might be making himself a sandwich—he liked peanut butter and jelly—something he'd begun to do. I was still awake when he came back to bed. I decided to speak to Anna in the morning.

While Alan was occupied watching one of his pre-breakfast shows—something farcical about a family of human-looking robots—I told Anna what I had seen. She was, at first, furious with him and, by association, with me.

"Get out of my way," she said. We were standing in the kitchen. She was in her nightgown and robe. Her hair, which she'd started to grow out, was in an unruly intermediate stage and, especially in the morning, made her look ashen and wild. "I'm going to talk to him."

"Maybe *we* should talk first," I said.

"You just let him do it?"

"What do you mean '*let* him'?"

"You didn't say anything?"

"I didn't have to. He stopped when I came in. Turned off the TV. Packed up. Went to bed."

"What did he say?"

"He said nothing."

"Did you see what he was watching?"

"Some."

"How bad was it?"

"I guess it was pretty bad," I said. "I don't know how to rate it."

"This is not good," she said. "I have to talk to him."

"What will you say?"

"I have no idea. I didn't expect this. Did you expect this?"

"I had no expectations," I said. "You raised boys."

"They didn't do this."

"Masturbate?"

"Pornography," she said. "Just let me think a minute." She opened a cabinet and took out a tumbler, then took some orange juice out of the refrigerator and poured herself a glass.

She took a sip and made a face. "Oh, that's tart," she said. She put the glass down on the counter. "We never had this problem." She shook her head. "Forgive me. I shouldn't have snapped at you. It's not your fault."

"I'm pretty sure it's not," I said.

"What do you think about this?"

"I don't know what I think," I said. "It's awkward."

"Did you do this?"

"Do what?"

"Watch pornography?"

"It never interested me." I said.

She put the carton of juice back into the refrigerator and poured the juice from her glass into the sink. "This stuff is awful," she said. "Let's remember not to get it again." She rinsed the glass under the tap, then put it in the drain board. "This may be my fault."

"How could that be?" I said.

"What I did for him."

"Oh," I said. "I don't think so." It occurred to me that this must be the way parents talk. "It's no one's fault, Anna."

"I'm not sure," she said. "What do I say to him?"

"I don't know. Tell him why you find it objectionable. Tell him how it makes you feel to know he's watching it."

"What if you spoke to him?" she said. I had never before seen her flinch. "You're a man."

"It would be more powerful, I think, coming from you." This was not only a dodge; I believed it to be true.

I saw her gather herself. She straightened her spine, set her jaw. She really did these things. "I'll clean up," she said, "get some clothes on. Then I'll talk to him."

"Do you want me there?"

"You choose," she said.

Anna reappeared when Alan and I were sitting at the table having breakfast. I'd cooked some oatmeal for the two of us. Alan had come to take his with raisins and brown sugar; I liked mine with just a jigger's worth of milk. Anna had showered and dusted herself with a fresh-smelling powder. She smelled clean. She'd brushed her hair and put on lipstick. She had on a flowered, knee-length skirt she'd not worn in my presence, and a white cotton man-tailored shirt, short-sleeved, open at the throat. Her feet were bare. It was the heart of the

Winnipeg winter, and she was dressed for a Virginia spring. She had no intention of going out this way. She looked good. I thought she looked as good as I'd ever seen her look.

It seemed to me that a small part, at least, of Anna's response to Alan's brief experiment with pornography—it was brief: after Anna spoke to him, he did not watch it again—had to do with her having hurt feelings. She was, it remains reasonable to believe, the first, and for a time afterwards, the only woman Alan had ever seen, and, more to the point, the only woman with whom, however qualifiedly, he'd been sexual. (The instance, I suspect, more momentous for Anna than for Alan.) By now, though, six months on, she'd been eclipsed in Alan's adult imaginings, if not in his child's heart—superseded in youth and beauty and sexual appeal (cast aside?)—by two generations of younger women, both those he saw on television, before and after midnight, and those he saw on the streets of Ottawa and Winnipeg. I don't know how Anna really felt about this. I never asked her, and she never spoke of it.

When the breakfast mess had been cleared and washed—Anna skipped breakfast that morning—the dishes put away, she asked Alan to sit with her in the living room.

"Why?" He said this without peevishness.

"I want to talk to you."

"Okay," he said.

Alan sat down in the middle of the couch, his customary spot, facing the TV, which was not on. Anna sat beside him, turned sideways so she could face him. He continued to look straight ahead, not intending by this, I'm quite sure, to be rude. I sat down in the wing chair between the windows. My aim was to help if Anna needed me— she didn't—otherwise to remain unobtrusive.

"Alan," she said. "I want to talk to you about something that's making me sad."

"Are you sad?" he said.

"I am," she said. "But I'm not angry. I want you to know that. I'm not angry with you."

"Okay," he said. So far, he didn't seem much perturbed.

"I don't like what you watch on television," she said.

If he looked any way at all, it was mildly confused.

"I mean, what you watch at night."

Still, there was no sign he knew what she was talking about.

"What you watch when we're asleep."

He smiled. He was interested now.

"I don't like you watching it."

"I want to fuck a girl," he said.

"Now just hold on," she said. She put her face closer to his. "In the first place, we can't have that kind of language. You and I have talked about this. I'm sure you remember. Do you remember?"

"Yes," he said.

"Then you must stop. Right now. No more of that."

"How do *you* say it?" He included me in this question.

"I don't say it," I said.

"That's a very good question," she said to him, making it clear she'd not found my response productive. "Someday, maybe it will be soon, you will meet a girl." I believe this was something she'd planned to say as the happy end of her disquisition. "You will get to know her. You will like her, and she will like you. If you're kind and gentle and considerate, which I know you will be, and if you're lucky, she will love you. You are always lucky to be loved. If you love her, and if, after a time, she wants to do what you want to do, then you will do it. What the two of you will do will be something fine and good and sweet. When we talk about that, we say 'making love.'"

"Which is not what you've seen on TV," I said.

Alan paid no attention to me. You could see him trying to make sense of what Anna had said. By this time Alan had more than a nominal understanding of what love was—I believe, in his way, he loved Anna—but the idea of *making* it appeared to stump him.

Finally, in frustration—it was cumulative—he said, "I want a girl to fuck." This was so heartfelt as to be inoffensive. "Why can't I have one?"

Anna softened even further. "You will have one," she said. "Someday you will. I promise. And no more of that language. Okay?"

"Yes," he said.

Anna set out the arguments, moral and political, against pornography, a term Alan hadn't heard before, and one she didn't insist he acquire. The arguments were familiar—the objectification, the dehumanization of women, the promotion of violence against them, the devaluation of sex, of physical and emotional intimacy, the suffering and sadness all around, etc. In her brief, Anna took pains to use language that was simple and clear. I found the arguments none the less compelling for their familiarity and simplicity. I can't say how Alan found them, though, as I've said, they certainly, and immediately, had the desired effect. What surprised and impressed me most was that Anna was willing to talk to Alan about, citing him as an example, her first boyfriend, the one she'd met in college, a psychopath and pornography addict, named Wilf. Without going into detail, she spoke about his cruel treatment of her, but also, with some charity, about the great waste and tragedy of his life. (The next time we were alone, I asked her if she knew what had happened to Wilf after college. She said she didn't know, and didn't want to know.)

When it was clear that Anna had said all she felt she needed to say on the subject, I said, "That was good. You did that well."

"Thanks," she said. "I hope so. I'm not sure."

"No," I said. "That was very skillful."

"Did I make any sense?"

"I think you did. Perfect sense."

"What do you think?" she asked Alan. "Is there anything you don't understand? Do you have any questions?"

Alan was hard to read. He had listened patiently and attentively, I thought, but he sat there largely without affect.

"Did you understand what I was saying?" Anna said

"Yes," he said. He might have. Then, looking straight at Anna, he said, "They like it."

"Who does?" she said.

"The girls. They like making love."

"How can you say that?" she said.

"They smile," he said. "They all smile."

Before we left Ottawa for Winnipeg—the drive was long, and we spent a night in a Thunder Bay motel—the Tall Man took our green Chinese car, which was a piece of junk that, in our care, had gotten junkier, and, in its stead, gave us a relatively new and spruce Tagore van. At the end of our stay in Winnipeg, the van, which we hated to lose, was replaced by an Oldsmobile Redux, a ponderous old sedan. We were in the Redux, on the way from Winnipeg to Regina. Anna was driving, and Alan was asleep in the backseat. It was the beginning of March and still very cold. A sunny, dry day, but the roads were dusted with snow blowing off the fields, the air glittery. In the interests of furthering my education, and passing the time, Anna was talking about what might have happened—was, she said, about to happen— had the government not taken cloning out of the hands of the corporate practitioners: the cloning process commercialized; cloned children commoditized, for sale.

"Take this hypothetical case," she said, "which would not have been hypothetical for long. An infertile couple, decent, civilized folks, who, after trying unsuccessfully a number of other possible solutions, want to clone a child. They are sad, frustrated, desperate. It is impossible not to sympathize with them."

"Not impossible," I said.

"All right," she said. "Fine. They go to a doctor who specializes in cloning. When they take this step, it is no longer extreme or outside the law. They are acquainted with several couples who have done it, though for our couple—let's give them this—it is a last resort. The doctor listens to their story. He has heard it many times before. He invites them to consider cloning a child from a donor cell that is unrelated to either of them, or to anyone in their immediate family."

"In their case," I said, "presumably an improvement."

"You're joking, but that's exactly the point," she said. "Anyway. The couple has considered this. The doctor suggests that a child of their own choosing might well be preferable to a child of their own. They are open to this suggestion."

"Why?"

"Why not?" Anna said. "Since it was now possible, and safe, why would they *not* choose to have a baby better, more perfect, than any, even with all the luck in the world, they could make on their own? That the doctor would make this same argument to a couple who were not infertile does not occur to our guys. Why should it? They can't think of a reason why they would not choose a better baby. They like the idea of a better baby. The idea of it brings them relief, and makes them feel proud."

"It would not be theirs," I said.

"That's one way of looking at it. She would carry it. Deliver it. Nurse it. They would raise it. They would love it."

"Still."

"Still," she said. "So the doctor shows them a catalog of donor cells he has available for purchase. There are donor bios they can read and color mug shots they can look at. The clinic has tissue samples of each available child in its deep freeze. Our couple is given a price list. They choose the best baby available, or the best baby they can afford. Let's say they are wealthy, that money is no object, and let's say that for them beauty is the prime virtue. So they choose to clone, to buy, as their child, Clarissa Harlowe."

"Clarissa Harlowe?"

"Whatever you want to say about her acting, she was generally held to be the most beautiful woman of her generation."

"She was a heroin addict," I said.

"Makes no difference. So let's say we really like this couple and want them to be happy. Let's say we think they deserve happiness."

"She was decapitated."

"It doesn't matter. She was beautiful. They want a daughter, and, above all else, they want their daughter to be beautiful."

"They want her to be Clarissa Harlowe?"

"They do" she said, "and they believe that because they will bring her up, she will be *their* Clarissa Harlowe. Now suppose everyone, or even, say, one percent of those who wanted a beautiful daughter—this, too, would have been possible—chose to clone Clarissa Harlowe."

"You're exaggerating for effect," I said.

"I'm not," she said. "But, beyond the ungodly circumstance of there being, at any one time, thousands of Clarissa Harlowes, young and old, preening around the country, hundreds in the same city, dozens in the same town, and the not inconceivable event of two or more of these beauties bumping into one another—what happens to our notions of beauty? of talent? of individuality? of the self?—the point is that in the way cloners exert control over the cloned, cloning is despotic. To take just this example, cloning gives us an unnatural opportunity to have our way, to work our wills on the identity of our children. The enlightened notion that all children, no matter who they are, should be wanted children would, with the possibility of cloning, inevitably mutate into the belief that only those children who fulfill *our* wants, *our* needs, would be worth having."

Here's what I was thinking, somewhat off the point, in the passenger seat of the Redux: if Alan were my son, that is, if he were a clone of my dead son grown into a man, and I'd had him made to replace the son I'd lost, I'd miss him, my lost son, all the more.

When we'd been in Regina several weeks and had settled in to our town house on St. John Street—after six months at very close quarters, Alan and I were thankful each to have his own bedroom—I got it into my head that, some night after Anna was asleep, very much on the sly, I would take Alan to a brothel.

I felt sorry for the boy. He'd been eager to placate Anna and had done as she'd asked: since his talking to in Winnipeg, he'd watched no pornography and, so far as I knew, and perhaps prematurely, he'd quit masturbating. In his work with Anna, he'd made geometric progress. (When the Tall Man came on his monthly visits, Alan still refused to do anything but sit silent on the couch.) Anna had recently begun reading *Great Expectations* with him. With her help he was able to withstand the language and keep pace with the plot, and seemed to enjoy the book. (Anna told me he found the novel's more realistic portraits—Pip, for instance, Joe and Mrs. Joe, Estella—no less fictive or fantastic than its out-and-out grotesques.) He was still somewhat slow of speech—his speech showed signs of echolalia—and self-conscious about it, but when he relaxed and got going, when he was in

the mood to talk, he was thoughtful and clear and even at times simply eloquent. Except when he was upset, or frightened, he was reasonably poised and self-contained. There was nothing about his behavior
readily apparent to distinguish him from most other sensible young
men his age, and he could be counted on to behave well with us in
private, and—he had not yet been by himself—with us in public. He'd
worked hard to make himself passable, I hesitate to say it, normal.
There was something sad about his diligence: no one, really, to appreciate the effort and the results but Anna and I, and our responses were
not the ones he was interested in. Virtual sequestration, along with a
broad-based abstemiousness and chastity of all sorts, had been my
chosen state going on forty years. But Alan, who'd spent all but the
last seven months of his life as a clone living with other clones in cap-
tivity (you supply the joke about the American polity), was young and
virile and, suddenly, desperately heterosexual. If there was something,
and there was, Miss Havisham–like about my life since Sara's death
(to my credit, I'd exacted revenge on no one but myself), Alan had
been given no choice but to live, living with us, the life of Rapunzel.
In my opinion he needed, now that he knew what one was, and had
seen what they could do and have done to them, needed before very
much longer, a girl. A girl, such was my thinking, who knew her craft,
who would treat him well, and with whom he would be safe.

I'd never been to a brothel. That I knew of, I'd never seen a pros-
titute and suspect I wouldn't recognize one if she stepped up and
licked my ear. On the rare and random instances when it had crossed
my mind, the thought of seeking comfort in a brothel elicited only
guilt and terror and disgust. But there I was, planning to act as pan-
der, and ready to pay Alan's way. In Regina, the legal brothels, female
and male, are confined, one hard upon the other, to a small subdis-
trict unofficially called "the Purg," which comprises two blocks of a
larger entertainment zone, with betting parlors, electronic cafés,
espresso bars, pot joints, retros, amusement arcades, multiscreen dig-
ital theaters, a VR Disney World for the kids, and the Globe, Regina's
one legitimate theater. I knew where it was, the Purg, up Scarth Street
no more than half a mile from our town house. We'd passed through

it several times during the day—soon after our arrival in Regina, we'd taken Alan to a movie, some deafening, frantic science fiction thing he didn't like, and which we didn't see through to the end—when there was nothing, no lights, no customers, no girls, to signal its function.

Alan and I were sitting in the living room, watching an informational program about the drought in the Northwest Territories attributable to a severe shortfall of snow there the past few winters. I was on the loveseat, Alan in a small club chair, his stocking feet up on an ottoman. It was after eleven o'clock, a weeknight in mid-March, still very much winter in Regina. Anna had gone to bed early. We were both bored by the show. Alan was restless.

"I have an idea," I said. "Might we turn off the TV?"

"I don't care if you turn it off," he said.

"If you're interested, I won't."

"Well, I'm not interested," he said.

"Anyway," I said, "I have an idea."

"What is your idea?"

"What if we took a walk? You and I? How does that sound?"

"How does that sound to me?"

"Yes," I said.

"I don't know how that sounds," he said. "Would she come with us?" With Alan, "she" always meant Anna.

"She's in her bed," I said. "We'll let her sleep. She's tired."

"She is tired," he said. This reads as if it might have been combative, but it was not. "Are you tired?"

"I'm not," I said. "Which is why I want to take a walk."

"With me?"

"Yes."

"Not with Anna?"

"No. With you. If you want to. Do you want to?"

"I don't know if I want to," he said. "Is she fast asleep?"

"I think she is," I said.

"Is it bedtime?"

"Well, yes. It *is* bedtime. So we can go to bed. If you're tired. If you're not tired, we can take a walk. If you want to."

"I don't know if I want to. You and I?"

"Yes," I said. "The two of us."

"The two of us never walked before."

"That's true. We haven't."

"It's dark."

"It is dark." It was hard for me not to fall into his pattern. Anna had no trouble resisting.

"It's cold."

"Listen, Alan, we don't have to go."

"All right," he said.

"Does that mean you don't want to go?"

"It doesn't mean I don't want to go," he said. "Where will we go?"

"Well, I have an idea about that."

"What is your idea?" he said, and we were back where we started, which often happened when I talked with him.

"What would you say if we took a walk to a place where you could be with a girl?"

"I would say I would like to be with a girl," he said.

"I know you would."

"You know I would. What kind of girl?"

"A pretty girl."

"I would like her. What's her name?"

"I don't know her yet," I said.

"I don't know her either," he said.

"We'll meet her, and then she'll tell you her name."

"When will I meet her?"

"When we get where we're going," I said.

"Where are we going?"

"We're going to a place where there will be a girl for you."

"A pretty girl," he said.

"That's right."

"For me."

The night was cold—Alan insisted on wearing his Jets cap—but there was little wind, and the air was clear and dry. By the time we started our walk it was midnight. Not accustomed to being out so late, to being out at any time unaccompanied by Anna, Alan was edgy and stayed close by my side, though not close enough that our bodies might touch. Near the town house the streets were quiet, which helped calm him. We'd walked about a quarter of a mile with not a word spoken between us, the lights of the Scarth Street entertainment zone, within it the Purg, just visible ahead, when I was given a rare moment of clear-headedness, in which I saw, with absolute certainty, the idea of taking Alan to a brothel was, in the real world, a bad one, that acting on it would be utterly inappropriate and irresponsible, and that the consequences of our proceeding as planned would be, for all of us, very sad. Alan might experience some ephemeral sexual satisfaction, but the price paid would be high: disillusionment, several kinds of sadness, embarrassment, disorientation. (He did not know enough for self-loathing.) If he wanted more, he'd be a long time getting it, so there'd be frustration and anger, and a good chance he'd revert, now with greater urgency, to pornography. There's no telling what the effect would be on his feelings about women in general, or on his feelings about Anna, the way he treated her. Anna would be angry and hurt. She'd rightly blame me—she'd be furious—and whatever trust had accrued between us would be breached irreparably. That my motives had included no self-interest (nor an ounce of wisdom or sense) would get me no leniency. She'd want to throw me out, make sure somehow I'd have nothing more to do with Alan. Alan would, in all the important ways, be innocent, of course, but would she be able to forgive him his betrayal—I believed that's how she'd read it—his transgression, when it came down to it, his desire?

We had come to an all-night retro at the edge of the entertainment zone. We could see two men sitting inside at the counter. From where we stood, the booths along the front window appeared empty.

"Let's duck in here for a minute," I said.

"Is the girl in there?" Alan said.

"No," I said.

"Has she left for a minute?"

"No, Alan. I'm afraid this is not the place with the girl."

"I'm afraid I don't want to go in it."

"Just for a minute. We'll get warm. We'll have a snack." I tried to make it sound exotic. "A late-night snack."

"No, thank you. I don't want a snack. Where is the place?"

"It's farther along. I'm not sure where it is."

"You're not sure."

"I've never been there."

"I've never been there either," he said.

"I know. Let's just go in. I want to talk to you."

"You want to talk to me about the girl?"

"Yes."

"Do you know where she is?"

"No," I said.

"Is she farther along?"

"I think she is."

"I want to go farther along," he said.

"Give me a minute, Alan. I want to talk. Please come inside with me."

"All right," he said. "A minute."

We sat down across from one another, by the window in one of the booths. Formica tables edged with aluminum, red leatherette seats and backs. The waitress, who'd been behind the counter talking to the two men, came over. She was middle-aged and looked tired. She was wearing a gray pinafore with a white collar. Pinned to her breast pocket was a white plastic nameplate with "Josie" printed on it. You were meant to know that wasn't her real name, but part of the overall mock-up. Her hands were red and chapped.

"Have you got any pie?" I said.

"We're picked pretty clean," she said. She was more affable than I'd expected. "We've got a couple of pieces of apple, some cherry. There may be a piece of banana cream left."

"Do you want some pie?" I said to Alan. He looked at his reflection in the window and did not answer.

"Give us two pieces of the apple pie," I said.

"You want ice cream on that?" she said. "Steamed cheese?"

"You do steamed cheese?" I said.

"Yeah. You want steamed cheese?"

"We do," I said. "And bring us two Cokes."

"*Please*," Alan said.

As the waitress went to put in our order, two couples came into the retro, their entrance presaged by an inrush of cold air. The men looked to be older than Alan, in their late twenties, early thirties; the girls with them were younger, eighteen or nineteen at most. Alan was sitting with his back to the door and couldn't see them at first. The two men were dressed well, both wearing dark wool greatcoats, scarves, and leather gloves. The men were hatless, and their ears were bright red. The girls had on luminescent, neon-colored ski parkas with fur-trimmed hoods, thick wool mittens, and shin-high, fleece-lined boots. They had their hoods drawn tight, and I couldn't see their faces. They made a lot of noise coming in, laughing, carrying on. Whatever they'd been doing, they'd had fun and more than a few drinks. One of the girls was clinging to the man she was paired with, her mouth on his neck. As they moved by us the cold air poured off them. They stopped just past our booth, standing over my shoulder, without once glancing at us, or otherwise acknowledging our presence. One of the girls put her mittened hand on my arm to steady herself. They took off their coats. Alan could see them now. The men were wearing business suits. The girls had on cocktail dresses, provocative flimsy things—their necks, shoulders, arms, legs left exposed—ludicrously wrong for the weather. The girls were pretty. They both immediately fluffed their hair. They sat down in the booth next to ours, at my back.

I was sorry to see them. Their presence would make it all ways harder, if not impossible, for Alan to hear what I wanted to say.

"Alan," I said.

"What?"

"I want you to listen to me."

He was smiling. "I like them."

He spoke softly. In any case, they were paying no attention to us.

"Because they're pretty," I said.

"They are pretty."

"And silly."

"Why?" he said.

"The way they act," I said. "As if they don't know any better."

He looked at me perplexed. He scratched the side of his head. I was saying things now I wasn't sure I had any right to say, wasn't sure I meant. "They should know better."

"Better than what?" he said.

"This."

"They are young girls," he said. This remark was descriptive, not by way of apology for them.

"True."

"Are they cold?"

"I'll bet they are."

"I'll bet they are," he said. "Their arms."

"Alan. Will you listen to me?"

"Yes."

"I want you to know I've changed my mind."

"To what?"

"I was wrong," I said. "This is a bad idea."

"A bad idea to be here?"

"No. Not to be here. This is fine. I'm happy to be here with you."

"I'm happy to be here."

"I'm glad. What I mean is, I was wrong. It was a bad idea to get you a girl."

"It was a good idea," he said. "You were right."

"I was not right. I can tell you, Anna would not like it."

"I can tell you, I would like it."

"I don't think you would," I said. "Anyway, it's wrong. It's not the way it should happen."

Alan was keyed in to the sounds coming from the adjacent booth. I was grateful when he said, "What is the way?"

"I don't know," I said. "You remember Anna said it will happen when it happens." There could be no solace in this tautology—Anna hadn't said exactly that—and he did not respond. "You will meet a girl. I can't tell you when. You will. But for tonight, it's not a good idea."

"It *is* a good idea," he said.

"It's not. I should never have proposed it."

"It's *my* idea," he said.

"I have to say no. I'm sorry. We can't."

He thought for a moment, then looked away. He'd said what he was going to say, and so had I. Neither of us was in the least satisfied, though I was relieved to have it over. I was surprised he'd quit so easily. The waitress delivered our Cokes and pie. Alan ate his quickly, without looking up.

The pie was delicious, as good as I remembered it.

"How do you like the pie?" I said.

"Fine, thank you," he said.

It was after one when we got back to the town house. I was exhausted from the walk and the cold. It had been a long day, and by the end of it I'd made a cruel mess of things. We went in quietly, but Anna was up. She was waiting for us, sitting in the near dark—there was a light in the kitchen—on the couch in the living room. She was in her robe, her feet bare. There was a cup of tea on the low glass table in front of her.

"Hello," I said. "I'm sorry you're awake. We tried to be quiet. Shall I turn on a light?"

"Please don't," she said.

Alan sat down beside her on the couch. She leaned in towards him. She put her hand on the top of his head and kissed his cheek. "You're up late, mister."

"I want to go to bed," he said.

"Go on then," she said. "Brush your teeth."

"Good night," he said to her.

"Good night," she said. "Sleep tight."

"Good night," I said to Alan.

He left the room.

"Where were you guys?" Anna said, not threateningly.

"We took a walk." I was flooded with guilt. "Alan was restless, and we took a walk up Scarth Street a ways."

"I know that," she said. She took the reader from the pocket of her robe. "I have to admit I was glad to have this thing. I would have been really worried."

"Sorry," I said. "It was spur of the moment."

"You stopped for a while. Where were you?"

"Are you angry with me?"

"I'm curious," she said. "Where'd you go?"

"It was cold. We were hungry. I was hungry. We stopped at a retro."

"In the entertainment zone?"

"Barely," I said. "We had Cokes. I introduced Alan to apple pie with steamed cheese. I used to eat it with my father."

"You let him have a Coke?"

"I guess that was dumb."

"He'll be up all night."

"I hope not," I said. "Why are *you* awake?"

"I got up," she said. "I don't know why. I looked in on Alan. He wasn't there. I went to tell you, and you were gone. I was concerned. I got out the reader to see where you were. Then I waited for you."

"There was no need."

"As it turns out," she said. "So you guys had a good time?"

"I think we did. I hope so. All's well that ends well."

"What do you mean?"

"Nothing," I said. "I mean we had a good time."

"That's good," she said. "I'm happy to hear it."

The next night, after midnight, Anna woke me.

"What?" I said.

"You need to get up," she said. "Alan's gone."

"What do you mean?" Even half-asleep I knew exactly what she meant.

"He's up on Scarth Street again."

"Okay," I said.

"Not okay. You need to get out of bed. It's snowing. It's cold. We need to go get him. There's no telling how he's dressed. He took money from my purse. You need to show me where he is. So get up."

I got up. "Let me get my clothes on," I said. "I'll be ready to go in one minute. How much money did he take?"

"A lot," she said. "We need to bring him back before the group decides to get involved."

"Might they?"

"He's been out two nights in a row. Do you know where he is?"

"I hope I do," I said.

"What does that mean?"

"I mean I know where he is if he's where we were last night."

"Where else would he be?"

"I don't know. There's a lot up there."

"Does he know that?"

"I don't know what he knows," I said. "Is he moving around?"

"No," she said. "He's stopped."

"Okay. Let me put my clothes on, and we'll go get him."

"Just be quick," she said.

It was snowing heavily and colder than it had been the previous night. Anna walked fast, and I had trouble keeping up with her. I was afraid Alan had gone out on his own to find a brothel. I was more afraid he'd found one. If we were lucky, he'd be lost, wandering dazedly through some arcade or huddling in an alley. I considered telling Anna what I'd done, what I'd not done but planned to do, but there was a chance he had gone back to the retro, hoping to see the girls from the night before, and on that chance, I kept quiet.

When we got to the retro I was comforted to see him through the window. He was sitting in a booth, the same one we'd had the night before, but he was on the opposite side, where I'd sat, facing the door. He didn't see us standing outside. He was alone. Apart from him, the retro, what we could see of it, was empty. He was wearing his Jets cap. On the table in front of him was a Coke and a piece of some sort of pie, both apparently untouched.

"There he is," Anna said. "I see him."

She rapped on the window. Alan turned and looked out at her. "He's all right," she said.

"Good."

She moved quickly towards the entrance. "Come on."

"You go," I said.

# Eleven

As I wrote in the previous chapter, I remember the Tall Man's last visit in Regina—I suppose I could be brought to remember them all—in small part because it was the occasion on which Anna asked him for more money, but largely because it was right before we left for Calgary and thus at the end of what were for us, though they might not have seemed so then, relatively happy times. Right before my heart attack. Right before we told the clone what he was. I remember it was also shortly after the Tall Man had gone that Alan, for the first time, asked for money of his own.

He told us he hadn't liked having to take money from Anna's purse; he knew what stealing was. Nor had he liked her response to his having taken it. All the boys he saw on the street—touchingly, he thought of himself as a boy, for which skewed sense of himself we were probably responsible—had their own money. "You have money," he said to Anna. "When you want more money, you ask the Tall Man"—in fact, it was Alan who came up with this designation—"and he gives you it. Ray has money. Why don't I have money?"

"This is something we should talk about," Anna said.

In the course of his lessons, Anna had explained to Alan about money. It provided an excuse to work with him on math skills (supposedly my job), but also Anna thought he needed to know how to handle money. The math was not a problem for him—he was able to pay for his pie and Coke up on Scarth Street, and he was adept at making change—it was the concept of money as a medium of exchange, which, at its most fundamental, he found foreign. It made no sense to him that you could give something intrinsically worthless—a piece of paper, a small round of common metal—and get something of value in return.

I listened to their conversations on the subject. I wanted to say to Alan, but didn't, that the only thing worth getting, besides, say, food and shelter and medical care, you can buy with money is time. The truth is, in the years since Sara's death, I have had a surfeit of discretionary, say even disposable, time to myself, and it has been a purgatory. I would have been happy to have had less time. I am not unhappy now, finally, to be running out of it.

"This is something we should talk about," Alan said.

"What would you buy?" I said to Alan. "Please don't say you'd buy a girl."

"I *would* buy a girl."

"I know you would," I said.

"You would not buy a girl," Anna said. "We would not permit it."

"Not to keep, you know," Alan said.

"I know," Anna said. "But no. Put it out of your mind."

"It is in my mind," he said.

"I'm sorry," Anna said.

Alan mulled over his next move. "If you give me money," he said to both of us, "I will buy a computer." (His first "If . . . then" construction. He'd certainly understood causation before this, but now he'd acquired its rhetoric.) "I want a computer." He knew what a computer was, knew everyone had a computer, but it was certain he had no idea what he could or would do with one.

"Computers cost a lot of money," Anna said.

"Ray has a lot of money," he said. Then, to me: "If you give me your money, Ray, I will buy a computer. And I will buy a whistle."

"A whistle?"

"Yes. I will buy a referee's whistle, a silver whistle, and I will blow it."

"I will buy you a whistle," I said.

(I did buy him a whistle, at a sports shop before we left Regina. It came with a lanyard. He wore the whistle around his neck and blew it at odd moments, only in the house. He blew it once when Anna was slow to bring him his dinner, but she quickly put a stop to that.)

If we would not give him money, then he would get a job, he said. He knew what a job was, understood the concept of work for pay. We believed he'd worked much of his life, though whatever he did inside the Clearances—he would not speak of it—he did for no pay. Anna had bought a book called *When I Grow Up*. It was a primer on jobs. It described, with celebratory illustrations—every job equally worthy and appealing, salary never mentioned—a wide range of occupations, and grouped them alphabetically, multiple jobs listed under all the letters but X (only X-Ray Technician). Over several weeks, as a part of their work together, Anna read through the book with him, taking her time, a letter or two a day. For a few days, in the middle of this process, Alan declared he wanted to be a journalist, his decision based entirely—the book was outdated—on a colored drawing of a handsome, well-dressed man standing in front of a camera holding a microphone. Under Z there were, as you'd predict, Zoologist and Zookeeper. At the head of the Zs, the book's climax, was Zamboni Driver, and Alan was decided.

"You *have* a job," Anna told him. At the time I thought this could have been a risky way to take the conversation.

"I don't have a job," he said.

"You do," Anna said. "Your job is to learn."

"That's not a job," he said.

"It is. It's an important job."

"Then give me money," he said.

"It's not that kind of job," I said, trying to be helpful.

"What kind of job is it?" he said.

"It's the kind of job you do but don't get money for."

"That's not a job," he said.

"It's your work," I said.

"*My* work is teaching you," Anna said.

"Is that your job?" he asked her.

"It's not really a job," she said. "It's my work. It *was* my job."

"*What* was your job?" he said.

"I was a teacher."

"You were a teacher?"

"Yes," she said.

"Did they give you money? The people you teached?"

"The people I taught," she said.

"Did they give you money?"

"No," Anna said. "The children I taught did not give me money. The school paid me. Ray was a teacher, too."

"You were a teacher?" he said to me.

"I was."

He waited for me to finish my sentence, then prompted: "A teacher."

"Yes."

"Did the school pay you, too?"

"They did pay me," I said. "I'm retired now."

"What did you say?" he said, though always when he said this he meant, "What do you mean?"

"I don't teach anymore," I said. "I've stopped."

"You've stopped?" he said.

"Yes. Anna's retired, too," I said.

"She's stopped?"

"Yes."

"You teach *me*," he said to Anna.

"I do teach you," she said. "But it's not a job."

"He gives you money," Alan said.

"Who does?"

"The Tall Man."

"He gives me money so we can live. So we can buy food."

"You don't have a job," he said, "and the Tall Man gives you money. Ray doesn't have a job. *He* has money. He has a lot of money. I want money."

Q.E.D., I thought.

Before I go further with my report, I want to speak about your expectations for the clone. Your expectations for him, I mean, before he was introduced, when he was, for you, still "the clone"—or, thinking with the government, "the copy"—as, before I met him in Ottawa, he was for me my clone, my copy. I am speaking, very broadly, about your *literary* expectations, those expectations you would have brought to this account derived from types you've encountered in books you've read, movies and television you've watched, not a bit of which, judged by someone fit to judge, might actually qualify as literature.

Alan was not a figment of anyone's imagination, not a figure of fantasy, not allegorical. He was not a noble savage, though he evinced some nobility and some savagery both. The world in which he found himself was not imaginary, but for him it was quite new. It was not unmitigatedly wonderful. Some things were indeed marvels to him, young girls especially, and mirrors, and television, and ice hockey, and sex between women and men, and chocolate chocolate-chip ice cream, and Anna, perhaps most marvelous of all. (What was I to him? It would be hard to say. Not a marvel.) But to most of what he saw outside the Clearances, when he was not afraid or otherwise repelled by it, you'd have to say he was indifferent, surprisingly incurious. He was not a wild child, not a boy who was raised by wolves. The question of who, if anyone, raised him, remains unanswered. Perhaps he would have been better off had he been raised by wolves. He was not a monster, not murderous or malformed. I suppose he *was* analogous to Frankenstein's lugubrious hodgepodge, inasmuch as they were both products of man acting against Nature, usurping God in the creation of life. But Alan was not made from spare parts; he was made to be a source of them. While it has become possible, with cloning, to revivify the dead, Alan was not a revenant, no Rip Van Winkle—notwithstanding in his presence *I* was made to feel like one—though, by his very essence, he was a creature *of*, though not exactly *from*, the past. Like all clones, he was retrograde; his existence was reactionary: by suppressing diversity, it impeded the evolution of the species. He was not one of those pathetic, lovable, slow-witted lugs who persist in literature and film, who are too good for the world and often inadvertently dangerous to it. Alan was not a danger to anyone else, however much the government feared him. Except in this way: if, as Anna's group hopes it will, the process that began with the discovery of Alan outside the Clearances results in the abolition of human cloning, what will we complicit originals do with the two hundred and fifty million clones already in existence? Would there be any humane, ethical choice other than to let them live among us? What would be the consequences? Mass confusion? Mass hysteria? Mass schizophrenia? The collective disintegration of self? Internecine warfare, twin against twin? The reinstitution of slavery? I don't know that Anna's group has answers to these questions. Would we relocate them? Find them a place where they might live, like us, but apart? Greenland? Madagascar? The precedents, and the prospects, are appalling.

On his last visit to us in Regina, as he was about to leave, I asked the Tall Man about the clone's navel.

Anna and I had talked about this. We knew that as a fetus Alan must somehow have been fed "in utero," though her group believed his generation of clones was never actually inside a human womb. Anna knew that in the womb the umbilicus (her word) grew outward from the embryo and attached itself to the uterine wall. But if Alan was not of woman born, how, why, would he have a navel? There was a simple answer, which, because of the sadness of it, and because, finally, it explained nothing, we were not ready to settle for. If the umbilical cord formed in the fetus, then it was reasonable to assume it would form whatever the circumambient situation. Whether there was a uterine wall for it to attach itself to would make no difference. The umbilicus would be there, part of the fetus, though, if an alternative way of feeding the fetus had been devised, snaking hopelessly, uselessly about. And useful or not, it would be present at birth. Anna speculated that whatever stopgap incubatory apparatus the government had developed must have included some input jack through which the fetus could be fed, and to which the umbilicus deludedly attached itself.

"Why does he have a navel?" I said.

"I'll give it to you straight, Ray," the Tall Man said, speaking my real name. "We don't know. But I'm touched by your interest."

At the beginning of June, we would be met by the Tall Man when we arrived in Calgary, a beautiful city, set spectacularly, that was not kind to us. He was waiting out in front of the apartment on 14th Street SW, a crummy place where tribulation gathered. The meeting was brief. The Tall Man handed us the keys. He helped us up with our bags. Then he left. As he was leaving, he gave Anna an envelope with cash in it, less than she was hoping for.

I imagined it would be good, constructive—in the worst case harmless—to take Alan to a baseball game. I had happy memories—the most vivid in too meager a store—of going with my father, several times a summer, to watch the Fisher Cats play in Manchester. Our hockey night in Winnipeg had been for Alan, for Alan and me, an unalloyed success. He knew nothing about baseball, had never seen it played. The game was not fast or violent; I didn't expect him to be thrilled. But after his two demoralizing outings in the Purg, I wanted him to have, with me, the author of the fiascos on Scarth Street, an encouraging, wholesome, uncomplicated time.

By the third week of May, the weather in Regina, which had persisted wintry through much of April, turned warmer. At a Sonic near our town house, where, to get out of the way, I often went for lunch, I bought two tickets for a Saturday night game, the season opener, between the Regina Red Sox and their rival in the East division of the Western Major Baseball League, the Melville Millionaires.

The day before the game, Anna, Alan, and I drove out to the mall. I told Alan I wanted to buy him a mitt. We were in the Redux. Anna was driving, Alan beside her. I was in the back.

"A mitt is a baseball glove," I said to him. "I want you to have it for the game."

"A glove?"

"A kind of glove. Big." I held up my hand, stretched out my fingers.

"Like for a goalie," he said.

"Yes. So when you catch the ball it won't hurt."

"I would like one."

He held up his right hand—like me, he's a lefty—as I had done. Stretched his fingers. Then he flicked at the bridge of his nose with his index finger and twitched back one corner of his mouth; this meant, at once, to denote and caricature his unease. Whether the result of instinct or observation—surely instinct—so many of the ways he used his body to communicate, his gestures, facial expressions, postures in conversation, were, as Anna never failed to observe—she catalogued our similitudes—exactly mine. "Will I have to play in the game?" he said.

Anna laughed. "No," she said. "You'll just watch."

"I won't know how to play baseball."

"Don't worry," I said. "We'll sit in the bleachers."

"What did you say?"

"The stands. We'll sit in the stands. We'll watch the game. You can wear the glove . . ."

"The mitt," he said.

"The mitt. So if the ball comes to you, you can catch it."

"The ball will come to me?"

"If you're lucky."

"Will I be playing in the game?"

"No. You'll be in the stands."

"The bleachers," he said.

"If a ball comes to you, it will be foul."

He looked at me.

"If the ball comes to you," I tried again, "it will be out of the game."

"If the ball comes to me," he said. "it will be out of the game."

"Yes."

"Will I catch it?"

"Maybe you will," I said.

"If I wear the mitt," he said.

"Yes."

"If I wear my mitt, and I catch the ball, will I be in the game?"

"No," I said. "You'll still be watching. With me."

"But I will catch the ball."

"Help me," I said to Anna.

"If a ball comes to you," she said, "if you catch it, you can keep it."

"I can keep the ball?"

"Yes," she said. "It will be a souvenir."

"What did you say?"

"Something you can keep."

"I can keep the ball," he said. He thought for a moment. "Will Ray have a mitt?"

"No," I said. "I won't have one."

"If the ball comes to you, how will you catch it?"

"You will catch it for me."

"Will you be there?" he said to Anna. "In the bleachers?"

"No," she said. "Just you and Ray. It will be boys' night."

"Ray's not a boy."

"Man's night," she said.

"If I catch the ball," he said to Anna, "I will give it to you."

I had not worn a mitt in fifty years. I wanted to get Alan, if they still made them, a Wilson A2000, the glove I wore, as did most of the kids I played with. I was pleased to see they did still make them, though it appeared they came now only in lurid colors—reds and blues, oranges and purples. That they had in stock only two left-handed fielders' mitts, and neither of them an A2000, didn't matter, because Alan decided he wanted a catcher's mitt—jet black with a bright red pocket, and wrong-handed—and would not be talked out of it. I bought him the glove, and a can of tennis balls, as well.

The next day, Saturday, was mild and sunny. In the late morning, at my urging, the three of us went to Victoria Park. I had in mind to give Alan a chance to catch and throw before the game that night. Just to put him in the mood; I had, I assured myself, no ambitions for him. He brought along his catcher's mitt. I brought the tennis balls, and Anna packed lunch.

We played catch on the grass. We stood in a triangle, more or less isosceles, with me at the apex. I threw a tennis ball to Alan, doing my best to hit his glove. After retrieving the ball, he, in a manner of speaking, threw it to Anna; she threw it to me. Anna could really play. She was skillful and puppyish. She whipped her throws, caught equally well with either hand. She bounded around. She was full of laughter. I was stiff, virtually immobile, sulky. I couldn't bear to see Alan wearing that ludicrous glove on the wrong hand, looking as if he was up to his wrist in a big round doughy loaf of black bread. He was, of course, totally inept. Every time he waved his glove at the ball, the glove flew off. He had no idea how to throw: he corkscrewed himself trying to replicate the motion—he wisely took Anna for his model—and never once got the ball near her. We tried reversing the direction of the ball—I threw to Anna, she to Alan, Alan to me—to no effect, except to further fray my patience. Our game lasted only a few minutes. Alan was quickly discouraged, and seeing Anna throw and catch with such ease embarrassed him. It embarrassed me, too. We ate lunch. Anna took a picture of Alan and me, standing shoulder to shoulder, Alan without his mitt (he would refuse to take it to the game). Somehow she got him to smile.

The stadium—it was hardly that—was in a sport park on the Ring Road. I'd estimate it seated a thousand, no more. The stands, ten rows deep, went from foul pole to foul pole. There were no bleacher seats. The outfield fences were wire, maybe six feet high. Beyond them—a difficult background for the hitters—you could see other fields, in use that night by the local little leagues, and a large municipal pool complex. The scoreboard was freestanding, set on stilts behind the left field fence. The field looked rough—the grass scraggly and not quite green, the infield dirt uneven—and hastily readied. The game started at seven. It was not quite dark when we got there, but the lights were on. I had planned to arrive in time to watch batting practice, but, after the morning's disenchantment, I was not eager, and Alan had pretty much to be bribed with unfounded promises of hot dogs and Cokes and ice cream.

The stands were half full. We had good seats, on the first base line, fifth row back, behind the home dugout. We might well have got a foul ball in our vicinity, had we made it through the game. Near to us the fans were: men my age and older, sitting singly or in pairs (some of these, likely, scouts); families—Dad, Mom, and kids—or fathers with their sons; relations and friends of the Red Sox players; and, for Alan, most agitating, a pack of girls, a dozen of them college and/or high school age, noisy, immodestly dressed, and almost uniformly pretty, who were, no doubt in various ways, attached, or hoping to attach themselves, to one or more of the players. Alan spent most of his time—we stayed through three innings—watching these girls make themselves conspicuous. (He didn't say anything about them, as if he thought I might not notice.)

Before the game, there was a brief ceremony on the field, during which the new players on the Red Sox roster were introduced to the home fans. This was a showcase league, wood bat, the players all college kids, most of them from Saskatchewan. Two were small-college players from L.A., one from Puerto Rico, and one, the centerfielder, from a bible college in Oklahoma, his last name Mantle (spelled Mantel). By the time the first pitch was thrown, Alan was restless and hungry.

The game moved slowly, both pitchers, at the start of the season, having trouble finding the plate, the only real action coming when Mantel misplayed a fly to left center that went for a triple. At the end of the third inning, the score was 4–2 Millionaires. I tried to explain to Alan what he was seeing on the field, to give him some sense of the game's intricacy, but he did not even pretend to be interested.

Between innings, the girls, as one, headed for the concession stand just inside the gate behind home plate. Alan watched them go.

So not to embarrass him, I waited several minutes—hard to watch him struggle—then said, "Are you hungry?"

"Yes. I am hungry."

"Shall we go get you something to eat?"

"I will go," he said. "Give me some money. I will go."

"I'll go with you," I said. "I'm hungry, too."

"I will buy you something."

"I want to see what they have."

"I will see what they have," he said. "I will buy you something. I want to go."

"By yourself."

"Yes," he said. I could see the conversation was upsetting him, but I didn't feel easy about his going on his own.

"Why don't we go together? Maybe we can find you a souvenir."

"I don't want a souvenir," he said. "I'm hungry. I want to go by myself."

"I can't let you do that," I said.

"Why can't you?"

"I just can't. It's not a good idea."

"Anna would let me."

"Anna would not let you," I said.

He covered his eyes with his hands. He made no sound.

"What's wrong, Alan?"

He took his hands away. Maybe he was hoping I'd be gone.

"Why am I with you, Ray?"

"Here, you mean? Why are you with me here?"

He did not answer.

"Would you want me to leave? Would you want to be here by yourself?"

Though, as I would see, my question was off the point, he answered it. "No. I would not want to be here by myself. I would like to go by myself."

"I'll tell you what," I said. "What if I give you money, we go part of the way together, then you go the rest of the way by yourself?"

"Because you will watch me?"

"I won't be too close," I said. "I'll just be around if you need me."

"You won't be close?"

"Not too close. Do you want to do that?"

"Yes. I want to do that."

"Let's go then," I said.

We went together, or nearly so, Alan walking a couple of paces ahead, until we were, say, thirty yards from the concession stand, the girls there, lolling about, obscuring whoever it was working behind the counter—they were in no hurry to get back to the game—at which point I said to Alan, who was nervous and self-conscious, visibly torn, "Okay. You're on you're own. If you want to go."

"I do want to go," he said.

"Then scoot."

"Will you watch?"

"Do you want me to?"

"I don't want you to," he said.

"I won't then. Go on."

Alan walked towards the stand, optimistic, needful—a hapless combination—oblivious to the risk. I couldn't help but watch. He stopped several feet short of the girls, the ruck of them, and stood, waiting his turn. As I've said, he is a good-looking boy, nothing anomalous about his appearance, and a few of the girls took notice. A leggy, dark-haired girl wearing a halter top and, insistently (even from a distance), no brassiere, smiled at Alan and said something to him. I could not tell whether or not he responded to her, but he looked back at me. He saw me watching and shook his head. I turned away. After a minute or so, I heard the girls explode in laughter, which I could feel, somehow, was not affectionate. I looked back. They were all looking at Alan, who stood looking at them. The dark-haired girl said something I couldn't hear, but I could see Alan re-coil as if he'd been kicked. There was another blast of laughter, unmistakably derisive. Alan jerked himself around, nearly stumbling, and came towards me. He walked fast, looking down at his feet, his arms stiff at his sides.

When he got close, he said, without looking up, "What do I do, Ray?"

"Come here," I said.

"I am here," he said. "I don't know what to do. You tell me."

"Come here to me." I looked to see if he was crying. I had not seen him cry. He was not crying, but his face was flushed and contorted. Over his shoulder I could see the girls watching us, making sport. I put my arm around him and, with some difficulty, drew him to me. I'd not been this close to him before. We were briefly—he would permit it for a space of seconds only—and literally, cheek by jowl, my arms around him, my hands on his back. He was substantial, rock-like, though the skin on his face against mine was smooth, boyish. He had no smell. His breath was shallow. Against my chest, I could feel his heart beat fast. He broke free, shook me off.

"Don't, Ray," he said.

"Sorry. Are you okay?"

"I didn't know what to do."

"That's all right," I said. "Shall we go home? Do you want to go home?"

"Do you want to go home?"

"I think I do," I said. "I've seen enough."

"I've seen enough," he said.

"Why don't we go home?"

"Okay," he said.

We did not speak again until we were in the car and pulling away from the field.

"I don't like baseball," he said. "Do you like it?"

"I do like it. But it's fine you don't."

"I don't know what to do there," he said.

"I don't know what to do either," I said. "We're even."

"What did you say?"

"We're alike. Neither of us knows what to do."

"Are you a retardo, too, Ray?"

"What's a retardo?"

"I don't know what it is," he said. "Do you know what it is?"

"I don't. Where did you hear it?"

"I heard it from the girl," he said.

"It's a silly thing to say. A silly word."

"She was beautiful."

"You're right," I said. "She was."

"You saw her?"

"I did," I said.

He sat with that information for a while, then said, "Are all the beautiful girls mean?"

"Some are," I said. "Not all. It's hard to be beautiful."

"Are they all mean to me?"

"No."

"Was your wife a beautiful girl?"

"She was."

"She wasn't mean."

"No," I said. "She wasn't mean."

"She's dead."

"Yes."

"Did a girl ever say you were a retardo, Ray?"

"I'm sure they did."

"They said it?"

"Lots of times."

"They said it to you?"

"Yes."

"How did you feel when a girl said it?"

"How do you feel?" I said.

"I feel bad. I feel sad." He put his hand on his stomach. "In my belly I feel sore."

"That's just how I felt," I said.

"That's just how you felt?"

"Yes."

"I didn't know that," he said.

"Now you do."

"Know," he said. "Now I do know. Don't tell Anna what she said, Ray. I don't want her to know I'm a retardo."

"You're not a retardo," I said. "She knows you're not."

"She knows I'm not a retardo?"

"Of course she does. She loves you."

"Don't tell her what she said."

I parked the Redux on the street two blocks from the town house. Alan made no move to get out.

"What's up?" I said.

He did not answer. He was crying now. He was surprised by it and confused. (I had never seen myself cry. It was disconcerting. Alan's face was utterly changed, ugly, doughy and squashed, as if it had not yet been shaped.)

"Why don't we sit a minute?" I said.

He pressed the heels of his hands against his eyes. (I don't know if this was something I did; I hadn't cried in forty years.)

"I am crying," he said.

"I can see you are."

"Don't see me."

"No," I said. "I'm glad to see you cry."

"You are glad to see me cry?"

"I have never seen you cry. I'm glad to see it."

"I have never cried," he said, with which declaration he stopped crying.

"It's good to cry. You cry, then you feel better."

"I don't feel better."

"Are you sad about the girl?"

"I am sad about the girl," he said.

"That's understandable."

He looked at me.

"I understand," I said.

"I did not cry about the girl."

"What did you cry about?"

"Why am I with you, Ray?"

I thought I understood this time.

"You don't mean here and now," I said. "You mean, why are you with me always."

"Why am I with you?" he said. "Why am I with Anna?"

"You are with us so we can take care of you. So we can show you, teach you, what to do."

"So you can watch me?"

"Well, yes."

"Why don't I know what to do? Am I a baby?"

"No. No. Of course not. You're a young man. You're a remarkable young man. You've made remarkable progress."

"I have made remarkable progress?"

"You have," I said. "Anna thinks so, too."

"Why don't I know what to do?"

"You do know. Most of the time you know. There are times when you don't. And we show you. That's why you're with us."

He shook his head.

"Why am I with *you*, Ray?" he said. "Why am I with *Anna*?"

"Oh," I said. "That's a complicated question."

"It's a complicated question?"

"It is," I said. "I think it's one Anna should answer."

"Do you know the answer?"

"I do. I do know the answer. Just not as well as Anna."

"Will Anna answer the question?"

"She will," I said. "She will."

"When will she answer the question?"

"I don't know when," I said. "When she thinks the time is right."

"When she thinks the time is right?"

"Yes."

"When is the time right, Ray?"

"I don't know."

"I don't know either." Alan opened his door. "I am a tragedy," he said.

\* \* \*

Two nights later, Alan asked us a different question, which, finally, amounted to the same question. He'd been watching television, some half-hour show he looked at regularly after dinner, a lame-brained, desperately unfunny comedy—you may know it—about a family made up of three detestable children, and two young, libidinous, rather caustic working mothers, one black, one white. (I have, as I've acknowledged, no sense of humor. This is true, too, of Alan, though in a much more literal way. He lacked any concept of humor. He didn't understand that this show, and all the others like it, were meant to be funny. "Who is laughing?" he asked once when the laugh track kicked in. "Why are they laughing?") Despite the alternative model that seemed to precipitate it, Alan, in framing his question, held faithfully, longingly, to the conventional understanding of the family he'd acquired since coming free of the Clearances. "Who is my mother?" was the way he posed it. "Who is my father?" There's no telling how long he'd been thinking about this question before he asked it. He did not ask *what* he was. He did not know nearly enough about what was possible in the world for that question to occur to him. However he would ultimately put it, it was a question we'd known was coming. We'd given it, and our response, a great deal of thought. This was a less collaborative process than I'm suggesting: it was Anna who'd tell him, and she decided we'd tell him the truth, as simply and as clearly as we could.

Before Anna could begin to answer, he said to her, "You are not my mother." He said this calmly, definitively.

"I'm not," Anna said. "No."

"You are not my father," he said to me.

"No," I said.

"Who is?" he said. "Where are they?"

Alan was not upset. He was curious, determined to find out what he wanted to know, and it was clear he'd not be put off.

"These are good questions, Alan. Important ones," Anna said. "I've been waiting for you to ask, hoping you would. If you will just sit at the table and give me a minute. I need to get something, then I'll be back, and I'll explain everything to you."

I've made her sound condescending. She was not a bit condescending. As always, she was kind and straightforward.

"What will you explain?" he said.

"I'll answer your questions. I'll tell you everything you want to know."

"You will tell me who my mother is? You will tell me who my father is? You will tell me where they are?"

"I'll do my best," she said. "Just sit down and give me a minute. Then we'll talk. Okay?"

"Okay," he said. "Can I have a Coke?"

"Sure," Anna said. "Get yourself a Coke. Are you still hungry?"

"I am still hungry," he said.

"Get yourself a cookie, too, then."

"What cookies are there?" he said.

"What have we got, Ray?" Anna said.

"I think there are vanilla fingers."

"I like those cookies," Alan said. "Vanilla fingers."

"Okay. Have a Coke and a few cookies," Anna said. "Just not too many. I'll be right back."

Anna went upstairs to her bedroom: as much, I knew, to collect her thoughts as to get the book she was carrying when, after five minutes, she came back down.

"Okay, I'm ready," she said.

"I'm ready," Alan said.

"Good," she said. "I've got a book for us to look at."

"What book do you have?" Alan said.

"Let me sit down, and I'll show you." Anna took the chair from the head of the table and pulled it around to the table's side, so she could sit next to Alan. In front of him there was a now-empty plate and a can of Coke. I'd been sitting across from him as he ate his cookies, but when Anna sat down, I moved to a chair across the room. I'm not sure why I did this. Maybe it was simple skittishness, or, let's call it by its right name, cowardice, but I thought it would be harder for him to hear what he was about to hear having to look straight at me.

"It's a book about how babies are made."

"I know how babies are made," Alan said.

"I wondered if you did," Anna said.

"I do."

"Will you tell me what you know?"

"Why?"

"So we can talk about it."

"I don't want to talk about it," he said.

"Why not?"

"Babies are made in the woman's stomach," Alan said. "Then the woman goes to the hospital and the baby comes out and it cries."

"That's right," Anna said. "I wonder if you know how the baby gets inside the woman's stomach."

"From fucking," he said. "Fucking puts it in there."

Anna let the profanity slide. "It is true," she said, "that sometimes when a man and woman make love, a baby is made. Not all the time, but sometimes."

"Sometimes a baby is made," he said.

"When the woman's body is ready to make a baby."

"Then they fuck," he said.

"Here," she said. "Let me show you in the book."

She paged slowly through the book with him, beginning with the section after conception. There were drawings and color photographs of the fetus in the womb at various stages in its development. There were drawings of the birth canal, photographs of the moment of birth, and of the mother (and sometimes father) with the infant just after. Alan was patient and polite, as he almost always was with Anna, but you could tell this was not what he wanted to know. I confess I doubted the wisdom of using a book on human sexual reproduction to introduce the subject of Alan's birth.

Anna closed the book. "Do you have any questions? So far, I mean?"

"I do have questions so far," he said. "Who is my mother? Who is my father?"

I stood up and approached the table. We had not planned for me to participate in this way, and I saw some misgiving on Anna's face.

"Your mother was my mother," I said to him. "Your father was my father." I could not tell what Anna thought of this tack. "You and I had the same mother and father."

"We had the same mother and father," Alan said.

"We did. Yes."

"Your mother was my mother."

"Yes."

"Your father was my father."

"That's right."

Alan thought a moment. Anna put her hand on his.

"You are my brother," Alan said, with neither perceptible joy nor relief nor sorrow.

"We *are* brothers," I said. "We are identical twins."

"What did you say?"

"'Identical' means we are exactly alike."

"We are exactly alike."

"In most ways, yes. We are."

Alan shook his head, not quite in horror. "You are old, Ray."

"I am. Getting older by the minute."

"I am not old."

"No, you're not old," I said. "You're young."

"You don't look like me."

"I don't now. When I was your age I looked like you. Though you look better than I did."

He turned to Anna. "He looked like me. Is it true?"

"Yes," she said. She had no choice but to go along. "He looked very much like you. But you *do* look better than he did."

"We are brothers," he said to me.

"Yes."

"Why are you so old?"

"Because I was made a long time before you were made. You were made a long time after me."

"Do you have any other brothers?"

"No."

"Do you have any other brothers?" he said to Anna.

"I don't have any brothers," she said. "Or sisters."

"Do you have any sisters?" he asked me.

"I don't."

"Do you know your mother?"

"I did," I said. "Yes."

"Do you know your father?"

"I did know him. He died when I was very young."

"Did your mother die?"

"She did," I said. "But later. When I was twenty-two."

"I am twenty-two," he said.

"You are."

"Did I know my mother?" he said.

"No."

"Did she know me?"

"No."

"Was I made in her stomach?"

"No."

"Were you made in her stomach?"

"Yes," I said.

"You were made a different way," Anna said.

"How was I made?"

And it was here Anna explained to him the process of cloning, the insertion of the nucleus of a donor cell into an egg cell from which the nucleus has been removed, etc. I was impressed, and touched, by the care Anna took in her explanation, by how she was able to translate a fairly technical business into language and concepts Alan might, but probably didn't, understand.

When she'd finished, Anna said: "You are what is called a clone. All those boys, all those men you were living with before you came to us, they were also clones, like you."

"I am a clone," Alan said.

"A copy," I said.

Anna made it clear she did not find my use of the government's euphemism helpful or acceptable. "The word 'clone' comes from a word that means 'twig,'" she said.

"The word comes from a word?"

"Yes," she said. "The way you come from Ray. They took a twig from Ray and made you from it."

"What is a twig?"

"It is a small part of a tree. A small branch. Part of a branch."

"I come from a tree?"

"You come from Ray."

"Am I real?"

"Yes," Anna said. "You are very real."

He put his head in his hands. I had never seen him do this. We were quiet for a minute.

He lifted his head and looked beseechingly at Anna. "What am I?"

"You are a person. You are a wonderful boy. A beautiful boy."

Again he put his head in his hands. (He did not get this from me.) This was not in any way a pose. He was thinking hard, and this seemed to help him do it.

To both of us he said, "Did you find me?"

"You found us," Anna said.

"Did you look for me?" He said this to me.

"No," I said.

Then, to Anna: "Did you look for me?"

"I waited for you," she said. "I watched for you."

"Did you miss me?"

"I didn't know you. I'd miss you now if you weren't here."

I'd been standing, awkwardly, by the table. I sat down now, across from Alan, so there'd be less of me for him to look at.

"Did you make me?" he said to me.

"I did not make you. I agreed to have you made."

"You agreed to have me made."

"I said it was okay to make you."

"You said it was okay."

"Yes."

"Who made me?"

"People who knew how to do it," I said.

"Say who they are," he said.

"They are scientists," Anna said. "You know what a scientist is."

"I do know what a scientist is."

"They made you," she said.

"They are not my mother."

"No," she said.

"Who is my mother?"

"Your mother was Ray's mother," Anna said.

"I was not made in her stomach."

"No," Anna said.

"She didn't know me."

"She didn't."

Right here I considered apologizing to Alan. "I am sorry I had you made." I didn't say it, because I wasn't confident that, once it had been said, I could keep control of its meaning. I *was* sorry. For the first time, really. Up to then I'd have contended, however he'd been made, now that he was outside the Clearances it was better for Alan, for all of us, that he existed. In my most complacent moments, watching him, I was gratified to think I had given him life. Removed as I'd been from the process. Now he looked undone, and I thought it would be good to stop there. For the time being, at least. I don't know if Anna thought the same. We had told him who and what he was, and given him more than enough to think on. Imagine hearing that, for Pete's sake. "You're a copy." Like being told you are a figure in someone else's dream. He'd been unnaturalized. Reconceived. De-selfed. Subhumanned. Interesting that the churchy words seem apt: he'd been desecrated, dis-graced, unhallowed. What covenant for him? Maybe I'm wrong. How could any of us know how he was feeling?

Alan was not ready to stop. "Why did you make me?" he said to me. "Why did they make me?"

I told him the truth. "I don't want to say."

"Will you say?" he said to Anna.

"I will," she said. "It is a terrible thing, why they made you."

"Why did they make me?" he said.

"They made you for Ray," she said.

"They made me for you."

"Yes," I said.

"Why?"

"So that . . ." Anna began.

"I should tell him," I said. "I am responsible."

"What did you say?"

"I am to blame," I said. "It is my fault."

"It is your fault," he said.

"Yes," I said. "They made you for me, and it is my fault."

"Why did they make me? Now do you want to say?"

"I don't, but I will. They made you for me, so that if I got sick, or hurt, you would be there to help me."

"I would be there."

"Yes."

"Where?" he said.

"Where you were," I said. "Before you came to us."

"I would be there to help you."

"If I lost an eye," I said, "they would take your eye and give it to me."

"They would take my eye."

"Yes. If I needed a kidney, they would take your kidney and give it to me."

"What is a kidney?" he said.

"It's a part of your body that cleans your blood," Anna said. "You have two of them."

"They would take my kidney," he said.

"Yes. If I needed a lung, they would take yours."

He looked at Anna. "How many lungs do I have?"

"You have two lungs," she said.

"They would take one," he said.

"They would take two," I said, "if I needed them."

"I am a thing you eat," he said. "I am food."

"You are not food," Anna said.

"If I were sick," he said to me, "would you help me?"

"I would now," I said.

"How many lungs does Ray have?" he said to Anna.

"Two."

"If I needed a lung, would they take one of yours and give it to me?"

"No," I said.

"Why not?"

"Because I was not made to help you."

"I was made to help you," he said.

"Yes."

"I am a bag of things you use," he said.

"No longer," Anna said.

Anna intended her remark to be definitive.

Alan stood up and knocked over his chair.

"I did that," he said.

"Don't worry about it," I said.

"You're okay now," Anna said.

He picked up the chair and threw it against the wall.

"I did that."

"You did," I said.

"Don't tell me," he said.

"You're okay," Anna said. "You are safe."

"I am safe," he said.

"Yes," I said.

"Nothing will happen to you," Anna said.

"Nothing will happen to me."

"No," I said.

He took the baby book off the table and threw it the length of the apartment.

"That happened," he said.

"It's okay," I said.

He looked at me. "What do you want?"

"There is nothing I want," I said. "Except for you to be safe."

"Nothing," he said.

"Nothing but that," I said.

"I am going to bed," he said to me. "I don't want you to come in."

Anna stood up. "Alan."

"Not you," he said.

The next morning Alan would not speak to us. He would not look at me. After breakfast, he went to his room, and we did not see him again until lunch, which we passed in silence. After lunch—he did not eat much—he was back in his room until dinner. Anna was worried that, left alone, he might do something to injure himself. She went up to check on him every hour or so, but he would not open his door or in any way respond to her. It was only when he came out to use the bathroom we knew he was all right, by which I mean alive. At dinner he was aggressive, barking orders at us, eating as noisily, as crudely as he could, muttering obscenities between mouthfuls.

"You are angry," Anna said. "You should be angry. But we are your friends. We are here to help you. We are angry, too."

"Shut up," he said to her. "You whore. You hag."

"Stop that," I said. What kind of father would I have been? How would I have treated my son?

"It's all right," Anna said.

"It's not all right," I said.

Alan called me a "fucking ass fuck." Then he said to me, "I am ashamed of you."

I thought I saw him beginning to tear. He ran upstairs to his room and shut his door. We didn't see him again until morning.

He had a good heart, and woke the next day repentant. He called for Anna from his bedroom. She went in and sat down beside him on his bed. She held him for a long time. They held each other. When they came downstairs, it was clear they'd both been crying.

"I'm sorry, Ray," he said.

"I'm sorry, too, Alan," I said.

At the breakfast table he had questions. Among other things, Anna explained the meaning of the numbers on his arm. (He had seen them all his life and hadn't before wondered.) Anna told him about the Dolly Squad, downplaying the menace. She told him about her group, about her participation in it, about their mission to abolish human cloning, and, towards that end, about their plans for him. When he had asked his questions, and she had answered them—one question she couldn't answer was, "What will they do with the other clones?"—he stood up from the table. He looked down at us, and said very quietly, "I don't want this."

In a matter of days we were in Calgary, living in a cramped and tatty two-bedroom, ground-floor apartment on 14th Street SW. Save for the motel room in Thunder Bay, where we spent only one night, this was the shabbiest accommodation we were to have in Canada. Alan and I had to share a bedroom again, which, after what we'd told him—installing a sudden, awful, untenable intimacy—was harder for him, and so for me, than it had been in Ottawa, when we were virtual strangers, and he was new to the world, alienated and, especially to me, openly hostile. Who, what, was I to him now? The drive from Regina to Calgary had been a long one, twelve hours, almost five hundred miles, the three of us in the cab of a clattery quarter-ton pickup the Tall Man had foisted on us before we left Regina. Sitting by the window—depending on which one of us was driving, either Anna or I was in the middle, knees to chest—Alan was quiet and somber. We were all somber. The truth, set loose as it was, had made us fragile and, in a way none of us intended, dangerous to one another.

A week into our time in Calgary I had another heart attack, this second one more serious than the first. Alan and I were out on the street in front of the apartment, waiting, neither of us, I remember—I remember little else about this day—feeling much like talking. Anna had gone to get the truck. It was morning, early June, the day warm and sunny. To the west we could see the mountains, which still had snow. Calgary was a sorrowful place for us, but its situation was sublime. Our plan that morning was to drive downtown to a jewelry store on Stephen Avenue. Just the night before, trying to come up with some way, however symbolic, of substantiating his identity, Anna had decided we would buy Alan a signet ring, engraved with his initials, AG. She ran the idea by Alan and me. I thought it was a good idea, though I didn't expect it would make Alan feel much better about himself or his existential predicament. (That's exactly what it was. Did he exist, *could* he exist, if I also and already existed?) Alan was non-committal, willing but not enthusiastic. At that point we could have found nothing about which he would have been enthusiastic. Except, perhaps, somehow contriving it that I, or he, had never lived.

Anna pulled up in the truck. I opened the door to climb in. I did nothing more strenuous than that. Then, as Anna told me afterwards, I collapsed, smacking my head on the running board as I went down. All I know about what happened next—up until the time I awoke in Calgary General—Anna told me when she came to visit.

The first time she came to the hospital I was heavily sedated and un-responsive. On her second visit, two days after the incident, though I was still in bed, hooked up to a network of wires and tubes, we were able to talk.

"You let out a moan," she said, "a great shriek, as if your insides were being shredded. Then you collapsed. You gave your head a nasty whack when you fell."

"I've noticed," I said. "I'm sorry. That must have been scary to see."

"It *was* scary. Alan was horrified. When he heard you shriek and saw you fall, he started to scream. 'Help him! Help him! Help him!' He shouted this over and over again. He was wild. He was spinning around as if he were trying to find the direction from which help might come. At one point he ran out into the street and tried to stop a car."

"How did I get here?"

"It was an amazing thing," she said. "Out of the blue, this guy and his wife came running up. A young couple, not much older than Alan. They were two blocks off, they said, but they heard Alan's calls for help. The guy was trained in CPR, and he went to work on you. His wife called the police, while I tried to get Alan under control. By the time the ambulance came, you were breathing."

"Poor guy," I said.

"I've got their names written down."

"I mean Alan."

"Oh. Yes. I know," she said.

"Just what we needed."

"Well, I will say your timing was bad."

"You'd think he'd be happy to have me out of the way."

"Oh, no, Ray." Anna said. "He loves you."

"I don't think so," I said.

"Of course he does."

"He loves *you*."

"I think he does love me," she said. "And you."

"Come on," I said. "I'm occupying his place. I'm the, what do they say, *bane* of his existence."

"That's true," she said. "Still, he does love you. I know he does."

"Where is he, by the way?"

"He's out in the waiting room. There's a pretty candy striper at the desk there. He's looking at her."

"He's okay by himself?"

"I think so," she said. "I hope so."

"Had you better get back?"

"I will in a minute."

"Are you concerned he'll talk about it?" I said.

"About being a clone?"

"Yes."

"I'm concerned, sure. I spoke to him about it. I explained it would be dangerous for him to tell anyone."

"He understood?"

"He seemed to," she said. "I don't think he'll say anything. I can't imagine he will."

"Did he want to come in?"

"He was afraid," she said. "He was afraid to see you."

"I'd like to see him."

"Maybe next time. Give him a chance."

When I first regained consciousness I was visited by the hospital's chief of cardiology, a haughty, elegant Egyptian in his early forties. He explained what had happened to me. I'd had a heart attack, which he described as massive. I was lucky to be alive. If it were not for the intercession of my Good Samaritan, I would be dead.

They'd found considerable scarring on the heart, he said, and he wanted the history of the prior incident. I told him I'd had the first attack a year ago in August.

"At that time, what did your physician tell you about your condition?"

He talked as if he were reading a questionnaire, as if neither I nor my condition was worth the time and energy it would take him to generate language afresh.

"He told me we'd need to wait for the inflammation to subside before we could assess the damage."

"What was his assessment?"

There was a chair beside my bed, but he chose to stand for the whole of our conversation.

"I didn't go back for it," I said.

"What do you mean?"

"I left for Canada before it was time. I've been here ever since."

"In Calgary?"

"In various places," I said.

"Did you think to consult a physician in any of these various places?"

"No."

"Are you currently taking any medication for your heart?"

"The doctor in New Hampshire prescribed some drugs. I took them until they ran out. I didn't refill the prescription."

"I have to say, Mr. Grey, you have behaved irresponsibly. You placed yourself in real danger."

"I know that."

"I will need the name of the doctor who saw you after your first attack. I'll want to speak with him. He's in New Hampshire, you said?"

"Yes."

"Although you live in Nebraska?"

"I do not live in Nebraska. I am not Mr. Grey."

"When you were admitted," he said, "they took the information directly from your driver's license."

"I understand. The information is false."

This appeared to interest him.

"What's all this about?" he said.

"I don't want to explain," I said. "I promise you I am harmless and have done nothing wrong."

The damage to my heart was extensive. "Your heart is shot," he said. In his opinion, there was no longer any question that I would need a transplant, and as soon as possible. He asked me if it were at least true I was an American citizen. I said I was. Then he asked me if I'd had a clone made. I said I had. He made no effort to hide his disapproval.

"Whoever you are," he said—I told him my name; he would need it if he were to speak with my doctor in New Hampshire—"whoever you are," he repeated, "we won't do the procedure here. I must tell you that no hospital in the country will do it." In Canada, he said, the waiting list for viable hearts was quite long, demand far exceeding supply. (Not so in America, of course. Plenty of hearts.) As (1) an American who'd (2) been cloned, I would be put at the very bottom of the list, and kept there. The best he could do would be to keep me stable until arrangements could be made for the procedure to be performed in the U.S.

"There is a university hospital in Missoula," he said, "and a first-rate hospital in Spokane. I know surgeons at both places, and both places are relatively close."

"You assume I want the procedure," I said.

"Yes, if you want to live, which I assume you do. You had a clone made."

"Twenty-five years ago," I said.

"You've had a change of heart."

It was a stupid joke. Tasteless. He knew it as soon as he said it. He neither laughed nor apologized, as if, by ignoring what he'd said, to disown it. A joke he'd used before, presumably in more hopeful contexts. I didn't mind the joke. What I found offensive was the man's faultless manicure, and his cuff links, and the fact that he enjoyed standing over me.

"I have," I said. "How long will I live?"

"Without the procedure?"

"Unless you can perform it here."

"I can put you on the list," he said. "That's all I can do. I can tell you, it won't happen."

"How long?"

"A month or two. Three months, at the outside. Providing you stay in bed, stay quiet, don't exert yourself, take your medication. I can't say for sure. Your heart could stop tomorrow."

"When can I go home?"

"Do you mean to New Hampshire? I'd have to advise against that. You won't survive the trip."

"I mean here. Calgary. When can I leave the hospital?"

"Have you got someone to care for you?"

"I do," I said.

"We'll want to watch you for a few days. Then, if you seem stable."

"All right," I said. "Put me on the list."


I waited for Anna's second visit—the second for which I was conscious—to tell her what the cardiologist had said. Alan had again decided to remain in the waiting room.

"Candy striper?"

"No," Anna said. "There's an old woman at the desk. She gave Alan a lollipop. They've got the television on. He's okay." She put a small duffle bag on the bed, at the foot. "I brought you some stuff. Pajamas and toilet articles. Magazines. Candy. Slippers."

"You brought candy?"

"I didn't know," she said, and sat down beside the bed. "I just threw in some things."

"Thanks."

"And I brought you your glasses." She took them out of her purse and put them on the bedside table. "He wants to see you, Ray. Don't think he doesn't."

"I don't think anything. I want to see him, too."

"Maybe tomorrow."

"When he's ready," I said. "Did the doctor talk to you?"

"I'm your wife."

"Right," I said. "Hold it. Let me raise my head up."

"Shall I get the nurse?"

"I can do it." I fumbled through the tangle by my left hand and, by touch, located the appropriate device. "There," I said. "What did he tell you?

"What did he tell *you*?" Anna said.

"All sorts of cheery things. My heart is shot. That's the delicate way he put it. I need a transplant. Without it, I won't live more than a couple of months."

"I am *so* sorry, Ray." She touched the back of my right hand, careful not to disturb the intravenous drip. "*Three* months he told me."

"At the outside. What did you think of him?"

"The doctor?"

"Arrogant jerk," I said.

Anna smiled. "You have trouble with men."

I thought about this. "Maybe I do."

"Have you always?"

"Maybe I have," I said. "Was Alan around when he spoke with you?"

"On the margins. I don't know what he heard."

A nurse I did not recognize came into the room. She spoke to Anna. "Mrs. Grey, your son is asking for you."

"Is he all right?" I said.

"Appears to be," the nurse said. "He asked me to get his mother. I told him it was okay if he came in, but he didn't want to."

"I'd better go," Anna said.

"Will you be back?" I said.

"Yes. Let me just see what he needs."

Anna was back within minutes.

"He wanted to tell me a joke," she said.

"A joke?"

"His first one," she said.

"Momentous," I said.

"It is," she said. "Something about two men and a duck. I didn't follow it. He thinks it's very funny. Requires quacking."

"Did he make it up?"

"I have no idea where he got it."

"How long do we have?"

"A few minutes," she said. "He's nervous, Ray. He told me the joke. Then he asked me how you looked."

"How do I look?"

"You look terrible."

"What did you tell him?"

"I told him you looked good. Like yourself."

"Half the truth."

Anna unzipped the duffle bag and began unpacking it.

"What are you doing?" I said.

"I'm putting your stuff away. So you'll have it."

"Stop," I said. "Sit here."

"I don't want to," she said. "I don't want to sit."

"Please."

She stopped unpacking, but did not sit. "What will you do, Ray?"

"About what?"

"About the transplant?"

"Are *you* asking me this question?"

"Yes," she said.

"You can't want me to do it."

"I don't know what I want," she said. She took a deep breath, then spoke, flatly, ticking off her wants as if she were ordering a meal. "I don't want to lose you. I know that. I want to keep the three of us together. I want to see my children again. My grandchildren."

"There's no way all of that can happen," I said. "You can't have all these things."

"I can't have any." This, too, said matter-of-factly.

"You'll see your children again."

"You think so?"

"That would be too great a price to pay."

"I was willing to pay it," she said.

I didn't know how to respond.

"Just consider it," she said.

"You can't mean this, Anna."

"I do."

"You can't. I can't take a heart. How could I do that?"

"You could. They've got plenty of hearts. They wouldn't have to kill a clone."

"You don't know that. You, of all people, don't need me to say this. However it goes, the heart would come from a clone."

"Someone else's." She was angry. "I don't care, Ray. I swear to you I don't."

"You *do* care. Of course you do."

She was quiet.

"That's not the whole of it, anyway," I said. "The truth is, Anna, three months sounds like just about enough."

I could see this hurt her, and I was sorry.

"What do we tell him?" she said on her way out. "I'm not sure he can handle any more hard news."

When Anna next visited me Alan came with her into the room. They showed up first thing in the morning. Though it was warm out, Alan was wearing his Winnipeg Jets jersey. He was nervous. He stood by the door and did whatever he could to avoid looking at me.

"I'm glad to see you," I said to him. I *was* glad. "You look sharp. I like your jersey."

"Don't say jersey," he said. "Say sweater."

If Alan was a citizen of any country, it was Canada.

"I like your sweater. So, are you coming in?"

"I am coming in," he said. "You got it for me. Do you remember that?"

"I do remember. That was a good night."

"How are you feeling?" Anna said.

"Good. Raring to go."

"What did you say?" Alan was in the room now, standing beside Anna, though still not quite looking at me.

"I'm eager to go."

Alan stated the obvious. "You are not feeling good. You are not raring."

"No," I said. "I'm not exactly raring. I'm tired. But I want to go home." To Anna: "Maybe tomorrow."

"Good," she said. "We'll be ready."

"Anna says you will be all right," Alan said. "They will give you a new heart, and then you will be all right."

"I hope that's true," I said.

"It's true," Anna said to Alan. Then, to me: "Of course it's true."

There was a TV bracketed to the wall opposite the bed. Alan looked up at it. "The TV's not on," he said.

"Turn it on if you want to," I said.

"I don't want to," he said. "I don't want to watch it."

"There's some Jell-O here I didn't eat. Would you like that?"

"No," he said. "What is Jell-O?"

I was unable to lift my hands, one still attached to an intravenous drip, the other to a monitor. I moved my head in the direction of the bedside table. "It's that green stuff on the tray."

"I don't want Jell-O," Alan said. "It looks like goo."

Anna laughed.

"It's good," I said. "You'd like it. It feels slippery and cool going down."

"Why didn't you eat it?" Alan said.

I had no answer.

"I don't want it," he said.

"One thing you can do for me," I said to Anna.

"Okay, but just one thing."

"I'd like to meet with a lawyer before I leave here."

"What for?" she said.

(I was reluctant to speak of this in front of Alan. I had it in mind to make my will. I'd decided to leave my estate—Sara's money, the house, the car—to Anna. Sara's brother and sister had been well provided for; Anna and Sara had been, when I met them, the closest of friends; if it hadn't been for me, their friendship might have been lifelong. If, as now looked unlikely, Anna were to predecease me, the estate would go to Anna's children, to be split three ways among them. Anna was able to find a lawyer who would come to the hospital. He drew up a simple will according to my instructions. He mailed a copy, which I will soon give to Anna, to the 14th Street address in Calgary, and kept a copy for his files.)

"There are some things I need to settle," I said.

Anna shook her head. "I don't want your money, Ray."

"Don't worry," I said.

Then Alan spoke to me. "Will they take my heart, Ray?"

"No," I said emphatically. "They will not take your heart."

"You are free now," Anna said. "No one will take your heart. No one will take any part of you."

"I am still a clone," he said.

"Yes," she said. "But you are safe with me. We are safe together."

Again, to me: "Whose heart will they take?"

"I don't know that," I said.

They stayed a while longer. No more was said on the matter of Alan's heart. Or mine. Then we said good-bye. Alan was somber. I tried to be as chipper as I could.

It was four more days until they discharged me. Anna had arranged to have a hospital bed delivered and set up in the bedroom I'd shared with Alan before I went down. Going forward I would share the room with Anna—Alan moving to the other bedroom—who now became my nurse, so that she would be near if, in the night, I needed her. Alan helped me from the car into the apartment. He was uneasy touching me, as if he was afraid I might shatter. I got into bed, and I have hardly left it these three months.

That first morning back, after breakfast, I asked Anna to get out the boot socks.

"What are boot socks?" Alan said.

"Wait," I said.

"Are they for me?" Alan said.

"Hang on. Will you get the socks, Anna?"

She took the socks out of the dresser drawer. "Now what?"

"I want you to empty them."

"Boot socks." Alan said. "What's in them?"

"Money," I said.

"Is it money for me?" he said.

"Some of it."

"What are you doing, Ray?" Anna said.

"I know what I'm doing."

She emptied the socks onto her bed. There were six stacks of bills, each stack held together by a thick rubber band.

"I don't want the boot socks," Alan said.

"Fine," I said.

"I would like the money."

"I know," I said. Then, to Anna: "Will you take five thousand dollars and put it in one of the socks?"

"Five thousand?"

"Yes."

"You're a sweet man," she said. "But this is crazy."

"We both know I'm not sweet," I said. "And this makes perfect sense."

Anna counted out the bills and put them in a sock.

"Can I have the sock, please?" I said.

Anna handed the sock to me.

"Come here," I said to Alan.

"All right," he said. He came closer.

I handed him the sock. "This money is for you." I said. "You can spend it however you like, so long as Anna says it's okay. Do you understand?"

He took the money out of the sock and held it in his hand. "This money is for me?"

"Yes."

"I can spend this money?"

"Yes. So long as Anna says it's okay."

"If she says it's okay, I can spend it?"

"Yes," I said.

Alan looked at Anna. "No girl," he said.

"No girl," she said.

"There is one thing," I said, "I want you to buy right away. Today."

"You want me to buy it today?"

"Yes. I want you and Anna to go out today and buy a computer."

"I want to buy a computer," he said. "I told you that. Do you remember?" He said this without any enthusiasm, and with more than a hint of recrimination. As if to say my offer was not so much too little as it was too late.

"I do. I want you to buy a computer. Anna will help you pick it out. It will be your computer. But I will use it for a little while."

"It will be my computer, but you will use it?"

"Yes," I said. "For just a little while. Then it will be yours."

"It will be my computer?"

"In a little while," I said.

# Twelve

"You're going to write the report, " Anna said.

"I was thinking I would," I said. "If I can remember how to write."

"Good, Ray. That's good."

"I've got nothing better to do."

"No. You want to write it."

"I suppose I do. I'm not sure why."

When Anna had satisfied herself I was comfortable and safe in my bed, that I would stay put, she and Alan went out and bought a computer. They picked one Alan liked the look of—they paid for it with Alan's money—and Anna set it up.

(I *am* comfortable. As comfortable waiting for my heart to quit in a rented hospital bed in a crap shack in Calgary as I have been anywhere else in Canada. As I have been anywhere else. From my mother I know the Germans have a word, *heimweh*, for the kind of homesickness you feel, even when you are at home. Everywhere you go you find what you find everywhere you go. After Sara died, I have been, without respite, homesick, with no notable increase in the feeling since we washed up here. Moribund heart or no.)

"Besides the obvious, 'Can I write the thing?'"—I had the computer in front of me (the bed came with a narrow rolling table that could be placed across it)—"the question is, 'Will I have the time?'"

This was the middle of June.

Anna would not speak of this imminence. "Listen," she said. "You'll want to use pseudonyms. For all of us."

"What shall I call you?"

"You can call me anything you want?" She smiled. Ruefully. "Not Twink."

"Not Twink. No."

"Make me lovely," she said. "Make me sound lovely."

"You are lovely, Anna."

"That's a lie. That is such a lie. You are such a liar."

"You *are*," I said. "I think so."

"I've been thinking about a name for you," she said.

"What is it? Shitheel?"

"I was thinking 'Ray Bradbury.'"

"Why that?"

"He was a writer. We had his books in the house. My mother read him as a girl. He wrote mostly science fiction."

"Was he good?" I said. "Because I won't be good. This won't be science fiction."

"I'm sure he was good," she said. "I never read him, but my mother liked him. I always liked the name. Sounds confident. Authoritative. Honest."

"I am none of those."

"Become them," she said.

"I want my real name, Ray," Alan said. He was lying on the other bed—it had for a short time been his, but since my return from the hospital, it was Anna's—his clothes on, and his shoes, the pillow laid over his eyes. This was how he was to spend his days, much of them, from then on: lying in that bed—in effect, however dashed he was, keeping me company—while I worked on my report. I wondered what name he had in mind.

"I want to be Alan," he said.

His real name. Even I could see the sad, bitter irony here.

"You will be Alan," I said. "I promise."

Unhappily, for all of us, after he'd bought the computer—he has yet to take possession of it, and no longer cares—there was almost nothing Alan really wanted to buy.

"I want to buy a car," he said, several days after I'd given him the money. He was at his post, splayed out on Anna's bed. I'd begun writing, and was glad for any interruption.

"You don't know how to drive," I said.

"You can teach me to drive. You are a teacher."

"I can't get out of bed."

"When you are better you can get out of bed. Then you can teach me." He took the pillow off his eyes and sat up. "I have an idea. Anna can teach me. Anna is a teacher. She can drive. She can teach me."

"Maybe she will," I said.

Anna heard her name spoken and looked in.

"Maybe I will what?"

"Maybe you will teach me to drive," Alan said. "You are a teacher. I will buy a car, and you will teach me to drive."

She looked at me.

"Don't look at me," I said.

"First I'll teach you to drive," Anna said. "Then we'll see about a car."

"First you will teach me to drive?"

"Yes."

"Then we will see about a car?"

"We'll *see* about it," she said. "I'm not promising anything."

"We will see about it," he said.

The next Sunday morning, in an effort to lift his declining spirits, with the concomitant risk of inflating his hopes, Anna drove the truck over to the middle school not far from our apartment, so Alan could practice in the parking lot. He drove around the lot with Anna beside him. "I had to give him almost no instruction," Anna told me later that night. Alan was in his room. We were in bed. She in hers, etc. We no longer worried about him sneaking out: he had given up that ghost. "I found myself hoping if I let him alone," she said, "he'd drive us into a brick wall, and we'd be finished with it." I laughed. "I mean it," she said. "He drove in wide circles, then narrowed them. He spent a few minutes in reverse. I think, actually, he'd be a good driver. He fooled with the knobs and switches. He turned the lights on and off, flicked the brights. We couldn't see the lights in the sun. He tried the radio, which, of course, didn't work. He honked the horn. When he had done all he could think to do in the parking lot, he looked at me and said, 'Thank you for teaching me.' Then he got out of the truck, and I drove us back to the apartment. There is nowhere he wants to go."

Anna took him to the mall for what she promoted as a "shopping spree."

"We look in all the stores," she told him. "If you see something you like, something you want to buy—if it's a reasonable thing, if you can afford it—you can buy it."

"Is that a shopping spree?" he said.

"That's what I call it," Anna said.

"I will spend *my* money?"

"Some of it," she said. "If you see something you like."

"Will Ray go on the shopping spree?"

"I can't," I said. "I have work to do." Almost unimaginably, this was now the truth.

"He has to write his report," Anna said.

"I know that," Alan said. "Will he remember?"

"Will I remember what?" I said.

"My name."

"You will be Alan," I said. "I'll remember. When you get back, you can show me what you got."

They were back in two hours, more quickly than I'd expected. I was dozing when they came in. I found I could work for an hour, an hour and a half, then I had to rest.

Alan came into the room ahead of Anna. "Ray is snoring," he said. Without another word to me, he slumped onto Anna's bed, unfurled himself, and dropped a pillow over his eyes.

"How was the shopping spree?" I said to Anna. She was in the doorway, holding a large plastic shopping bag loaded with stuff.

She shook her head. "It was good."

She shook her head again.

"Do you want to show me what you bought?" I said.

Without taking the pillow from his head, he said, "Did you ask *me* that question?"

"Yes."

"I don't want to show you what I bought."

"What if Anna shows me? I'd like to see."

"No," he said.

"I'll put the bag in your room," Anna said.

"Thank you," he said.

When that night, after reading with Alan, Anna came to bed—it was, again, awkward for me to sleep with Anna in the same room, but her presence, as nurse-at-ready now, was reassuring, and the medication I took before bed made it easy for me to sleep —I asked her what had happened.

"He's got a bagful of junk," she said. "And he knows it's junk."

"Just junk?"

"He bought himself a camera."

"That's good," I said.

"That *is* good," she said. "We'll need to download the pictures onto the computer."

"All right."

"And he bought some sort of contoured pillow for his bed."

"Okay."

"A pair of mirrored sunglasses. A backpack. The rest is junk. A pen in the shape of a hockey stick. A pair of alligator slippers."

"Made of alligator?"

"Chenille. Alligator heads you stick your feet into. He bought a pedometer."

"What for?"

"I have no idea. For something to buy. He bought a doll."

I had visions of something inflatable. "What kind of doll?"

"A cheap little plastic thing. Like a Dolly doll."

"Not here, surely," I said.

"No. This is 'Pony Girl.' I assume for the Stampede. Different dress, same exact doll. He had to have it," she said. "Of everything he bought, the doll was the thing, the only thing, he seemed really keen on. I had to push him to buy the camera. We went into four or five stores where I thought he might find something worth buying. He got discouraged, pretty quickly lost interest, asked if we could stop. We had something to eat, then we came home."

"Sounds grim."

"Not grim so much," she said. "Sapped. Lifeless. You could see him trying to be good company, indulging me. Finally, he asked if there was something I wanted, something he could buy for me. The whole time he was very polite, concerned I not be disappointed in him."

"Listen, Ray," Anna said the next night. The bedroom was dark, the shades closed, as much to muffle the street noise as to keep out the light. We kept our door open so we could hear Alan. There was a night-light in the bathroom down the hall, but the bathroom door was closed, and the pallor didn't quite make it to our room. No light shone from beneath Alan's door across the hallway. I had fallen asleep. Anna may have had to say my name more than once. "Ray. I need to talk to you about Alan. Are you awake?"

"I'm awake," I said.

"Have you got your wits? I need you to know how he's feeling."

"I've got them. Shoot," I said.

"I will shoot," she said. "He was traumatized by what happened to you. Seeing you go down like that in the street. He thought you had died. We both did. Then seeing you in the hospital, lying there so weak and frail. It scared him. And coming, the way it did, on the heels of his finding out who and what he was. He was shattered. Wrecked. How could he have been anything but?"

"That's a rhetorical question, right?"

"Come on," she said. "Just listen. I can't say exactly what you are to him. His twin, technically, only technically his brother. 'Original' uncomplicates your relationship. 'Friend' is grossly inadequate. He loves you. I know this to be true. As much as he is able to love. In the way he is able to love."

"What do I say?" I said.

"When you were in the hospital, I did my best to bolster him, to piece him back together. First thing I did, I bought him the signet ring."

"He's not wearing it."

"As soon as he put it on, which he did grudgingly, I could see it was wrong. It was an old man's ring, incongruous on him. He wore it the first few days, to please me, then managed to lose it. I combed the apartment, which I see now was cruel. He pretended to help me look. I think he dropped it down a vent. We went for a walk in Prince's Island Park. We had lunch in a different restaurant each day. I could hardly get him to eat. One morning we drove up into the mountains. We went bowling. Nothing helped. I thought about buying him a puppy."

"Don't. Good lord."

"I won't," she said. "He slept a lot. Too much. You see it. When he wasn't asleep, all he wanted to do was talk."

"About?"

"He wanted to know about you. Not just about your heart, though I had to keep reassuring him you weren't going to die, that you'd be coming back. He wanted to know about your life."

"What did you find to tell him?"

"He asked how we'd met. He was interested in that story. I wondered how you'd tell it."

"I don't know how I'd tell it," I said. "I was a jerk."

"Not when we met. That story's sweet. He wanted to know what college was like. Where we slept. What we ate. How and what we were taught. Did we ever get drunk?"

"Did we?" I said.

"I was abashed by the truth of it, which is that I never did get drunk. I never have been drunk. Not even alone with my husband.

You have to wonder why not. He wanted to know if we'd made love. I told him we hadn't, and that, at the time, I regretted it."

"You didn't miss anything," I said.

"That I regretted it still. Afresh. He wanted to hear about Sara, and about why you had never had children. I told him Sara died in childbirth. I described Sara to him as I remembered her. He asked about New Hampshire. I told him I'd been there only briefly, and that he should ask you about it when he saw you next. Has he asked you about it?"

"He hasn't yet," I said.

"He was interested to know what you looked like back then. How you combed your hair. How you dressed. I told him you looked like him, which he already knew, and that your wardrobe hadn't changed a bit.

"He asked me about your parents. *His* parents. I had to tell him I didn't know anything about them. Except I remembered how troubled you were when your mother died. More troubled than sad, I thought."

"Probably true," I said.

"He asked about me, too, of course. He was especially interested in my life as a child, about what it was like to grow up with a father and mother. It puzzled him to hear my father left us when I was very young. We talked about marriage. He wanted to know how old I was when I got married, and how old you were. Had I wanted to marry you? I told him I'd considered it, but that it had not been up to me. We talked about divorce. He wanted to know how many times you could do it. He asked if I'd ever had cancer. I said I hadn't. It turned out he was under the impression that, sooner or later, everyone had cancer. He wanted to know what menopause was. He'd heard about it on TV. Had I ever had menopause? I sure had, I said. I told him more than he wanted to know about that."

"Sounds grueling," I said.

"No. Not at all," she said. "It's exhilarating to have someone to talk to who is so interested."

"I'll bet it is," I said.

"That wasn't a dig."

"It's true," I said. "I don't listen well."

"Well, he stayed interested and engaged no matter what the subject, so long as I was talking about my life, or yours. About life as we'd known it."

Again she was silent. We lay in the dark for a minute or so, and I tried not to fall back asleep. It was nonetheless jarring when she spoke.

"Still, all the conversation seemed to make him no less sad, no less discouraged. I tried to get him to speak about his life, before he came to us. I thought, after I'd spoken so freely, jabbering on about *my* life—whatever else you want to say about it, it's been full—if ever he'd be willing to talk about what it was like for him inside the Clearances, that might be the time. I was wrong. 'I don't remember,' God help him, was all he'd say."

We are into September. I began writing this report in June. If, by some miracle, I live through November, I will be sixty-seven. Already I have made it to an older age than either of my parents. I have outlived my wife and son by nearly four decades. Today, not pressing our luck, Anna threw a party. A cake—decorated with plastic hockey players and a net—candles, and pointy hats. She decreed it everyone's birthday, Alan's and hers and mine. I was able to get out of bed and sit for a few minutes at the table. Anna and I each had a small piece of cake. We sang "Happy Birthday." Alan would not eat or sing.

The Tall Man did not show up at the end of the month as we'd come to expect, then surprised us with a visit two weeks later, in the middle of July. We had not seen or communicated with him since early June, our first day in Calgary. He came in the morning, early, when Anna and Alan were still in their pajamas. I am all but perpetually in my pajamas. They'd been reading *Adam Bede*, which both of them preferred to Dickens, though parts of the book, one character in particular, infuriated Alan. I haven't read Elliot. We'd just sat down to breakfast, mine a somewhat rare appearance at table.

"Good morning," the Tall Man said. "I hope I'm not too early."
To me, he said. "Glad to see you up and about. How are you feeling?"

"Same," I said. "Tired."

"Are you able to work?"

"Some," I said.

"How's it coming?"

"I don't know how to answer that."

"Is there something I can read?" he said.

"When I'm finished."

He smiled. "I'll look forward to it."

"Would you like breakfast?" Anna said to him. "I can fix you
something."

"Thank you," the Tall Man said. "I've already eaten breakfast.
It's my meal of the day. I'm religious about breakfast."

"Don't come here," Alan said. He had not looked at the Tall Man
since his entrance, and, so far as I can recall, had never spoken to him.
"It is not time for you to come. We are eating. Do you see?"

"I do see." The Tall Man smiled. "It's you I've come to see. I
thought we should talk."

"Ass fuck," Alan said.

Anna said, "Alan."

"Now that's impressive," the Tall Man said. "A year with you,
and he says, 'Ass fuck.'"

He meant this as a joke, I thought, but it lacked all light and
warmth.

"Don't talk to her," Alan said.

"Where might we go, he and I?" the Tall Man said, again to Anna.

"Stop talking to her," Alan said. "Talk to *me*."

"That's why I've come," the Tall Man said.

"That's why you've come," Alan said.

"To talk to you. Yes."

"To talk to me."

"Yes," the Tall Man said. To Anna: "This repeating he does.
What's it called?"

"Echolalia," Anna said.

"He's got a mild case," I said, as if we'd actually got a diagnosis.

"Interesting," the Tall Man said. "And tedious."

"Stay with it," I said. "He'll surprise you."

"Shall we talk?" he said to Alan.

"No," Alan said.

"Why not? Do you not want to talk to me?"

"I want you to leave," Alan said.

"I'll leave after we talk."

"I want you to leave now."

"You've come at a bad time," Anna said.

"I need to talk to him. To see what he can do."

"Ass fuck," Alan said again.

"Besides that," the Tall Man said.

"He's been really dark since Ray got sick," Anna said.

"What did you say?" Alan said.

"I said, you've been sad since Ray got sick."

Alan didn't confirm or deny this assertion. Instead—perhaps he was offended by Anna's apologizing—he went to his room. We heard him shut his door.

"Dark," the Tall Man said.

"Maybe another time?" Anna said.

"There's not much other time left," the Tall Man said.

"Next time," she said, "I'll make sure he speaks to you."

"Listen," he said to me, "I know you've been in the hospital. I know about your heart attack." He sat down at the table, and I took this as the kindness it was: he was much less fearsome sitting down, which, of course, he knew. "I also know you decided against a transplant."

He was sitting close, speaking quietly.

"I did."

"It might have been the strategic thing to do," he said. "To go back to the States. Get the transplant. It might have confused them."

"The Dolly Squad."

"Then again, it might have led them straight here."

"I wasn't thinking about them. Should they actually exist."

"They exist, and, I'm sorry to say, they're after you, too, now."

"They'd better come quick," I said.

"They're trying," he said.

He shifted in his chair, trying to find a comfortable position. He was unable to fit his legs beneath the table. He pushed his chair back. Finally, and with considerable effort, even for me painful to watch, he managed to cross one leg over the other.

"So," he said, "I'm sorry this happened."

"Thanks."

"I want to tell you I respect your decision. I'm sure it wasn't an easy one. It was admirable. There's no other way to see it. But I have to say this. It's one thing to make the decision for yourself. Anna's husband, for instance. Quite another to make the decision for someone else. Denying them available care."

"You're speaking from personal experience."

"I am."

Anna took Alan to the library. He didn't want to go, but Anna got him out the door. Her program for cheering him up had begun to wear on them both. There is a satellite branch quite near us, but they went to the Central Library on Macleod Trail. A new building. Lots of steel and tinted glass and a shadeless plaza with a fountain in its center. "Ill-conceived," Anna said that night. She was talking about the fountain. "Cruel, really. Figures of children linked round a jet of water, dancing in the spray. The figures are sentimental. They've put a metal sign in front of the fountain: 'Do Not Play In The Water.' What were they thinking? Hot as blazes, and poor Alan in his long sleeves. I showed him the sign. I pointed out the provocation. He understood, but he didn't react."

She hoped Alan might enjoy—she told me she'd known this hope was unrealistic—or at least be diverted by seeing all the books. It was something to do. They took the bus, still a novelty for Alan, who insisted they sit in the very back. At the library, already crowded when they got there, it turned out the books were hard to find. Except for a capacious children's section—which, in addition to toys and stuffed animals and child-scaled furniture, was, Anna said, brimming with books, and, on this summer day, with parents and their kids reading them—the rest of the main floor was given to rows and rows of partitioned carrels, each with its own computer and headphones.

"We went to the information desk," Anna said. "I asked the librarian where the books were. 'Is there a particular book you want to see?' he said. I said, 'No. We just want to browse.' He said, 'I'm sorry, but the stacks are not open to the public. The catalog is on-line. If there's a book you want, just click on it, and a staff person will bring it to your carrel. It doesn't take long.' 'Is there no way to see the books?' I asked him. 'I'm here with my son. I want him to see what a library is like.' The old man smiled at us. 'This is a library,' he said. 'I mean a library with books,' I said. He repeated that the stacks were private. I asked him, by the way, where they were. 'They're on three levels,' he said. 'Basement. Sub-basement 1. Sub-basement 2. Only library staff is allowed down there.' 'Listen,' I said to him. 'We just want to look. I promise we won't disturb anything. We won't touch the books. We'll be five minutes, tops.' The man said he couldn't let us go. 'What if someone goes with us? Just for a minute.'"

"You wore him down," I said in the dark, from my bed.

"I did," she said. "'I'll tell you what,' he said. 'I've got a break coming in ten minutes. If you guys want to wait, I'll take you myself.' I thanked him. 'So long as it's on the q.t.,' he said."

"He said that?" I said.

"He was sweet. Alan was not happy having to hang around. He found the men's room, and he stayed in there. I had to call in to get him out. There was a door near the information desk. The librarian opened it with a key attached to a wooden paddle. We followed him down one flight of stairs to the basement, where he unlocked another door, and we were in the stacks. 'Literature and History and Philosophy on this floor,' he said. 'You guys go and have a look around. I'll stand right here. You can take your time. I've got a few minutes.'

"I led Alan down the central aisle, to give him a sense of the size of the place, which was huge, cavernous, maybe a hundred yards square. Low ceilings. No windows. There was metal shelving, I'd say ten feet high, on all sides, with almost impassably narrow aisles between the rows. A few yards from the end—we could barely see the librarian—we turned off into the thick of the stacks. We walked, single-file, about twenty yards in the near dark. Though the books were close on either side of us, it was difficult to read their spines. I slid a book out at random. It was something by Henry James."

"What luck," I said.

"I turned to show the book to Alan. I can't really say what I wanted him to see—at that point I wasn't sure why I'd brought him there—and I knew nothing about Henry James to tell him. Have you read James?"

"Not a word," I said. I used to feel some regret about all the books I hadn't read.

"Then the lights came on above us. The librarian called out, 'Is that better?' Though the place was dead quiet, we could only just hear him. I looked at Alan. I held out the James to him. What did I expect him to do with it? He didn't look at the book. He was upset. His face was white. I thought he might be about to throw up. I reshelved the book. 'What's wrong, Alan?' I said. 'I want to go away,' he said. He was frightened. 'Do you mean you want to go home?' I hoped that's what he meant. 'Will you tell me what's wrong?' 'I do want to go home,' he said. 'Then we'll go home,' I said. 'I don't want to be in here,' he said. 'We'll go then,' I said. 'Let's go.' I took his hand and led him back out to the central aisle. I tried to put my arm around his waist, but he wouldn't have it. We walked towards the librarian. Alan walked fast. 'Is your son okay?' the old man asked when we got close. 'Are you okay, son?' 'We're okay,' I said. 'I think we're ready.' 'It can be pretty spooky down here in the dark,' the librarian said. 'I don't like it much myself. I should have turned the lights on sooner.' 'No, no,' I said. 'Thanks for bending the rules.' The librarian smiled. 'Bending, hell. We broke them.'

"I tried to talk to Alan while we were waiting for the bus, but he wouldn't speak to me. He didn't say a word all the way home. Did he say anything to you when we got back?"

"Not a thing. He came in, lay down on the bed, put the pillow over his eyes, went to sleep. What he always does. What do you think it was?"

"Well, I don't think it was the dark. He doesn't seem to mind the dark. Do you think he does?"

"I don't," I said.

"In fact, if I'm right, it was worse for him with the lights on."

"What's your idea?" I said.

"I think it was the shelves. So many of them. Packed in tight. Floor to ceiling just about. All the books on all the shelves."

"And this . . . ?"

"And this reminded him of his life inside the Clearances. How he was kept. How he lived. How he slept. More than reminded him. Took him back. Do you think this is too farfetched?"

"I don't know, Anna."

"No. You weren't there. It must have felt like he was back."

Anna urged Alan to try out the camera he'd bought. To placate her, he took a few pictures: of me in my bed; of Anna standing in front of the living room window; of Anna and me, Anna sitting beside me on the bed. He took two pictures of the television, one with it on, one with it off. He took a strange picture of himself in the mirror, wearing the mirrored sunglasses, taking the picture. He took a picture of his empty bed. We downloaded the pictures onto the computer, and we looked at them together. For the most part, they were clear and sharp and relatively well-composed. The mirror shot—Alan's unwitting experiment in infinite regression—was unreadable. They were, without exception, uninteresting and dull, which Alan—an aficionado, after all—could plainly see. He insisted we delete the whole batch. I said I would. He watched to make sure I followed through, but I contrived to keep the one of Anna sitting beside me on the bed. Which, for all I knew, might have been the one he most wanted scrapped. Anna suggested they go over to Prince's Island Park, where the photo

opportunities would be plentiful. Alan refused. After the library outing, he resisted leaving the apartment, and almost never did.

The Tall Man returned the third week of August. We could no longer
predict or prepare for his arrival. We'd finished lunch. I'd got back into
bed, thinking I might push through another hour on my report before
I napped. (My naps, now, were long and deep, mini-comas from which
I surfaced—so that I might eat—groggy and disoriented.) The day outside, Anna informed me, was inhumanly hot. The apartment's air-conditioning, mostly notional, could not begin to keep up. Alan was
stretched out on the other bed in shorts and a T-shirt; Anna had provided him with a drawer full of short-sleeved things he could wear inside the apartment. He had come to us thin, without an ounce of fat
on him, but strong. He was markedly thinner now. He was lying on
his back, his head on the contoured pillow he'd acquired, his hands
beneath his head. I could see a segment of his tattoo. He had his mirrored sunglasses on (he wore these more and more)—obviating the
need for the pillow over his eyes—and it was impossible to tell where
he was looking, or if he was awake. (I hated these glasses: to see myself reflected in them was unnerving.) The Tall Man, who wore the
same thing whatever the weather—a kind of coolie's uniform: gray
chinos and a blue work shirt, the sleeves rolled up above his hypertrophied forearms, muscly and thick-veined—had come to speak to
Anna. Before he did, he looked in on me.

"How are you faring?" he said.

"Faring all right," I said.

"Do you get out of bed?"

"On occasion."

"Then you might want to come into the living room. Hear what
I have to say to Anna."

"And Alan?"

"Either way," he said.

Alan had been awake and wanted no invitation. He had taken it
on himself to protect Anna from the Tall Man, and, still wearing his
sunglasses, sat down, inscrutable, on the couch close beside her. Hot

as it was, I put a robe on over my pajamas. What the Tall Man said to Anna—you could tell he took no pleasure saying it—when we'd all gathered, was this: we would have to leave Calgary at the end of September. Anna, who must have been expecting something of the sort, told him this would not be possible. I could not be moved. The Tall Man said he understood. That, in negotiating for us an extra month—getting us four months instead of three, as had been the rule—he had bought us as much extra time as he could. And in doing so, he assured us, he had put our lives, and his own, had put the whole enterprise, at unacceptable risk. When the time comes, he told Anna, you and the clone will have to leave Ray here.

"We'll have someone from the group move in with him and see to his needs while he finishes his report."

Anna told him she refused to leave me behind.

"You'll have the choice," he said to her. She could stay with me, or move on with Alan. He didn't say where they'd be going, but, given the pattern, we assumed it would be somewhere in British Columbia.

(I will not live beside the sea.)

"I won't leave Ray," she said.

"That will be your choice. Just know this: if you decide to stay, we'll have to take the clone."

"I won't leave, too," Alan said.

I was touched by Alan's pronouncement, even though I knew it spoke more to his concern for Anna, and her predicament—if he could effectively refuse to go, he would release her from the need to choose—than to his wanting to stay with me.

"I won't leave," Alan said again.

"That's all right, Alan," Anna said to him. "You don't need to worry. We'll work something out."

Alan stood up and approached the Tall Man, so that he was standing directly in front of him. "I won't leave."

"Alan," Anna said. "Come back now. Sit here."

"I'm not afraid of you," Alan said. His head came up to the Tall Man's chest, and he looked, next to him, in all ways impotent and small.

"You should be, son."

"I'm not your son," Alan said. "I am no one's son. I am not afraid."

"Then take off those damn glasses," the Tall Man said. "Let me see your eyes."

Alan took off the glasses and looked straight at the Tall Man. "Do you see my eyes?"

"I do."

"I am not afraid."

The Tall Man studied him. "I can see that."

"I don't care if I die," Alan said. "Did you know that?"

"No," the Tall Man said.

"Do you care if you die?"

"Yes, I do," the Tall Man said.

"Then you should be afraid of me."

"Maybe I should."

"I know what you want me to do," Alan said. "I know what you want me to do. I won't do it. I won't do it for you."

"You won't?"

"No," Alan said. "I won't do it."

"Yes, you will," the Tall Man said. "Believe me. You will do it."

"I *don't* believe you."

The Tall Man put his hand on Alan's shoulder. There was nothing rough or threatening about this gesture. Alan moved out from under his touch. "That was good, son," the Tall Man said. "Well done. Well spoken." He turned to Anna. "Devil his due," he said. "You've done well." He looked at me. "Both of you."

That night, when Alan had gone to bed, I told Anna I was proud of him. I knew Anna was fretful. She'd left the oven on, the milk standing out, the door to the freezer open, neglected to flush the toilet. Such undomesticated things as she never did. She'd snapped at Alan for the most trivial offense (I don't remember what it was), and for the first time, she'd sent him to his room. I'd meant to find something positive to say about what had transpired.

"You're proud of him?"

We were in bed, the lights off.

"Yes. I am."

"Who cares about your pride? What difference can it make? If I lose you, Ray."

"As, one way or the other, you will."

". . . I will have lost, or be lost to, all and everyone I loved." She shook her head, as if chasing off a bad dream. "You don't want to know this."

"Listen, Anna. There'd be no percentage, no special virtue, in your staying with me. It is Alan who needs you."

I needed her, I *need* her, too, though she can do me much less good, and, whatever my needs, they will be short-term. Which is what I told her.

"You need me," she said.

I am not so insensible that I didn't understand what she wanted me to say.

"I do." I was glad I couldn't see her.

She claimed she couldn't say what she would do, but we both knew, if it came to that, she would go.

The next day was hot again. Outside the streets were baking, and there was not much relief to be had inside the apartment. We were already jagged, the freakish (for Calgary), insistent heat another edge.

That's not quite true. I didn't seem to register the heat. What the Tall Man said did not signify a change in *my* prospects. It remained probable I would die before the end of September, and that Anna, without having to choose, would go on with Alan to British Columbia, to wherever they were sent. It was hard to know how Alan was feeling. He spoke even less frequently, only in terse pellets of speech. He spent most of the day silent and supine on Anna's bed. I could never tell if he was looking at me, watching me work (the pretext for this proximity was that he was helping with my report). He wore the mirrored sunglasses all the time now. He came out for breakfast with them on, and wouldn't take them off, supposing he did take them off, until he went back into his room at night. It was Anna who was

jagged, vexed, working full tilt, if I know her, to find the solution to
a problem that would, in short order, solve itself.

In the late afternoon—by then it seemed as if the air-conditioning
had capitulated—Anna came into my room (*her* room as well) to say she
had a favor to ask of us, Alan and me.

"Is he awake?" she said.

"I don't know," I said.

"Alan," she said. "Are you awake?"

"Yes," he said.

"Would you mind sitting up?" she said.

"Why?" he said.

"There's something I want to ask you and Ray."

Alan sat up.

"I'd like it if you'd take off your sunglasses," she said.

"I wouldn't like it," he said.

"Will you do it anyway, please?"

"I won't do it," he said. This was neither defiant nor belligerent.

"Leave them on then," she said, "but listen. I didn't get any sleep
last night. The heat."

"And I was snoring," I said.

"You always snore," she said. "Last night you were extravagant."

"It must be the medication."

"Do I snore?" Alan asked.

"You don't," she said.

"Why don't I snore?"

"Because you're young and fit and good-looking," I said.

"Is that true?" he said to Anna.

"It is true that you're young and fit and good-looking," she said.
"Maybe it's true that's why you don't snore. Now listen. I want to
sleep by myself tonight, boys. I'll sleep in your room, Alan. You can
sleep here, on my bed. Do you mind? Just for a night or two."

"I don't mind," Alan said, which surprised me.

Anna went to bed early. Alan stayed up a while in the living room
by himself. It was past eleven when he came in. I'd been asleep for an
hour. Alan switched on the ceiling light, a garish bulb in an open fix-

ture that did nothing to soften the glare. I was sleeping on my back, which is how I start out, and the light woke me.

"Turn the light off, will you?" I said.

"I won't turn the light off," he said.

"Why won't you turn it off?"

"I don't want it off," he said. "I want to talk."

"We can talk in the dark," I said.

"I won't talk in the dark," he said. It began to seem he might be being disagreeable for sport, or reviving, in a more articulate version, an erstwhile mode of behavior. "I don't want to go to sleep. I don't want to go to sleep in this bed."

"Why not?"

"Because you snore," he said.

"Where will you sleep?"

"I will sleep on the couch."

He was wearing a green T-shirt and, in lieu of the shorts he routinely wore inside the apartment, a darker green bathing suit. (He still would not undress in front of me.) Anna bought him the bathing suit thinking she might be able to find him a place to swim. Though minor, still another sadness. We surmised Alan had never been swimming, didn't know how to swim. There was the problem of his tattoo. Anna hoped to find, in her words, a swimming hole, where she might take him after dark, so that he could wade and paddle around, get a feel for the water, cool off. Alan expressed no interest in swimming, but he liked to wear the suit. It was loose and baggy and didn't necessitate his wearing underwear.

He had his sunglasses on, and his Jets cap. That he had aspirations to, but no sense of, fashion is understandable. The same could not be said for me. He sat down on Anna's bed, his feet on the floor. He leaned forward, halving the space between us. I turned on my side to face him.

"Did you ever make love to a woman, Ray?"

He took something out of the side pocket of his bathing suit, but I couldn't yet see what it was.

"Yes," I said. "What have you got there?"

His response was to hold up a small pink plastic figure I was slow to recognize.

"What *is* that?" I said.

He didn't say, but, whatever it was, he continued to hold it up so I might see it.

It was, I saw, the Pony Girl doll Alan had been determined to buy on his shopping spree. He'd taken off the doll's pony dress, a pinto shift with hood. What remained, what he was showing me, was the doll undressed. There was no attempt at anatomical correctness. The doll was a cheap, junky plastic thing: head (it had no hair; it was meant to be seen with its hood up), arms, legs, undifferentiated torso; the whole figure no more than five inches tall. I knew it, of course, as a Dolly Doll: the same plastic figure dressed, shift and hood, in imitation fleece. Each year, come Dolly Day, they sell millions of these things.

"Oh, right," I said. "The doll."

"To a woman?" he said.

"Yes."

As we talked, Alan dismembered the doll, pulling off its arms and legs and head—all affixed to the torso by a kind of ball-and-socket snap joint—then put it back together. He performed this action repeatedly, deftly, without looking at the doll in his hands, the action unmistakably reflexive and unconscious.

"You made love to Anna," he said.

"I mean my wife."

"Her name was Sara," he said.

"Yes."

"You made love."

"Yes."

"How many times did you make love?"

"I don't know," I said. "We were married. A number of times."

"How long were you married?"

"Seven years."

"You made love a number of times."

"Yes."

"How many times?" he said. "One hundred and forty-four times?"

I couldn't help but laugh. "Where did you get that number?"

"It's a gross," he said. "One hundred and forty-four."

"I know," I said.

"How many times? One hundred and forty-four?"

"I don't know, Alan."

"Did you also make love to Anna?"

He kept working away at the doll, pulling it apart, snapping it back together.

"No," I said.

"I mean before."

"Before I was married?" I said. "No. Never."

"Will you make love to her?"

"I won't make love to anyone."

"Will I ever make love to a girl, Ray?"

"Maybe you will."

"Maybe I will," he said. "Is it good?"

"Making love?"

"Yes."

"Sometimes it is," I said.

"Sometimes it is."

"Yes."

"Sometimes it's good," he said.

"Yes.

"Sometimes it's not good?"

"Yes," I said. "I suppose sometimes it's not good. I mean, it's not always the same."

"It's not always the same."

"It depends on a lot of things. How you're feeling. How she's feeling. What time of day it is. The weather."

"It depends on the weather?"

"In a way," I said. "Yes. It does. It depends on a lot of things."

"Does it hurt?"

"Does it hurt whom?"

"Does it hurt the girl?"

"It can," I said.

"Why can it?"

"If you're too rough," I said.

"I wouldn't be too rough," he said.

"I'm sure you wouldn't."

"I wouldn't hurt her."

"Listen, Alan," I said, thinking, too late, I ought to end the conversation, which could lead only to more frustration and sadness for him. "It's not something to get all worked up about."

"I am all worked up."

"I know you are. I'm sorry."

"You're not worked up about it, Ray, because you're old."

"You may be right."

"I may be right," he said. "When you were my age, were you worked up about it?"

"Not really," I said.

"Did you love Sara?"

"Very much."

"Do you love me?"

"I do love you," I said, before I had a chance to think about it.

"Do I love you?"

"I don't know."

"I don't know either," he said. "Do I love Anna?"

"She loves you. I know that."

"I know that, too," he said.

He didn't say anything for a minute. He may have been thinking about what I'd said, and/or coming to grips with my uselessness. Then he stood up and walked to the door. He turned to look at me. He held up the doll, intact.

"I made this," he said.

"I know," I said.

"You don't know."

"I was watching you."

"You weren't watching me," he said.

"I was."

"You weren't watching me. You weren't there," he said. "I made this doll."

He turned off the light.

# Thirteen

We are just about out of time.

It is the 25th. We have—thirty days hath September—after this one, six days.

As I write this, Anna is in the kitchen making dinner, opening and closing cupboards and drawers, clanging pots, rattling flatware, trying desperately to keep herself occupied. Alan is in Anna's room. He locked himself in there this morning, when the Tall Man left, trailing havoc, and has not come out.

We have gone from the soup to the shit.

The Tall Man showed up about the time we'd finished breakfast. Alan was at the table looking over the Michelangelo bible, which I inscribed—beneath the Kolberg's inscription to their daughter—and gave to him as a gift. "To Alan:" I wrote. "My roommate, my brother, my friend. With admiration and affection. Ray." Beneath that, "Calgary" and the date. Uninspired stuff. I'd bought the thing as a prop, under duress, and was merely handing it down. I watched Alan read the inscriptions. He made no comment. He seemed interested in the color plates. It had long been my plan to give him the bible when the time came.

"I'm sorry," the Tall Man said. "Again I've come at your breakfast."

"We've finished," I said.

"Sit down," Anna said.

"Thanks, I won't," he said. "I'll not stay long. I've come to tell you, I regret to tell you, that your decision is academic now."

"What do you mean?" I said.

"I mean you can stay with Ray." Glancing at Alan: "We've decided to take him."

Alan did not look up from the bible.

"Take him?" Anna said.

"We think he's ready."

"You can't take him." Anna said.

"Of course we can."

"He's not nearly ready," Anna said. "I need more time with him."

"We think he's ready. You have until the first of the month."

"That's not enough time," she said. "I promise I'll tell you when I think he's ready. I won't need too much longer."

"It's not your decision," he said. "I'm sorry. But there's no surprise here. This was the plan all along. Just a matter of when. I'll be back for him on the first. At noon. We'll expect you to have him packed."

"Please don't do this," Anna said. "Don't take him from me. There can't be such a rush."

I was, belatedly, about to say something—no doubt callow and inflammatory—when Alan stood up.

"Listen to me," he said.

"I'm listening," the Tall Man said.

"I will not go with you."

"You will go," the Tall Man said.

"Where will you take him?" Anna said.

"I can't tell you that."

"Let me come with him," she said. "I can still be of use."

"I'm sorry," the Tall Man said. "I did what I could. It's my sense that you, *and* I, have become a nuisance. You can take consolation in this: he will be very useful. Very effective."

"I will not be useful," Alan said.

The Tall Man smiled. "You will not only be useful, son, you will be revolutionary. Transformative."

"What did you say?"

"You will change everything."

Late in the afternoon Anna came into my bedroom. She woke me up. We had not spoken since the Tall Man's visit.

"I've been trying to think of a way to keep them from taking him," she said. "Some way to forestall it. He won't go willingly. We know that. They'll have to take him. I'm afraid they'll hurt him. Or he'll hurt himself."

I humped myself up into a sitting position, my back against the crummy headboard.

"I should just take him and go," she said. "Right away. Leave the country. We could move from place to place. You could help us, Ray. You could give us some money."

"I would," I said. "Of course. If that's what you decide to do."

"I don't know," she said. "I don't even know how far we'd have to go, or if we *could* go far enough." She sat down on Alan's bed. "He won't go," she said. "I know he won't."

"Why won't he?" I said. "With you he'd go."

"I don't think so. Not now. I'll tell you, Ray. I think he's decided to die."

"What makes you think that?"

"I just think so," she said. "Watching him, this morning."

"I didn't see that, Anna," I said. "He seemed pretty combative."

"Maybe I could inflict some injury. The way boys used to shoot off their toes. I could do something that would make him useless."

"Like what?" I said. "Cut out his tongue?"

"I couldn't do anything to cause him pain."

"I know you couldn't."

"Not even to save him from pain? Not even then?"

"I don't know, Anna."

"Here's what I know," she said. "I'm his friend. Maybe his first friend. I'm his teacher. But I have no rights in this matter. I am not his mother. I'm not his wife. Or his lover."

"Still," I said.

"I am furious, Ray. With the Tall Man. With the group. I'm more furious with myself. My complicity. My naivete. For this, for them, I was willing to leave my own children behind. What sort of mother does that? For any reason. For any cause. For someone I'd never met. No matter how much he was you. What do I do, Ray? What would you do?"

"If I were you?"

"Yes," she said. "Tell me something."

"I would let him go. I would let them take him. You've done what you could. You've given him a year. You've cared for him very well. You've cared for me. Christ, you've been magnificent."

"Thank you, Ray."

"I'd let him go, Anna. And me. I'd let me go. I'd go back to my children."

"I'd be putting them in danger," she said.

"Ahhh," I said. An old man's sound. A dismissive sound my father—he didn't live to be an old man—might make when he wasn't as sure as he wanted to seem. "There's got to be some way to do it."

At dinner that night, last night—I write this after breakfast the following day, September 26—Alan offered me his heart. Anna and I were at the table. I was eating dinner; Anna couldn't bring herself to eat. Alan remained locked inside her bedroom. She'd announced three times at the bedroom door that dinner was ready. He did not respond. She was concerned he might do, might already have done, something to himself.

"I don't hear him in there," she said to me. She pushed her chair back and stood up. "I'll be right back."

She left the apartment. She was gone several minutes. "I went around the side of the building," she said when she returned. She was daunted, out of breath, this woman who never flagged. "I thought I'd be able to see him through the window, but he had the curtains drawn.

A light was on. I rapped at the window, called his name. What do we do?"

"I guess we wait," I said. "He'll come out. He'll get hungry, and he'll come out. You should eat something."

"What if he's not all right?" she said. "Shouldn't we try to open the door?"

"How would we do that?"

"We could jimmy the lock," she said. "There's a little hole in the knob. I've got a bobby pin."

Before Anna's idea could be tested, as if thinking about fooling with the lock was enough to open the door, we heard Alan come out. He looked fine—calm and steady-eyed. I found his composure worrisome.

"Oh, thank goodness," Anna said.

He approached the table. He did not sit down or speak. He stood facing us.

"Are you hungry?"

A simple question that, in the circumstances, sounded discordant.

"I am not hungry," he said to her.

"Sit with us," I said.

"I won't sit with you." He looked at me, and said quietly, as though he didn't want Anna to hear, "I want to give you my heart."

"No," Anna said.

"I want you to take my heart," he said to me.

"No," Anna said more emphatically.

Alan persisted, not looking at Anna. "I want to give you my heart, Ray."

Anna stood up. "Absolutely not," she said. I was not surprised by her choice—or by how unhesitant and unqualified it was—and took no issue with it. "You just put that out of your mind," she said.

"It is not *your* mind," Alan said.

"I don't care," she said. "I don't want you to say that again. I don't want you to think it." She tried to take him in her arms, but he deflected her.

"I will think it," he said. He hadn't raised his voice.

"You will not think it," she said. "You will not say it." She turned to me. "Ray?"

"Listen to me, Alan." I stayed sitting. "I'm touched you would make such an offer. I'm happy, and I'm sad, at the same time, that you would say you want to give me your heart. I am happy you like me enough to say it. You are very generous to say it. It shows you are a good man. Which I already knew about you. But it makes me sad to hear you say it. I can't take your heart. I won't take your heart, because I like you, too. And because it would not be right." I looked at Anna, who seemed to want me to enlarge. I could think of nothing else to say. I resorted to the sentiments and language of movies, and, though Alan would not have known this, debased us all. "You are a young man," I said, "and you have most of your life left to live. I am an old man. I have already had my life. It would be wrong of me to take your heart, and I won't do it. But I am grateful to you. You are noble and very brave."

I looked at Anna. Then, to Alan: "Okay?"

"No," he said. "I am a clone."

"That is true," I said. "But you can be whatever you want."

"I can be nothing else."

"You can," I said.

"I can't be you."

"You wouldn't want to be."

He looked at Anna.

"Please," he said.

"No," Anna said.

He looked at me.

"No, Alan," I said.

That stood as the last word. Alan went back into Anna's bedroom and locked the door.

I've had a night and most of a day to think about Alan's offer, to which my response, in the moment, was derivative and glib, incommensurate. It is now late in the afternoon, and, except to use the bathroom—during these excursions, we thought it better not to waylay him—Alan has been locked inside Anna's bedroom. We have not seen him eat in at least a day. Anna is afraid he is starving himself.

The first thing to say about it, his offer, is that it was no mere gesture. If I was willing to accept his heart (Anna would have killed me first), he would give it to me. He understands about death, and, from his conversations with Anna subsequent to our telling him who he was, he knows he would surely die if his heart is taken. By any measure, his offer was heroic.

What I can't quite work out is why he made the offer. Even if Anna is right, and he does care more about me than he lets on, that doesn't explain why he is willing to die so that I might gain a few more unproductive, superfluous years.

There is this: Alan's willingness to sacrifice himself for me, and by doing so, to live out his purpose as a clone, is nothing short of revolutionary, and, thus, paradoxically, fully human. It would be almost certainly the first and only time a clone would have served his original by choice, as an act of free will. The first time, for that matter, a clone would have exercised his free will in *any* meaningful way. He might not be able to articulate it, but I think on some level Alan knows this.

This, too: having heard us talk about it, Alan understands that, when he somehow came free of the Clearances, he became, irreversibly, a grave and intolerable threat to the government. So that now, wherever he goes, they will pursue him without letup until he is captured, and that, once captured, he will be executed. He knows, too, more proximately, what his life will be like for however long he is to survive under the protection of Anna's group. If they have him—they already have him—and have their way, he will be "celebrated" wherever they permit him to surface. He will be the public face of the movement. He will be required to speak out against the idea of cloning and clones. To speak out against himself. To be his own nemesis. Safe to say that Alan would want neither of these alternatives. I believe he preferred to help me, rather than to die at the hands of his makers, or to be pitilessly traduced at the hands of his keepers.

I don't mean by this in any way to devalue his offer, just to understand it. I think if he was able or willing to talk about it, he would acknowledge that, given the alternatives he is facing, his decision to give me his heart was not simply "heroic." I think his decision was meant to approximate an instance of altruism, to (forgive me) replicate it, and thereby to enter, or almost enter, the human community of human selves. Which community, which version of selfhood, he idealizes and sadly overestimates. But I believe he sees giving me his heart as the only way he can participate in a human life he will, otherwise, have no chance to live.

If Alan was in my position, needing a heart, and I was in his, with a healthy heart to give, would I make the offer? I would not.

Three days have passed. It is now September 29. The interim has been fraught. I have not written a word.

When Alan reappeared—he'd stayed closeted and we'd not seen him since he'd made his offer the night before—it was dinnertime, on the 26th. We'd finished our meal, but were still at the table. Alan sat down as if nothing of moment had passed between us. He asked Anna if there was anything left to eat.

"You must be starving," she said.

"I am starving," he said.

Anna made up a plate and put it in front of him.

"Thank you," he said. "This will taste good to me."

I believe, at this point, Anna knew what was coming next, what Alan had decided to do. I was happy to see him eating, as was Anna, but I—not the deepest diver—did not think to think about any decision he might have been meditating.

His demeanor, I would have said, was pleasant and entirely unforeboding. When he'd done eating, he said there was something he wanted to ask us. He was courteous enough to include me, but it was Anna he wanted to speak to.

"How do I die?" he said to her. He was calm. He might have been asking where we kept the cereal.

"What are you asking me?" Anna said. She knew full well.

"I'm asking you, 'How do I die?' I don't know how to die. How do you do it? You tell me."

"There is no reason for you to die," she said.

"There is not no reason," he said. "How do you do it, Anna?"

This exchange began a discussion about Alan's determination to die that lasted the better part of two days, and was exhausting for Anna, less so for me (Alan was inexhaustible), and in which discussion—I participated, between irresistible naps, as a kind of subaltern—we were able to say nothing either to dissuade or divert him from his resolve. Afterwards, Anna insisted we agree to talk no more about it, so as not to wreck the time we had left, however it ended.

At some latter point in the conversation, Anna did reluctantly address his initial and persevering question. "When the time comes," she said to him, "if you still want to do it, I will find a way for you."

"I will still want to do it," Alan said.

"I hope you won't," she said. "I pray you won't."

"When will the time come?"

"We have until the thirtieth to decide."

"What day is today?" he asked me, the mathematician.

I thought about lying to him, rigging the game, but I told him what day it was.

"We have four days," he said, and from that moment, he kept scrupulous track.

Anna tried to find ways they could pass the time they had left together with some steadiness, some peace of mind—*her* steadiness, *her* peace of mind; Alan was steady and at peace—ways, more or less, to keep him, them, occupied. (In bed most of the time, I was not much of a diversion.) "I feel like Scheherazade," she said to me, then had to explain the allusion. She knew her plan—wholly ad hoc, seat of the pants—in the end amounted to nothing other than a plan to turn him over to the group. She needn't have tried so hard. She was not happy or at peace, not for a moment, no matter what they did. However short the time would be, for her it was purgatory. And Alan, irrespective of her efforts, was, except for scattered moments of frustration,

happier than we'd ever seen him. He was unfailingly good company.
He spent some time sitting on the bed opposite mine—Anna had re-
installed herself in my bedroom—and, in my presence, he did no
brooding or stewing, showed no fear or regret. Admirable boy, he was
self-contained. He didn't speak of his, if he followed through, impending death. He grew increasingly, unnervingly peaceful, until, at the
last, he was so serene, Anna said, it broke her heart.

The 28th was a Sunday, and Anna took him to church, a Lutheran
church not far from the apartment. "Besides us," she told me later,
"there was almost no one there. I gave no commentary on what was going on. Where would I have begun? We had not talked about God.
Maybe that should have been the first thing we talked about."

That evening, the three of us were at the table, having dinner
together. Alan asked us what was the best time we'd had together,
Anna and I, when we were young. Anna told him about the day we
spent driving around northwestern Iowa in my old Volvo, and about
stopping at that roadhouse in Le Mars for steaks and sweet potato
fries. Alan wanted to know if sweet potato fries were different from
the french fries he ate at every opportunity. Anna told him. She told
him, also, that years later, long after I'd left Iowa for New Hampshire,
with Sara, that she and her husband would go dancing at that same
roadhouse.

"I would like to dance," Alan said.

I thought he was merely musing. So did Anna, apparently.

"I would like to dance," Alan said again, looking at Anna.

"With me, you mean?" she said. "You want to dance with me?"

Once, early in our domestic adventure with Alan, Anna told me,
"There are too many times with him, when I say something, some-
thing I believe is innocent, guileless, and I hear how flirty it sounds."
There was nothing flirtatious about her now.

"Yes," he said. "I would like to dance."

Anna found some music on the radio, and they danced in the living room of the apartment. I recognized the song they danced to. It
was "Dandelion Wine." Anna tried to teach him the box step, but he
couldn't get it. He was clumsy and self-conscious—the floor was car-

peted, which didn't help—and seemed to have almost no rhythm. I was self-conscious, too, watching them dance—I was surprised he'd let me watch—and would have been, in his place, equally clumsy. Alan quickly got frustrated, and they stopped.

Anna was desperate he not feel defeated. Before he could go to his room, she said, "Hold on, Alan."

"What?" he said.

"Would you like a girl?" she said. "Would you like me to get you a girl?"

"You're a good dancer," he said. "I'm the bad one."

"You're not bad," she said. "You're inexperienced. You haven't danced before. You'll be good. But I don't mean that."

"I won't be good," he said. "What did you mean?"

"I mean, do you want me to get you a girl?"

"A girl to dance with?"

"A girl to be with," she said.

Alan looked at her. He was incredulous. You could see him think it over. Then he said, "No, thank you."

When Alan had gone to his room, Anna turned to me and said, "Can you believe it?"

"Can I believe what? That you offered to get him a girl? Or that he turned you down?"

"Both," she said. "Either. If he'd wanted me to, I would have figured out how to do it. You would have told me."

"I wouldn't have known," I said.

"Well, I would have done it. I think I would. Can you believe it?"

"No," I said.


Alan is dead. He died last evening, the 30th of September, at approximately ten o'clock. He was twenty-one, or twenty-two. We can't be sure how old he was. Anna and I were with him. He'd decided to die, and we cooperated, helped him do it.

We'd thought it through. The three of us. Alan was thinking clearly. I was floored by the clarity, the acuteness of his thought. He was calm and, in his fashion—which I'd grown accustomed to and, impersonating him in this report, fond of—articulate. He was analytic. "It was like listening to you," Anna said before she left. "The way you talked, back in Iowa, when you used to talk, when you were interested in ideas, in people. Like you at your most alive and direct, least qualifying."

By the end—some days before the end, really—Alan had become fixed, unshakeable in his intention. There was nothing we could say, nothing we could do, except refuse our help, to stop him. (It's not clear how he might have proceeded without our help.) Anna's position— she held it to the end—was that she didn't want him to do it, no matter what might happen once they took him. Still, when it came time, she helped him. Because—about this there was no doubt—she loved him, and didn't want him to suffer. I had no position. I preferred neither of the possible outcomes, found them both objectionable. ("Objectionable?" "Prefer?") There was no choice to make—his was a choiceless choice—but I think, in part, perhaps, because *I* was ready to die, he made the right one. But I didn't want him to suffer. I would try to be of use.

We were with him. Anna handed him the pill. She filled the glass with water. Menial tasks that made her his executioner, me her accomplice. Say what you want, we are responsible for his death. I watched him die. His head was in Anna's lap.

Anna thought to make the night of the 30th routine and uneventful, slow and sleepy and idle, on the ghost of a chance that Alan had lost track of the date. I believed what she had in mind for the next morning, should we all get through the night, was to plead with the Tall Man to give her just a little more time.

We ordered out for pizza and ate it in front of the television. I can't tell you what we watched. I watched Anna. She was agitated, alert to Alan's mood and behavior, tracking the time.

A little before nine, Alan stood up. "I'm going to my room," he said.

"Are you going to bed?" Anna said.

"I'm not going to bed."

"Will you come back out?" she said. "Shall we wait for you?"

"Yes," he said. "Wait for me."

It took Anna only a few minutes to clean up from dinner—she went at it as though her life, somebody's life, was at stake—just a pizza box to flatten and dispose of, three plates and glasses to wash. As she finished, Alan came back into the room. He was wearing my clothes. A pair of my dark dress slacks, a white button-down shirt of mine, and my sport coat, the glen plaid. He was in his stocking feet, in his own socks. He was holding one of the two ties I'd brought with me. I'd not worn either of them.

"You look smart," I said.

"What did you say?" he said.

"You look good," I said.

"Handsome," Anna said.

He held the tie out to her. "I don't know how to tie it. Will you tie it?"

"If I can remember how," she said. "What about you, Ray?"

"You do it," I said.

"I used to do this for my husband," she said, "and for my boys. It's been a while." To Alan: "Come here to me."

He did as she asked.

"First we need to unbutton your collar."

"My collar is unbuttoned," he said.

"I mean these two little buttons here." She undid the buttons at the points and turned up the collar. He tilted his head all the way back to give her room to work. "There," she said. "Now turn around."

"Why?"

"That's the only way I know how to do it," she said.

He stood with his back to Anna. She reached around his neck and tied the tie. She made a simple knot, nothing fancy. It was better than I could have done. "Face me now," she said. She buttoned the collar down, then pulled up the knot and straightened the tie. "Step back," she said. "I want to look at you."

Alan stepped back.

"Not such a good job," she said. "Let me try again." She was using whatever was at hand, rallying what little remained.

"No thank you," he said. "Don't try again."

"You look sharp," I said again.

From this point on, I would only watch.

"Very snazzy," Anna said.

"Did you find a way for me?" he said to Anna.

I'm sure her instinct was to feign ignorance, but, to her credit, she didn't. "I don't want to, Alan. I don't want you to do this."

"You said when the time came you would find a way for me. The time came."

"Please," she said.

"I say 'Please' to you."

"Let's sit and talk," she said.

I felt my heart sag.

"What is the way, Anna?" he said. "How do I die?"

Anna sat down on the couch. Alan remained standing. "Did you find a way?" he said.

"I have a way," she said.

"What is it?"

"Give me a minute," she said. "I need just a minute."

"All right."

"Sit beside me. For just a minute."

Alan sat down. She took his hand in both of her own. "His hand was dry and cool," she would tell me later.

"I don't want you to die," she said.

"I want to die," he said.

"I know you do. I know you do."

"What is the way you have?"

"Sit here," she said. "Stay here with Ray." She got up and went into the bedroom that was again Alan's. She'd put the envelope of pills the Tall Man gave us in a dresser drawer, underneath her socks. She took one of the two pills out of the envelope, and put the envelope back in the drawer, not bothering to hide it. There is no other way for me to imagine this.

She came back into the kitchen and filled a glass with tap water.

"Come with me," she said to Alan. He followed her to the bedroom. I followed him.

"Have you got the way?" he said.

"I do," she said.

"I don't know how to do it," he said.

"I know you don't. I'll help you. Why don't you lie down?"

"Lie down on the bed?"

"Yes."

"In my clothes?" he said.

"Yes."

"Is that how you do it?"

"That's how you do it," she said.

He lay down on the bed.

"Take this," she said.

If this were going to happen, I wanted it over with. She handed him the pill and, without looking at it, he put it in his mouth.

"Drink some water," she said.

Alan raised himself up, and he drank.

"Is this how you do it?" he said.

"Yes." She sat down beside him. "Put your head in my lap."

"Okay," he said. "Do I close my eyes?"

"You can close your eyes," she said.

He closed his eyes. "Thank you, Anna."

She put her hand on his head. "What a fine boy you are." She stroked his hair. "What a good man."

I'm not sure he heard her say these things.

I left her alone with him and went to bed.

The Tall Man will be here at noon.

I have just enough time to end this.

I had not taken my medicine, and I did not sleep.

I had not before watched anyone die. Let alone . . . I don't know how to finish that sentence. I did not watch my father die. Or my mother. I was asleep in a chair beside her bed when Sara died. I stayed with her afterwards. I never saw my son.

I was sad to see Alan die. I was also relieved. That he would not have to face what he was facing. That Anna would not have to see him taken. That it was over for him, and for us. Above all, I confess, I found Alan's death, the manner of it, his manner in it, instructive and inviting.

It was three in the morning when Anna came in. I could see her by the dim light of the lamp she'd left on in Alan's room. She sat down on the other bed.

"I'm awake," I said. "If you want to talk."

"Thank you," she said. "I do want to talk."

"Then please."

She did not respond.

"I am sorry, Anna. Are you okay?"

"Not really," she said. "Are you?"

"I'm okay," I said.

"I didn't cry," she said. "I haven't cried."

"If you want to, go ahead."

"I sat stock still," she said. "His head was in my lap. I looked at him. His eyes were closed. I was grateful for that. I didn't move. I was afraid to move. As though I might wake him. I didn't sleep, or only minutes at a time. I don't know. After a couple of hours, he was stiff and cold. I may be wrong about how long this took. I thought about taking the second pill myself. That would have been melodramatic. It would have been perverse. I want to see my children again. I'm ashamed to say I allowed myself to feel some relief."

"Of course you did," I said. "How could you not?"

"No. And I took comfort—I'm ashamed to say this, too— reminding myself that I love my sons and daughter, my grandkids, more than I ever loved Alan. If I loved him. I told myself I was now free to go back to them."

"You are," I said. "You will."

"I'm not free," she said.

She stood up and began to undress. She took off her blouse. "What am I doing?" she said. "I'm so sorry. I don't know what I'm doing."

"It's all right," I said. "Don't worry. It doesn't matter."

"Why doesn't it matter?" she said. "Because I'm an old woman?"

"Because I'm an old man," I said. "And we've been through it."

"We have," she said. "We have been through it. We did our best. Didn't we?"

"You did," I said. "You were great."

"Thanks. I couldn't have done it alone. You hear people say that. But I could not have done it alone."

"You could have," I said. "You pretty much did."

"Maybe I could have. But you've been a great help to me. You've been brave. And steady."

"I've been tired," I said. "Worn out."

She finished undressing.

"He was a beautiful, sweet boy, Ray."

"He was a good kid," I said.

Then she said, "I'm coming in with you. I need to be held. I need to be close to someone." Before I could object—I might well have objected—she got into my bed. "Not just anyone," she said. "I need to be close to you. Do you mind?"

"No. That's fine," I said.

It had been forty years since I'd slept with someone in the same bed. I was as unhabituated as one could be.

"I just want to be close," she said.

"It's okay," I said.

"Then relax."

"I'm worried I don't smell very good."

"You smell fine," she said. "You smell like an old man."

"Thanks."

"I'm no gardenia," she said.

"What if I snore?"

"I'll move over."

"What if you snore?" I said.

"You're out of luck."

We were quiet a while, then she laughed brittlely and said, "I'm a girl who'll stop at nothing."

She didn't say another word. She began to cry. She tried to be quiet. I closed my eyes and listened to her sob. I held her. She held me. We were like two . . . I don't know what. Like two old stagers sharing a doom. Like failed conspirators. War buddies. Not like lovers. Or family. Like two old friends, come together one last time.

She fell asleep in my arms. In the morning, at six, when I woke her—I didn't sleep; sleep would have been superfluous—she was on the other side of the bed.

"What's going on?" she said. She was not fully awake.

"I'm sorry to wake you like this," I said, "but I need to talk to you. Can you get up?"

"Has something happened to Alan?"

"Nothing more."

"I feel like I should check on him," she said.

"I don't think you should, Anna. I don't think you should see him."

"What's happened, Ray? What time is it?"

"Six."

"Jesus."

"I'm sorry."

"No," she said.

"I can't talk like this," I said. "Here's what I want you to do. I want you to get out of bed and put your clothes on. Will you please do that?"

"All right," she said.

When she was dressed she said, "Can I go pee?"

"Sure," I said. "But come back."

She left the room. When she came back, I was sitting on the edge of my bed. She sat down on her bed. "That poor boy," she said.

"Listen to me," I said. I'd spent the night planning what I would say. "I want you to get your things together, a few things, and then I want you to get out of here. Right away."

"Whoa," she said. "Where am I going?

"Wherever you like," I said.

"I'll stay with you," she said.

"That won't be necessary."

"I want to," she said.

"I need you to go, Anna. I want to be alone now. I want to finish my report before the Tall Man gets here."

"And then?"

"Then I want to be alone. I'm tired. I want to rest."

"I'll let you rest," she said. "I'll help you."

"No," I said. "I won't need your help. You need to go. All right?"

"No," she said.

"Please, Anna, do what I say. Go into my closet and take out the duffle bag. Please do this."

She got the duffle bag.

"Put it on the bed, okay?"

She did that, too.

"Now take out my stuff," I said. "Just dump it on the bed."

"Tell me what I'm doing," she said.

"You're dumping out my stuff."

"Why?"

"I want you to leave the boot socks in the bag. That money is yours."

"I don't want the money," she said.

"So you've said. At the bottom of the bag there's an envelope. Do you see it?"

"Of course I see it," she said.

"Leave that in the bag, too. It's a copy of my will. If you lose it, the lawyer has a copy. My estate goes to you."

"I don't want it."

"Fine," I said. "Then give it to your children. Or put it aside for their children. Or give it to charity. You can do with it whatever you like. When you feel settled, contact the lawyer. His name and number are on the document. He's the executor. Tell him I've died. Tell him how to contact you. It'll take a year or so for the estate to clear probate. But you'll have the money in the socks to tide you over."

"You haven't died, Ray."

"I want you to put a few of your things in the bag, and then I want you to get out of here. Get a cab. Go to the airport. Get on a plane. Go somewhere nice. Fly to Vancouver. Or Victoria. Go back to Montreal. You liked it there. Leave the country. Go to Europe. Scotland. Italy. Go anywhere you want. Anywhere you've wanted to go." I admit talking to her like this, giving commands, taking charge—whether or not she was giving me, as a parting gift, the illusion of control—felt good. "When you get there," I said, "buy yourself whatever you need. A whole new set of clothes. A new suitcase to put them in. After a while, send for your children. Or you go to them."

"I don't know," she said.

"*I* know," I said. "This is what I want you to do, Anna. This is what I need you to do, right away. I don't want to discuss it. I just want you to do it."

"What about Alan?" she said.

"The Tall Man will be here at noon. He'll take care of Alan."

"He'll be furious," she said.

"I won't care."

"What if he doesn't show up?"

"We have that reader. Leave it with me. When you're gone, when I've finished the report, I'll push the button. If that doesn't bring him, I'll smash the thing. He'll get the idea."

"What will they do with him?"

"What can they do with him?" I said. "They'll bury him. Cremate him. Whatever they do."

"What if they use him?"

"How?" I said. "For what?"

"I don't know," she said.

"Don't think about it."

"How can I not?" she said.

I admit, too, I was surprised that without further argument, she seemed, then, to acquiesce.

I've nearly done.

I'd like to think that in this report I will have accomplished something worthy.

It took Anna about an hour to get her things together. She was in and out of Alan's room, which must have been terrible for her. I'd gotten back into bed and begun writing the last section of my report. She came into the bedroom. She'd washed and dressed and packed. She was ready to go. She sat down beside me on the bed.

"I'll get up," I said. "I'll see you off."

"You don't need to do that," she said. "I know the way."

She put her hand on my knee. "I'll miss you, Ray. You know what? I've spent too much of my life missing you."

"I'll miss you, too," I said.

"It's kind of you to say that."

"I mean it."

"And thanks for the money. The socks and the other. I won't know what to do with all of it. You're a generous man."

"Who would I leave it to?"

"No. I should have said that before. I didn't want to think of you dying."

"You don't have to think of it," I said.

"I've come untied, Ray. And I'm afraid."

"Me, too," I said, which wasn't the truth.

"Oh," she said. "What about the pill?"

"Do you want it?"

"I don't," she said.

"Leave it then."

She stood up. "I never had a chance, did I?"

"That's not how I'd put it," I said. "I'd say you lucked out. You deserved better, and you got it. You've lived an enviable life, Anna."

"I have," she said. She smiled. "I want more of it."

"Good. Good. Then go."

"I will go," she said. She moved towards the door. "I seem to lose you again and again. I'm happy to see I was right about you all along. You aren't such a shit."

"So *you* say," I said.

I will finish, then take the pill.

Sara and I had agreed that last Christmas not to buy each other gifts—the baby would be our gift to one another—but neither of us had any intention of abiding by the agreement. When I came down the stairs on Christmas morning, I saw, resting on the mantle, propped against the wall, a large, ornately framed Audubon print of a bald eagle. (She must have gotten up in the middle of the night to put it there.) My present for Sara was wrapped and underneath the tree, where I'd placed it the night before, after Sara had gone to bed. Christmas Eve afternoon—the last minute—I'd driven to Hanover. In a fancy shop there I'd bought her a pale green linen sundress. I liked her in that shade of green, and I liked to look at her in sundresses, to see her arms and neck and shoulders and legs exposed. And I wanted to remind her that she would once again be elegant and lissome, to remind her, in the teeth of winter, that spring would come again.

I have lived more than a year with Anna and the clone. I have lived. I have done that which was asked of me. I had forgotten who I once was, who once I might have become. I have been made to remember.

This is my report.

# Acknowledgments

$\mathsf{M}$y debts are many and large.

I am most grateful to Ann Patty, the book's first editor, and to Doug Stewart, my agent. Without these two wizards, there would be no book. I am grateful to my sons, Benjamin and Michael Polansky. It was in discussion with them this book was conceived and elaborated. And to Richard Florest, the book's second editor, who rescued it. Thanks to Judy Hottensen, Kristin Powers, and Katie Finch at Weinstein Books, and to Jamie Byng and Francis Bickmore at Canongate. I thank my longtime friend, Flip Brophy, of Sterling Lord Literistic, and Marcy Posner and Seth Fishman, of that same agency. Thanks to my brother, the composer Larry Polansky, for setting the standard high. To Alvin Handelman, my kinsman and colleague, for his support and advice, and to David Delvoye for reading a manuscript version. Substantial parts of this book were written at Melvyn's Cafe in Alnwick, Northumberland, and at the Copper Rock in Appleton, Wisconsin, and I am grateful to the proprietors and staff of these establishments for their patience and hospitality.

For some of what I know and say about human cloning, I am indebted to Leon Kass's fine essay, "The Wisdom of Repugnance: Why We Should Ban the Cloning of Humans." What I know and say about heart transplants, I owe to Jean-Luc Nancy's essay, *"L'Intrus"* (English translation by Susan Hanson). The description of how it feels to suffer cardiac arrest, I owe to Michael Wanchena. For my thinking on the subject of self-love, I am indebted to Harry G. Frankfurt's *The Reasons of Love*.

My apologies to Ray Bradbury; my intention was only to honor him. My apologies to Dr. Anna Lewis, whose friendship I have not forgotten. My apologies to Penelope Fitzgerald, from whom I stole a lovely metaphor.

Finally, I am grateful, for her faith and encouragement, to my wife, Julie Filapek, who gave me back my life and, as well, a daughter, the remarkable Sylvia, thief of hearts.